W.R

D0536520

THE GOLDEN HOUR

Also by William Nicholson

The Secret Intensity of Everyday Life
All the Hopeful Lovers

THE GOLDEN HOUR

William Nicholson

WATERFORD
NO 004852490
CITY LIBRARY

Quercus

First published in Great Britain in 2011 by

Quercus
55 Baker Street
7th Floor, South Block
London
W1U 8EW

Copyright © 2011 by William Nicholson

The moral right of William Nicholson to be identified
as the author of this work has been asserted in accordance with
the Copyright, Designs and Patents Act, 1988.

All rights reserved. No part of this publication may be reproduced
or transmitted in any form or by any means, electronic or mechanical,
including photocopy, recording, or any information storage and
retrieval system, without permission in writing from the publisher.

A CIP catalogue record for this book
is available from the British Library

ISBN 978 1 84916 391 0 (HB)
ISBN 978 1 84916 392 7 (TPB)

This book is a work of fiction. Names, characters, businesses,
organizations, places and events are either the product of the author's imagination
or are used fictitiously. Any resemblance to actual persons, living or dead,
events or locales is entirely coincidental.

10 9 8 7 6 5 4 3 2 1

Typeset by Ellipsis Digital Limited, Glasgow
Printed and bound in Great Britain by Clays Ltd, St Ives plc

'The only true voyage of discovery, the only fountain of Eternal Youth, would not be to visit strange lands but to possess other eyes, to behold the universe through the eyes of another, of a hundred others, to behold the hundred universes that each of them beholds, that each of them is.'

Marcel Proust, *A La Recherche du Temps Perdu*.

The story takes place over seven days in July 2010.

SUNDAY

1

She comes to the front door just behind him, and notices for the first time that the heels of his shoes are worn on the outer side. Funny the things you still don't know about someone, even after a year. No, it's more than a year now. It was a cold spring day when they first kissed, and now it's high summer. The latch of the door drops into the keep behind her with a solid clunk. Late afternoon sunshine warms her bare face, her bare legs. A summer to remember so far, blue skies over yellow fields, no rain for weeks. They say the trees are showing signs of stress.

Down the narrow lane lined with brambles, the blackberries still too small to pick. Andrew striding ahead, his stocky body proceeding with purpose, though she knows the way and he doesn't. Then where the lane meets the road he stops and waits, looking back at her. That ugly gentle face, the shine of his rimless glasses, those comical eyebrows. He can make his eyebrows go up and down independently of each other. She laughed when she first saw the trick, and thought perhaps she could love him. It was the way he kept a straight face while being so foolish.

'I was thinking,' he says.

Maggie raises one hand and looks away, shielding her eyes from the sun. She hears it coming, the way you know the phone will ring before it rings.

I don't want this.

This is the shock. She thought she'd made up her mind. Where has this come from?

'Take a right at the school,' she says. 'It's the field behind the school.'

They hear the distant sounds of the village fête in progress. A loud voice shouting indistinct words. The boom of a brass band. They pass a high hedge that conceals a flint-and-brick early-nineteenth-century cottage in which the windows have been replaced. The new windows are double-glazed, single-pane, plastic-framed, illegal.

'See those windows,' she says, pointing through the hedge. 'That has to be a listed building. That's a planning violation.'

Andrew looks.

'Ugh!' he says.

'It's like the house has been blinded. It's like it's had its eyes put out.'

This is genuine, she really feels it. Maggie Dutton, conservation officer, champion of oppressed buildings. Who will cry their pain but her?

'Will you report them?' says Andrew.

'Probably not. It's awkward when you live in the village. And it looks like it was done a long time ago.'

Not a true villager, only renting, the prices in Edenfield way too high for her salary. Two salaries combined would be a different matter, of course. In a week's time Andrew starts a new job, in Lewes. He's moving out of his flat in London, moving in with her. So it has been agreed. Arrangements have been made, friends have been told, parents have approved. This is the appropriate next step. And now, for no good reason, outrageously, she doesn't want it.

He's looking at her, smiling, but at the same time he's wrinkling his forehead the way he does, making deep lines between his eyebrows. Why is he smiling?

Because I'm smiling at him. I'm smiling at him because I'm afraid of hurting him. Afraid that if I hurt him too much he'll leave me and then I'll be hurt. Or is that what I want? Mum used to say, 'Don't you look at me like a naughty puppy.' And Dad would say, 'Go on, give her what she wants. You know she'll get it in the end.' But what happens when you don't know for sure what it is you want?

Dad called me 'dainty'. Christ I hated that, it's a cruel word. It means pretty but not to be handled too roughly. Not to be handled much at all.

'So about next weekend,' he says, not receiving the message.

'I can't think about that now,' she says. 'Later.'

They head on towards the fête. A mother she doesn't know passes them, trailing two unhappy children. 'Well, you can't,' the mother's saying, not looking back. 'Whining won't get you anywhere.'

Here's what happens later. We move in together. And later? We get married. And later? We have children. And later? We get old. And later? We die. And that's my life.

Ahead of her the high dome of Mount Caburn and the clean line where the land meets the sky. Maggie loves the Downs. Sometimes she climbs the sheep track to the top and stands face on to the wind watching the cloud shadows sail over the sea, and she feels as if she's escaped time altogether.

I can't think about that now, Andrew. I can't talk about it because how can I tell you that later turns into forever and how can I tell you that suddenly I'm not sure I want to be with you forever? Forever scares me. I can do tomorrow. I can do next week. But ask me for more than that and I don't know what to say to you.

Ashamed of her doubts, she slips her hand through his arm as they enter the school field where the village fête is in full swing. Then she feels she shouldn't hold his arm, not now. But she doesn't let go because she doesn't want to seem to be rejecting him. Because she is.

It's a lovely fête, small and humble and home-made. A hundred or so local people stand about, stupefied by the heat. Sheep bleat. Dogs bark. Boys shout. The dog show is attracting a crowd, many of them sitting on the straw bales that line the rectangular arena. Owners parade their dogs up and down, competing to win the prize for Dog Most Like Their Owner. One woman in black leggings wears long purple-and-black striped socks. So does her dog. The Wealden Brass Band plays 'Don't Cry for Me, Argentina'. The sound of smashing plates punctuates the mellow horns. One pound gets you four balls to throw at the crockery. Little girls race by with painted faces. The sun streams down on fat men in shorts. People line up under the chestnut tree to place their bets on the runners in the sheep race.

Mrs Jones from the village shop is serving tea and lemonade and lemon drizzle cake.

'You should have heard Billy's speech,' she says. 'He got stuck in the middle.'

Billy is Lord Edenfield, formerly of Edenfield Place, a bulky stooping figure accompanied by a stout woman with black hair and a ringing laugh.

'Is that Lady Edenfield?' says Maggie.

'That's her. His housekeeper as was.'

The village scandal, except it's not a scandal at all. Why shouldn't a lord marry a housekeeper?

'You should hear how she bosses him,' says Mrs Jones. 'She's got him where she wants him all right.'

Andrew looks across the field and sees Lady Edenfield's laughing face.

'I expect she makes him happy,' he says.

That's Andrew for you. Always looking on the kind side. Old ladies adore him. Sometimes catching sight of him when he doesn't know she's watching, like when he gets off the train at Lewes station and makes his way down the steps to the car park where she waits, engine running, radio playing, she sees him as others see him, a serious young man with a purposeful air striding towards some meaningful encounter. But then he comes close up and somehow he loses focus. Getting into the car he's already softer, floppier. When he leans across to give her the expected kiss he looks like a teddy bear, which is one of her affectionate names for him, though she's forbidden him to use it about himself. Teddy bears, after all, are cuddly but not sexy. Teddy bears get left behind on the bed in your childhood bedroom when you grow up and leave home.

Maggie scans the crowd. A total stranger, a friendly looking man in a cream jacket by the Catch-a-Rat stand, meets her eyes and smiles.

Did I invite that?

Thoughts clatter through her mind like dominoes falling. If I'm not moving in with Andrew, then we've got no future together. If we've got no future, it's over. If it's over, I'm single again. If I'm single again, I'm looking for a new man.

Please don't tell me I'm back on the market.

She feels a wave of panic wash over her. Thirty years old and starting again.

I can't do this.

After all, it's not as if anything's actually been said. Here's Andrew by her side just like before. No bridges burned. All she said was, 'Later.' Except now he knows she's avoiding the issue, and why would she do that if there isn't a problem? Barely a word spoken but so much understood.

He gets her a lemonade. He shows no sign that he might

be angry with her. Or hurt. Would it be easier if he did? Fleetingly she imagines a different Andrew, one who would swear at her, saying, 'What the fuck's going on?' After all, they have only one week to go. There is a case for urgency. He could stand in front of her, eyes no longer seeking to please, and say to her, 'Fuck all this talk of later. We sort this out now.' Except Andrew's eyes do seek to please. They're fine eyes, large and amber-brown behind his rimless glasses. When his eyes are on her they're forever watchful, checking to see what mood she's in, trying to anticipate her wishes. This has the effect of making her petulant.

I have a bad character.

This was always her mother's warning to her. 'You watch out, Maggie,' she would say. 'It's all very well being pretty and getting what you want, but it'll ruin your character.'

'They have a sheep race,' Andrew is saying to her. 'This I have to see.'

They cruise the rough-cut field. Henry Broad is wandering about looking lost. Maggie barely knows him, but they talked once at a village party and discovered a mutual love of history. He's bald, with a long worried face and intent eyes.

'Isn't this something?' he says, gesturing round him. 'We're back in the Fifties. Retro chic, marinaded in irony.'

Maggie doesn't follow this at all, but she decides she likes Henry.

'Whatever you say, Henry.'

'Can I test my theory on you? You have to name your favourite film, or book, or music.'

'Is it a trick question?'

'No, not at all.'

Maggie's mind goes blank. What music do I like? What films? There's so much, and yet nothing comes to mind.

'I can do it,' says Andrew. '*Once Upon a Time in the West*, Sergio Leone's masterpiece.'

Maggie suppresses a spasm of irritation. This is one of the things about Andrew that she doesn't like. He keeps lists.

'Can I have a graphic novel for a book?'

Henry Broad looks baffled. 'I suppose so. Why not?'

'Neil Gaiman's *Sandman*.'

'Oh, Andrew,' says Maggie. 'No one's ever heard of that.'

'Actually it's a classic, and a huge seller.'

'Great,' says Henry. 'I'm not sure whether that proves my point or not.'

'What point?'

'My idea is that we like the art we like because it projects the picture of ourselves that we want to project. So if you secretly love *The Sound of Music*, you might conceal that and say you like *Brokeback Mountain* best, because it makes you appear cooler.'

'I liked both of them,' says Maggie.

'Well, I expect I'm wrong.'

Henry drifts away.

'Were you trying to appear cooler?' Maggie says to Andrew.

'I'm not sure,' he says, furrowing his brow, considering the possibility. Always so scrupulously fair.

Maybe it's a male thing, this keeping lists of what you've read and seen. Or a child thing. Small children are forever asking, What's your favourite colour? What's your favourite animal? And now with Facebook everyone has to reduce their personality to a few bullet points. My music. My photographs. My friends.

I don't want to be on a list.

So what do I want? Who do I want?

Three very pretty girls are running about by a line of straw bales, calling out to the crowd, taking money for betting slips. They're all wearing very short shorts, long bare legs, bare feet:

the three daughters of the local farmer, Martin Linton. Martin himself is knee-deep in sheep in a pen in the shade of the chestnut tree. This is the sheep race.

The oldest of the Linton girls, Lily, is maybe fifteen, but is practically a young woman now, meaning she has very evident breasts. The men standing round can't keep their eyes off her. The man in the cream jacket too.

I'm over thirty. What chance do I have?

She moves so she comes into Cream Jacket's eye-line and he gives her a nod, acknowledging that a connection now exists. Maggie turns quickly to smile at Andrew.

'Are you going to have a flutter?'

'I have to study the form first,' says Andrew.

Maggie glances back towards Cream Jacket. He's moved away.

So is this it? From now on, every man I meet between the ages of thirty and fifty I'm going to flirt with, asking myself: Is he free? Do I fancy him? Does he fancy me?

Maggie knows she's attractive to men, with her smiling eyes and her sweet face and her petite figure. They always think she's younger than she is, and usually make the mistake of thinking she needs to be protected. But if it's big boobs you're after, forget it.

Andrew's gone off to examine the runners in the sheep race. Rosie and Poppy Linton are now on either side of him, competing with each other to take his bet.

Jimmy Hall comes shambling up to Maggie.

'Too bloody hot,' he says.

His sagging red face shining with sweat.

'What's the news, Jimmy?'

Jimmy Hall edits the local weekly newspaper, which means he writes all the stories too. From time to time Maggie has provided carefully worded quotes about conservation matters.

'We've got a film star coming.' He lowers his voice as if it's a secret between them. 'Colin Firth.'

'Coming here?'

'Filming all next week. On the Downs. There'll be crowds.'

'Do you think so?'

'Oh, you're too young,' says Jimmy Hall sadly. 'He was Darcy.'

Andrew is making a ludicrously thorough inspection of the field. Each of the seven sheep in the race is daubed with a colour on its back. Laura Broad, Henry's wife, who is standing nearby, is also hesitating over which sheep to back. Looking up, her eyes meet Maggie's and she smiles. She and Maggie once spent a whole train journey to London talking about how the past lives on for them in *things*. Laura's special expertise is in old manuscripts and rare books.

'Hello, Maggie,' she says. 'Heavenly day.'

'A pound on Lewes Lady,' says Andrew.

Lewes Lady is the sheep with blue on its back.

'A pound on Lewes Lady for me too,' says Laura.

'Crikey!' says Martin Linton. 'It's a ring! Poppy, shorten the odds on Lewes Lady. The big money's coming in.'

Laura gives Andrew a smile.

'You look as if you know what you're doing,' she says. 'I'm sure you're an expert.'

Andrew puts one finger to his lips.

'Ssh! Don't give me away. I'm here incognito.'

Maggie plays along with the joke.

'Andrew Herrema, the world's foremost sheep-racing expert.'

Laura laughs. 'Are you really called Andrew Herrema?'

'Yes,' says Andrew. 'It's not easy having a name that sounds like a typo.'

'Any relation to Menno Herrema?'

'My uncle,' says Andrew, surprised. 'Or he was.'

'Yes,' says Laura. 'I heard he'd died.'

So it turns out that Andrew's uncle was a collector of first editions, and Laura knows all about him.

'He had the best collection of Golden Age detective fiction ever. Where is it now?'

'Well,' says Andrew. He gives a quick glance at Maggie. 'I've got it.'

'You've got it! Are you a collector too?'

'No,' says Andrew. 'All that stuff does nothing for me at all. But my uncle cared about it so much.'

Maggie is surprised and puzzled by that look of Andrew's. There's something here that he believes affects her. But what?

Henry Broad joins them.

'Guess who's coming to the garden party?' he says to Laura. 'Nick Griffin of the BNP. I just heard.'

'Oh, Lord!' says Laura. 'Will there be demos and so on?'

'I very much hope so,' says Henry.

Laura explains to Maggie and Andrew, looking apologetic.

'We've been asked to one of the Buckingham Palace garden parties. God knows why. Ten thousand long-serving councillors and us.'

'And Nick Griffin,' says Henry. 'It might even get interesting.'

'Henry,' says Laura, 'I want to ask Maggie and Andrew over for dinner.' To Maggie and Andrew, 'How about Saturday?'

'Fine with me,' says Andrew.

Before Maggie can qualify this thoughtless response, the sheep race begins. Everyone crowds round the short hurdle-lined track to urge on their favourite. Martin Linton opens the gate and comes out rattling a yellow bucket of sugar beet. The sheep follow. Martin lopes down the track, and the sheep break into a waddle, still packed close together. The crowd starts to shout. The sheep become alarmed, and break into a run. The crowd goes moderately wild. The sheep scramble over the straw bales placed in their way, and so the field spaces out.

'Come on, Lewes Lady!' cry Andrew and Laura.

Lewes Lady does not win. Andrew and Laura share a rueful grin.

'I'm beginning to think you may not be the world's foremost sheep-racing expert,' Laura says.

'Damn!' says Andrew. 'Exposed again.'

'But you're on for Saturday, then?'

Maggie feels trapped. What on earth was Andrew thinking of, saying, 'Fine with me'? But of course he spoke to please. His automatic reflex, which is to be obliging, overrode his common sense. So now, because Andrew is such a sweetheart, because everyone loves Andrew, she will have to be the witch, the bitch, the one who gives offence.

'Let me check my diary when I get home,' she says to Laura. 'We'd love to come, I'm just not sure what's happening next weekend.'

She catches sight of the man in the cream jacket over by the Bonfire Society stall. He has his hand on the arm of the woman beside him, they're laughing together at something. The sun goes behind a cloud, and all at once it feels cold.

'Let's go,' Maggie says to Andrew.

Too many dogs and children.

As they head back across the field she says, 'I never knew you had an uncle.'

'I hardly knew him. Turns out he left me this collection of books. Agatha Christie, Margery Allingham, Dorothy L. Sayers, that sort of stuff. I don't want it at all, but I feel I should honour his memory or something. Apparently the collection's worth a lot.'

'Like how much?'

'Maybe sixty or seventy thousand.'

'Good God!'

'I was going to tell you. As a sort of nice surprise.'

Because seventy thousand is house-deposit money. Settling-down money. So I should be grateful and happy. But nowadays we leave it too long. We know each other too well. When the moment comes the excitement's long gone, and you're left thinking – is this it? And that means you're a spoilt bitch. He's solvent and loyal and kind, what more do you want?

Just – more.

Maggie knows she should ask how it's a nice surprise, but she can't. The words won't come out. A stubbornness has got hold of her and won't let her go. She feels as if Andrew is making her walk backwards into a windowless room, and even his silence, his not-pursuing of the unspoken topic, is herding her through the doorway. Once inside the door will shut and she'll never be able to get out again.

His mobile rings. He checks the number and takes the call, with a quick shrug of apology. She hears his calm voice reassuring a panicked client.

'Have you tried rebooting? Just switch it off at the main switch and then on again.'

This is his work, trouble-shooting problems with computer systems. Five o'clock on a sunny summer evening, no time for anyone to be sitting in front of a screen.

'I'm not at my laptop right now. Give me half an hour and I'll call back and log into your system.'

He puts his phone away.

'Sorry about that.'

Behind them in the emptying field the band is playing 'My Way' to the sound of smashing crockery. The sun is out again.

The husbands and wives and children and dogs are heading for their cars.

Because of all that she hasn't said, Andrew understands that something has gone wrong.

'I shouldn't have said we were okay for Saturday evening. I wasn't thinking. But she seems nice.'

'She is nice. They're both nice.'

'I think she wants to talk to me about my uncle's collection.'

Suddenly, urgently, Maggie wants to be alone. She doesn't want Andrew to stay for supper, as he usually does. She doesn't want to have to face the question of what to do next Saturday, because once begun, that discussion has no escape route. Nothing whatsoever has happened, but Maggie feels an extraordinary degree of turmoil. It's not just her future with Andrew that's hanging in the balance, it's her entire sense of herself. Because Andrew is so sure and so generous, she feels tight and mean. Because he's so steady in his love, she feels incapable of love. She's appalled at herself for wanting him to go, but that is what she wants. Now. At once. What excuse can she give him? There is none.

'I'm feeling a bit anti-social right now,' she says. 'You know how I get sometimes.'

'Yes,' he says.

For a moment it seems like he'll say more, but he doesn't. She realises she has no idea what's going on inside him. He could be angry. He could be disappointed. He could be unaware.

They're walking back to the cottage.

'Maybe I should head on back,' he says. 'Back to London, I mean.'

At once she feels intense relief. Then in quick succession, gratitude that he's made it easy, guilt that she's hurt him, resentment that he makes her feel guilty, and shame that she's taking it out on him. The usual suspects.

'I could run you into Lewes. Put you on the 6.20. If you really don't mind.'

'Give me a chance to catch up on some work.'

'If you really wouldn't mind? For some reason I've just run out of energy.'

'No problem. You get an early night.'

He's so understanding. That's a good thing, isn't it? It's not as if I want some selfish bastard who only ever thinks of himself. Except somehow in this scenario I get to be the selfish bastard.

Look, here's what I want. I want a man who's loving and loyal, but not too eager to please me. I want to want to please him, but I don't want to have to please him. I don't want to be possessed like a chattel, but I do want to be possessed like a woman. I want him to love me out of his strength, not his weakness. I want him to adore me, but for his adoration not to trap me. I want him to lead his own life and let me lead mine, but I want us to live our lives together.

Am I making impossible demands? Dad always said I behaved like a spoilt child. So who spoiled me, Dad? How else am I supposed to behave? This isn't about who lays the table. This is my life. This is happy ever after, if that's not too much to ask.

So now what? Watch something mindless on TV. Go to sleep lying across the bed. Wake up and not have to smile.

2

Ask yourself this, Justin. When were you last hit by a genuinely new, really big, game-changing idea? Television still has the power to do that. I'm talking about setting the agenda. Getting everyone buzzing, challenging, taking sides. And it all starts in Vienna, in 1913.

Henry Broad walks home with his wife Laura, his mind buzzing, challenging, taking sides. The route home is familiar and requires no mental attention. He is preparing for his meeting on Tuesday with a Channel 4 commissioning editor, at which he will pitch a new series idea. But no sooner has he begun to address the editor in his mind than he is caught off-guard by the mental image of a large rabbit grazing on his lawn. Not a hallucination, a memory: he saw the rabbit yesterday evening. He is overwhelmed by a surge of anger. How is this possible? The garden is rabbit-fenced. He's found no breach in the fence, no burrow holes in the long grass of the orchard. And yet they're getting in. This means they'll start breeding in the garden. By next spring the rabbits will have taken over.

I truly believe, Justin, that this idea is both original and compelling. Ask yourself—

The low sunlight glints silver on the elm leaves. A cool breeze is getting up. Is this the end of the recent warm spell? What is one to think about global warming? It's not the science that's become murky, it's the morality. You worry about taking plane flights because you want to believe you're a good person. Then it turns out to be more complicated than everyone supposed, and you take the flights anyway because really there's no other option, and you're left feeling a little grubby, a little hypocritical.

And why do I feel this constant louring sense of foreboding? Surely not intimations of mortality. I'm only fifty-four, for fuck's sake. And I'm swearing more than I used to. Is that part of the general decline of civility, or fear of my own fading vigour? Once upon a time we swore on the name of the Creator. Now we appeal to the great god Fuck.

Will the great god Fuck save me from the coming cataclysm?

Terry Sutton is outside his terrace house washing his car, a red Toyota Corolla. He's stripped to the waist, revealing that he has tattoos right up his broad back. His hair is shaved close round the sides and left longer on top, like a brush.

'Not at the fête, Terry?'

'Chance'd be a fine thing,' says Terry.

'Those bloody rabbits are still getting in,' says Henry.

'See you at home,' says Laura, walking on briskly down the lane. Laura is bored by Henry's war on the rabbits.

Terry squeezes out his cloth and straightens up, flexing the aching muscles in his back. The tattoo is an eagle with spread wings, holding the globe of the world in its claws. Beneath it a scroll bears the legend: *Pain passes, pride is forever.*

'Seen any droppings?' he says.

'A few. In the orchard.'

'So they're coming in from the meadow.'

'Yes,' says Henry. 'But how?'

'Oh, they're clever little buggers.'

A white Ford Transit pulls up. A small young man in a grey tracksuit gets out. He has blond hair and a boyish face, the skin scarred with the remains of acne. He smacks one hand on the bonnet of the red Toyota.

'Waste of time cleaning this wreck, Tel.'

'Tell you what,' says Terry to Henry. 'I'll run the Nipper through your orchard, see what she finds.'

The Nipper is Terry's dog, a Jack Russell.

'That would be great,' says Henry. 'I'm up in London on Tuesday and Thursday this week. But any time you can make.'

He gives Terry and his friend a nod and heads on home. His thoughts revert to his programme proposal.

Call it the elephant in the room, Justin. The thing we all pretend isn't there. It's not just about history, it's not just about art, it's about all of us today, and our conspiracy to conceal the truth. The great unmentionable. You know what that is, Justin? We don't know any more what's good and what's bad. We don't even know what we like. We rely on a small band of experts to tell us what to admire, but we've no idea why. And there's a reason for this, Justin. It started in Vienna, in 1913.

Apparently young people don't watch television today. It's all Facebook and apps and smart phones. The days of the great television essays are over. Kenneth Clark's *Civilisation* is a museum curiosity, a footnote on the now-defunct twentieth century. And with *Civilisation* goes civilisation. The dark clouds gather. The storm approaches.

What is this storm? How is it possible to have a feeling of dread and yet have no idea what it is you fear?

Henry comes to a stop at the back gate to his house. There before him lies the small orchard. Beyond it the square lawn with its two handsome flower borders, the flame-orange crocosmia in the last of their glory. Above the border rises the brick terrace, where a grey teak table stands with its attendant chairs, and a big sun-umbrella now mottled with mildew. The last few weeks have been so warm they've had meals out on the terrace. The back door stands open, the door that leads into the kitchen, where Laura will even now have begun making supper.

Is this what I fear to lose? This sturdy russet house flanked by elms and limes, protected by lines of ancient hills. Yes, this too shall pass. But not yet, my friend. It'll see me out.

Pain passes, pride is forever. In your dreams, Terry. Pride is as mortal as all the rest.

The thought brings in its train a low hiss, like the soft rustle from far off that tells you the rain is coming. So is that it, pride? Some damage to my *amour-propre*, some loss of status? All too likely, but no surprise there. I've been anticipating my descent to the scrapheap for so long that I shall feel quite at home there. I see myself stretched out at my ease on some broken-springed sofa, dreaming of ragged-trousered philanthropy. No cause for nameless dread there.

But there it is again, the distant hiss. The terror to come.

He crosses the garden quickly and enters the house by the back door. Laura is on the phone to her sister Diana. Carrie is by the fridge, looking for something to eat.

'So you'll be here by lunchtime, then?' Laura is saying. 'I've asked another couple to dinner.'

Henry touches Carrie's arm, making her jump. He worries about her, she's so withdrawn these days.

'I'm going to get myself a drink. Want anything?'

'No thanks.'

And she's gone. All she ever does when she's home is sit in her room alone and strum on the guitar she's never learned to play properly. Nineteen years old, surely she should be out with her friends. But you can't ask. It's her life.

He pours himself a glass of wine and goes in search of the *Sunday Times*. Increasingly this is the form of escape he craves:

sunk deep in an armchair, legs stretched out before him, wine glass balanced on the chair arm, newspaper spread over his lap. Henry is addicted to reading the papers, though quite what it is he gets out of them he'd be hard put to say. It's not as if he cares much about the events of the day. You tell yourself you need to stay informed, but it's a lie. What you seek is distraction.

You see a photograph of Prince William playing cricket, and you feel a ridiculous twinge of affection, for cricket, or royalty, or both. You read that Muslim bus conductors are ejecting guide dogs from buses, because they believe dogs are unclean. Is that wrong? We believe smokers are unclean. We eject smokers from buses. Nothing is entirely right or entirely wrong. It all floats by the idle gaze, triggering little puffs of disapproval or amusement. After a while the accumulation of information, like alcohol in the bloodstream, results in a fuzzy sense that nothing matters much at all.

Rail fares are going up. A nine-year-old boy has died, strangled by a swing. Four soldiers have been killed in Afghanistan.

Where does it go, all this information? What part does it play in my life? *You never actually own a Patek Philippe. You merely look after it for the next generation.* They tell you that to persuade you to spend an absurd amount of money on a watch. A watch! Since when did watches become the primary display of male status?

Laura appears from the kitchen.

'Diana howled with laughter when I said we were going to the Buckingham Palace garden party. She says they're for lollipop ladies.'

'She would.'

'I've still no idea what I'm going to do about a hat.'

Henry is baffled as to why they've been asked, but it seems

WATERFORD NO 00852490 CITY LIBRARY

churlish to refuse. It must be some form of minor recognition for his services to television.

'The whole affair will be ghastly,' he says. 'We'll never get near the Queen. Or the cucumber sandwiches.'

'Oh, Henry. You know perfectly well you want to go.'

'Well, I am curious.'

He turns round to look at her. She's smiling at him, standing against the window, the evening sunlight glowing in her pale hair.

'Did you mind me asking Maggie and her boyfriend to dinner?'

'I was a bit surprised.'

'I really like Maggie, and we've never asked her round. And the boyfriend owns a rare collection of first-edition Golden Age detective fiction. He's not at all interested in it, he's obviously going to sell. Why shouldn't I handle the sale for him?'

'Oh. I see.'

'What do you think I should cook? Do you think we should ask another couple? We'll have Diana and Roddy, of course. Six isn't much of a dinner party.'

Henry groans. Laura's sister Diana is not his favourite person.

'Oh, God. Is it a dinner party now?'

'Stop it, Henry. Stop acting like an old fart.'

Laura goes back into the kitchen, leaving Henry to his newspaper. But the pleasure has gone out of reading it. He sits looking through the French windows at the garden, now striped by the long shadows of the elms. He thinks about the concert in Vienna's Musikverein in 1913, when Schoenberg premiered his *Gurrelieder*. The composer expected boos and cat-calls. Instead, the bourgeois Viennese audience he so despised rose to their feet and cheered. It was a triumph. Schoenberg was appalled. He bowed to the musicians, but he turned his back on the applauding crowd. 'If it is art, it is not for all,' he wrote later. 'And if it is for all, it is not art.'

The artist turned his back on the applauding crowd.

This image fascinates Henry. He wants to recreate it on film. The rejection of the popular. There it is, in a single gesture, the fork in the road that became a chasm, that robbed art of its audience.

Am I acting like an old fart?

Admit it, Justin. This is a big idea. This is a fucking big idea. Why has high art become synonymous with difficulty, inaccessibility, a refusal to please? I know the answer, Justin. The great god Fuck has whispered it in my ear. I may be middle-aged and I may deal in concepts that require more than one hundred and forty characters to express, but I'm still sparking. I can still light fires.

Carrie comes in, treading as if she has no weight.

'Dad, I need driving practice. I've got my test in just over two weeks. I really need more time in the car.'

'Yes, darling, of course,' says Henry. 'We'll find time.'

'I mean now.'

'Now? We're about to have supper.'

'No, we're not. We could do half an hour.'

'I've just had a glass of wine. I've finally sat down. Let's do it tomorrow.'

'Okay. Fine. Tomorrow.' She adds without bitterness, floating the observation in the air, 'It's always tomorrow.'

She drifts back up the stairs to be alone with her guitar. Henry feels guilty, then resentful, then tired. It's summer, for God's sake. Summertime's for sitting about doing nothing. It's officially allowed.

Laura looked so beautiful haloed by sunlight. I should have told her so. Why does one never say these things? It's not become less true over the years, it's become more true. Almost twenty-seven years now, if you count from when we got engaged.

A thought strikes him. He picks up the newspaper and checks the date: July 18. So this coming Saturday will be July 24.

'Laura!' He gets up, goes to the kitchen doorway. 'You know what this Saturday is?'

'What?'

'It's the anniversary of our engagement.'

She turns round, looking perplexed.

'Our engagement?'

'Twenty-seven years ago this Saturday I asked you to marry me. Not a very important anniversary. But even so.'

Laura looks down at her left hand. There on her fourth finger is the antique ruby ring they went out and bought together, after she'd said she'd marry him.

'You don't usually remember that sort of thing.'

Now's when he should say it, how beautiful she looked in the sunlight. But the words won't come out of his mouth. Instead he says,

'So we should have a not very important celebration on Saturday.'

'Well, we are. We're having a dinner party.'

'Oh, yes. So we are.'

He goes back to the living room and sits down again. As he reaches for the newspaper he glances out into the garden and there it is, right in the middle of the lawn. A huge rabbit.

He rises at once, and opens the French window on to the terrace, careful to make as little noise as possible. He keeps his eyes fixed on the rabbit as he treads softly across the brick paving. The rabbit senses him, turns, and bolts. At once Henry sets off in pursuit, not to catch it, but to see where it goes. The rabbit dives beneath the hedge into the orchard. Henry, panting, bursts into the orchard after it, and sweeps the far fence with his gaze. Nothing. The rabbit has vanished.

He paces the wire netting that protects the orchard from the meadow beyond, looking for holes in the wire or in the ground. He finds nothing. There is no way a fully-grown rabbit can escape. So it must still be here, among the apple and plum trees.

Slowly Henry's agitated breathing returns to normal. He claps his hands, hoping to startle the hiding rabbit into breaking cover.

The rabbit stays silent, invisible.

Returning to the house, Henry asks himself why he cares so much about rabbits getting into the garden. There are obvious answers, of course. Rabbits can do a great deal of damage. But it feels like there's more at stake, that the power of the rabbits to penetrate all the defences he erects against them threatens his security at some deeper level.

I suppose it's a phobia or something, he tells himself. I suppose the rabbits represent the encroachment of − of what? Of unemployment? Of old age? Of the gradual erosion of status, purpose, self-respect? If I can't hold the breach against the rabbits, what hope of standing firm against the onrush of the years?

Ridiculous, of course. Fifty-four is hardly old age. No, it's not dread of decline, not yet. It's a different kind of challenge, one not fully identified, not named. You spend the first two decades of your adult life becoming something, then a third decade being that something, then the arc of your life begins to turn downward. It's not that you stop, it's that you're no longer on your way to somewhere. You're there; or perhaps you're already leaving.

That's the question. How do you manage your life when the best of it is already in the past? Too late for ambition, too early for death. A wise man would say now is the time to live most abundantly. But we're not built for stasis, we're built for motion. So we dream on.

Are you following me here, Justin? Modern art defines itself as that which repels the bourgeoisie. The bourgeoisie redefines its taste accordingly and applauds only when discomforted. So the golden thread between art and delight is broken, and in its place we forge an iron chain, between art and status.

3

Sitting in Terry's kitchen, Dean can see his own shadow cast across the table by the low rays of the sun. He doesn't like the way his ears stick out. That's why he could never shave his head close up the sides the way Terry does. He doesn't like anything about the way he looks, if you want the truth. Twenty-nine years old and people think he's still a kid. Terry's one year older and he could be his dad. But you know something? So fucking what. It's not what you look like that does the business. Take Brad. Nothing special about Brad. You'd never pick him out in a crowd. But Brad's a professional. He could kill you with a fucking Get Well card.

Dean hasn't yet decided he'll do it but he's here, isn't he? Sitting in Terry's kitchen looking round, noticing how nice Terry and Julie have made it, it's got what you call character. All these pretty touches. The old iron range is still there in the chimney recess, but now it has a crowd of ornaments on its hob, a white-and-gold jug, little china birds, one of the old glass milk bottles. For real cooking they've got an electric stove with a flat glass top that's easy to wipe clean. Julie keeps it all very clean. My house, she says to Terry, my rules. Funny how it's the women who own the houses these days.

Even so, thinks Dean, I like ours better. There's an armchair in the kitchen for starters, a chair you can get comfortable in, right by the radiator so you can warm your hands when you come in on a cold day. And the mugs are hanging just where you want them when it's time for tea. And they're big generous mugs. So it's all comfortable and big and generous, because that's Sheena. People make jokes when they see Dean and Sheena together, they say, What's that you've brought with you, Sheena, your dinner? I'm trying to fatten him up, says Sheena. I don't know where he puts it.

Everyone loves Sheena. But no one loves Sheena as much as me. You couldn't. You'd have to be dead. I love Sheena more than I love being alive. You can't say better than that.

Terry is supposedly repainting the kitchen unit doors while Julie and the girls are away. Just white again, but Julie doesn't like scuffed paintwork.

'The paint's no fucking good,' Terry says. 'They've got new rules from Europe about how to make the paint and now it's no fucking good.'

Terry hasn't asked Dean if he's come over because he's agreed, but maybe he's just assuming it.

I've not said I'll do it, says Dean to himself.

'What's wrong with the paint?'

'Doesn't cover, does it? Doesn't stay on. Doesn't dry. Come on, lads, what the fuck else is there for paint to do?'

The *News of the World* lies on the breakfast bar beside the tin of paint and the jar of water for the brush. On the front page there's a photograph of a blonde in a nightie holding up one arm to show her injuries. Dean can't read but he knows what the story's about. It's about Raoul Moat.

'What do you reckon to that, then?' he says, pointing to the paper.

'Fucking nutter,' says Terry. 'But I'll tell you what. He fucking stood up for himself.'

He opens the *News of the World* to a middle page where Raoul Moat's letter to his girlfriend is displayed. He reads some lines aloud.

' "You can kill a person without ever physically harming them, you just make them harm themselves. That is what the police and the social services have done to me." '

'What do you reckon to that?' says Dean.

'Well, he's got a fucking point, hasn't he?'

He closes the newspaper. Dean looks again at the young woman with the wounded arm.

'I could never hurt my girlfriend,' he says slowly.

I could never hurt Sheena. Not that warm soft body. You lay a glove on her, I'll kill you.

'Course you wouldn't,' says Terry. 'No more would I. But she was going with another feller. He's doing time, and she's jumping this other feller. What would you say if that was you?'

'I'd never hurt Sheena,' says Dean. 'No matter what.'

'Course you wouldn't.'

'And I'm not doing time. Never again. I promised Sheena.'

'Nor me, mate. Nor me.'

He doesn't mean to tell Terry but it comes out anyway. And they are best mates. He wants Terry to know that if he's going to do this job it's only for one reason.

'I want to marry her, Tel.'

'Hey! Good one! Congratulations, mate! About fucking time. How long is it?'

'Three years. Coming up four.'

He can feel himself blushing like a kid.

'I want to do it right. Propose and everything. With a real ring.'

'You're a fucking romantic, Deanie. That's what you are.'

'Did you propose to Julie?'

'Not exactly, mate. It was more like, guess who's up the duff?'

'Didn't you want to marry her?'

'Not bothered either way. Can't see the point, myself. But Julie wanted it.'

Dean stares at him, not understanding. He's wanted to marry Sheena for so long. Ever since he met her, really. He wants to say to her, Till death us do part. But for years he didn't dare ask, still hasn't asked.

She's too good for me, that's the truth. Christ knows why she puts up with me, but she does. I'll stand by you, Dean, she says. You're my boy. No one's ever loved me like she does.

'So have you got a ring and all?' says Terry.

'Not yet.'

Terry gives a little nod like he's putting two and two together.

'How much you want to spend?'

'Maybe five hundred. I don't want any cheap shit.'

'What if she says no?'

'Then I'm fucked, aren't I?'

It's not like he hasn't thought about it. Why would Sheena want to marry a loser like him? Only because she's got the biggest heart in the universe. But she might say no.

'Five hundred's no problem,' says Terry.

Now they're into business talk.

'I haven't said I'll do it,' says Dean. 'I made Sheena a promise.'

'So don't tell her.'

'There's no fucking work, is there? What am I supposed to do?'

'Fucking right,' says Terry. 'And it's not like you'd be hurting anybody.'

It's an insurance job. Jimmy Dawes has this RS Cosworth he can't shift, not at a fair price. So he needs a lad to take it and roll it. Then the insurance writes it off and pays up. Top-of-the-range motor in its day, should clear four or five grand. So Jimmy Dawes pockets the money and passes some of it down the line. No aggravation, no harm done.

'You know what else? If I could, I'd buy Chipper a BMX.'

Chipper is Sheena's boy but Dean loves him like his own. A smart kid, and proud as shit. Never asked for a BMX, but you can tell how he hates it, waiting on the charity of other kids for a ride. Can't do stunts on the ramps in case he damages some other kiddy's bike.

'How much for a bike?' says Terry.

'Five hundred,' says Dean.

'Five hundred! For a kid's bike!'

'That's cheap, mate. You can spend five thousand on a BMX. And the rest.'

'So it's five hundred for the ring or five hundred for the bike. You got a choice there. Jimmy Dawes says he'll give us a grand for the job.'

Takes two to roll a car, one to drive, one to follow. You don't want to be walking home.

What would Brad do? He'd say you do what you have to do. It may not be pretty, but if the job gets done who's counting?

'Cash?'

'Of course cash.'

'You'll never tell Sheena?'

'Swear on my mother's grave. Not that she's dead yet. Worse luck.'

Dean's gaze falls once more on the front page of the *News of the World*. He's telling himself he hasn't said yes yet.

'My dad used to beat up my mum,' he says. 'Went for her with a hammer once.'

'Your dad was a nutter.'

'Christ I hated him.'

'Couldn't take his drink, your dad.'

Dean and Terry go back a long way, kids growing up on the Landport Estate. Terry's got out, nice little house, nice little village, bit of gardening, bit of hedging. But you don't make a grand in cash gardening and hedging. And the Landport Estate's not so bad. Sheena calls it her island. Come off the Offham Road and down the ramp and you're in a different country. Roll an artic across by the Tally Ho and you'd be cut off from the rest of the world, all on your own between the Downs and the river. You could declare independence and make your own laws, the Republic of Landport. Dean grew up on Evelyn Road and now he's living on Stansfield Road, which is all of a couple of hundred metres away, so he hasn't exactly moved far. Except Evelyn Road was hell and Stansfield Road is heaven because it's where Sheena lives, and he's going to ask her to marry him, and she has to say yes or it's over. Nowhere to go from there. The end.

Terry says, 'So are you on, mate?'

Dean nods and it's done. He was always going to say yes, why else is he here? But he's shaking.

'We go in your van,' says Terry.

'Why my van?'

'Because I'm going to roll the Cozzie, aren't I? Or do you want to do it?'

'No. You do it.'

'So fair's fair.'

Share the risk, share the reward. Won't be the first time. But it will be the last.

Ask Brad. You have to know when to quit. Thirty-seven combat operations for Special Forces and who even knows his name? But when you're pinned down by enemy fire and there's no way out, you want Brad in that foxhole by your side because he's smart and he's fast and he's a survivor. He'll do whatever he has to do and you won't hear him speak of it again. You could meet him in the pub and chat to him for an hour and you'd never know. Just don't get in his way.

'I'm only doing this for Sheena,' says Dean. 'You know that?'

'So you can propose. With a real ring. You're such a fucking romantic, Deanie.'

4

Evening is the best time for watching rabbits. At the back of the new house, which is actually a very old house, there's a field where sweetcorn grows. The stiff straw-coloured stalks with their sheathed cobs are nearly as tall as Caspar himself. Everyone tells him he's average height for an eight-year-old but he can see just by looking that he's one of the smaller boys in his year. If you go right through the middle of the standing corn you can't see anything but the corn and the blue sky above so you could be anywhere. Keep straight on walking over the crumbled stony earth between the lines and you come to the end of the field. Here there's a bank covered with brambles, with small trees growing up out of the brambles. In the bank are the rabbit holes.

You have to come up to them very slowly and make no noise, which is actually impossible, but you do everything in slow motion as if you're in a film. Then just where the corn ends you sit down on the last raised furrow and you wait. The rabbits are all in their holes where they've run while you're stamping and crashing towards them, because however careful you are, to them you're a huge heavy frightening giant. Rabbits are gentle, timid creatures, they don't hurt anyone. They don't eat other animals, not even worms. Other animals eat them. But they can hear everything. They can hear when your tummy rumbles. And they're so fast. If you startle them they vanish and you don't even see them go. They've got special eyes, they can see in all directions at once. But there's something they can't see, which Cas has learned all by himself. If you stop moving and just stay still, after a while they can't see you any more.

So he sits and waits, breathing softly, his hands clasped round his knees. He likes to try to guess which hole the first rabbit will come out of. From where he sits he can see two holes clearly, and another three through a fringe of grass and bramble. He thinks a lot about what it must be like underground, where the rabbit holes go. He imagines each hole is like a door, and each door leads to a passage, and each passage leads to the same big burrow with a round curving ceiling, which is like the living room. Running off the main burrow he imagines lots of smaller burrows, which are the bedrooms. The most rabbits he's counted outside this warren at once is nine, but there's probably lots more.

A flicker of movement. A whiskery rabbit nose peeps out of a hole, sniffing for danger. Cas sits motionless. Watching the first rabbit come out is the best bit. You can tell how timid they are, how ready to run at the slightest sign of danger. That makes the slow creeping out all the more exciting.

The rabbit is fully out now, crouched on the edge of the hole, on the little slope of bare earth that's always littered with droppings. Strange that they should do their poos on their doorstep. You'd think they'd want to go off into the nettles and make their mess in private. The rabbit crouches there, trembling, nose twitching, ears scanning from side to side. The soft sleek grey fur on its flanks moves in and out as it breathes. Then up it rises onto its haunches, front paws folded before its chest. Now it's a sentry rabbit, doing guard duty. The bulbous all-seeing eyes take in Cas, hunkered down on the edge of the field of corn, but because he doesn't move, he's invisible.

A few moments go by, then the rabbit drops down again, and starts to graze. Two more rabbits come out of the holes, moving more confidently than the first. How do they know it's safe to come out? The sentry rabbit sent no signal that Cas heard or saw. But now there are four rabbits, all with their heads down, nibbling away at the grass. The evening sunshine falls on them as they graze, making their coats gleam.

One of them hears a sound, and starts up into the alert position. The other three freeze. A soft whirr of wings high above: a sparrow-hawk circling overhead. The sentry rabbit doesn't look up, but his sticky-out eyes can see the hawk even so. A flash of white scut, and he's disappeared down the rabbit hole. The other three go within the same instant. The hawk flies on, no more than a speck against the great blue sky.

Cas hears the sound of a car driving down the lane half a mile away. He hears an aeroplane's low whine, heading south towards France. He hears the breeze clicking the stiff leaves of the corn.

Then a voice calling. Too far away to pick up words, but he knows both the sound and its meaning. His mother is calling him home for supper.

He jumps up, suddenly aware how hungry he is, and runs home through the rattling corn.

Sunshine pours through the open window onto the kitchen table. A plate of lasagne waits for him, and a glass of apple juice. His mother is at the sink, cleaning the pans used for cooking.

'You can eat in the garden if you want,' she says, not turning round.

'It's okay.'

Cas likes to eat at the table. It's the table they had in the kitchen of their old house, so it's familiar but it's also strange. You sit at the same table, there's a window in front of you like before, but what you see out of the window is completely different.

'Been watching the rabbits?'

'Yes.'

'You and your rabbits.'

Actually it was one of the reasons they moved house, or that's the family story. Cas's famous passion for wildlife. 'Cas will love it,' they told each other, his mum and dad. 'There'll be badgers and woodpeckers and squirrels and rabbits.' He hasn't seen any badgers or woodpeckers, but he has seen the rest. The other reason for the move is so that Mum and Dad can have space to do their work. Dad is going to have a big new study in one of the empty buildings across the yard. Then Mum and Dad will each have their own places to go and they won't get cross with each other so much.

His dad comes into the kitchen.

'Is it too early for a drink?'

'Help yourself,' says his mum.

His dad gets a beer out of the fridge and drinks from the bottle, which Cas knows his mum doesn't like.

'I'm worried about Bridget,' says Cas's mum. Bridget is Granny's carer. 'She says Mum's getting very difficult.'

'She's always been very difficult,' says his dad.

Cas hears everything. He knows how his mum finds Granny difficult, and how she feels bad about that, and how she thinks she should be a better daughter. He knows other things too. He knows they're worried about money because of buying the new house. He know his mum worries she might lose her job at the *Telegraph* and has to work extra hard to keep it. He knows his dad feels angry because his film story about the sheepdog has been changed. The people in the film are arseholes, he says. They don't care what he wants, they make him do what they want, and so he's sad and angry.

All these things Cas knows because he sits quietly in their midst and they forget he's there, just as the rabbits do. And at night as he lies in bed waiting to go to sleep – it takes longer to go to sleep in his new bedroom – he tries to think of ways to make them be happy again. He doesn't like it when Dad does something that makes Mum snap at him, especially when he can see that Dad only does it because he's feeling sad about his film.

This sunny summer evening he eats his supper and listens as they talk past him.

'I should go over and see her,' says his mum. 'I don't go and see her nearly enough.'

'You could go every day and it wouldn't be enough,' says his dad. 'She's a bottomless pit of need.'

'Even so. I'm the only family she's got.' She's finished her washing up at the sink but she's still standing there, head drooping. 'It makes me tired just thinking about it.'

'Why don't you have a drink?'

'Because I don't want to turn into an alcoholic.'

That's a criticism of Dad. Mum thinks he drinks too much.

'Well, just feeling guilty's no use to anyone.'

That's a criticism of Mum. But what Mum wants is for him to give her a cuddle and say he understands. She doesn't want to be told what to do. She knows what she's going to do. But now she's going to get cross with him.

'I don't ask you to deal with her. It's not your problem.'

'Of course it's my problem. You think I like seeing you beating yourself up day after day? Liz, she's got a carer. She's fine. You have to let go.'

'Let go? You think I'm doing this for me?'

That's her angry voice. Now Dad's going to get cross back.

'All I know is every time you go over to your mother you come back upset and angry, but when I try to tell you that's not helping either her or you, you tell me you've got no choice. But you do have a choice. If it's a destructive relationship, then maybe you should cut it out.'

'Cut it out? She's my mother.'

'Yes, I know. That's the last word. That's the trump card. Mothers have to be loved by their children. It's a law of nature.'

Cas shifts slightly on his chair, making the chair legs scrape on the floor to remind them of his presence.

'Well, anyway,' says his mum, 'I just don't know what I'll do if Bridget leaves.'

Cas feels his dad crossing the room behind him, coming close.

He's going to touch me now. This is what he does sometimes to calm himself down. Puts an arm round me, ruffles my hair.

'How's the rabbits, Cas?'

His hand stroking Cas's back.

'Okay,' says Cas.

'Heard them say anything yet?'

This is a question Dad and he puzzle over from time to time, how the rabbits talk to each other. They must squeak or something. But you never hear it.

'Not yet.'

'I learned something the other day about rabbits.' He goes on stroking Cas's back as he speaks. 'You know how sometimes they hop about as if they're mad? It's got a name. It's called a binky. Or maybe it's a verb. The rabbits are binking.'

'Binking?' Cas laughs at that.

'It means the rabbit's happy.'

'Well, it would,' says Cas.

After supper he's allowed to watch TV. Flipping channels he finds *Grease* halfway through, and settles down to enjoy it, even though he's seen it before. Actually he likes films better if he's seen them before. His mum comes in to make sure he's all right and she stands there watching it for a bit with him, a smile on her face.

'I never dared admit it,' she says, 'but all I ever wanted to be was Olivia Newton-John.'

'Watch it with me,' says Cas.

'Too much work.'

'Mum,' says Cas, 'next time you go to see Granny, I could come too.'

'That's a lovely idea, darling. I'm sure she'd love that.'

Cas has two lovely ideas. One is that he can make Granny be happy about her carer, Bridget, and that will make Mum happy. The other is that he can make Dad be happy about his sheepdog film. Then when both Mum and Dad are happy, he'll be happy too.

5

Oh, those tractors! They drive too fast down these narrow roads, but complain to the farmer and you might as well be talking to yourself. *She* thinks I don't notice when she changes my pills, but I do. Why would anyone do that? She's not a doctor, she's got no right, but try telling her that! Elizabeth won't hear a word against her, but she doesn't see what I see.

Mrs Dickinson sits on a green plastic garden chair, her bent upper body tilting a little to one side. The sun has just set, but she can still make out the busy forms of the guinea pigs moving about in their run. She watches the guinea pigs a lot these days. They eat grass, they scuttle in and out of their house, nothing of any great interest, but how else is she to pass the time? She is the prisoner of her ageing body. She can still walk with the help of a stick, but not far. Her hands can no longer undo buttons, or use a pen. She is permanently tired. Television bewilders her, the pictures jump about so much, and she can't hear what they're saying. Reading is now beyond her. Somehow she loses track of what she's read after just a few lines. It's become hard to hold a thought in her head for more than a few seconds. Not that her head is empty. Quite the opposite. As she sits in the garden for hour after hour, watching the pigeons, or the guinea pigs, or just the leaves on the trees shimmering in the breeze, her mental world is tormented by nagging voices, as if she is the host to a discontented mob.

Where is *she* now? She'll be shuffling about in the kitchen, moving everything round so I won't know where anything is. She knows I don't like it, which is why she does it. There should be two guinea pigs, where's the other one gone? She's killed it, she's fed it poison, it's the sort of thing she'd do. Ah, there it is. Am I supposed to sit out here in the garden till I die? She'd like that, she wants me to die, then she can have my house. That's her plan, and has been all along. Well, I'm not dead yet.

Bridget Walsh, Mrs Dickinson's carer, comes out of the house into the twilit garden.

'Better be getting in, Mrs D,' she says in her flat tones. 'Getting quite nippy out here.'

'I won't,' says Mrs Dickinson. 'You can go away.'

'No, I can't,' says Bridget. 'I have to see you safe in bed.'

'I'm not going to bed,' says Mrs Dickinson.

She's tired and she longs to be in bed, but stronger than her need for sleep is her will to resist her carer.

'I'll give you a few more minutes, then,' says Bridget.

She climbs over the little fence into the guinea pigs' run and starts shooing them into their hutch.

'Don't do that!' says Mrs Dickinson.

'You know they have to be shut up,' says Bridget, chasing the guinea pigs inside and closing the hutch door.

'I said don't — I said don't—'

Mrs Dickinson is overwhelmed with rage and frustration. She wants to rise up out of her chair and strike Bridget's pale puffy face, but she lacks the strength. How dare she disobey an order! Who does she think she is?

My jailer, that's who she is. My prison guard. Oh, she knows just what she's doing. Those piggy eyes don't fool me. She thinks she can break my spirit. She thinks she can turn me into a puppet who does her bidding. She's got another think coming. I'm not dead yet.

'I'll go and make a hot-water bottle for your bed,' says Bridget. 'Then I'll come back out and help you inside.'

'Go away,' says Mrs Dickinson.

Bridget goes into the house.

It's getting hard to see in the garden now, and the air is cold. Mrs Dickinson longs to be in bed with her hot-water bottle, but she refuses to give in to her jailer. This is a battle of wills that she knows she can't afford to lose. Once she starts doing what Bridget tells her to do it'll all be over.

Shivering now, she looks at the shapes of the chestnut trees against the darkening sky. There are two, standing like sentinels at the bottom of her garden. Every year they grow taller and reach out further. The rest of the garden – well, what can you say? A boy comes once a week for what he pretends is three hours, Elizabeth pays him for three hours, but he does nothing. So naturally the garden is dying, uncared for, reduced to bald lawn. All her plants, so lovingly chosen and tended over the years, all gone. The path to the back gate choked with weeds. No one goes that way any more. And to think that for years she and Perry came and went through that gate twice a day.

Oh, Perry. It's all over now. I'll be coming to join you soon.

A wave of misery sweeps over her.

What am I supposed to do?

This is the question that torments her waking hours. Old age has taken away her ability to do things, but not her will. Always such a busy person, such an effective person, always more to do than there was time to do it. Well, when you live on your own for as long as I have you learn to do things for yourself. Many's the time I've got out a screwdriver and tightened a loose door hinge, and if I haven't paid all the bills and always on time I don't know who has. So what right does she have to treat me like a baby? I go to bed when I choose to go to bed, not when some bossy little woman tells me.

Apparently I'm supposed to be grateful, but I don't know for what. All I do is sit in a chair in the kitchen. Then for a change I go and sit in a chair in the garden. Why doesn't anyone understand that it's driving me insane? They think if they put me to bed and get me up and feed me that I'm well looked after. But count the hours in the day. Count the minutes in the hours. All those endless minutes, and I'm living through them, doing nothing.

Don't tell me my brain's not working properly. I know what's going on. I'm not gaga yet. She'd like you to think so, that's her story. 'Mrs D's not all there,' she whispers, but I can hear her. And why can't she call me by my name? I'm not Mrs D, thank you, I have a name like everyone else. And I'm all there all right, as you'll find out soon enough.

Oh, Perry. Can you hear me, Perry? I think of you all the time. I think of the walks we had together. I hear your bark. I see you curled up on your rug by my chair. You understand, don't you, Perry? You know I'm living in hell.

Bridget comes out with a torch. The beam of light causes the night to fall.

'Time for bed, Mrs D,' she says. 'I have to be off. I'm an hour late already.'

'Then be off,' says Mrs Dickinson.

'Now don't be silly. You know you can't go on sitting out here.'

'Phone Elizabeth. Tell her to come round. There's something I have to tell her.'

'Now, Mrs D, you know your daughter can't just come round whenever you want.'

'Do as I tell you!' says Mrs Dickinson. She hears her own voice rising to a shriek. The effort of it leaves her breathless.

Bridget stands there for a moment, the beam of the torch wobbling about over the grass. Then without another word she goes into the house.

Maybe she's walked out.

Mrs Dickinson's heart lifts in momentary exultation. Her one desire these days is to force Bridget to quit her job. She's asked Elizabeth to sack her, but Elizabeth says, 'Don't be silly, Mummy. She's wonderful.' If she's so wonderful, why do I hate her? Why do I want to kill her? You try living with her. You try being ordered about all the time and talked to as if you're a baby. Just because she gets me meals doesn't mean she keeps me alive, you know. Exactly the opposite. She's slowly killing me. She wants me dead. But she doesn't know me. I'm a survivor. Rex thought I'd just give up and die when he left, but I didn't, did I? I'm still here. So just let her try, that's all.

Bridget comes out again, invisible behind the glare of the torch.

'Your daughter says she can't come round right now and could I get you to bed before I go.'

'Why can't she come round?'

'Don't know. So come on, I'll give you a hand.'

A white hand looms towards her. Mrs Dickinson twists her body away.

'Now come on, Mrs D. I haven't got all night.'

'I have.'

'You know you want to go to bed.'

'Just go away. Leave me alone.'

'I can't leave you here. You'll catch your death.'

'Good.'

A silence falls. Mrs Dickinson waits, hearing Bridget's heavy breathing, wondering what she'll do next. A secret exultation fills her. She's never staged such a show of total defiance before.

'Well,' says Bridget. 'I can't force you.'

Mrs Dickinson says nothing. Victory is in her grasp.

'I should have been home an hour ago. You know my hours. If you won't go to bed, I can't make you.'

'No, you can't.'

'So what are you going to do? Put yourself to bed?'

'Yes.'

'Well, then. You'd better do that.'

Mrs Dickinson keeps her head down and waits. Then the beam of the torch is swinging away. Bridget's footsteps return to the back door.

The old lady listens, not moving. She hears Bridget pass through the house. She hears the front door open and close. She hears a car engine start up, and drive away. She hears the sound of the car fade into silence.

Bridget has walked off the job! She can't come back after that.

Mrs Dickinson sits in the dark garden and savours her victory. A flock of rooks passes overhead, squawking, to land in the distant elms. If she stays quiet she can hear the soft scratch of the guinea pigs in their hutch as they make their nest in the straw. She wonders if Bridget filled her hot-water bottle before she left.

Why didn't Elizabeth come? She didn't even give a reason. Because she hasn't got a reason. She just couldn't be bothered. My only child, and she can't be bothered to come when I call. For all she knows I'm dying. Except of course Bridget would have told her it's nothing. The old bat making a nuisance of herself over nothing.

I shall kill that woman. If she comes back.

Now she does feel cold. Suddenly it's more than she can bear. She knows she must get herself into her warm bed.

She grasps the arms of the garden chair, shuffles her bottom to the edge of the seat, and pushes. Up she goes. There. Who says I need help? She turns herself slowly to face the house. The light in the kitchen window throws an illuminated rectangle across the stone-paved path. Moving slowly, probing with her stick, she sets off on the journey to the back door.

Walking is hard work. Not just the effort required to pull one leg ahead of the other: there's the constant worry over maintaining your balance. You take it for granted all your life, but it turns out that staying upright is a feat of skill that requires constant responses from muscles all over your body. This common act of crossing the garden is now fraught with danger. Get the movement of an arm or the lean of the back just a little wrong and you fall. So everything has to happen very, very slowly.

She reaches the back door at last. The door is standing as Bridget left it, half open. She puts out her left hand to support her weary weight on the door handle. The door swings back under the pressure. And down she goes.

Falling has its own familiar pattern. The first terrible moment of helplessness. Then the slithering crumpling descent, in which many parts of your body are bumped, but you feel no pain. Then seeing the floor and the walls at odd angles, and not quite knowing where you are. Then twisting your head about you and seeing an arm, a leg, all in strange places. Then the throbbing sensations in various unidentified regions of your body, and the rush of sudden weakness that makes you lay your head down again. Then the pain.

Maybe you've broken a hip. Maybe you'll have to go to

hospital. Maybe you'll have a general anaesthetic and die. Or not die, but lie in bed for weeks and weeks, and die later.

Falling is the prelude to dying.

She lies still for a few minutes longer. Then she starts to wriggle her limbs. They all respond. Bruised but not broken. So she begins the slow arduous process of raising herself up off the ground.

The first stage is to get into a sitting position. This she achieves by pushing against the doorframe. But getting up on her feet is another matter. Not that she's a heavy woman, there's not much of her at all. But try lifting yourself up when there's nothing to pull on and you'd think you were tied to the ground with leather straps.

She heaves and strains, and feels what little strength she has left draining out of her. She could try crawling, but that means turning onto her knees, and one knee hurts. There's a dustbin nearby, she could pull herself up on that, but it's not quite within reach.

So there she sits, in the open back doorway, with the cool night breeze sucking the heat from her body, and the bruises from her fall pulsing in her thigh, her knee, her elbow. Tears form in her eyes, but she's too tired to cry.

It's all Bridget's fault. She left the door half open. She made me fall. She left me to cope on my own. How wonderful is that, Elizabeth?

She knows now what it is she must do. She must press the red panic button that hangs round her neck. She's not injured, it's not an emergency. But if she stays here all night, who knows what state she'll be in by the morning?

Don't fall, Elizabeth says. Whatever you do, don't fall. Well, now I've fallen. You try staying on your feet all day at my age. Try doing anything at my age.

She fumbles for the string round her neck, pulls out the heavy plastic fob. Her stiff fingers feel for the dome of the button. She presses. Then she presses again, and again. Nothing happens, it makes no sound. Now all she can do is wait.

A few minutes go by. Then her phone starts ringing. It rings and rings, then falls silent. Another minute. Then the Lifeline speaker by the phone wakes up with a cackle. A boomy echoey voice says, 'Mrs Dickinson? Are you all right?'

'No,' she says. 'Send someone.'

'Mrs Dickinson?' calls the voice. 'Can you hear me?'

I can hear you but you can't hear me. My voice isn't strong enough. I'm by the back door. My knee hurts. I want to be in bed.

The crackling and booming ceases. Silence returns. Nothing to do now but wait.

She feels the need to sleep. It tugs at her like a child. Then she feels another need, to be held, to be cuddled, to be comforted. Take me in your arms. Make me safe, make me warm.

Love me.

She finds she's crying. Angrily she pushes the tears from her face. She doesn't want pity. But just because she's old and her body is failing doesn't mean she has no need of love.

How did this happen? How did I get so there's no one who loves me? It must be my own fault, but I don't know what I did wrong. Rex pretended to love me, then he left. Elizabeth does her duty, but she finds me a burden. The grandchildren never visit. Perry's gone. All I've got is Bridget, and she hates me. Am I such a despicable creature? Am I so worthless that no one in all the world loves me?

Then she sleeps a little, sitting in the doorway. As sleep relaxes her, she tips slowly to one side, and feeling herself falling again, she wakes.

Time passes. Impossible to say how long.

Then the sound of a car, and footsteps, and the front door opening. Someone coming through the hall, into the kitchen.

Elizabeth.

'Oh, my God! Are you all right?'

Elizabeth takes her hand and helps her up. Mrs Dickinson feels tottery, her legs seem to have forgotten how to support her. But with Elizabeth's help she makes it to her bed in the room that used to be called the study. Elizabeth talks all the way in that tight high voice she uses when she's stressed.

'What happened? Why on earth didn't Bridget get you to bed? How long have you been there? Thank God you pressed your button. What can Bridget have been thinking? It's almost ten o'clock. What on earth happened?'

Mrs Dickinson is too tired and too cold to speak. She lets her daughter help her get undressed and into her nightie. All she wants is to be in bed.

'Are you sure you haven't broken anything? Does it hurt anywhere? Why wasn't Bridget here?'

'She left.'

'She's supposed to help you go to bed. She knows that.'

Now Mrs Dickinson is in bed and beginning at last to feel warm again. Funny how cold you can get even in mid-summer. She hears her daughter fussing round her, tugging at her bedclothes, asking her about Bridget, but she no longer has the energy to speak. Elizabeth sounds very angry with Bridget, which soothes the old lady. Yes, she thinks as she lets herself slide into sleep, Bridget abandoned me. She failed in her duty. She wants to tell Elizabeth more, now that at last she's begun to understand. How Bridget hates her and torments her, and wants her to die. How Bridget has been plotting to steal her house. How unhappy and lonely she is. How long the day lasts. How she wants so much to be cuddled. How easy it is to fall. But she says none of these things, not aloud.

She sleeps.

6

Dean drives his van up the Offham Road and waits at the junction to pull out onto the main road. A blaze of approaching headlights. Terry's in the seat beside him. A truck rumbles by.

'Done this before, Tel?' says Dean.

'Not as such,' says Terry.

Out on the A275 between night trees, the van's engine struggling, needs retuning. Needs scrapping, more like, but where's the money coming from for new wheels?

Dean has a plan, a dream you could call it. Buy a new van, new tools, set up as a Mr Fixit, come to your house, fix anything. Fencing, walling, drive maintenance, rubbish clearance, all the little jobs the big boys won't touch. His name and mobile number on the side of the truck: *Dean Keeley, No Job Too Small*. Sheena thinks it's a good plan, she's backing him all the way. Not like there's much work going on the building sites these days.

'You're lucky you got out,' he says to Terry, meaning out of Landport. 'Nice place you've got now.'

'It's okay,' says Terry.

'Doing good for yourself.'

'Tell you what, Deanie,' says Terry. 'Makes no fucking difference where you live, they still treat you like dirt. They've got the money and you don't, that's what it's all about. You and me, we could work till we drop, we'd never make that kind of money. And you know how they get it? They're born with it. They're fucking millionaires from when they're babies.'

'But at least you're picking up a few jobs round your way.'

'Oh, right. His lordship tips me a tenner to chase away his rabbits. Her ladyship never says a word to me, not even a fucking nod. I'm telling you, that woman can't even see me. And guess where all her money comes from? From her dad. Like I said, fucking millionaire babies.'

'Just luck in the end,' says Dean.

'We do what we can, don't we, mate? Even up the odds.'

Ahead on the left looms the cut into the hillside that's the old chalk pit. The van's headlights sweep the high grimy white cliffs. The windows of the Chalk Pit Inn glow bright and cheerful. Half a dozen cars parked outside.

Terry jumps out.

'Give me half an hour,' he says.

Dean swings the grumbling van onto the road again and heads back into Lewes. Just before the Neville Estate begins he turns off up the rutted track that climbs the hill to the racecourse. Up here on bare downland there's not exactly any roads, you just drive. He follows the tyre marks in the beam of his lights, careful to stick to the run where others have been. Just before the training gallop he swings the van round full circle to look back down on the lights of Lewes. Here he settles down to wait for Terry.

Towns look different at night. And different from high up. There's the castle, you can usually find that, high on its mound. And the river, and the lights of the Malling Estate rising up the flank of the Downs beyond. This is the landscape of his entire life.

Maybe I should have got away long ago, run away to London, made my fortune. Some chance. I got away all right, to Rochester

Borstal, to Camp Hill. At Camp Hill they give you a whipping you don't forget in a hurry.

When Dad was on the booze any little thing would set him off, and then I was for it. Send me up the road to fetch Grandad's belt. Bring it home, bend over. Eight whacks on the bum. Then take the belt back to Grandad. Grandad never said a word. Funny, that, how he never said a word. You're ten years old and you've got a dad who belts you and no one ever asks why. You don't even ask why yourself.

Terry's always been a good mate. He knows I need the money, but I promised Sheena no more hooky business. A promise is a promise. All I'm doing is bringing the van onto the racecourse so Terry can have a ride home. That's all. Terry gets that.

'You're not breaking any promise, Dean. You're just helping a mate.'

So Dean watches and waits. A half moon low in the sky, some stars. His phone rings. It's Sheena, wanting to know when he'll be home.

'Just having a drink with Terry,' he says. 'Don't wait up.'

Never before been anyone who wants him to come home.

'Love you, hon,' he says.

'Love you, babe,' she replies.

No one knows him the way Sheena knows him. No one else in the world he trusts, unless you count Brad. But Brad's a loner. You'd never say hand on heart that Brad loves anyone. He'll pull you out of a burning house. He'll take a bullet for you. But you'll never see him smile and you'll never hear him cry.

He sees headlights coming up the track, and there's this roaring animal of a car shuddering to a stop in front of his van. He gets out.

'Fucking hell!'

'This,' says Terry, 'is a four-wheel-drive turbo-charged '92

Cozzie with whale-tail spoiler. And there's only seven thousand of them in the universe.'

'And you're going to roll it?'

'That's the job, kiddo.'

'You saw Jimmy Dawes?'

'I saw Jimmy Dawes and I didn't see Jimmy Dawes. He comes into the pub to buy a packet of fags and I go outside and there's the Cozzie with the keys in the ignition just like he said, and I'm away.'

'And you're going to roll it.'

Dean strokes the sleek spoiler. Seems a dumb way to make a few grand, but what do I know?

'What's she like to drive?'

'Like sweet fucking,' says Terry. 'Ride of your life.'

He gets back into the car and eases it up the track while Dean watches. There's a slope down to one side of the track, and that's where the Cozzie's going to roll. Lie it on its back and it's a write-off. That's official, insurance rules.

Terry cuts the engine and gets out. The Cozzie's right by the edge of the slope. It's not like he wants to go down with it. But the ground is rutted, and the wheels won't roll.

'C'm here, Dean! Give us a hand!'

Together they push the car sideways on to the slope.

'You wearing gloves, mate?'

'Course I'm wearing gloves. I'm not an idiot.'

'Okay, okay. Just looking out for you. Give it some welly, now.'

They push some more and the car gets two wheels down the slope and starts to tilt. Then all at once it's rolling. They stand back, hearing it bump down the slope. There's some louder thumps, not as much as you'd think, then silence. Too dark to see how it's landed.

'Get the van.'

Dean goes back and drives the van round so its headlights shine into the valley. There lies the Cozzie, wheels in the air. Terry jumps into the van beside Dean. Dean's impressed.

'How'd you know she'd roll?'

'That's a steep slope, mate. Send her down sideways, she's going to roll.'

Dean drives them back through town, taking Terry home to Edenfield. Once they're out the other side of the tunnel Terry pulls out his phone and makes a call.

'Jimmy?' he says. 'Job done.'

Dean can hear the sounds of the voice on the other end but not the words. He feels Terry tensing up beside him.

'You can't do that,' Terry says. 'You can't do that.'

He listens some more, then he ends the call without another word, thrusting his phone deep into his pocket.

'The fucker,' he says. 'The fucker.'

'What?' says Dean.

'He just fucked us.'

'How? What'd he say?'

'He said, I quote, You call me again, I'll get the police on you.'

'The police?'

'He said, I quote, I got witnesses you left the pub just before my car was nicked.'

'I don't get it,' says Dean. 'That's what he wanted.'

'He fucked us,' says Terry savagely. 'That's what he just did.'

'But why? You rolled it like he wanted.'

'Oh, sure. Too fucking right. So now he'll claim on his insurance and get his five grand. And we get fucking zip.'

'But he can't do that!'

'He just did it.'

Dean takes in the full scale of the calamity.

'So we don't get paid?'

'Good old Deanie. You're there, mate.'

Dean is shocked. You don't just break your word. There are limits.

'Fuck all we can do about it,' says Terry.

'Break his fucking legs,' says Dean, his outrage growing.

'This is Jimmy Dawes, right? He's got family.'

Dean knows. You don't pick a fight with the Dawes boys. So that's it. It's over. He had this sweet dream they'd drive over to Jimmy's place and Jimmy'd come out smiling, a fistful of fifties in his hand.

I should have known. I never get the luck.

They drive up the main road to Edenfield in silence. When Dean drops Terry off at his house, Terry squeezes his arm and says, 'I'm sorry, mate.'

'Not your fault,' says Dean.

But he's choked.

'I'm just a fucking loser,' he says. 'Always was. You should have got someone else.'

'Luck of the draw,' says Terry. 'You're no more a loser than me or anyone else.'

'I've been shat on all my life,' says Dean. 'I've done time. I've tried doing myself in. I can't win, Tel. They won't let me. I'm fucked, mate. Always have been.'

'Except you've got Sheena.'

'I'm telling you, if I lose that woman, I'm out of here. I'm gone. I'm finished.'

'Want to come in for a beer?'

'No. I'm off home.'

That's when Terry gives him this look that comes out of nowhere. Like he actually cares.

'I'm going to see you right, Dean,' he says.

'Forget it.'

'So you can buy that ring.'

'Not your problem, mate.'

'I'm on this job, gutting this house. I could do with a hand. I reckon I can get you a couple of days at a hundred a day.'

'You reckon?'

'Why not? Gets the job done faster, doesn't it?'

'I'm up for that. Cheers, Terry.'

'I'll give you a bell first thing in the morning. Now fuck off home to your woman.'

Dean gives him a wave and drives off. As he drives he thinks about how Jimmy Dawes screwed them over and he can still hardly believe it.

He must just think we're dirt under his feet.

He gets home and parks the van by the recreation ground. The lights are still on in the house but Sheena's gone to bed. He shuts the house down quietly and goes up to their bedroom. She's not asleep.

'How was Terry?' she murmurs.

'Terry's good,' he says.

He undresses and washes and gets into bed. He feels her warm soft body roll close against him. This evening his big chance has gone bad and all his plans are shot to fuck, but what remains is that look on Terry's face, and the way he's trying to help.

Terry gets it. He knows what it means to me.

Knowing someone understands you turns out to be stronger than knowing someone else thinks you're the dirt under his feet.

7

It's just on midnight and the MV *Seven Sisters* is churning past the lights on the end of the jetty and entering Newhaven harbour. It's been a smooth crossing from France. The truck drivers and the car drivers have all descended to the car decks, while the few foot passengers remain on the top deck, pressing themselves to the iron railings, watching the lights of the town approach.

'I'm hungry, Mum. When will we be home?'

A boy of about six clings to his mother's legs, barely able to stand with weariness.

'Not long now, darling.'

'Can I have a chocolate milkshake when we get home?'

'When we get home it's straight to bed for little boys.'

The boy starts to cry.

'Don't cry, darling. We're almost there. You've been so good.'

A young man standing beside them says without turning his head to look at them, 'Is crying bad?'

The mother becomes confused.

'No, not really,' she says.

The young man has long hair and a beard. He wears loose soft clothes, and has a small backpack by his sandalled feet. He looks down at the boy with intent, dark eyes.

'Then you can cry all you want,' he says.

The boy tugs at his mother's hand.

'Mum,' he says. 'Is he Jesus?'

'No,' says the mother. 'I don't think so.' To the young man, 'You're not Jesus, are you?'

'Would you like me to be?' says the young man.

Now he's turned his gaze on the mother. She's in her late twenties, fair, pretty. She gives him a cautious smile.

'Not really,' she says.

The big ship starts to roar and judder as the engines are thrown into reverse. The quayside rotates round them.

'Back from holiday?' she says.

'My life is a holiday,' he says.

'Lucky you. I can only manage a week. If you can call it a holiday with his lordship here.'

'His lordship? Your son is a peer of the realm?'

'He's a peer of something.'

She laughs, relaxing under the young man's gaze. She can sense that he finds her attractive. For her part she finds him bewitching. The way he says funny things without smiling. The way his eyes hold hers without looking away.

'Backpacking,' she says, glancing down at the bundle by his feet. 'I did that once. Me and a friend went to Rhodes. Those were the days.'

'These still are the days,' says the young man.

'Mum,' says the child, pulling at her hand. 'What's his name?'

'I don't know his name,' she says, giving the young man a quick smile. 'We'll have to ask him.'

'Toby,' says the young man. 'What is your name?'

This is addressed to the young boy, but in a serious, almost formal manner, as if he really wants to know.

'Harry,' says the boy.

'Well, Harry,' says the young man called Toby, 'if I tell you something very special, will you remember it?'

'Yes,' says Harry.

'You have a very beautiful mother and she loves you very much. But she has her life and you have yours.'

Harry pulls his mother's hand once more.

'What does that mean, Mum?'

'Nothing,' says his mother. 'Nothing at all.'

But she's holding tight to the ship's rail and not looking at the young man who said she was beautiful.

Now the ship has docked and the ramp is being lowered. Orange lights flood the concrete quay. The smell of exhaust fumes as the great trucks come rumbling out of the lower decks. The big blue trucks of J. C. Fiolet, the big red trucks of Norbert Dentressangle.

The foot passengers pass back into the boat's interior and bump their wheeled suitcases down an iron stairway. The mother and child go first, the strange young man following. Out on the quay there's a white bus waiting to carry the foot passengers the short distance to Passport Control and Customs. Gulls sweep overhead, mewling their harsh cry. The air is heavy with diesel and salt.

On the bus the little crowd of foot passengers slump with weariness. The young man remains standing.

'So where do you go from here?' says the mother.

'I have no idea,' says the young man.

'You must have some idea. You can't go nowhere.'

'No,' he replies, in that careful thoughtful way he has. 'I can't go nowhere. But I can go everywhere.'

His eyes are on hers, looking down at her. Again she gives a quick uncertain smile.

'You're a joker,' she says.

'I am.' He doesn't smile back, just holds her eyes. 'I'm a joker.'

The bus stops and they all get out. They file past a booth

where a man checks their passports, then through the Customs hall alongside slow-moving cars. Then into a bleak terminal building, and so out the other side into an immense and mostly empty car park, lit orange by street lights.

Harry and his mother go to a waiting car. The driver doesn't get out to greet them or help them with their bags. The young man, his pack now on his back, walks alone up the pavement past a fenced-off compound. The concrete yard beyond the fence is cracked, and weeds grow thick in the crevices. The windows in the abandoned industrial building are arched, as if it wants to be a church, but the glass is broken. Creepers have climbed the drainpipes and started to crawl over the corrugated iron roof.

A sign directly ahead says *Toutes directions*. The adjoining land, between the road and the railway line, has gone to waste. Thin dark weeds trap plastic wrappers, bright dots of colour in the night.

A car slows as it passes, and the young mother calls out.

'You want a lift? We're heading for Brighton.'

'Thank you, no.'

He offers no further explanation. The car drives on.

Toby Clore, returning from abroad, notices every smallest detail of his homeland. England is as ugly as ever. The ugliness not in the buildings or the landscape, but in the absence of joy.

Toutes directions. He follows the arrow. To his left a raised roadway over which the occasional car passes. Late at night now, and the pavements are empty. A steady stream of trucks rumbles by from the ferry. A road sign ahead offers Brighton, Seaford, Eastbourne. He was not telling the truth when he said he has no idea where he is going. He has several ideas. The strongest of these is that he is not going to Eastbourne, where his mother lives, even though he has no money left and no means of supporting himself. Then after this comes a lesser idea, that he will make his way to the village of Edenfield. He went to prep school nearby, and has friends who live there. He has come back to a world where he is known.

He follows the road, now passing through an industrial zone. Many of the yards are abandoned, their offices boarded up. The Travis Perkins yard is stacked with building materials laid out in rows behind a high fence. A sign on the fence reads: *Anything you need to transform any landscape.* A grand promise indeed.

Give me a fleet of bulldozers, Travis Perkins. Give me flame throwers, and a giant incinerator. Let's take this landscape back to the Stone Age and start again. Oh, and this time leave out the people.

The long road stretches out ahead, lit by the white glow of truck headlights, the red glow of tail lights. How far is it to Edenfield? Five or six miles, no more. But not tonight.

He veers off the main road up a fork to the left. Here there's a car graveyard where the cars have been lifted up as if by a tidy giant and stacked close together in layers. On top of a blue steel container there sits a yellow Skoda pickup, wheel-less and gutted, with a message painted on its doors: *If your car has a drama get your parts from Motorama.* This is a vehicle-dismantling yard.

A gap in the fence opposite leads to a stile. Toby climbs the stile, seeking some sheltered spot where he can lie down to sleep. Beyond the stile is the railway line, straight and gleaming in the moonlight. A red stop-light in the distance. He crosses the tracks, follows a narrow path round a building site. On one side a dense hedge, on the other, beyond a chain-link fence, a man-made mountain of fresh earth. He has no idea where he's going, only the knowledge that where there are stiles there are footpaths, and where there are footpaths there are places people like to walk to.

The path climbs a rise, and all at once he's out of the dark tunnel, and there before him is the river. The dark gleam of water is edged with a broad band of chalky mud, all clearly visible in the light that never entirely leaves the sky. Town light, moon light, star light.

He walks the high embankment, following the river inland. Ahead he sees some kind of shelter in an open field. He tramps through dry thistles which scratch his calves, and comes to a strange brick ruin built on a wide concrete apron. It's low but substantial, a flattened pyramid of bricks, like a sacrificial altar. Beyond it is another ruin, made of upright iron girders supporting immense concrete beams and a concrete roof. There are no walls, only a strand of barbed wire fuzzy with sheep's wool. The underside of the concrete roof drips with white stalactites that crumble at the touch. Some of the concrete beams have collapsed, and lie at an angle.

There are sheep here, huddled up, asleep. They become agitated as Toby approaches, but he moves slowly and makes no noise and keeps himself some way away from them, and they settle down again. He takes out a ground sheet from his backpack and lays it on a patch of rough grass in one corner of the shelter. Then he stretches himself out on the ground, with his pack as his pillow, and composes himself for sleep.

He hears the breathing of the sheep, and the rumble of the trucks on the distant road. I'm back in England, he thinks. Safe, small, joyless England. Why have I come back?

The demon commands. I obey.

Then a smile forms on his face in the night, even as his punished body cries out for sleep. He's remembering the little boy on the boat.

Maybe I am Jesus. Maybe I've returned from the wilderness to bring new life. The gospel according to Toby.

Sleep now, Toby. Sleep, demon.

MONDAY

8

Maggie Dutton wakes with a headache, a dull pain behind her ears and eyes. It's hard to get out of bed. Her head has grown too heavy to lift. Later it's hard to go in to work. Her feet stick to the ground.

What am I afraid of?

She loves her job. Ask anyone who knows her and that's what they'll tell you. Lucky Maggie to be paid for her passion. But a job isn't a life, and all of a sudden Maggie's in hiding from her life.

She swallows two paracetamol. One sticks briefly in her throat, leaving behind its bitter taste.

This has happened before. Call it a panic attack. The form it takes is a voice in the head, not her own voice, the sound of the heavy pain behind her eyes, saying, *You're losing it. You're losing it all.*

So she grips her hands tight on the kitchen table, on the steering wheel of the car, on the strap of her leather satchel, not knowing she's doing it. Fear of losing it all.

Feathery clouds in the pale blue sky as she walks from the car park past the railway station. Nesting rooks rising and falling in the tops of the sycamores that line Southover Road. She tries calling her best girlfriend Jo, but gets no answer and doesn't leave a message. Her head is still hurting as she keys in the code and goes through the glass doors and climbs the wide stairs to the second floor.

Sam is already there, stirring his first cup of coffee of the day, the cramped little office wrapped round him like a coat. He looks up as Maggie enters and she can see from his eyes that he can't see it, the panic. He looks instead to see how she sees him, a sweet boy with more than a crush on her. It happens when you're squeezed together in a tiny office day after day.

'Good weekend?' he says.

'Not bad.' She drops her heavy satchel, sinks down into her chair, presses her fingers to her temples. The tray of new applications looks fuller than it was last thing Friday. There are Post-It notes on her desk with messages.

'Oh, God. The Westmeston barn conversion again.'

'It's the glazing bars. They want a decision today.'

'Get me a cup of coffee, Sam. I haven't woken up yet.'

'Coming up.'

For a few moments she has the office to herself. The pain is passing at last. So what was that about? Not about Andrew, surely? It's true she had half assumed he'd call when he got back to his place yesterday evening, and he didn't. But what's the big deal with that? She's been wanting to cool things down a bit. Slow things down.

Nothing has slowed down. Suddenly her life is going by at double speed, fast-forward to somewhere unknown. In seven days' time Andrew starts a new job just up the road here in Lewes, and if he's not living with her then they've split up, and if he's living with her then they're getting married.

That's stupid, isn't it? How can your entire future come down to a decision you make in six days?

Yesterday it seemed simple. Yesterday it was just a matter of stopping the door closing on her. But he always calls in the evenings when they're apart, and yesterday he didn't call. What does that mean? Is he hurt? Is he angry? She doesn't want to hurt him or anger him.

So what do I want? I stay with Andrew for the rest of my life, and know it could have been so much better. Or I split up with Andrew and risk spending the rest of my life alone.

Sam returns with a mug of hot strong coffee.

'You look like hell, if you don't mind me saying so.'

'I feel like hell.'

'You know what, Maggie? You should marry me.'

Five years younger than her, so he can joke about it.

'What makes you think I want to marry anyone, Sam?'

'Oh, you know. People do.'

'Actually I'm okay with the marrying. But living with someone, that's hard.'

'You know why?'

'No, Sam. Tell me why.'

'Because you're a control freak. You need someone submissive who adores you.'

He poses with his hands spread, a soppy grin on his face. Maggie laughs. The panic is subsiding.

'I'd drive you nuts.'

'You don't know till you try. And I don't care that you're older than me. Actually, that's what I like about you.'

'Shut up, Sam. We've got work to do.'

But Sam's ridiculous act is doing her good. Shaming how much we all like being flattered.

So the day's work begins. There's the amended plans for the Southease bridge to check, and a batch of new plans for the alterations to F-Wing at the prison. Four household extension applications. Two conversions of outbuildings. Phone calls have been logged over the weekend from neighbours reporting suspicious work on nearby properties.

'Have you checked the addresses, Sam?'

'No, not yet.'

'So what have you been doing?'

'Drinking my coffee. Tending to my boss's needs. Anyway, I only just got in.'

You can never tell what time anyone's got in now that they all work flexitime. But she knows Sam's not a slacker. He's already pulled over the list and opened up Map Explorer to check if any of the reported addresses require planning permission or listed building consent.

John Randall looks in from the Development Control Office outside. He's holding a stapled batch of papers.

'PPS5,' he says. 'You need to run your eye over this.'

'I thought I had,' says Maggie. 'What's the problem?'

'Policy HE1.3 is pretty racy stuff.' Randall lifts his eyebrows as he speaks. He's a humorist. 'Heritage assets and climate change.'

Maggie takes the papers and reads the policy clause.

Where conflict between climate change objectives and the conservation of heritage assets is unavoidable, the public benefit of mitigating the effects of climate change should be weighed against any harm to the significance of heritage assets in accordance with the development management principles in this PPS and national policy on climate change.

'Terrific,' she says wearily. 'So that's a big help.'

'If you ask me, I'd stay with PPG15.'

'I love PPG15. But that's not much use either.'

'The department's had a letter from the agent for the Harvey's site development. The one you warned off making direct contact with the AAP. He's threatening legal action.'

'There's a surprise. Funny how it's always the crooks who send in the lawyers.'

'You are covered, Maggie?'

'It's all in the email record.'

Randall leaves. Maggie checks her diary. She's due to make her first site visit at 10 a.m., a house on Chapel Hill. She settles down to work through her in-tray.

Jo rings, responding to Maggie's missed call. Maggie takes her phone out into the little meeting room they call the Goldfish Bowl. Jo's just about the only person in the world she can tell.

'I've been going insane, Jo. Tell me I'm not crazy. I think maybe I am crazy. You know Andrew's got this new job? He starts next Monday. The idea was he was to move in with me. I mean, why wouldn't he move in? It makes all the sense in the world. Except yesterday I panicked. Now I come out in a sweat every time I think about it.'

Jo as always says the obvious thing.

'Do you love him enough to marry him?'

'I don't know,' Maggie wails. 'And anyway, it's not just that. It's what if I don't find anyone better? If I don't find anyone better then I'll settle for Andrew.'

'You know what it says in the paper today?' says Jo. 'It says women are at their most beautiful at thirty-one. You're at your peak.'

'Oh, Jo. I do love talking to you. Are you free at lunchtime?'

Not the kind of conversation you can squeeze into a few minutes. It turns out Jo is out all day at some rehearsal and won't be home till late tonight, so they fix to meet for lunch tomorrow.

Back in the office Sam asks to come with Maggie on the site

visit, but she says no. She needs him to stay and keep on top of the phones and emails. Work is piling up.

'I don't know what happened to this recession,' she says.

'You could look in on South Street while you're out,' says Sam. 'Some kind of unauthorised work at Dean House.'

Walking across Lewes Maggie's spirits rise. She loves Lewes. Compared to Cardiff, where she worked before, which is almost all Victorian and Edwardian stock, Lewes is a treasure trove of architectural styles. Walk down just about any street and you'll see buildings studded with Caen stone robbed from the Priory at the time of the Reformation, flint walls over three hundred years old, mathematical tiles from the eighteenth century, Victorian decorative brickwork, right up to the blight of modern through-colour render. There's a Georgian house on the High Street with a black mathematical tile high over a top window, look with binoculars and you can see a cat's paw printed in the ceramic glaze, made the day the tile was set out to dry two hundred years ago. When you know what to look for it's as if the streets are talking to you, as if all the people who ever lived here for the last thousand years are watching you go by. It actually gives her goose bumps to find a house like Castle Lodge where the knapped flints run round the corners. That's difficult work. All other flint walls trim the windows and the corners with brick. But all those years ago someone said, I don't care how long it takes, nap me flints on two faces and damn the expense. Then at the opposite end of the spectrum you have the prefabricated flint-and-concrete blocks used in the development of Baxter's Printworks in St Nicholas's Lane. No conservation officer can have authorised that abomination.

Down Friars Walk into the pedestrian area of Cliffe, where most of the buildings date from the 1970s. What went wrong in the twentieth century? Something happened that broke the link between an area and its buildings. From about 1950 onwards each new shop, each new house, arrived like a foreigner, an emissary of some alien power seeking to infiltrate and corrupt the town. These newish buildings attempt a disguise, they wear some trappings of the region, a dormer window, a tile-hung upper wall, but applied so cheaply and so out of proportion that no one is fooled.

She walks on over the bridge into Cliffe High Street. Here the authentic town returns again in earnest. The street has recently been repaved to make it more pedestrian friendly, but cars are still allowed to pass down it in one direction, which makes a nonsense of the good intentions. The whole of the centre of Lewes should be car-free, the town would spring alive, but the traders won't hear of it. They can't believe people will ever get out of their cars.

As she turns into South Street, it's not hard to find the building work underway. A big yellow skip stands outside the house, and men are at work within. Maggie examines the contents of the skip and sees torn sections of lath-and-plaster internal walls. She takes out her warrant card from her bag.

A dust-covered builder responds to her knocking. He's a powerfully built man with his head shaven at the sides. Maggie shows him her authorisation.

'Maggie Dutton, Planning Department,' she says, keeping her voice neutral. These moments can get confrontational. She catches the flutter of a net curtain in the next-door house. That would be the caller.

'What about it?' says the builder.

'I have to ask you to stop work here,' says Maggie. 'Under the Planning, Listed Building and Conservation Area Act 1990 it's a criminal offence to carry out works that affect the special interest of a listed building without listed building consent.'

The builder stares at her, silent with shock. She's so small and so pretty men usually can't take in that she's giving them orders.

'Nothing to do with me, love,' he says at last. 'Talk to the owner.'

'Under the act,' says Maggie, 'the builder is just as responsible as the owner who instructs him. The penalties range from unlimited fines to imprisonment.'

The builder dabs at the plaster dust in his eyes. From the upper floor comes the sound of banging.

'Stop work?' he says. 'You serious?'

'Yes,' says Maggie.

The builder turns and calls up the stairs behind him.

'Yo! Dean! Give it a rest, mate!'

A second builder appears, equally dusty, a younger man with a scarred face.

'What's up?'

'Lady says we have to stop or she'll put us in prison.'

The second builder throws down the hammer he's holding.

'Fucking great,' he says. 'That's all I fucking need.'

'This house is a listed building,' says Maggie. 'The owner needs listed building consent to make these alterations. He can submit an application, but until and unless it's approved all work must stop.'

'So how long will that take, then?'

'Around eight weeks. Could be longer.'

The younger builder slumps down on the bottom step of the stairs.

'Why me?' he says. 'When do I get a break?'

'I'm sorry,' says Maggie. 'The owner should have known the procedure.'

She takes out her little digital camera.

'If you don't mind, I'll take a look inside.'

They stand back to let her in. She moves quickly from room to room, photographing the work. Then she leaves a card for them to give to the owner and goes on her way.

The curtains flutter in the neighbour's house. Her phone buzzes. A text from Jo.

Sun says average number of sex partners for women is 7. Way 2 go.

Maggie smiles as she texts back.

How do U no?

Leave out a few short-lived mistakes and it's four. Andrew's been the longest. They'd been friends for ever before they got together. All the time she was with Nigel she was telling Andrew what a prick Nigel was, and then when they broke up Andrew took her for a walk in Regent's Park. The roses were in bloom in the long rose beds, the air was heavy with the scent of roses, and he asked her if she only liked pricks, and she had to laugh. He was always so easy to be with. You don't get aggravation with Andrew.

You don't get excitement.

So what do I want? To be worked up into a froth of passion? You can't live like that. Life is mostly the everyday stuff. We expect too much.

If women are at their most beautiful at thirty-one, I've got nine months to go. If my allocation of sex partners is seven, I'm due three more.

When it's right you don't have these doubts, do you? You just know. You take one look and you just know. That's why it's called falling in love. So how do you do that?

9

Carrie Broad sits on her bed gazing into the mirror on the inside of her open wardrobe door. She sees her pale face. The mole on her upper lip. Her high white brow, her hair pulled back and up, tied in a prudish bun. She stares into her unblinking grey eyes.

This is me.

She raises one hand and gives a token wave of greeting. The hand in the mirror waves back.

I'm saying hello.

She goes on staring at her reflected image, knowing that soon the face in the mirror will take on an existence of its own and will cease to be her, or she will cease to be it. This separation is what she needs. Cut loose from her visible self with all its disappointments she can be a nothing. She can prowl the world seeing but unseen, knowing but unknown.

The wardrobe mirror grows until it fills the room. The girl with the blank face becomes a stranger.

Bye. See you. Don't see you.

She reaches for her guitar and settles it onto her lap. Picking out chords with her fingers, improvising a tune that she will never be able to repeat again, she sings a song written by the girl in the mirror, the one who has gone away. The song is called 'It's Over Now'.

'I died and went to heaven
Like they said I would
And there I met my friend the Artist
Waiting for me.
He said to me, Look down
And I looked and saw my life
Like a river running to the sea.
And my friend the Artist said to me
Do you see it now?
Do you see it now?
It was always going nowhere
Always going nowhere
But it's over now
I know it hurts
But it's over now
I know you lost
But it's over now
We're above the clouds
Beneath the sea
My friend the Artist said to me
And you're beautiful
You're beautiful
Now you've died and gone to heaven
And there's no one left to see.'

After the song has finished she goes on playing chords on the guitar, letting the sounds tremble in the air. Her guitar is her shield, no one can hurt her. Her songs are the way she knows that someone feels what she feels, even if that someone shares her name.

'Get in my car
Hit the open road
Distraction's what I need
Drive myself to distraction . . .'

That makes her laugh. She sees the girl in the mirror smiling and she looks away. That's the loser who's failed her driving test twice so far. Only way she'll ever hit the open road is with her head.

She pushes the guitar away and jumps up, suddenly filled with determination. Third time lucky.

She goes downstairs and finds her father in his study.

'I really need driving practice, Dad. You said you would.'

Her father groans and holds his head in his hands.

'Not now,' he says. 'I've got this meeting tomorrow. It's really important. I'm sorry, darling.'

'But I've got my test in two weeks.'

'Wednesday. I promise.'

He gives her a pleading look and she knows she has to back off. That's the trouble with her father. He's got his own problems.

Suddenly he's up out of his chair like he's been stung. He's staring out of the window.

'Rabbit!'

There's a rabbit on the lawn, nibbling the grass.

'Carrie! Wait here! I'm going out of the side door, and down to the orchard. Count to twenty, and then shout boo!'

'Why?'

'To make the rabbit run.'

He goes into the hall. Carrie watches the rabbit and counts slowly to herself. The rabbit goes on grazing, all unaware. As Carrie gets to thirteen, the phone rings. Somewhere in the house her mother answers it. As she gets to seventeen, the front door bell rings.

Eighteen. Nineteen.

'Carrie! Get the door! I'm on the phone.'

Carrie opens the window and shouts, 'Boo!'

The rabbit looks up.

'Boo!'

The rabbit lopes off towards the orchard.

Carrie goes to the front door. There outside is a young guy with long hair and a beard and a backpack. He looks at her without speaking, as if he's trying to find something in her face. His black eyes scan her all over, then come to rest on her eyes. She stands there and lets him examine her, feeling herself starting to tremble. But she doesn't break the eye contact. It's like looking in the mirror.

See you. Don't see you.

'I'm a friend of Jack's,' he says at last.

'Jack's not here. He's in Turkey.'

'Then I'd better be a friend of yours.'

'Why?'

'I need food,' he says. 'I need a shower.'

All at once she sees beneath the beard and the long hair a face she remembers from the past.

'You're Toby.'

'Yes.'

'I'm Carrie.'

'Hello, Carrie.'

Neither of them has moved. Neither of them has broken the intense eye contact.

Her father bursts into the hall from the back door.

'You'll never believe it! I wouldn't believe it if I hadn't seen it with my own eyes! The rabbits are climbing the fence!'

'Dad—'

'The bugger took a run at it and up he went! Like a bloody lizard!'

'Dad, this is Toby. He's a friend of Jack's.'

'Hello, Toby. Did you know rabbits could climb fences? It's a new one on me.'

'He needs somewhere to stay. I told him he could crash here. Is that okay?'

'I expect so,' says Henry. 'Ask your mother.'

'She's on the phone. He's a friend from Underhill.'

'Fine, fine,' says Henry. 'I have to go and call Terry. We need to raise the fence.'

He disappears into his study.

'So it's fine,' says Carrie. 'You'd better come in.'

Toby picks up his backpack and comes in.

'Thanks,' he says.

'You said food.'

'Right. I could do with something.'

'When did you last eat?'

'Saturday,' he says. 'Or maybe Friday.'

'Oh my God!'

She takes him into the kitchen and starts hunting round for something quick and easy to feed him.

'How about a cheese and tomato sandwich? Or would you rather have cornflakes? I know. I'll get you a glass of milk.'

'Yes,' he says simply.

So she pours him a glass of milk and fills a bowl with cornflakes and while he eats that she sets about making him a cheese and tomato sandwich.

He eats slowly, intently, quietly.

'So what happened?' she says. 'Did you run out of money?'

'Yes,' he says.

'That must have been so scary.'

'No.'

'Where've you been travelling?'

'I walked up the river bank. That was this morning. Yesterday was France.'

'And now you're going home?'

'No.'

She watches him eat with the pride of a mother watching her child. He looks so thin, so unloved. He'll need a shower. His clothes will need washing.

'How long have you been travelling?'

'Long time.'

Every word he speaks excites her. He doesn't say so much, but it's the tone of his voice. It's like he doesn't care what impression he makes. He thinks before he speaks, as if to check that what he's about to say is correct as far as he knows. And those eyes! She feels as if he sees right into her.

Her mother, off the phone at last, comes into the kitchen. Carrie introduces Toby as if she's been expecting him.

'This is Toby, Mum. He's Jack's friend from Underhill. Dad says it's okay if he crashes here.'

'Toby?'

'Toby Clore.'

'Yes, of course,' says Laura vaguely. 'That was Liz on the phone. Alice's mum.' She explains for Toby's benefit. 'Alice is Jack's girlfriend. They're in Turkey right now. Alice texted her mother to say they're standing in the Roman stadium in Aphrodisias. Apparently it's the largest Roman stadium anywhere.'

Henry Broad comes back.

'I've found out how the rabbits get in!' he announces to Laura in triumph. 'They climb the fence! I've just been on to

Terry. He's going to build a slanting top section to the fence. Like this.'

He holds his arm up at an angle.

'Jack's in Aphrodisias,' says Laura. 'Liz phoned. I asked Liz and Alan to come to dinner on Saturday. They can help us celebrate.'

'Celebrate what?' says Carrie.

'Oh, it's all rather silly. Saturday's the anniversary of our engagement. It's not at all important.'

'I like that,' says Toby. 'If you think about it, every single moment of our life could be a celebration of every other single moment.'

He says it as if he expects to be taken seriously. It's like he comes from some alien civilisation and has never encountered humans before.

'Where should Toby sleep?' Carrie says. 'He could have Jack's room. Or a spare bedroom?'

'Whatever you like, darling. How long are you staying, Toby?'

Toby lowers the sandwich from his mouth and gives Laura a slow smile.

'Not long at all,' he says. 'Couple of nights. If that's okay.'

'He can go in Jack's room,' says Carrie. 'He's Jack's friend.'

Henry has now had the opportunity to take in their unexpected guest.

'So you've been travelling,' he says. 'Gap year, is it?'

'That sort of thing.'

'So which college are you heading to?'

'No college.'

'Oh, right. Straight into earning your living, eh?'

'No earning. Just living.'

He says it so simply it silences them all. Carrie is entranced. Everything he says and does seems to her to be perfect.

'You must have indulgent parents,' says Henry.

'I suppose so,' says Toby. 'I never met my father. I haven't spoken to my mother for years.'

Another silence. Toby finishes his sandwich.

'Come on,' says Carrie. 'I'll show you where you can sleep.'

He follows her upstairs. Jack's room looks uncharacteristically tidy. His teddy bear has been put on the neatly made bed.

'You can use my bathroom,' says Carrie. 'It's still called the children's bathroom. I'll get you a towel.'

'That's your room, is it?'

He's looking through the half-open door of Carrie's room. On the far wall hangs Anthony Armitage's portrait of her. Toby is staring at it. He moves to the doorway to see it better. He looks from the portrait to Carrie.

'It was done ages ago,' says Carrie.

'It's good,' says Toby.

'Yes. It's good.'

She leaves him to have a shower and a rest, but as he does so she tracks his every sound. She can't help herself. He fascinates her. She hears the splash of the water and its gurgle as it drains. She pictures him naked, glistening, towelling himself. She hears the bathroom door open, and his light footsteps, and the door to Jack's room close.

Will he lie down on the bed and sleep? For how long?

She tries to recall him from prep-school days, but she barely knew him. He was Jack's friend. She's not heard Jack mention him since.

The things he says. *No earning, just living.* And those eyes! He's not beautiful, but he's something else that's so much more potent. He's unique. He's like no one she's ever met.

She wonders what he makes of her. Just some boring girl. Carrie knows there's nothing special about her, not at first glance anyway. She's not pretty and she's not a clever talker. Whatever she has that makes her interesting is hidden from view. She's never shown her songs to anyone, or sung them to anyone.

I'd better be a friend of yours, he said. And he liked the portrait. Not many do.

Then there are footsteps across the landing and a tap on her door.

'Yes?'

He looks into her room. His hair is wet from his shower, slick to his head, and he's wearing Jack's bathrobe. He looks fresh and young.

'You think Jack would mind if I borrowed some of his clothes while I get mine washed?'

'No, of course not,' says Carrie.

'Okay if I lie down for a while?'

'Sleep as much as you want. Do you want to be woken for lunch?'

'For supper, maybe.'

He goes back to Jack's room. Carrie sits on her bed and shivers.

I was wrong. He's beautiful.

She puts her arms round herself and hugs herself tight. She rocks from side to side on the bed. She's trying to stop it happening but already it's too late. She's caught. It's going to hurt and there's nothing she can do to stop it.

10

The programme went out yesterday evening on Radio 5, but thanks to the wonders of the Internet she can catch up with it today in the privacy of her study. Not her study: Liz Dickinson is anxious not to let it be established that this former back pantry is adequate as her work space. She's only camping here until they can convert the old cart lodge into an office for Alan. Then she in her turn can take over the room that seems to have been known, by the previous occupants, as the parlour. What on earth do you do in a parlour?

She navigates on her laptop through the BBC website. The programme is called *Men's Hour* and is billed as the male rejoinder to the venerable *Woman's Hour*. Mark, her section editor, has asked for five hundred words.

Before clicking on Listen Again, putting off the moment when she has to concentrate, Liz calls her mother's carer, Bridget, again, and again she gets no answer. Then, seeking further cause to avoid her work, she remembers that she hasn't checked with Alan about Saturday evening. She jumps up and crosses through the living room, where her son Caspar is lying on the floor making something strange out of Lego. You pay a fortune for private education and they spend half their life on holiday.

'Mum,' he says, in a reasonable sort of voice, 'I need to take more exercise.'

'What are you talking about, Cas?'

'I thought you could take me to the skate park.'

'Not now, darling. I just can't.'

This is the one downside to their move, from Cas's point of
view. He had just started to get good on his skateboard. Liz
recalls guiltily that promises were made.

'Maybe Dad can take you.'

She finds Alan staring out of the parlour window.

'The Broads have asked us to dinner on Saturday. I said yes.'

'Why? What about Cas?'

He sounds aggrieved, as she knew he would.

'You like Henry. We'll find a baby-sitter.'

'Look at that!' he says, pointing accusingly out of the window
at the golden day, at the sun on the distant Downs. 'How am
I supposed to work?'

'Don't work,' says Liz. 'Go and watch them shooting your
film.'

One of Alan's screenplays is actually being filmed at last, and
he's so conflicted about his work that he won't go and visit the
set. He keeps shifting his reason for not going, but Liz knows
him well. The screenplay changed so much in development that
he feels it's no longer his baby, or perhaps that it's some kind
of bastard baby. He talks about it angrily, as if he hates it. Liz
tries to be sympathetic, but as a working journalist herself she's
all too used to the compromises of the game. You do the work,
you take the money, and you move on.

'They don't want the writer hanging round,' says Alan.

'They're not going to send you away. Come on. Go and say
hello to your dog.'

The dog, a sheepdog, is the only part of the story that has
remained from the long-ago first draft. Now in its final form

it's a talking dog. This has become something of a family joke. Cas wants to know how it talks.

'It won't really talk,' says Alan. 'It's just film trickery.'

The fact is he's embarrassed. In the film the dog swears.

'Go on,' says Liz. 'Take Cas.'

'Maybe tomorrow,' says Alan.

He's done nothing at all to settle himself in the parlour. It's a pretty room, square in shape, with two deeply recessed windows that look out towards the Downs. Being Alan, he finds the view distracting. When the cart lodge is converted he's going to have a window that looks across the yard towards the house. This conversion is more Liz's idea than Alan's. Left to himself he would never change anything.

'You haven't picked up a call from Bridget, have you?'

'I haven't picked up a call from anyone.'

Alan never answers the phone if she's in the house. What does that say about him? You could call it a kind of trust, that he's content for her to be the gatekeeper to his life. But it feels more like evasion.

'I don't know what's happened to Bridget,' says Liz. 'She just abandoned my mother last night.'

'You'd better ask her.'

'I've left endless messages. I don't understand. I thought she was more responsible than that. It means I'll have to go round and deal with Mum myself.'

Alan nods, but he's not listening. He heard it all last night, and gave such sympathy as he could then. His mind's on other things. Or avoiding other things.

'If you won't go and see your film, then take Cas to the skate park.'

'Yes, okay. I don't mind doing that.'

Liz returns to her desk. She picks up a biro and clicks on the programme and starts listening again. A little to her surprise, it turns out to be quite interesting. Andy McNab, once of the SAS, talks convincingly about how he loves his wife but 'wants the chance to hang out with his mates'. He wants to be all lads together. Her mind drifts. She thinks about Alan. Why doesn't he have a gang of mates? He never goes to the pub. Maybe that's why he gets so low. Maybe he needs male friends. What is it men talk about when they're on their own? In the old days, when the ladies withdrew from the dinner table, leaving the men to their port and cigars, what did the men talk about? Politics? Sex?

Liz's biro scribbles away, jotting down thoughts in note form to work up into her article.

Can men and women ever really be friends? Isn't it always about something else? A silent dialogue conducted alongside or beneath the audible conversation, an exchange of signals sent and received. Am I still attractive? Do I still exist as a sexual being? God knows, it's not as if we want to be forever seducing. But helpless in the grip of our self-doubt we smile and dimple in mixed company. Is that why we prefer to gather in gender-segregated groups? The girls out on the town, the lads watching the match, the hen party, the stag party, which by the way should be called the cock party. There's a comfort in not being on show, and why shouldn't the boys feel it as much as the girls? The laddish pubs and the gentish clubs, not bastions of male superiority after all, but hiding places.

Men's fear of women. A theme to write up one day. Look at the great world religions, Christianity, Islam, Judaism: all obsessed with maintaining men's dominance over women. No wonder they're all in crisis. Women priests, homosexuality, child abuse, abortion, contraception, veiling, stoning for adultery. What is organised religion but an enormous prison built by men to contain the threat of women?

A little over-ambitious for five hundred words. She has paused
Listen Again to make notes. Now, before she can resume *Men's
Hour*, the doorbell rings.

Why is it always me who gets interrupted? Why does Alan
assume I'll answer the doorbell?

Liz realises then that she's criticising Alan to herself a lot of
the time these days, and it scares her. She doesn't want to turn
into a nagging wife. Also she has only to think back nine years
to her former life to regain the shock of gratitude his love once
gave her. And truth to tell, she still experiences a little tremble
of happiness every night when she gets into bed and there he
is – always in bed first – and she feels the warmth of his body
beside hers. Not exactly a sexual happiness: it's more a kind of
comforting, a nightly reminder that she's not alone. And there's
the sex, too. So much chatter about sex these days it's hard to
know how important it really is. Americans say to each other
in bed, 'Do you want to fool around?' Sex as folly, sex as a
childish game.

We fool around, Alan and me, and as the years go by it seems
more and more precious.

Liz opens the front door and there's Bridget, her mother's
carer.

'Oh, Bridget! There you are!'

'I thought I'd best come round,' she says.

She speaks slowly and ponderously, as if this is an official
matter. Liz takes her into the kitchen and puts on the kettle for
tea. Bridget sits down at the kitchen table, folding her hands in
her cumbersome lap. She wears tracksuit trousers and a fawn-
coloured woollen cardigan with a zip.

'What on earth happened, Bridget?' says Liz.

She intends to put the question in a neutral tone, but somehow
her actual feelings come through. Bridget senses the accusation.

'I did as I was asked,' says Bridget, her broad fleshy features setting into a stubborn scowl. 'Your mum, she can be a devil.'

'You know I found her on the floor? God knows how long she'd been there. She says you walked out on her.'

'She told me she'd put herself to bed. You go away, she told me.'

Bridget has gone a little pink and is breathing faster.

'She told you she'd put herself to bed?'

'I do my best,' says Bridget. 'I like to give good service. She asked me to go and I went.'

'But Bridget, you know she needs help going to bed.'

'I know it, of course I know it. Time to come to bed, Mrs D, I told her. But she won't do it. You go away, she says to me. No please or thank you, like I'm a dog to be shooed out of the house. And then I was an hour past my time, and I've got a life too, not that you'd know it. Come to bed, Mrs D, I told her. Go away, she says. What am I to do? I can't pick her up with my own arms and carry her to bed like a baby. She's got a will, that mum of yours, oh she's got a will. I can't make her do something if she don't want to do it. I didn't like leaving her there in the garden, it was dark by the time I left, but what was I to do? Stay there all night? You know I take my responsibilities serious, Liz, you know I do. But your mum, she's got a deal of spirit, don't get me wrong, but oh, she's got a will.'

'She refused to let you put her to bed?'

'Again and again and again.'

Liz feels gripped by a helpless rage. After all the efforts she's made to find a carer, after the false starts and the wrong choices, she had thought that at last it was working. Bridget might not be the most lively of companions, but she is conscientious and reliable. And now it's all going wrong.

'Do you know why she didn't want you to put her to bed?'

'She gets a devil in her, is all I can say. She's like a naughty child, that's what she's like. She won't be told. But she speaks her mind all right. I'm not going to speak to her disrespectful, but she can treat me like dirt.'

'Oh, she is a menace!'

Liz speaks both to herself in her dismay and to Bridget, signalling that the accusation of neglect is withdrawn. Bridget lifts her head higher and speaks in almost official tones. She has clearly prepared these words.

'I've been and spoke to my sister Janet in Hove, Janet always did have the sense in the family. Janet says I'm not to put up with it. Janet says if that's how I'm to be treated, then I'd best take Mrs D at her word and see myself off. If I'm not giving satisfaction, then there it is. There's only so much a person can do.'

'Of course there is,' says Liz, wanting only to appease.

'And she won't take her medication sometimes. Takes it and drops it on the floor. The other day I made her a shepherd's pie, lovely it was, fresh out of the freezer, and she never touched it. Well, it's a waste, isn't it? And of course it's a worry. Won't take her medication, won't eat her food, won't go to bed. It's not right, not at her age.'

'I'll talk to her, Bridget. I'll sort it out.'

'If I'm not giving satisfaction, I don't want to stay on. The Lord knows I do my best. But Janet says I've no call to stay on and be spoken to like that.'

'Of course not, Bridget. I'm so sorry. I'll make sure it doesn't happen again. You're so reliable and you keep everything so tidy – really we're so lucky to have you. My mum knows she needs you, really.'

'If I say I'll do a thing, then I do it. I was in this morning and not a word. It was just like nothing had happened. I put out her toast and she ate it up. Then off I went, and still not a word. I went to Hove and spoke to Janet. So as soon as you can find someone else—'

'No, no. I'll never find someone as reliable as you, Bridget. I'll go over as soon as I can and talk to her.'

'If I'm not giving satisfaction, I don't want to stay on. Don't get me wrong, but it's no pleasure doing a job if you're spoken to like you're dirt.'

'I'll make her understand, Bridget. I don't know what I'd do if you left us. Don't worry about it. I'll talk to her. Please?'

'Well, seeing as you don't have anyone.' Bridget allows herself to be persuaded. 'But if she tells me to go away again, I'll take her at her word and not trouble her no more.'

Bridget leaves. Liz feels so agitated by the encounter that she goes through to Alan again, even though she knows she's running out of time to file her five hundred words.

'My bloody mother!' she says. 'Turns out she sent Bridget away last night.'

'You know why? She doesn't want a carer. She wants you.'

'Well, she can't have me.'

Caspar squeezes into the space between them.

'I know who can babysit me on Saturday,' he says. 'Granny. I can go to Granny's.'

'Good Lord! Do you want to?'

'Yes,' says Cas.

'She's too old, darling. And she's not being at all nice to Bridget.'

'She'll be nice to me,' says Cas. 'And Bridget could be there too.'

'We'll see,' says Liz. 'Don't worry about Saturday. We'll sort something out.'

To Alan she says, 'I'll have to go round there and try to knock some sense into her. This is the last thing I need. I'm already late with my piece for today.'

'Do your work,' says Alan. 'Forget your mother. One visit won't solve anything. She's just something you have to endure, like the weather.'

'God, she drives me crazy.'

Back at her desk, Liz starts up the radio programme once more. She listens to a man called Louis confessing that he wishes he'd shagged around more when he was younger. It seems he was held back because he thought his knob was too small.

Liz stops the playback and puts her head in her hands. For God's sake. What is it with humanity? What makes people so ignorant, and fearful, and self-destructive? Surely there's enough misery in the world without dreaming up ways to make it worse.

She picks up her biro and writes at the bottom of her page of notes: *Men fear women because their knobs are too small.* So why would that bother them? Because they fear the loss of sexual power? If so, here's the news, guys. It's on its way. The day will come when you'll no longer be able to get it up. It's called old age, and it happens to every single one of us. You want to get angry about that? You're going to be old for a long, long time. How long can you stay angry? So let it go, guys. In the end all our knobs are too small.

11

Laura emails a friend who specialises in crime fiction to get a price indicator on the Menno Herrema collection. There are several serious buyers out there, and Golden Age mystery novels are much in demand. Get a bidding war going and you could end up doubling the standard dealer estimate. Laura wants a figure to dangle before Andrew on Saturday.

That done, she sits down at the kitchen table, pulls a lined pad towards her, and writes at the top: Dinner for 8. She has a menu to plan.

Laura is a good cook and she takes pride in her food. She wants to present a dinner that will be seen to be special, while at the same time not straining to be praised. The food is to be fine but not showy. But this is not a family supper, and she will feel inescapably on show, so she does not want to subject herself to any unnecessary last-minute stress. Dover sole for eight, for example. Or soufflé. Not that either are on her mental list. But the object is to have as much done ahead of time as possible, so that once the guests arrive there is nothing left to go wrong. Against this one must set the need to present each dish at its right moment, which will almost certainly mean last-minute cooking of some parts of the meal. And that will mean cutting herself off from the conversation at exactly the time when it's most relaxed, which is over the pre-prandial drink.

Then there's the weather. The forecast is for the hot weather to continue, so Laura's first thought is to eat out on the terrace. But by nine in the evening it can get quite cool. Should she make a hot main dish, say, a roast leg of lamb, to bring warmth as the air cools? Or should she go for a cold main dish, say, Thai beef salad, to acknowledge the alfresco nature of the evening? Or is it is madness to plan to eat outdoors when the temperature may plummet and the wind get up? July can be so unpredictable. Everyone is saying the hot weather must break soon.

She thinks then that it would be nice to make a summer pudding. There are still redcurrants and blackcurrants in the fruit cage, and though the crop of raspberries is just about over she has some frozen from last year. If she's to make summer pudding she'll have to buy the white bread today or tomorrow to give it time to go stale. If the bread isn't stale it forms a gluey rind and fails to soak up the juices of the fruits. The bulk of the shopping will have to be done on Friday, for maximum freshness.

When the sun is shining the garden looks lovely in the early evening. The light falls on the great brow of Mount Caburn, rising up behind the house like a guardian rampart. Laura visualises her guests moving about the terrace, drinks in hand, enjoying the warm summer air, chatting to each other in a relaxed manner. So a starter that can be eaten standing up, then. Not canapés, this isn't a drinks party. But something bite-sized, that doesn't require a plate. Bruschetta?

Each decision affects the rest. If the main dish is elaborate, the starter should be simple, even homely. Perhaps a sardine pâté, made with fresh sardines, she could make that in the morning, it's just fish paste really, but no one would think it was bought pre-made from M&S. The whole trick is to present food that is easy to deliver on the day, but which requires skill and originality in the making beforehand. The art that conceals art.

Laura catches herself thinking this, and realises she's smiling in that way you smile when you want to deflect attention. And it's true that she would never reveal to anyone just how much the success of a dinner party matters to her. It's as if it's a secret addiction. And as with all drug habits, it's not the narcotic that's shameful, but the neurosis that drives the user to reach for the drug. In her case, the need to project a certain self-image. The need for control.

Why should this be a source of shame? No one accuses a businessman of being neurotic when he plans his appointments and ticks off his objectives. But have a few friends round for a meal and it's supposed to happen in some spontaneous manner, without forethought. Like sex, which is supposed to be the result of the passion of the moment. You don't schedule sex. Except quite often that's exactly what she and Henry do. He'll say to her, 'Carrie is going to be out on Friday evening, let's have some time to ourselves.' That way they can both look forward to it, and make the time, and enjoy it. But she'd never tell any of her friends this. Somehow the acts in the arena of private happiness are not supposed to be rehearsed. Home life is natural, it's organic, it's free range. Why? Because it's our refuge from the disciplines and efforts of the world of work. We come home not to do, but to be.

When they have friends round for a meal, she often says to Henry, 'What shall I cook?' He usually replies, 'Don't do anything grand. Just a bowl of pasta.' He too lives in this dream world where home life follows a natural rhythm like the seasons, and good things grow and ripen in their time, and have only to be plucked and enjoyed. To be fair he does cook from time to time, and in what he would call an 'instinctive' way. This means he never uses recipe books, and he picks from the ingredients he finds in the larder and the fridge. No making of lists, no thinking ahead, no shopping. When he lays his triumphant dish on the table there's a look in his eye that says, 'There, no need for all the fuss.'

Laura goes in secretly for a considerable amount of fuss. Perhaps if she exposed the process to Henry he'd be more grateful. But something in her wants to protect the illusion that her excellent meals are a last-minute improvisation; as indeed they sometimes are. The vanity of the expert. The hours of practice kept out of sight, so that the public performance will be nonchalant, without signs of strain, graceful. Like the way she ticked the box for Yes when he asked her to marry him.

She blushes a little as she remembers. There's something here of which she is still ashamed.

Henry managed the proposal in such a Henry-ish way. They were having lunch in a pub, nothing grand, the Dove, by the river in Hammersmith. He was telling her about the research he was doing at the time, which was all about the history of tests and examinations. He was explaining the terms used in multiple choice tests, the *stem*, the *key*, and the *distractor*, most of all the distractors, the false answers designed to be so plausible that you might be fooled into picking them. To illustrate what he was saying he pulled out a paper napkin from the holder on the table and wrote her an example.

Even before he had begun to write on the napkin she knew what was coming. This is the part she doesn't want to think about: how she was able to respond so seemingly without hesitation. All the calculation and the compromise had taken place earlier, out of sight.

He wrote on the napkin: *Will you marry me?* Next to this he drew two little boxes, with the choice of answers beside them.

Yes and *No*. No distractors after all. He then turned the napkin round to face her, held out the pen, and fixed her with his hesitant smile.

She ticked Yes.

She kept the paper napkin, of course, but she can no longer remember what she did with it. She's looked through the bottom left-hand drawer of her desk where she keeps all her personal and family papers, but it's not there. She tries to remember when she last saw it. She remembers taking it from the pub table all those years ago and putting it in her handbag, but after that there's nothing. This makes her feel guilty, as if she has deliberately airbrushed the history of Henry's proposal from her past.

She hears Carrie and Toby come downstairs and is struck by a sudden thought.

'Carrie!' she calls out, catching them as they're crossing the hall. 'Are you going to be in on Saturday evening? And will Toby still be here?'

'Don't know,' says Carrie.

'But I need to know.'

'It's Monday, Mum! We could all be dead by Saturday.'

With that she goes out, and Toby follows her, and the door shuts after them.

This is unacceptable, surely? The very least Carrie owes her is information about when she expects a meal to appear before her. If she and Toby are to join the dinner party, that means she's shopping and cooking for ten, which is quite different to eight. What if Toby has some quirky faddishness over what he eats? It seems to Laura to be highly likely. In which case she needs to know. Carrie is not being fair, or grateful.

Henry appears with that look on his face that says his mind is elsewhere. He's come to make himself a mug of coffee, and to filch a Maryland cookie. In theory he has given up eating cookies mid-morning, as part of a programme to lose his paunch; also in theory he goes for a run twice a week. The intention remains, and is honoured by his secretive pocketing of the cookies, as if taking them without being seen means he can eat them without gaining weight. In the same spirit, while never actually going for a run, he has a way of talking as if he's always on the point of it. 'I'll see if I can find time for a run after lunch,' he says. Or, 'It's just too bloody hot to go running today.'

'About Saturday evening,' he says. 'We shouldn't be having people round. It should just be you and me. It's our anniversary.'

'Too late now.'

'We can tell them not to come.'

'No, darling. We can't. Diana and Roddy are coming down for the weekend. People make plans. You can't just ring up and say you've changed your mind.'

'What if there was some crisis?'

'But there isn't.'

Henry takes two biscuits in a way that shows he thinks she can't see, and turns to head back to his study.

'Carrie won't tell me if she and Toby are going to be eating with us on Saturday night,' Laura says. 'How on earth am I supposed to plan my menu?'

'Two more can't make that much difference,' says Henry.

This makes Laura even more cross.

'What utterly stupid things you say, Henry. If there are ten guests and I've bought eight fillet steaks, what are the other two supposed to eat?'

'Don't buy fillet steaks. Make a stew or something.'

'A stew! In July!'

'Well, I don't know, Laura.'

He retreats.

Alone in the kitchen she pulls out recipe books and spreads them across the table to begin the long process of deciding on a menu.

Maybe I'm neurotic, she thinks to herself. Maybe I'm a control freak. Too bad. That's just how I am.

She checks Hugh Fearnley-Whittingstall's suggestions for July in *The River Cottage Year*. Baby courgette salad. Beetroot salad. Not at all what she's looking for. She looks in Nigel Slater's *Kitchen Diaries*. Red mullet – far too much anxiety at the last minute. Lamb rolls – what on earth are lamb rolls? Vietnamese beef salad – which turns out to be Thai beef salad under another name – but grilling the beef would be such a last-minute worry. The barbecue is simply not reliable.

Why not do the obvious? July is the time for new-season lamb. Can I get enough for eight out of a leg of lamb?

12

Alan understands Cas doesn't want him hanging round watching him in the skateboard park, though he doesn't say so. He takes his skateboard through the gate and closes the gate behind him, not looking back. Alan lingers for a moment watching his son's lithe body twist and turn on the board, until he's lost to sight in the crowd of other boys. All boys here, on bikes and boards. A male environment, the concrete ramps bright with graffiti, jagged letters that spell out illegible tags.

He crosses the grass to the riverside path and follows it, walking slowly, killing time. On the far side of the river, glimpsed between trees, stands a line of abandoned industrial buildings, grey corrugated iron, fading signs. Ahead on the hillside a tall phone mast poking through the treetops. The tarmac of the path is uneven like the blankets on an unmade bed. He feels the ground with his feet as he walks, half-expecting it to respond to the pressure of his weight. He finds himself thinking about *ground*, how we presume it to be solid, sustaining, the base and foundation of all things. And yet it's only a layer on a layer on a layer. Much like blankets on a bed.

There are gulls on the grass of the little park, moving about, stabbing at the earth. Gulls are supposed to be seabirds, they're supposed to catch fish. Nowadays they live on garbage.

Above the park rises the whaleback hump of Malling Hill.

Further south, further east, and the Downs meet the sea in the ripple of cliffs called the Seven Sisters. Here above the meander of Cuckmere Haven the film unit is shooting the opening scene of *Rockefeller*. Everything about this project has caused Alan grief. It began as a gentle fable about a banker who abandons the high-stress world of the City to become a shepherd. Now it's a comedy about a talking sheepdog who becomes a successful City trader. The biggest joke in the screenplay comes when the dog, under pressure at the trading desk, starts shouting 'Fuck!' This is supposedly Alan's creation.

My big moment. A dog that says 'Fuck!'

He's ashamed and he's angry, without quite knowing where to direct his anger. At himself, obviously, for colluding in this nonsense. But also at his producer, and the studio above her, for having such a low estimate of their public. And maybe, if they turn out to be right, at the public, for living down to such cynical estimations.

Then again, the situation is more complicated than that. There are one or two moments, one or two lines, that he's proud of. And there's the dog.

Throughout the two years Alan has been working on *Rockefeller*, the eponymous dog has slowly become real to him. When the decision was made – not by him, though he didn't fight it – to give the dog the power of speech, some deep buried knowledge woke within Alan. He knew just how Rocky would speak. The lines flowed. The character was already there.

Rocky is smart and cynical. He is permanently amused by the way those round him underestimate him. He rarely troubles himself to correct them, because he has no interest in their approval. He finds the antics of most humans absurd, in particular their infantile pursuit of immediate gratification. When introduced to the trading desks of a City bank he can see at once how to win at the game they play there, but he has no interest in becoming rich. He loves his master, Hector, but he can't help treating him, as he treats everyone, as he treats the sheep at the start of the film, as foolish creatures incapable of knowing what's good for them.

Alan loves Rocky. This is another reason why he doesn't want to visit the set. The Rocky in his head and in his heart can never be matched by any performing-dog reality.

Finally, truth to tell, he knows he's not wanted. Jane Langridge, the producer, extended a half-hearted invitation. Come any time, Alan, it's always chaos on set, don't mind if I don't stop for a chat. Gorgeous Flora actually took the trouble to warn him off. Don't bother, Alan. You'll hate it.

He hasn't told Liz this. A man is entitled to keep one small corner of the world where he gets respect.

At the end of the path he turns round and walks back. Now he has the Tesco clocktower ahead. A crowd of boys on bikes comes clattering past him, making for the skateboard park. He follows them with his eyes, searching to pick out his own son in the melée.

Odd to think that his screenplay is actually being shot. He has come of age as a screenwriter. Now when people say, 'Oh, what would I have seen of yours?' he'll have an answer. Even if it's an answer given with a shrug that says, Yes, I know, it's not exactly great art. That won't stop people being impressed. It stars Colin Firth. It's a real movie. No one cares if movies are good any more. All they'll want to know is what it was like meeting Colin Firth. How to explain that he's never actually met him?

He can see Cas now, in the middle of a cluster of bigger boys on bikes. Good to see him talking with other boys, he doesn't get out enough with his friends. That's one of the disadvantages of sending him to a posh little school like Underhill. There's no neighbourhood. His classmates all live in country houses scattered round an area twenty miles wide, and all social contacts have to be fixed up in advance. So much driving!

Cas, who loves animals, knows all about Rocky. 'Put on your Rocky voice,' he says. So Alan makes his voice gruff. 'Baa! Baa! That's all I hear all day! Where's a fellow to go to get a decent conversation?' But Cas has never asked to be taken to the filming. It's as if he senses his father's fear and doesn't want to expose him to pain. Or is that ridiculous? Cas is only eight.

He's watching Cas as he approaches, seeing his skinny frame and his innocent serious face listening to the big boys.

For this child I would do anything in the world.

Alan loves his son so much it scares him. He knows Cas believes in him, with that baseless admiration small children have for their fathers, and it hurts him deeply to think how little he deserves to be admired. But even in the time to come, even after his son has learnt to see his littleness, Alan knows he won't be able to stop loving him.

Something's not right about the group of boys. They're pushing closer to Cas, and he's moving back against the railings. Alan increases his speed, walking fast now towards them. He senses that Cas is frightened. He can hear voices, but he can't make out words. One of the boys has his hand out, gesturing at Cas. Cas is looking from side to side, as if seeking escape. What are the big boys doing? They're not so big, maybe eleven, twelve years old. There's four of them.

'Cas!' Alan calls. 'You okay?'

The boys turn to look.

'What's going on?' says Alan, coming up on the far side of the railings.

'Nothing,' says one of the boys.

'It's okay, Dad,' says Cas.

'Your dad, is he?' says the boy. He's quite tall, with black short-cropped hair and a narrow face. He wears a navy-blue T-shirt and jeans. Cas gives a nod.

'You can ask him, then, can't you?'

The other boys grin at this.

'Ask me what?' says Alan.

'Nothing,' says Cas.

'You play, you pay. Pound a go. That's right, an't it, boys?'

'Right,' they say, nodding and grinning. 'You tell him, Chipper.'

'Of course he doesn't have to pay,' says Alan angrily. 'This is a council park. It's free.'

'Not any more it's not,' says Chipper. 'It's a quid a go. So who's going to pay, you or him?'

The other boys look from their leader to Alan and back, ecstatic at his boldness.

'No one's paying anything,' says Alan. 'Come on, Cas. Let's go.'

But Chipper and the boys on bikes are blocking Cas's exit.

'He's had his go,' says Chipper. 'He has to pay.'

Alan jumps the railing and storms forward.

'You get out of the way or else!'

'Or else what, Mister? You going to hit me? You going to assault me?' But he and the others are backing away. 'You a paedo? You a dirty old man?'

'Yes, I'll hit you, you little fuckers!'

He raises a threatening fist. He wants to hit the boy called Chipper. He wants to smash his grinning face in.

They back off, but not very far. They know he won't hurt them.

'He's a paedo,' says Chipper. 'Watch out, Darren. He'll have your trousers down.'

The other boys are squirming with laughter.

Alan takes Cas's hand and marches him out of the railed area. Cas carries his skateboard under his other arm. As they pass the boy called Chipper they can hear his mocking sing-song.

'Paedo! Paedo! Paedo!'

Cas tugs his hand away, but he keeps pace by his father's side. He says nothing. They walk rapidly from the recreation ground to the Tesco car park where Alan's car is waiting.

'Little bastards!' says Alan. 'I'm sorry, Cas. Did they threaten you?'

Cas says nothing. They put the skateboard in the boot and they get into the car. Alan glances towards Cas as he starts up the engine. He's got his face down.

Once they're out of the car park and crossing the Phoenix Causeway Alan reaches out a hand to touch Cas's arm. All he means to do is show his love and concern.

'You okay?'

Cas nods dumbly.

'They scared you, didn't they?'

Cas shakes his head.

'Some of those kids are bloody little savages,' says Alan. But he can feel that Cas is not with him. Maybe he's misread the situation.

'You didn't mind me chasing them off, did you?'

Cas says nothing. Now Alan is filled with doubt. He had acted instinctively, in defence of his son. Without quite putting it to himself this way, he had assumed Cas would be proud of him. No one messes with my dad. That sort of thing.

'Cas?'

Still nothing. He has his head turned away now, looking out

of the window. Nothing to see except the grey-brick terraced houses of Lancaster Street.

'That was mugging, what they were doing. Demanding money. I should report them.'

'No!'

It comes out low and fierce. He's clutching his hands into fists.

'Okay. I won't.'

They drive on in silence. Alan struggles with a wave of dismay. He can feel it now. Cas's resentment is not against the bullies, it's against him.

'I had to do something, Cas.'

'I would have been okay,' says Cas.

'They would have made you pay. They weren't going to let you go.'

'I'd have been okay,' mumbles Cas again.

Alan knows then he's lost. He meant to be strong, he meant to be a hero to his son, but instead he made himself ridiculous. Those boys had no fear of him, they knew his threats were empty. Kids have to sort these things out among themselves. He shouldn't have intervened.

'Sorry,' he says.

He'd like to say so much more, how he's not really an aggressive man, nor even very courageous. How he'd attack anyone and anything if he thought his son was in danger. He wants Cas to know this and to feel safer because of it, but he can't say it now. They were only kids having fun. He made himself ridiculous, and now his son is ashamed of him.

It's what dads do, Cas. They fight for their sons. Don't punish me for that.

They're driving up the Offham Road, heading out of town to the little hamlet of Hamsey where they now live. On either side the trees close out the sky, forming a green tunnel that flickers with trapped sunlight. One sunny day has followed another, for weeks now. They say the fine weather will break soon.

As they make the steep turn onto the lane called the Drove, there before them lies the river valley, with the square tower of Hamsey Church on its knoll rising up out of the river. The quieter slower life of the lanes brings with it a change of mood. Cas lifts his head up, straightens his back.

'You know your dog film,' he says.

'Yes.'

'Maybe we could go and watch them doing it.'

Alan feels a wave of love pass through him. This is Cas's equivalent of the reached-out hand. He won't say he's sorry the way Alan said he was sorry, his pride won't allow it. So this is how he makes amends. This is how he gives me back love.

'Okay,' Alan says. 'I'd like that. But I warn you, filming is ultra-boring.'

'I don't mind.'

They drive on down the lane and Alan's mind is filled with wonder. At the complexity of people's feelings, and the delicacy with which they negotiate each other's tender bruises. He also wonders at himself. Now that he's to visit the filming at the request of his son, all his hesitations drop away. Cas is his chaperone and his alibi. He goes not to please himself, who will not be pleased, but to please his son. It's so much more straightforward doing things for other people than for yourself.

'We'll go tomorrow,' he says. 'I'll find out when's a good time.'

13

Dean Keeley gets home early because Terry's job rolled over and died and now what the fuck does he do? There's no one in the house and without Sheena it feels empty and sad so he goes up the road to the Tally Ho for a drink. There's a pikey from Crisp Road in there and he keeps staring at him. He's got these teardrops tattooed on his cheek, one drop for each man he's killed, or maybe one drop for each year he's done inside, who knows? So Dean drinks up and moves on. Heading home past the house where he grew up he passes the old jockey who used to beat his wife. He's walking his greyhound, whistling as he goes. Go out in the garden when you were a kid and there he'd be, whistling.

The old house is in a bad way, paintwork gone on the window frames, curtains closed. Not that it was ever much. Half the estate kids went to Wallands, half to the Pells, here was no-man's land, caught in the middle. Not such a great place to grow up. Terry was sitting pretty in Horsfield Road, clear Wallands territory. Always had the luck, did Terry. Not that I grudge him.

Sheena's house is something else. Dean still thinks of it as Sheena's house because she's the one who got the money together to buy it. And because they're not married. Stupid when you think about it, what difference does a ring make? My mum and dad were married and look what a fucking joke that was. But it does say something, doesn't it? It says you belong together. All those forms you have to fill in, you put Married.

Sheena fills in forms for Dean. She doesn't mind that he can't read. One day she's going to sit down and teach him, she's promised him.

'You'll have a job,' Dean says. 'I'm thick as fuck.'

'No you're not,' says Sheena. 'You just never got taught right.'

Sheena keeps the house very clean. Dean has learned to wipe his boots when he comes in and hang up his coat and not leave coffee mugs out when he's finished with them. He doesn't exactly get why any of this matters but it's how Sheena likes things and so that's what he does.

The house is empty. Chipper's off somewhere with his mates. Sheena's at work. Dean thinks he might as well check in with Brad, see what's doing.

In the lounge, in the corner on the far side of the big couch, there's a small square table. On the table stands a wooden Triang fort. It has a ramp up to its entrance arch, and six battlemented towers surrounding a chipboard yard. Dean got it on eBay for £4.99, a low price because the paintwork is badly worn in places. It's identical to the toy fort he used to play with in his grandad's house. The soldiers too are almost the same: grey-green plastic figures in helmets, holding rifles, Second-World-War vintage. He has twenty-one soldiers. Some aim their rifles from a kneeling position, some standing. Some are running, some are hurling grenades. One of them is half crouching, a Bren gun to the fore, about to explode into action. This is Sergeant Barry Bradford of Special Forces, assigned to Fort Hawk under secret orders. His fellow soldiers know nothing of his true mission, and they don't ask. Push

Brad too much and he'll look at you in a way that makes you back off.

Dean settles down in front of the fort. He lines up a squad of eight men in the yard and stands his one officer before them.

'We're going for the big one,' the officer tells his men. 'Our job is to blow the bridge.'

'Blow the bridge? That's a suicide mission!'

'So we find a guy who doesn't want to live.'

Step forward Sergeant Barry Bradford.

'One man! It's impossible!'

'Maybe it's impossible,' says Brad. 'But the bridge goes.'

That's how Brad is. He never explains, never boasts. He just goes out and does the job.

Chipper comes in from the front door and crosses through the lounge to the conservatory with a nod towards Dean. He starts picking himself out a fishing rod from the rack.

'You off down the Pond?' Dean says.

'Yeah,' says Chipper.

'If you hook a carp,' says Dean, 'throw the bugger back.'

'The Polacks eat them,' says Chipper.

'And the pikeys shoot them with catapults. But we don't.'

You have to keep up standards. Dean's a proper fishermen and he's taught Chipper. They've walked up the river to the Mills many a time, spent the day together catching the odd roach.

If me and Sheena got married I'd be Chipper's dad. There's a strange thought. Most of the time it just feels like we're mates.

Chipper's on his way out the back, through the conservatory, when he says, 'About the bike.'

'What about the bike?'

'You said maybe you could help me out.'

'Maybe I can.'

'Lowest price on the new Kona Cowan 2010 is £529.'

'Lot of money, Chipper.'

'That's nothing. Custom-build a top-range bike and it'll cost you five thousand.'

'Fuck off! Who pays that?'

Chipper gives a shrug as if to say, There's things I could tell you.

'Same difference,' he says.

The lad's right. Might as well be five thousand as five hundred. It's all out of sight.

Alone in the house again Dean returns to the fort. The eight men in the squad cluster round Brad.

'So what's the plan, Brad?'

'Cover me as I go in,' says Brad. 'I'll do the rest.'

'How are you going to get out, Brad?'

'That's my problem.'

Dean lifts the toy soldiers down from the fort to the carpet, and sets them going on their mission. The enemy-held bridge is the edge of the carpet, where it gives way to the tiled floor of the conservatory. The squad takes up an advanced position behind the leg of an armchair. Brad sets off on his own, crossing open terrain, and gains the protection of the doorframe. He radios the squad to mount a diversionary attack, and readies himself to blast his way in.

'You'll never make it, Brad,' the captain signals back. 'There's a hundred of them, and no cover.'

'You do your job,' says Brad, 'I'll do mine.'

You can call it luck if you like. People say Brad's got nine lives. But Brad knows it's something else. He doesn't feel fear, and that means he stays sharp and he stays steady. There's a reason why he doesn't feel fear. He doesn't give a shit whether he lives or dies.

You don't get rich doing what he does. You don't get famous. But you get the job done and there's a satisfaction in that. These rich bastards you read about, what do they get for their money? Robbie Williams gets back together with *Take That* and they get fifteen million each. What do they do with it? Piss it away on drugs. Buy themselves bottles of champagne for ten grand. You can buy a fucking car for that. Terry's right, they've got the money and you don't, that's what it's all about. There'd be enough for everybody if there was some justice in the world. It's not like I'm afraid to work. Give me a job and I'll do it. All I want is a few hundred quid, a ring for Sheena, maybe a bike for the lad. I just need a bit of luck.

Brad's different. He doesn't give a shit. You don't impress Brad with your Rolex and your Ferrari. Just look into his eyes and you'll see. There's a man who knows his own worth.

The front door opens and closes. Sheena back from work, surprised to find him in.

'Got sent home early,' he says.

Sheena was so pleased he'd got work he can't bring himself to tell her he's out of a job again.

As soon as she's home he starts to feel better. The house isn't right without Sheena. Very first time he saw her in the Tally Ho the afternoon of Bonfire Night, she was still with her Scotch boyfriend back then, he knew right off she was the one. Not that you'd call Sheena a looker. She's too big-boned, her face too broad for some. And she's that bit older, she's got five years on him. But when those brown cow-eyes of hers catch a look at you, you feel it all right. She's one of the sort that makes everything all right. The aggravation drops off you and you feel the way you always knew you could feel if only you could catch a bit of luck.

He watches her now as she moves about making everything be the way it should be. She puts on a kettle for a cup of tea and while it's boiling she does a little tidy-up. She leaves the toy soldiers where he put them, but Chipper has dumped a pair of trainers in the conservatory, and she doesn't like that. She holds them up to show the holes in the soles.

'Look at that! New eight weeks ago! You know why that is? It's those bikes. They use their shoes as brakes.'

Sheena doesn't like the bikes. She thinks Chipper will injure himself, the stunts they pull on them. Most likely he will, but you can't stop him.

She sees him watching and comes over to give him a cuddle.

'You still my boy?' she says.

'You know it,' he says.

'Oh, my legs ache,' she says. 'On my feet all day.'

She works at the checkout desk in Boots. But however tired she is, Sheena always keeps herself busy. Now she settles down with her cup of tea and turns on the TV. It's showing *The Weakest Link*. She takes out her sewing box. She's making a new war bonnet for Dean, for the bonfire procession, because his old one got burned. Turkey feathers sewn into leather straps, over ninety feathers, and the beadwork all done by hand exactly the way the Sioux women do it. It's going to have a peacock quill on the back.

Dean watches with awe. How did she learn to do Sioux beadwork? It seems to him that she can do anything. No one pays her millions. There she sits, her hands so busy, her beautiful eyes steady on her work. She's wearing a sleeveless top in this warm weather, and her bare arms are soft and white.

'So what have you been doing, Deanie?'

'Gutting this house,' says Dean. 'Nothing much.'

'It's a job,' says Sheena. 'Better doing something than nothing.'

'Won't last long.' Better to prepare her. 'Looks like the owner didn't get planning permission.'

'Oh, no! That's too bad.'

She's not overly concerned. Jobs come and go.

'You can kill a person without ever harming them,' he says.

Sheena looks up from her sewing.

'Raoul Moat said that,' Dean says. 'He's right.'

'He's dead,' says Sheena. 'That's where that gets you.'

'What he did to his girlfriend. I could never do that.'

'I should hope not.'

She's back at her feathers. Nothing really bothers Sheena. She's steady. She's a rock.

Later that evening they're watching *Corrie* when Dean's phone rings and it's Terry.

'Been thinking, mate,' he says. 'First the Cozzie, then the job. I know you could do with the money.'

'I'll work it out somehow,' says Dean. 'Not your problem.'

He walks out of the lounge and into the narrow front hall.

'You with Sheena right now?'

'Not any more.'

He opens the front door and steps out onto the street. A warm night. Kids sitting on the pavement in a huddle, laughing softly together. A car crawls by, hunting for a space to park.

'Here's the thing,' says Terry. 'If you need the cash quick, there is a job you could do.'

'I'm not doing another insurance job.'

'Nothing wrong with an insurance job, pal. The mistake we made was getting mixed up with Jimmy Dawes. But shift the goods on your own account, the insurance covers the loss, and you keep the cash.'

'I promised Sheena,' says Dean.

'I know,' says Terry. 'Just an idea.'

'If I get nicked again, it's over, Tel.'

'You won't get nicked. I know the house, don't I? I'm doing a fencing job there. I'll call you when it's clear. You'll be in and out in five minutes. Leave everything neat and tidy, her ladyship claims on her insurance, no harm done. But it's up to you, mate. I'm just trying to help out.'

'Appreciate that.'

'Think about it. Thursday would be good.'

After the call is over Dean stays out on the street, thinking about it. He has a whole lot of questions to ask Terry, such as access to the property, valuables inside and so on, but they all come second. First is the question, Am I going to do it?

He hears Sheena calling from inside the house. He goes back to the lounge.

'That was Terry,' he says. 'Looks like the job's down the toilet.'

He marvels at the ease with which he lies.

'Something'll turn up,' she says.

'That Terry,' says Dean. 'He's like a brother. He really watches out for me.'

'I remember Terry Sutton when he was six years old,' says Sheena. 'He was a rackety kid, always in and out of scrapes.'

'Not any more.'

'Oh no, not any more. Julie sees to that. Where would you boys be without us?'

Dean drops down onto the soft couch by her side and she pushes her workbox away so the needles won't prick him and takes him in her arms.

'Don't you ever leave me, girl.'

'Here I am, babe,' she says. 'Here I am.'

14

Roddy Dalgliesh moves through his own house like a ghost. He wants something but he's not sure what it is. Then he identifies the desire: he wants a drink. His son Max is in the kitchen, with his girlfriend Polly, sitting facing each other across the table but separately occupied. Max is intent on the screen of his laptop, Polly is thumbing the keys of her BlackBerry. Neither of them looks up or acknowledges his presence. Roddy finds communication with Max impossible these days. His son intimidates him. He's so self-confident, so good-looking, so everything he never was at his age. He has Diana's slender form and fine features, not his own squat body and pug-like face. His girlfriend Polly Lyman scares him even more, with her serene certainties: a vegan, a climate warrior, and disconcertingly lovely. Roddy recalls his own solitude and awkwardness at the age of twenty-one, and can only marvel.

He clinks ice into a glass, adds a modest shot of Scotch. Carrying the glass in one hand, silent and unremarked, he passes from the kitchen to the living room, where Diana is curled up on a sofa reading *Wolf Hall*. He stands for a while as if gazing out of the window into the street, but she does not lift her eyes from her book. He sips at his Scotch. He exhales a sigh, which comes out as a low hum of sound.

'Don't stand there moaning, Roddy,' says Diana. 'Either come in or go out.'

He moves on into the hall.

Perhaps I am a ghost, he thinks. Perhaps I'm invisible. But there before him in the hall mirror is his own reflection, his face too fleshy, his eyes too small, his hair too thin: an undistinguished man in late middle age.

After the Middle Ages comes the Renaissance. Roddy nods at his reflection, as if sharing with it a secret, and heads down the half-flight of dark stairs to the back door.

Five days to go.

At the far end of their small town garden stands a timber-walled felt-roofed shed. It has one window, shuttered by a cream-coloured roller blind, and one wall of shelves packed with books. Under the window, a table heaped with books. In the remaining space, which is very limited, an armchair with a shelf beside it, on which stands a brand-new digital radio. Behind the chair, leaning over it like an inquisitive neighbour, is a high curving reading light of the kind that is advertised for 'Serious Readers'.

He sinks down into the armchair, setting down his glass on the shelf. He turns on the reading light, and then turns it off again, choosing darkness. He turns on the digital radio, which after its puzzling fashion thinks for a while before deciding, one might suppose reluctantly, to produce some sound. He recognises the lush melancholy of the music. It's Rachmaninov's Second Piano Concerto, live from a Prom. He drinks his Scotch slowly as he listens, and allows his thoughts to drift.

How much longer can he go on living this life? It amazes him that he hasn't been found out and expelled. From his job, his marriage, his family. Not that he's been remotely culpable. He continues to put in his hours at the bank, apparently fulfilling some needed role as a species of mascot. 'Hairy times,' his boss Jock Sinclair said to him. 'Your great virtue is you're not flashy, Roddy. That reassures the clients.' Of course his virtue doesn't merit the bonuses that the traders get, but he still receives his salary. Among his colleagues he's seen as a loser, virtually on the breadline. To his own parents, both retired teachers, he's rich beyond their dreams.

His children never see their grandparents. It's not so far to go, St Albans. He used to make half-plans to take them, fix up a family trip, but Diana was never too keen, and the children were always busy. He reflects on his own childhood, and recalls long months of empty days. But perhaps it felt different then.

Five days to go.

Now that Max and Isla are both out of university he could jack in the job. Tell Jock Sinclair to fuck himself, unthinkable in reality but sweet to contemplate, except what's the point? He's more or less retired already. A ghost in the office. Strange how long you can live on after your own death.

There was a time, not so long ago, when Roddy's dream was to walk away from even more than his job, to escape the noise and clutter and live a life of utter simplicity. Like Thoreau he wanted to live in a hut in the woods, and empty his days along with his pockets. He thought he could hear a voice calling him, but from where and to where he did not know. All he knew was that it was not this. Not this life of pretence and hypocrisy.

Instead here I sit, drinking Scotch, listening to Rachmaninov in the dark, in the shed Diana made me buy, at the bottom of our garden in Islington. Not what you'd call a great escape.

Roddy smiles to think how little they all know. He's not stupid. He knows that to his family, to his colleagues, to all who know him, he's good old Roddy, decent but dull, someone you don't want to get stuck with at a party because he mumbles in a way you have to strain to hear, and anyway he has no small talk. And all the time, within him, a whirlwind of change is lifting him up, preparing to sweep him away.

What will happen will happen. I no longer have power in my own life. The decision is made. On Saturday I will open the door outside which I have been standing for so long. After that, I am in the hands of another, and in the hands of God.

He wonders whether he should write something down, much in the way people write suicide notes to be found after their death. What was it Virginia Woolf wrote? 'I can't go on spoiling your life any longer.' This is no suicide, this is the choosing of life over death. I can't go on spoiling my own life any longer. But there will be explaining to do, and once that door has opened, such a wind may blow through it that all his familiar world will be blown away. Diana will never understand. The children will never understand. This may prove to be a form of self-exile. But if so, he will not go into exile alone.

As for the hurt and the blame, it can't be helped. I am a leaf on a stream. I ask nothing and I refuse nothing. All I commit is an act of love.

Five days to go.

Curious how this decision has formed in his mind. At first it was no more than the theoretical notion that the time had come to speak. The feelings had matured into understanding, the understanding into intention. For a long time he has been hesitating on the brink of the next step, which is action. Why the hesitation? He has no fear of the outcome. Whatever comes of it is good, and can only be good, because he acts in love. No, he has hesitated because – because when the time is right there will be no more hesitation. And now the time is right.

This morning, lying in bed, awake before rising, he said to himself: I'll speak to her on Saturday. There was no hesitation about it. As soon as he made the decision he knew it was both right and inevitable. From that moment on, a deep calm settled over him.

He allows himself to think of her now. He sees her before him, turning to meet his gaze, smiling for him. Such a true smile. Of course she's beautiful, the most beautiful woman he's ever known, but it's nothing without that shaft of truth. She knows him through and through, of that he's certain. She has shown it in so many small ways, through little acts of sensitivity. She knows him because she feels him. This is the nature of true sympathy. And he feels her, and knows her, in a way that no one else does. So much passes between them without words ever being spoken. He sees her sadness, her loneliness, her self-doubt. Their times together have been short, but rich in connection. He feels the threads that tie them to each other drawing ever tighter, trembling, responsive to every smallest nuance. The last time they met, as they were leaving, she gave him a kiss on the cheek and said, 'Drive safely.' As she said it her right hand rested on his left arm. He could feel that pressure all the way home.

What will happen? There will be changes, of course. Those who understand nothing will call it a breaking-up of two marriages. But all that will follow is a process of things falling into their rightful places. Love is not to be legislated. Yes, there will be a time of confusion, but not for me, not for her. For us it will be a time of clarification, coming home. We should have done this years ago.

Roddy marvels that he can be so sure of her love when no promises have been exchanged. He has never been a vain man. He would never presume on another's love. For a long time, for years, it was more a wistful regret for a path not taken than a hope for the future. Then little by little he began to pick up

the signs. He became watchful, and subtle in his watching. She
has a tender heart, will never cause pain if she can help it, will
never betray another's trust. But she gives herself away even so,
in ways that are invisible to all but the most attentive eye. A
momentary smile, a question left hanging. 'You won't mind,
will you, Roddy? Roddy never minds.' Even, most precious of
all, a gift made – 'I got them for Roddy, I know he loves
Florentines' – the gift, so much more than the thing itself, being
her message: that she thinks of him when they're apart. As he
thinks of her.

The fine delicacy that links them also keeps them silent. They
both have to be mindful of others. But Roddy knows now that
his attempts to protect Diana have been misguided. What
protection can he offer where there's no love? He and Diana
should never have married, that much is obvious. Diana has no
comprehension of what goes on inside him. He doesn't blame
her for that. They're different sorts of people. He has failed her
as much as she has failed him. As for the children, how much
good does it do them to have a father who is a ghost in his own
house?

The house question will have to be resolved. Where will they
live? Roddy has no idea. Instead he has trust. If they act in
accordance with the force that governs all things, which you
can call love, or God, then they will be carried on the stream
of life to their next destination. All that matters is that they
cease resistance. Remove the stubborn opposition of the narrow
selfish will to the command of the greater force, life itself. And
why do we call it a command? Is water commanded to flow
downhill? Is the sun commanded to rise? Each acts as it is its
nature to act, neither willing nor unwilling. Not choosing, but
being.

This is the fruit of Roddy's many evenings alone in his shed.

Diana has made a great joke of it, that he goes to his shed to 'look for God', but it's no joke. He has looked, and he has found. In the early stages, he found God in releasing himself from false desires, from the cycle of ambition, frustration, anger and sadness. Then came a later stage, in which he found himself turning towards true desires. He told himself then: I will only know God when I learn to love.

I have never loved before. Not like this. Most people have never loved. They reach out for others, in their desperation, but that's not love. That's fear. In true love there's no fear. In loving her I feel no fear, and I know she too will be unafraid. The words must be spoken, then the door will open.

There's a question waiting to be answered about rooms. First the house, then the room. This is a question of intimacy. You can love without being intimate. We must be respectful of each other, and act with delicacy. There will be no bounds to our love, in time we will be all things to each other, but this too must be surrendered to the stream. Let the flow carry us towards each other in its own time.

Roddy sips his Scotch and listens to the surging music and allows himself to visualise a time in the future, the near future now. His picture of their life together is so modest it makes him smile. They're sitting in a simple room, each in an armchair, each with a book. He looks up from his book just as she looks up from hers. Their eyes meet. He says, 'Happy?' She replies with her sweet smile, 'What do you think?' He thinks she's happy too.

Five days to go. It would be good if he could find time to be with her before the social busyness of the weekend. Maybe he should find an excuse to go down by himself on Friday night. He could make that trip he's planned for so long, to Worth Abbey. Then they could talk on Saturday morning, before Diana drives down. He thinks of the words he'll use. It hardly matters. He's quite certain she knows already, and is waiting for him to speak. So maybe all he'll say is, 'You know, don't you?'

She'll say, 'Yes.' Or maybe she'll just nod her head.

Then there's something more he'll say, he knows it now. Not because the words need saying, but for the joy of saying them, and watching her beautiful face as she hears them.

He'll say, 'I love you, Laura.'

15

The client is called Gloria and she has a small cash business as a dog walker for the dog owners of Kentish Town. More specifically, for a cluster of upwardly mobile dog owners in Bartholomew Villas and Lawford Road, all of whom work long hours and invite each other to dinner in the evenings and share dog talk. Gloria's dog-walking service specifies a maximum of two dogs at a time and a minimum of one hour. Inevitably the paired dogs become friends, or their owners imagine so, and like to maintain the pairings. So Gloria has evolved a matrix to keep track of times, addresses, dogs, pairings, and fees to be charged. The matrix lives on her four-year-old Mac iBook. And something is wrong.

'This is a catastrophe,' she says, showing Andrew Herrema into her bedroom, which doubles as her office. 'This isn't just my life. There are twenty-seven dogs on my list, and I've no idea when to go where and with who.'

She's a large, soft-toned young woman who speaks in the voice of a little girl. Her flat is tidy and without personality.

'Let's take a look,' says Andrew.

He shouldn't be making calls like this, mid-evening, to clients who can barely afford the £60 minimum charge. He's not entirely sure why he agreed to come out. Perhaps it was the way Gloria had sounded so panicked on the phone. One of the unmeasured

rewards of the job is that sometimes you can bring joy and relief
to others with very little effort. At such times Andrew feels like
a doctor in the early days of penicillin. One magic pill and the
patient is cured. No pill for stupidity, alas. Sometimes he's been
called out to fix a dead computer only to find it's not been
plugged in.

He settles down in front of Gloria's laptop.

'What's the name of the missing file?' he says.

'File?'

'Or folder.'

'Folder?'

'The timetable you've lost,' he offers patiently.

It amazes him that some people can operate a computer at
all. As far as he can tell they strike at the keys blindly until
something happens that they recognise, but they never have any
idea how to replicate the result.

'It's not got a name,' she says, gazing at the laptop screen
with anxious longing. 'It's just how I keep track of my walks.'

Andrew tries 'Walks'. This produces nothing. Then he looks
in the Trash folder and finds a large number of auto-backup
files. Then he brings all current open windows onto the screen
at once, which produces a wall of postage-stamp-sized windows,
fifty or more, most of them duplicates.

'Goodness!' says Gloria. 'What's all that?'

'You've been creating copy versions of your files.'

'Have I? I didn't mean to.'

Andrew runs his eye over the clutter.

'You put the dogs' names in your diary, right?'

'Yes. All of them.'

'Give me a name.'

'A dog's name?'

'Yes.'

'Well, there's the Hammonds' dog, Posy.'

'Posy.'

He opens Spotlight, keys in 'Posy'. A list drops down, offering locations. He selects the first. A window opens, headed 'Monday'. It's a home-made calendar complete with times and names.

'That's it!' cries Gloria, her little voice shrill with astonishment. 'Where did you find it?'

'On your computer,' says Andrew. 'All you need to know is the name of the file. It's called Monday.'

'Why's it called Monday?'

'If you don't give a file a name the system automatically uses the first word or words you save.'

Gloria looks baffled, but also intensely relieved.

'You found it!' she says. 'I was sure I'd lost it forever. I'm so hopeless with these things.'

'Would you like me to show you how to find it if you ever lose it again?'

He talks her through Spotlight, but he can see as he demonstrates the simple process that her brain is resisting the information. This no longer surprises him. He's met it too often. In fact, he's learned a reluctant sympathy for the condition. It's not a kind of stupidity, it's a kind of panic. Gloria would like to understand her computer and knows it would be helpful to her if she did, but she believes at a profound unconscious level that she never will. Even as he repeats the sequence of mouse-strokes Andrew can see her eyes not seeing and her ears not hearing. Like an illiterate child faced with a page of print, the mind, overwhelmed by complexity, retreats.

'You know what?' he says. 'Just as a back-up, why don't you print out your walks diary? You could even make changes on it with a pencil.'

'But I spent so much,' wails Gloria.

'Just as a back-up. While you're getting used to it.'

Gloria sits staring at her lost file, breathing rapidly.

'Do you think so?' she says. 'I was so worried. I thought I was going to lose my whole business. It's taken me a year to build that up. Look, tomorrow's Lulu's big walk. If I'd not taken Lulu out, Mrs Garcia would have killed me.' She looks up at Andrew with wondering eyes. 'You're so wonderful.'

'Let's print a copy.'

He coaxes her old ink-jet printer into juddering out a copy on paper. Then, to be sure, he prints a second copy.

'There. Pin it on the wall. That way you'll never lose it again.'

'Oh, you are wonderful.'

He's giving her permission to walk away from the machine that so frightens her. This too is part of his job.

It embarrasses him to charge money for performing so trivial a task, but the company that employs him, through whose advertising Gloria found him, needs and deserves the revenue. Andrew has a highly developed sense of what is due.

'I'm afraid I'll have to charge you the call-out fee.'

'Oh my goodness, I should think so. You're a miracle worker. You've saved my life.'

She writes him a cheque. The company name on the chequebook is Glorious Walkies. His own employers go by the name of MacRescue. So many people offering so many services, the whole great city a web of intersecting needs being satisfied, every city dweller both a consumer and a producer. He'll go home on the Tube tonight, employing as he does so a host of drivers, maintenance men, supervisory staff. He'll send out for a pizza for his supper, so bringing work to fast-order cooks and delivery riders on Vespas. In this way the sixty-pound cheque from Gloria will spread its value ever outwards, playing its tiny part in the economy of London.

She shakes his hand as he leaves. Her grip is sincere, heartfelt, her gaze moist with gratitude. He's a doctor, he's a therapist, he's a priest. Of course, this is why he's come out in the evening when he'd rather be at home. He's a bringer of joy, a saver of lives. But even as he steps back out onto the street the beneficial effect is fading. While in front of a screen, wrangling problems that he can solve, he can believe that he's still in control. Away from the screen his life looms up before him, incomprehensible, unmanageable, and full of pain.

He takes the Northern Line south, taking care not to get onto the Bank branch, waiting patiently for the Charing Cross branch, which stops at Tottenham Court Road. Others may find themselves on the wrong train, but Andrew is not prone to mistakes of this sort. He has a methodical mind, and he likes to minimise errors where possible. His strategies include informing himself properly in advance (he always read manuals), setting himself attainable goals, and learning from his mistakes. None of this is of any avail in his present crisis.

He chooses to stand on the train, even though there are seats available. He plays a game that has almost become a habit. He lets go of the overhead handrail and maintains his balance by sensing and responding to the train's motion. Feet placed at a diagonal to the direction of travel, knees slightly bent, he rocks and sways like a surfer riding a wave. Just another exercise in control.

And now he's falling apart.

It came out of nowhere. As far as he's concerned, Maggie has been the one for him from the first time he met her. He's not been unduly demanding. He's not tried to rush things. She's known from the start that he's been looking for work in Lewes so that they can be together. So what's the problem now? What has he done wrong? Why has this, whatever it is, not come up before? What can he do to make everything be all right again?

The first and simplest step is of course to talk to her, but he keeps putting off making the phone call. He's frightened of making real something that may not yet be real. He dreads calling her and saying, 'What's the problem?', only to hear her faraway voice reply, 'What problem?' After all, he might have imagined it all. She might just have been tired on Sunday. It may all mean nothing.

Then why do I hurt so much?

The body feels the pain before the mind has traced the wound. This alone tells him the problem is real. As soon as she blanked him, walking to the village fête, the pain settled in his stomach, and it's never left. His usual strategies are rendered powerless. He would love to reboot himself, but he has no off switch. This is a glitch that can't be fixed. All that he can think – no, not think – all that he can feel is how much he loves her, how gorgeous she is, how happy she makes him, how empty his life would be without her.

He stares at the prospect the way Gloria stared at the screen, in bewilderment and panic.

Have I done something wrong? Has she met someone else? Has she grown bored with me? And if the answer is yes to any or all of these questions, what can I do about it? I can't be a different person. If I'm not enough as I am, it's over. There isn't any more.

At Tottenham Court Road he changes to the Central Line, making his way down long tunnels past the endless new works thrown up by the Crossrail project. The Central Line is his home line, its colour on the map and the metalwork in its carriages a cheerful red. The various colours of the tube lines carry emotions. The black of the Northern Line is the soot and coal of the north. The green of the District Line is leafy suburban spaces. The dark blue of the Piccadilly Line is the colour of the jetset, with its airports and its members-only clubs. But at the heart of the metropolis lies the main artery, the scarlet blood of the Central Line, that carries him home to Shepherds Bush.

All this is supposed to be about to change. Already, some weeks ago, he began to cut his ties to his present familiar territory, closing his eyes to the bright and tacky convenience shops in the Uxbridge Road, closing his ears to the roar of the QPR stadium. In their place he has begun to relocate his heart in the little Downland town of Lewes. Gavin, his flatmate in Ingersoll Road, has long known he plans to move out, and has arranged a replacement. Harvey at MacRescue has done the same. All this has taken place with Maggie's full knowledge. How is it possible for her to back out now?

Maybe he's imagining it. Maybe he's over-reacting. Maybe it's a wobble, nothing more. If so, why doesn't he phone?

He makes a decision as he comes out into the night air of Shepherds Bush Green: once he's home he'll call Maggie and find out what's going on. He has reached this decision before and has backed away, secretly hoping she'll call him first. The truth is he feels badly treated, and not a little resentful. He has done nothing to deserve this sudden change of heart. His own heart has not changed. This is Maggie's problem, and she should solve it. But he doesn't want any of these thoughts to be present in his voice when he calls her.

Just don't leave me, Maggie. Please.

As he crosses the bottom of Wood Lane his phone rings. His heart jumps. One glance tells him it's not Maggie. It's Jo, a mutual friend. Her voice on the phone sounds breathless.

'What's going on with you and Maggie?' she says. 'I talked to her today and she sounded all confused.'

'I'm the one who's confused,' says Andrew.

'So nothing's happened?'

'I took this job in Lewes. That's what's happened. But for some reason it's freaking her out, and I don't know why. Do you know why?'

'I don't know anything. But I'm having lunch with her tomorrow, so I thought I should check in with you first, in case there's something I'm missing.'

'If there is, I'm missing it too. Do me a favour, Jo. Tell me what she says. I know I should ask her myself, but I'm scared. I mean, it may just all be nothing. I don't want to over-react.'

'Of course it's all nothing.' Jo's warm voice brings the reassurance for which Andrew hungers. 'You two are so great together.'

'Tell her that, Jo. Tell her.'

'You bet I will.'

'And call me afterwards. Any time.'

'I'll do that. And you know what, Andrew? She's lucky to have you.'

'You don't think she wants to break up?'

'Are you nuts? No way! You're the best thing's ever happened to her.'

'Don't tell me. Tell her.'

But he likes it that she tells him. Jo is Maggie's closest friend and he wants her on his side.

By the time he's letting himself into his flat he's feeling far more hopeful about life. Jo's breezy certainty has put it all back into perspective. Maybe he should call Maggie after all. But then he thinks he'll wait for Jo's report after their lunch tomorrow. Just to be safe.

Gavin is stretched out on the couch watching an episode from the first series of *Entourage*.

'Sorted?' he says.

For a second Andrew thinks this question is about him and Maggie. Then he realises Gavin is asking about his call-out.

'In about one nano-second. The so-called lost file was on her desktop.'

'Nice work if you can get it.'

Gavin's attention is on the screen. Andrew goes into his bedroom to dump his bag. There's Maggie's picture by his bed. There's the card she gave him for his last birthday on his chest of drawers. There's the bathrobe they bought for him together, because she said his old one was too drab, and worse, too short. That was only six weeks ago. He remembers exactly how they stood by the rack in John Lewis and Maggie pulled out bathrobe after bathrobe and held them against him and studied the effect with a frown on her lovely face. He remembers how he felt owned by her, and how he liked that.

It strikes him now, gazing at the blue-and-white-striped bathrobe, that he offered no preferences of his own. He wanted for himself whatever she wanted for him. You could call that selfless, or you could call it spineless. It just happens to be one of those areas where he doesn't have any strong opinions. You can't go fabricating preferences just to make yourself appear more manly.

So is that it? Am I not manly enough?

TUESDAY

16

On Tuesday morning Toby wakes late and gets up slowly, dressing himself in Jack's clothes. Jack's jeans, a little loose on him, hitched round his waist with Jack's khaki webbing belt. Jack's blue polo shirt. Entering the kitchen where Laura is sitting at the table surrounded by recipe books making a shopping list, he announces, 'I am Jack.'

Before Laura can respond, Carrie, who has been waiting for him, comes in through the side door from the garden.

'Oh, hullo,' she says. 'You up?'

'I'm up.' He looks out of the window at the bright sun on the lawn. 'And the sun is up. Another perfect day in Paradise.'

Carrie fills the coffee pot to brew the strong coffee she has already learned he likes. Laura makes a token gesture of drawing the open recipe books closer to create space for his breakfast.

'It's okay,' he says. 'I'm far too late. And anyway, I want to take my toast and coffee out into the sunshine.'

Actually what he needs is a smoke.

Toby understands that Laura doesn't approve of him, and he accepts it. She's right not to approve of him. She thinks he'll be a bad influence on Carrie, and the demon thinks he will too. But the demon does as it pleases.

He watches Carrie as she moves about the kitchen putting bread in the toaster, taking butter from the fridge, marmalade from the cupboard, her lanky body making awkward movements, and he feels her awareness of his gaze like his arms round her body.

I could ask her for anything and she'd give it.

This is not a new phenomenon in Toby's life. Wherever he has found himself there is someone, usually but not always female, who takes on a role that is more than friend, less than lover: a follower, perhaps. The follower responds to his particular brand of indifference to the good opinion of others, which you might call arrogance, or callousness, by subordinating herself to his will. And it is after all a kind of trade. The follower offers submission and service. In return, he gives his time, his attention, and what they most hunger for, which is direction.

'So what are your plans, Toby?' says Laura. 'Though I don't know why I even ask. You'll tell me you don't believe in making plans.'

'I don't make plans,' says Toby. 'But it's not a belief. I don't think I have any beliefs.'

'So you don't care about your future?'

'I don't think I know what the future is,' says Toby. 'There's what's happening now. And there's all sorts of fears and hopes and anxieties about what's coming. But then it comes, and it's now again.'

'I don't know what that means,' says Laura. He can hear from her voice that she's irritated. 'I've invited some people for dinner on Saturday, which I suppose is the future. So now I'm making plans for what to cook. If I don't do that, they won't eat.'

'That would be quite interesting, wouldn't it? The guests come and you all sit down at the table, but there's nothing to eat.'

Carrie utters a short laugh.

'It would be ridiculous,' says Laura, returning to her list.

The coffee pot begins to rattle on the hot plate. Carrie has assembled breakfast on a tray.

'Come on, Toby. You're annoying Mum.'

'Sorry. I don't mean to.'

They go out onto the terrace and sit at the table in the sunshine. Toby sits with his back to the sun and Carrie has to shade her eyes with one hand to look at him.

'Why do you say such odd things?' Carrie asks him.

'They don't seem odd to me,' he says.

The coffee is dark and bitter. With each sip he feels stronger, surer. The marmalade is home-made, also dark and bitter. One of the many minor glories of England that he has learned to value by being away. Raised railway platforms, radio music without commercials, tap water you can drink.

He takes out his tobacco and his Rizla papers and rolls himself a thin cigarette. A banging sound is coming from the far side of the orchard. A man is at work on the rabbit fence.

'So how do you decide what you're going to do next?' says Carrie.

'I don't decide,' he replies. 'When next comes along, I do whatever there is to do.'

'But look.' She leans across the table, pushing the butter out of the direct sunlight into his shadow. 'You won't stay here for ever.'

'No.'

'So where will you go?'

He drinks his coffee and smokes his cigarette and gazes at her, smiling. The more he sees of her the more interesting she becomes to him. Too young, of course, but not weak. Nobody's fool.

'You look like your portrait,' he says.

She flushes with pleasure.

'The man who painted that was a great artist,' she says. 'One day he's going to be famous.'

'That'll be nice for him.'

'He's dead.'

He says nothing to that. He puts down his cigarette and spreads butter and marmalade thickly on his toast.

'You're quite greedy,' she says. 'And also lazy.'

He nods his agreement. He eats carefully, almost fastidiously, not wanting to get stickiness on his beard.

'Don't you care what anyone thinks of you?'

'No,' he says. Then almost at once, with a frown of annoyance, he corrects himself. 'Yes, I care very much what people think of me. The people I respect, that is. As for the rest, they're of no significance. Their opinions are formed on the basis of values I don't share. Why should their approval matter to me?'

He's aware that he's spoken with more energy than usual, and that this pleases her.

'That's so right,' she says softly.

'But you care, don't you?'

'Too much,' she says.

'I shall most likely go to Eastbourne next,' he says. 'Call on my dear mother, who hasn't had the pleasure of my company for far too long.'

'Why not?' asks Carrie.

Toby is surprised at himself, that he's brought up the subject of his mother. It seems he wants to talk about her.

'I've been travelling.'

'But you call her?'

'No. I've been trying to keep away. I'm training her.'

'Training her to do what?'

'To live a life that doesn't revolve around me.'

'What about your father? You said you'd never met him.'

'Did I? That's a lie, of course. You mustn't believe everything I say.'

He watches her processing this information, trying to decide whether or not to believe that he tells lies, or whether this is another lie.

'So you have got a father.'

'There is a rumour to that effect.'

She gazes at him intently, wanting so much to understand him, herself hiding nothing. She has no idea of the power of her vulnerability. Her clear grey eyes hold him and embrace him, making him the unconditional offer of herself.

Bang bang bang goes the man working on the fence.

'I wonder what you think of us all,' she says.

'I think you're lovely people, living in a lovely house, in a lovely country.'

'No, you don't.'

'Actually I do.'

'But you don't want to be one of us.'

'I don't want to be one of anything.'

Carrie's mother comes out onto the terrace.

'I'm going into Lewes. Is there anything you want?'

'I need more driving,' says Carrie. 'Dad promised me some time today.'

'He's in London all day. You can drive me into Lewes if you like.'

'No, it's okay.'

'Then do something for me, will you, darling? Take Terry a cup of tea.'

Laura nods towards the banging in the orchard. She goes back into the house.

'You're learning to drive?' says Toby.

'I can drive,' says Carrie. 'I just have to pass the bloody test. Can you drive?'

'Of course.'

Before she can ask any more he says, 'Let's take Terry a cup of tea. I want to see what he's doing.'

'Why?'

'It's work. I like work.'

'You're strange, Toby. I never know what you're going to say.'

She picks up the tray and they go back into the kitchen. Carrie puts the kettle on for Terry's tea. Toby looks at the *Guardian* lying open on the table. There's a story about space clouds, with a picture of a coloured night sky.

'Noctilucent clouds,' he reads aloud. 'Isn't that beautiful? We should get up in the middle of the night and look for them.'

'All right,' says Carrie. 'What are they?'

'Luminous clouds sixty miles up in the mesosphere. Noctilucent. That's a beautiful word.'

'Why did you grow a beard?'

'Beards grow all by themselves,' he says.

'So why didn't you cut it off?'

'Like everyone does.'

'Okay. I know. You're different. I get it.'

'I'm not sure you do get it,' he says.

She mashes the tea bag in the mug.

'Do you want tea as well?'

'No. But I'll come with you.'

'To see the work that so fascinates you.'

He likes this trick she has of pushing his own words back at him. It's like that card game where you pass each other unwanted cards and later get them back again. She's a listener, a rememberer. He likes that.

They go into the orchard, down the path mowed through the long grass, to the little gate into the meadow. There on the meadow side Terry is at work, stripped to the waist, his eagle tattoo glistening with sweat. *Pain passes*, it says, *pride is forever*.

'Cup of tea,' says Carrie.

'Cheers,' says Terry, putting down his tools.

Toby studies the brackets Terry is screwing to the fence posts. They project upwards and outwards, into the meadow.

'For the rabbits,' says Terry. 'Stop 'em climbing over.'

'Dad's having a war on rabbits,' says Carrie.

Toby looks round the meadow. The grass is long and yellow-brown, starved of rain. Over by the far hedge he sees rabbit holes. Then in a patch of nettles he spots a rabbit, sitting motionless, staring back at him.

'Will it work?' he says to Terry.

'Bloody better,' says Terry. 'Unless they're fucking gymnasts.'

Rolls of netting and barbed wire lie on the ground, alongside wire-cutters and a long-levered tool that Toby has never seen before.

'What's that?'

'Stretcher,' says Terry. 'Pulls the wire taut.'

As they make their way back again Carrie asks him, 'Why are you interested in tools?'

'I've always liked tools,' says Toby. 'They're made to do an exact job and they do it. I like that.'

'I bet you've never done any work with tools.'

'I cut up logs once, with an axe. For firewood.'

'Were you any good at it?'

'I got better.'

They're passing through the orchard. She sits down quite suddenly in the shade of an apple tree.

'Let's not go back to the house yet.'

So he sits down too, cross-legged like her. She starts pulling at blades of grass, breaking them off, throwing them away.

'I'm in a bit of a mess,' she says.

He says nothing. This is her show.

'Basically I don't see the point of my life. I know I should be grateful, wonderful home, wonderful parents and all that. I know I should just get off my bum and stop moaning and get a life and all that. But I can't seem to get motivated. Dad says to me, We can't do it for you. You have to find your own motivation. But I've looked. Where is it? I think mine's got lost.'

She mocking herself and hurting at the same time. She's making this appeal to him as if he's some kind of teacher. Also as a kindred soul.

'Mine's lost too,' he says.

'So how do you cope?'

She's stopped pulling at the grass. Her earnest gaze is fixed on him, her only hope. She gets more beautiful the more he looks at her.

'I don't cope,' he says. 'I stopped coping way back.'

'Are you really not going to uni?'

'I can't,' he says. 'I never took any A-levels.'

'Wow!' She's awestruck. 'You got off the train.'

'I did.'

'So now what?'

'That's what I'm finding out.'

'Aren't you scared? I'd be terrified.'

'It was being on the train that scared me. Who wants to go where that train's going?'

She's nodding and nodding.

'You can't imagine,' she says. 'Every word you say, it's what I think. But where do people like us end up? Don't we end up sad and poor and lonely?'

'We end up different,' says Toby.

He can see the hunger in her for all he has to give her. If he wants he can shape her soul. There's a powerful seduction in that, in being so yielding. He knows he should back off now, make more space between them. But the demon has other ideas. He holds out his hand, and at once she holds out hers to meet it. They press lightly, palm to palm, under the apple tree. Then their fingers interclasp.

Her eyes fixed on his. Her hand warm against his.

The offer of love is there, unprotected, without conditions, without limits. First love, timid but not yet wounded. The dappled sunlight falls through the leaves of the apple tree onto her solemn face. Yes, she's beautiful.

'Hello, Jack's sister Carrie,' he says.

This is what life is offering me. Why would I say no? This is my chance for today. Tomorrow is another universe.

'Hello, Jack's friend Toby,' she says.

17

'I don't believe it! You're kidding me!'

'If only,' says John Randall.

'No one in the department's been keeping back-up emails? Since when?'

Maggie is in shock. Her entire case against the Harvey's site agent rests on the exchange of emails in March 2009.

'It's up to you to keep your own emails, if they're likely to be needed.'

'But we keep getting those messages telling us the servers are full. We're supposed to delete any emails that are more than a year old.'

'So I expect that's what you did.' The planning director makes a wry face. 'Being a good girl.'

'Jesus,' says Maggie.

She's on her way out for her lunch break. Now caught in the door from her little office to the open-plan floor of the greater department, she looks round in bewilderment, as if hoping to find a solution among the work stations.

'What am I supposed to do now? Murray's the one bringing the legal action.'

'You'll have to withdraw the accusation. I'm afraid you'll have to offer an apology.'

'Apologise to that smarmy crook? Not in a million years.'

'I'm sorry. What can I say?'

He's on her side, she knows. He shares her frustration. He'll give her time to come round. And even as she says 'Never!' Maggie knows she will have to bow to the inevitable. Grovel to the inevitable. Eat the dirt that Murray kicks in her face. Life is made up of these little defeats. She feels like she has the job of protecting the white cliffs of England from the merciless power of the sea. She stands there, back to the roaring waves, arms outstretched, embracing the high bare chalk, and the water crashes over her, and the cliffs crumble under her hands. It's an ocean of money that roars at her back, money and contempt for the past and indifference to the future. One day the sea will break through the last of their gallant inadequate defences and will erase all record of those who have lived before. Then Murray and his children and grandchildren will live in an interminable present, and will never even know what they have lost.

'I'm going out,' she says. 'I may be some time.'

She climbs Watergate Lane, passing the deep scary gorge that takes the London railway line into the tunnel below Lewes; past the high wall of the gardens to Pelham House. She touches the wall as she goes, in habitual homage to its construction: parallel bands of brick set in napped flint, with here and there single bricks marooned in a sea of flint. The bands of brick converge as the lane rises, making the great wall on its skirted base seem to have grown naturally from the ground.

At the top by the Post Office Jo is waiting for her, boldly dressed as always, today in a sleeveless red top and black-and-white-check palazzo pants. Jo is almost exactly Maggie's age, but their friendship is based on how different they are in every way, a topic that never ceases to amaze and amuse them. Where Maggie is slight, bordering on petite, Jo is generously built, sexy, almost but not quite pretty, and without fear or shame.

She wears strong colours and outsize costume jewellery, and conducts her life in a series of glorious, often unscrupulous, impulses which generally come to grief. She makes an erratic living as a singer, having come up through the Glyndebourne chorus, though as she likes to say, she hasn't yet come up far enough. She lives with a cat in a flat in the new development where Baxters used to have their printworks.

She flourishes their lunch, bought at Beckworths Deli, and contained in a brown paper bag.

'Two slices of tomato and mozzarella pizza, a brownie, and an apple juice.'

'Oh, you angel.'

Maggie shows her the sign on Beckworths' front wall saying that this used to be the old Church House of St Michael's, in 1545.

'Crikey!' says Jo. 'And now it's selling pizza.'

'We're going to St Michael's,' says Maggie. 'I'm going to show you my secret place.'

She leads Jo up the High Street to the church with the big black clock that projects high over the pavement. The way into the church is across a miniature brick courtyard.

'We can't eat our pizza in a church,' says Jo.

Maggie leads her into the church's shadowy interior and then out again through a side door. Here nine broad steps of stone and brick rise gently before them, lined on either side with gravestones.

Maggie stops before one of the gravestones to show Jo. She reads out the worn lettering aloud.

'In memory of Thomas Evans, Collector of Excise. He had but recently been appointed to Sussex Collection, and whilst travelling his first round was attacked by fever, which terminated in death on the 30th November 1837. Aged nineteen.' This is Maggie's surprise. 'Aged nineteen!'

'They died young back in the old days,' says Jo.

'But it's like a story. A tax collector, new at the job. His first round. He was probably all excited, his life before him. Probably thinking, I've got a great job, secure future, I can think of getting married, start a family. Then pop, he dies. Aged nineteen!'

'Now I'm all miserable.'

At the top of the steps they enter a walled grassy plateau where three mature yew trees spread their shade over a cluster of grey stone graves. The graves are raised like stone altars, their inscriptions smoothed to illegibility by wind and rain. To the left a narrow path through ragged shrubs leads to a further miniature graveyard, where a wooden bench has been placed beneath one of the yews.

'Maggie, this is heaven!' exclaims Jo. 'I never even knew this place existed.'

'It's a secret. You mustn't tell.'

They sit down on the bench, which looks towards the church's round tower with its spire of oak shingles. Beside it a lower tower, also shingle-roofed, carries the square bell-cage and the clock. On three sides the back windows of surrounding houses peer down at them; on the fourth, the high old stone wall of the castle.

Jo opens the brown paper bag and gives Maggie her slice of pizza. The clock clangs out the quarter hour. The sky above is overcast, the air warm.

'So what's up with nice Andrew?' Jo says.

'Oh, God,' says Maggie. 'I've been in such a state. I actually think I had a panic attack yesterday. Can you believe it? Is it possible to have a breakdown over something you've chosen to do of your own free will?'

'Don't ask me, girl. My own free will never ceases to fuck me up.'

'You know Andrew's said he'll take this job? Suddenly it's happening. He starts on Monday. And I go into a panic attack.'

Jo wants all the gory details.

'Like shortness of breath? Dizzy spells? You didn't swoon, did you?'

'More like this blinding headache.'

'No one swoons any more,' says Jo wistfully. 'You could do a lovely swoon, Maggie. Me, I'd be like a felled tree.'

'I think it's all about whether or not he moves in with me.'

'Is he moving in with you?'

'Why wouldn't he? That's why he's taken the job. So we can be together. But you know what's so stupid? We've never actually talked about it. It's been there all the time, kind of assumed, but there's been no actual, you know, conversation.'

'Hey, you don't have to tell me. Paddy and me, we never talked at all. We had sex without talking. If he'd talked I'd have found out what a jerk he was years earlier.'

Maggie knows Jo still pines for Paddy, however much she jokes about him. The sting is that she was the one who ended their relationship. This is the experience Maggie wants to tap: the woman who said no and lived to regret it.

'But the difference is,' says Jo, 'nice Andrew is not a jerk.'

'No, he's not a jerk.' Maggie has hardly touched her pizza. There's another symptom of her breakdown: loss of appetite. 'He's just nice. Is that a terrible thing to say?'

'There's worse than nice,' says Jo.

'But for all the rest of your life? That's what I keep thinking. This is it till I die. I mean, if you're making that kind of decision you're supposed to be really sure, aren't you? Like, over the moon and in love and so on.'

'It helps,' concedes Jo.

'When I think of marrying Andrew I start to feel all shut in, but when I think of never seeing him again I get this panic attack. Who am I supposed to believe, me or me?'

'Oh, boy. Don't ask me to take sides.'

'What would you do, Jo?'

'Me? My latest plan is to find myself a cripple in a wheelchair who can't run away. That way I don't end up alone.'

She's joking, of course, her opinions as fun and fake as her jewellery. But Maggie finds solace in her friend's shamelessness. It makes it easier to say the unsayable.

'Do you think anybody's better than nobody?'

'Definitely. One hundred percent. But that's not the question, is it? The question is, have you reached the end of the line? What we all need is a future flash that tells us, This is the last one. Turn this one down and you're on your own for the duration. But if he's not the last in line, hey, rock on. Out with the old, in with the new.'

'Do you sometimes think maybe Paddy was the last in the line?'

'Like, every ten minutes of every day.' She laughs at her own predicament. 'But Paddy was such a jerk.'

'He won't be the last, Jo.'

'You think? I'm a minority taste.'

Jo has had three boyfriends by her own account. Her time with Paddy was longer than the other two put together.

She breaks the brownie in half. Maggie waves her share away.

'Nice Andrew's not the last in your line, I'll tell you that much. Your line's got a way to go.'

'But it all takes so long, doesn't it?' With Jo Maggie feels free to admit the calculations that fill her waking hours. 'If I break up with Andrew, I have to meet some new guy. How long does that take? Give it three months, and that's being optimistic. Then you have to find out if he's really the one.

Another three months, minimum. That's six months. Then it turns out he isn't. So back to the store. Another six months. If you're really lucky, twelve months in you've got a good one. But you still need time, you have to try each other out, live together. Say, another year. Then you're ready. You decide to get married. That's a big deal, it takes time. I mean, you don't just go ahead and get pregnant right away. So there's another year. Three years, then nine more months, almost four years, and you've got a baby. And that's pretty much if everything goes right. By then I'd be thirty-four, and I'd have made it just in time. Or not. That's what makes it all so impossible. What if it's not? Then I'll be thirty-five, then I'll be thirty-six, then I'll be thirty-seven, and I'll be saying, why didn't I settle down with Andrew when I was thirty? By thirty-seven we'd have kids in primary school.'

'Oh, Maggie! Don't!' Jo makes a cross with her fingers to ward off the evil eye. 'I feel like you're walking over my grave.'

'But you do see the problem.'

'The problem is the air we breathe. The problem is our birthright. It's our inheritance. It's our curse.'

'So how does everyone else cope with it?'

'They fuck up,' says Jo. 'They compromise. They live with regret.'

'Do you? Over Paddy?'

'Sure. But I have a good time even so. I mean, like who said life was supposed to be roses all the way? I get a bit down sometimes. But then I wash my hair and pour myself a glass of Shiraz and think how much more other people have fucked up their lives than me. Then I feel almost fine again. I mean, hey, look around you.' She waves a beringed hand over the graves. 'This lot are actually dead. Compared to them, we're winning. And in case you hadn't noticed, the sun is shining.'

'Yes, I know. I should count my blessings.'

'So, count. One, you're not dead. Two, you're not crippled. Three, you're not old. Four – fuck it.'

'Right.'

Jo kicks her legs in front of her, doing dance steps in the air.

'So here's the question, Mags. Do you love him?'

'Do I love him?'

'Nice Andrew.'

Maggie thinks about it, thinking she shouldn't have to be thinking about it.

'I don't know, Jo. How do I know? Yes, I love him. But how do I know I couldn't love someone else much more? I feel like I could. I feel like there's a whole lot more of me not coming out to play, you know? Like loving Andrew only uses part of me.'

'Oho,' says Jo. 'Aha.'

'What does that mean?'

'It means I don't know what to say. What's nice Andrew got to say about it?'

'I don't know. We haven't talked.'

'You mean he doesn't even know you've got doubts?'

'Of course he knows. I've been ducking the conversation. He's not stupid. But I don't know what he feels about me ducking it.'

'So call him. Ask him.'

'Don't I have to sort myself out first? I mean, he's going to say, What do *you* want to do? I'm the one with the problem here. It's not like I'm asking him for anything that he's not already giving. It's not fair on him to dither about like this. Either I'm staying or I'm going.'

'He's Aquarius, right?'

'Oh, please.'

'You can mock. If I'd paid more attention to Paddy being bloody Pisces I'd have saved myself years of grief.'

'All right. He's Aquarius. So what?'

'You're Scorpio.'

'I hate being Scorpio. Who wants to be a scorpion?'

'Scorpios are amazing. Very sexual. Very insightful. Julia Roberts is a Scorpio.'

'She's not exactly got a brilliant history of relationships.'

'Been married eight years now. Forty-three years old. Three kids, twins Hazel and Phinnaeus, and three-year-old Henry. Two dogs. Does her own cooking.'

Jo is a devoted reader of celebrity magazines.

'Hazel? Phinnaeus?'

'When that marriage started, she was thirty-five. You've got five years at least.'

'What about Jennifer Aniston?'

Jo lets her head fall. This is a killer blow. To a generation raised on *Friends*, Jennifer Aniston's failure to find love is the ghost at the feast.

'I'll never forgive Angelina Jolie,' says Maggie. 'Never ever.'

'What I don't understand,' says Jo, 'is why she didn't stay married to Ross.'

They laugh together, at their own failed dreams, at the shared failed dreams of the world.

'So tell me what I can do,' says Jo. 'How can I help? Do you want me to call nice Andrew?'

'What would you say?'

'Hi, nice Andrew. How's it going? I hear you're moving down our way. That'll be nice. Then I leave a pause. Then I say, Won't it?'

'Then what?'

'How do I know? Maybe he starts crying down the phone.

Maybe he acts like there's no problem. Maybe he asks me what's going on with you.'

'What do you tell him is going on with me?'

'I say you're having doubts. Eve of wedding nerves. Julia Roberts walked out on Kiefer Sutherland three days before their wedding.'

Maggie thinks about that.

'Maybe you should. I just need time, Jo. Ask him to give me a bit more time.'

'You don't want to ask him yourself?'

'I don't want to have the conversation. Not yet. I want to know which way I'm facing first. You call him. Say I just need a bit of time on my own.'

Back in her office, tackling her ever-renewed in-tray, Maggie feels a little calmer, a little stronger. Jo will buy her some time. Maybe she should go home this weekend, home being the solid Edwardian villa in Oundle where her parents still live. Except that her parents adore Andrew and expect Maggie to marry him. She knows this even though they're too discreet to raise the subject. Maggie finds herself wondering about her mother's own marriage. Did she have doubts? Was Dad a compromise? Maggie in her turn has been too discreet to ask. You could say the marriage has worked well, in that it's quite impossible to imagine them apart, but they don't seem to talk much, or go out much together.

Then she remembers that she and Andrew are supposed to be going to the Broads for dinner on Saturday.

Have to find a way to get out of that.

18

Henry arrives a little early for his meeting and it seems that Justin Hamo is running a little late, so he sits down in the windy reception area and picks up a copy of the day's *Guardian*. He reads a story about vaginal gel as other visitors arrive, report to the reception desk, and hurry on to the lifts. Unsummoned, waiting in the lobby, he looks about him with a half-smile, to indicate that something quite other than the life of the lobby is occupying his mind, and that the little he does take in he finds gently amusing. Then, tiring of the strain of smiling to himself, he closes his eyes and lets it be seen that he has chosen this chair in this lobby as an opportunity to catch up on the sleep he so desperately needs. No doubt he's just flown in from LA, or more fashionably, Mumbai.

'If you'd like to go up now, Henry.'

The receptionist issues this message from her distant desk, not troubling to rise. She has never seen Henry before in her life, but they're on first-name terms.

He shares the lift with a young PA who is carrying a lunch order. The lift fills with the aroma of miso soup.

There's someone new to him in Justin's outer office, but she too is on first-name terms.

'Go on in, Henry. Sorry you've had to wait.'

In fact the wait is not yet over. Justin is on the phone. He smiles to Henry, waves for him to take a seat, without pausing in his conversation.

'Right,' he says. 'Right. I'm not arguing with that. Listen, the June numbers are spectacular.'

Justin is maybe thirty years old, he wears his hair shaved very short, which emphasises his dark bushy eyebrows and his dark piercing eyes. He plays with a pencil as he talks, rotating it end to end, tapping it on the glass desktop.

'Look, if it was up to me I'd strip the show daily from here to eternity.'

Justin is a powerful figure in the world of factual programming. Not the ultimate arbiter of what gets made and what doesn't, but his support is critical. When Henry's last series aired, Justin was a young assistant whose function seemed to be to act excited about whatever project was in hand. Now he has risen to the glass-topped desk.

His call ends. He bounds up to shake Henry's hand.

'Henry! Great that you're here. This job is insane. You know who that was? Midge Smith, who produces *Come Dine With Me*. Which by the way is now a global megahit and making us very happy. We don't want Midge to know just how happy because we have a renegotiation coming up and we don't want to give away the store.'

Henry has no idea why Justin is confiding to him what appears to be extremely sensitive information, but this is how it goes in the media world. The presumption of intimacy softens and illumines every encounter.

'So how's Aidan?'

Aidan Massey, historian and media star, until recently Henry's on-screen presenter and business partner. They are now moving on, as they say, developing new opportunities independently. Henry has not so far chosen to make this public.

'Still as thrilled to be Aidan as ever,' he says.

He and Justin share a grin, bonding over the tribal hatred among production staff for on-screen presenters.

'You should meet Simon Cowell,' he says. 'Talk about the court of the Sun King.'

'You're taking me out of my comfort zone there.'

Justin shoots his cuff, checks his watch.

'So talk to me.'

Henry has his proposal on paper. He takes a slim file from his satchel and lays it on the desk. This is no more than a nod to the decencies. The real presentation will be verbal, and of that probably the first five minutes are all that count. Television, like the movies, now starts with the pitch.

'I'm not going to pretend this is *Come Dine With Me*,' he begins. 'What I'm offering you will never give you high numbers. But Channel 4 needs more than numbers. You need to be seen to be setting the intellectual agenda. You need to be the market leader in the world of ideas. Am I right?'

'You are right,' says Justin.

He leans back in his chair and watches Henry closely, as if he supposes Henry is about to perform a conjuring trick.

'You want to capture the zeitgeist,' says Henry. 'You want to be the first to say what everyone's thinking but no one's put into words. And you know what that is?' He speaks slowly, emphasising each word. This is his headline. 'I. Don't. Get. Modern. Art.'

'Okay-ay,' says Justin, narrowing his eyes, zeroing in on his prey.

'I. Don't. Get. Modern. Music.'

'What modern music?'

'John Cage. Harrison Birtwhistle.'

'Oh, Jesus. No one gets that stuff.'

'So how come they're supposed to be the best? What are we missing? Are we stupid? How come the advanced stuff in every art form is either really hard to understand, or really unpleasant? What happened to beauty? What happened to melody? What happened to delight?'

'Okay-ay,' says Justin again, not committing himself to any form of agreement. This is as Henry has anticipated.

'I'm making three simple points,' Henry says. He holds up one finger. 'That's number one. We've lost confidence in our ability to make artistic judgements. We just don't know any more. Of course, we don't want to be caught out not liking the next great genius, just because we don't get it. We don't want to be like those simpletons who didn't get Beethoven, or Van Gogh. So we keep our mouths shut and wait to be told what we like. Because all on our own, we just don't know any more. So that's number one.'

'Number one,' says Justin. He too raises one finger, to show he's keeping up.

'Number two. Why has this happened? Why have we, art's audience, art's customers, art's consumers, lost confidence in our own judgement? Because something happened in the early years of the twentieth century. A war broke out. Not the Great War. This was an art war, and the first shot was fired in November 1913. The composer Arnold Schoenberg performed his latest work before a packed audience of the Viennese bourgeoisie in the great hall, the Musikverein. Vienna was the music capital of the world. They loved his work. They rose to give him an ovation. And what did he do? *He turned his back on them.*'

'Turned his back on them?' says Justin.

'Schoenberg believed that true art could not be popular. "If it's art, it's not for all, and if it's for all, it's not art." For me this single moment represents the start of the war between the artist and his audience. From now on the artist seeks to alienate his audience. Why? Because only by offending or shocking the bourgeoisie does the artist know he is being true to art. Any other path is artistic prostitution. The bourgeoisie seeks comfort. Art must make them uncomfortable. The bourgeoisie wishes to celebrate their way of life. Art must tell them that their way of life is shameful. Theodor Adorno, one of the greatest theorists of this new philosophy, declared that the job of the composer was to write music that would repel, shock, and be the vehicle for unmitigated cruelty.'

'Theodor Adorno,' says Justin, nodding.

Henry deploys his fingers once more.

'So number one: we, the audience for art, have lost confidence in our judgement. Unsurprisingly, because number two: artists no longer want to please us. They want us to be bewildered, offended and ashamed. So now we come to number three. Why hasn't the audience for art gone away? If art is designed to upset us, why do we run after it, and admire it, and buy it? Because – and this is the key to my whole argument – because art is no longer a deliverer of delight, as it once was. It is now a deliverer of status.'

'Status,' says Justin. 'Didn't Alain de Botton do something about that?'

'Yes. But his whole approach was quite different. Actually, I've tried this idea on Alain and he's right behind it.'

'Alain thinks you're onto something?'

'Absolutely. He gets it.'

This seems to make a difference to Justin. His scrupulously non-judgemental pose is being replaced with a marginally raised level of animation.

'Our taste in art has become central to our self-image.' Henry presses on. 'There is intense competition in the image wars. For the uneducated, a designer label does the job. For the smart set, it's art. We feel compelled to demonstrate by our taste in art that we are in the vanguard. We are not middlebrow. We are not mass market. So when the artists produce works that confuse or disgust the mass market, we embrace them. We love them. We hurry to admire works we neither understand nor enjoy because in doing so we separate ourselves from the middlebrow masses. At the same time we show, or appear to show, that we know something other people don't know. In 1918 Malevich painted White on White, which is one white square on top of another white square. If I stand before it in MoMA and announce that I'm profoundly moved, the person standing next to me, feeling nothing at all, concludes he must be a fool. In the same way, if I go to a performance of Boulez's Second Piano Sonata, and jump to my feet at the end with a loud bravo, those who found the music tedious and unpleasant will feel like fools. So in this way I can use my taste in art to raise my status. To set myself above others.'

'Okay,' says Justin, raising a hand. 'Wait a bit. Let me see if I have this right. All modern art is bollocks, and we only pretend to like it to show off.'

'There's good among the bad, of course. My point is that we no longer know how to tell the difference, nor do we need to know how to tell the difference.'

'But you, Henry Broad, you alone know?'

'That's not my point, Justin. My point is that art has become defined by its ability to drive away the mainstream audience.'

'Except for Tate Modern, which is a giant success. It's always packed.'

'Of course! That's the joke! The more artists strive to offend the bourgeoisie, the more the bourgeoisie run to embrace them. Why? Because the bourgeoisie – that's you and me, by the way

– we understand the game. We don't want to be philistines. We want to be in the vanguard. So off we go to gaze at the giantist sculptures of Anish Kapoor or Richard Serra, and we gawp at them and tell ourselves this is art, because the priesthood has so ordained.'

'The priesthood? Did we meet them already?'

'The curators, the collectors, the reviewers. The gatekeepers of the art industry. Nick Serota. Charles Saatchi, though he's past his sell-by date now. Larry Gagosian.'

'Larry Gagosian?'

'He's a dealer in New York. Look, Justin, the names don't matter. The point is the audience has lost confidence and no longer exercises any judgement. A self-perpetuating industry elite decrees who's making art worthy of our attention. The art colleges then churn out artists who emulate that brief. Do you follow the Turner Prize? It would be hilarious if it wasn't so tragic.'

Justin averts his gaze, as if Henry has accidentally unzipped his flies. Knocking the Turner Prize puts you in dodgy company.

'Isn't this all in danger of being a tad old-fartish, Henry?'

'Of course! You're experiencing the nervous sensation of the contemporary intellectual who doesn't want to be caught admiring the wrong stuff.'

'Or who wants to stay open to new experiences.'

'Come on, Justin. Fess up. We all have guilty pleasures. Is it Constable? Is it Tammy Wynette?'

'I liked *Mamma Mia*.'

'Only because it's camp.'

'Okay. Okay.' He pulls his chair up to his desk and makes a note. Getting down to business. 'Tell me about format.'

'Three times sixty minutes.'

'Who's the presenter? Alain de Botton? Aidan Massey?'

'No, this isn't Aidan's thing at all.' Henry wants to say, It's my thing. I've thought this up all by myself. I'll be the voice and the face.

'You know what?' Justin now has a faraway look on his face. He's slipped into creative mode. 'If we go for this, we have to deal with the old-fart thing head on. What this needs is a really cool young presenter.'

'Or no presenter.'

Justin doesn't even hear him.

'I'm thinking – can you guess who I'm thinking?'

Henry is entirely unable to guess.

'I'm thinking Russell Brand.'

'Russell Brand?'

'He's a comedian. A movie star. A contrarian. He's totally irresistible on camera. And he's an Essex boy. Oh, and he's a big David Lynch fan. I heard him talking about Transcendental Meditation.'

'Oh, well then. He's perfect for the job.'

Henry's sarcasm passes unnoticed.

'What do you say? He might just go for it.'

'I don't think so,' says Henry. 'I'm trying to construct a serious argument here.'

'Capture the zeitgeist, you said. That's Russell Brand.'

'Seriously, Justin. Seriously. No.'

Justin looks disappointed. He frowns. He puts down his pencil and pushes back his chair.

'Let's cut to the chase here, Henry,' he says. 'How old are you? Fifty-something?'

'What's that got to do with anything?'

'Put yourself in my chair. I go into the Channel meeting and I say I want to do a bunch of programmes by a middle-aged guy nobody's ever heard of saying he doesn't get modern art. How well do you think that's going to go down?'

'It's a new idea. I know that. No one's going to get it until it's out there. That's the risk you take.'

'New ideas come from a new generation.'

'What?'

'I'm just telling you how it is, Henry.'

'Say that again. I can't believe I heard you properly.'

Justin starts tapping his pencil again.

'Bring me the full package, Henry. I need a name.'

'Did you just tell me that only young people can have new ideas?'

'The concept could have legs. It's a stirrer, I can see that. Have the old farts been right all along? But if we're going to get away with it we need the right front man to take the heat. A young Brian Sewell. Maybe gay, maybe Asian. A Gok Wan of the arts. Who's the guy who's just done that Modern Masters series? Alastair Sooke. Is he gay?'

Henry watches Justin's hands as they rise and fall and slice the air before him, and a chill hopelessness seeps into his soul. Suddenly it all seems to him to be a farce. What possessed him to think he could sell a television essay on the arts on the basis of nothing but its originality, relevance and intellectual value? For a while, in the privacy of his study at home, he had persuaded himself that his thesis had enough shock value to force its way into the schedules. Now he sees it as Justin Hamo sees it, as a 'stirrer', a piece of mischief, not to be taken seriously.

So what have I got to lose?

'My proposal is that I present it myself, Justin. For the no-doubt unheard-of reason that all the ideas are in fact mine.'

'You want your moment in the sun, Henry. Don't we all? But you know that's not how it works.'

Henry shakes his head and says no more.

'I like your idea, Henry.'

'But you're not buying it.'

'Bring me the right face and I'll offer it. Hey, you're a pro. You've made more hours of heritage television than anyone still in the business.'

'Heritage television.'

'I'm not the enemy, Henry. I'm not a jerk. Do you have any idea how hard it is to get anything funded these days? You've lived through the golden age. You know that. What's the biggest audience you ever got?'

'Just over five million. For the first episode of *The Victorians*.'

'Five million! We'd die for that now! *Come Dine With Me* sometimes gets close to two, and that's one of our bankers. You've lived in heroic times, Henry. When gods walked the earth. We who come after have to make do with crawling through shit.'

So that's it. Not a yes and not a no. Except if it smells like a no and stings like a no and fills you with a no-like despair, then it's most likely a no.

Going back down in the lift, gazing at his own reflection in the bronze-tinted mirror, Henry sees an old man who's too tired to fight it any more.

I'm fifty-four. I'm having the best ideas I've ever had. After thirty years of letting others take the credit, I'm ready for my close-up. The Norma Desmond of heritage television.

He sees his own bitter smile in the mirror. Then the doors open and he's out into the glare of the glass and aluminium lobby. It's alive with the chatter of children, except they're not children. They're boys and girls barely older than Jack and Carrie. As he passes between them they don't even register his existence. This is who works in television now.

He pushes through the glass doors and crosses the glass bridge onto the street. Why are modern buildings made of so much glass? The message is one of transparency and openness. And it's true, you can see all the way in. But that doesn't mean there's anything worth seeing. This is a classic category error, surely. To make something visible is not to make it significant.

He stands on Horseferry Road, briefly unsure which way to turn. Not so far here from Buckingham Palace, where he'll be with Laura on Thursday. An honour, apparently, but for what? For his contribution to heritage television.

He turns right and makes his unhurried way towards Victoria. No rush, after all. The future stretches empty before him. Maybe find a café to stop for a coffee and a pastry. A pain-au-raisin or a maple pecan plait. Of all the pastries ever made, how is it that these two alone are to be found everywhere? Why not palmiers, millefeuilles, macaroons? Why is everything becoming the same? Why in an age of unfettered capitalism is there so little choice?

Suddenly he recalls how he told Justin that Alain de Botton approved his idea, and he feels a cold dread. The simple truth is that Henry only met Alain de Botton when he queued up to get his book signed at the Charleston Literary Festival. In the very short time he felt able to hold up the others behind him in the queue he tried out a truncated version of his idea. Alain de Botton listened politely and said, 'That's rather interesting.' Then there was another book to sign.

Justin's bound to meet Alain at some launch party or première. Those sorts of people are always meeting each other. Justin will say he's been hearing Henry Broad's new idea, as endorsed by Alain, and Alain will say, 'Henry who?'

Walking down Artillery Row he sees at the far end of the glass-fronted buildings of Howick Place, above a brown-glass raised walkway, the pink-and-white striped Italianate tower of

Westminster Cathedral. It looks lost, out of time, bewildered by the world in which it finds itself.

The darkness comes rolling down the London street towards him, a slow billowing cloud that he can no longer escape. The dread is upon him, and he sees it now, and knows its name. It is regret. He breathes its poison now, and feels it entering his body and taking possession of him. So many missed opportunities, so many wrong choices. His life lies behind him like a lost battle, hummocked with the bodies of the dead. So much hope, so much effort, so much illusion, and all amounting to nothing much. While the passion still burns bright you can look forward, you can say, The best is still to come. But when the light dies you turn and look back and you say, Is this all? Then the dark cloud closes about you, and you surrender. You lay down your arms. You are the prisoner of regret.

There's no escape, and no remedy. The clock won't turn back. Nobody gets their time again. This is the cruelty of regret, it lives in the past, but it corrodes the present and makes a mockery of the future.

A little hysterical, perhaps? An over-reaction?

But the plain truth is you can't fight it forever. You get tired. You get old. You want to go home, sit in an armchair with a glass of wine, read the paper. You want to slip into a waking sleep, and not have to care about any of it any more.

19

As Liz Dickinson parks outside her mother's house she feels her whole body tense up. Passing between the stone gateposts, with the bank of hydrangeas to her right and the brick path beneath her feet, she is seven years old again, returning from school. This is the house in which she lived as a child. Inside, beyond the grey-painted front door, her mother waits for her, unhappy and alone. Familiar sensations of pity and guilt bear down upon her as she turns her key in the lock, and enters the dark hall. As a child she would know from her mother's first words of greeting, from the tone more than the content, if this was a good day or a bad day. When it was a bad day, nothing was right. Tea would be dominated by tales of injustices done to her, respect not given, outrages left unpunished. Whatever the detail of the moment, each petty insult received was only a surrogate, as Liz well knew, for the original wound, her father's abandonment of them. In truth Liz had hardly known her father, and all her feelings about this abandonment came from her mother, who had enough feelings on the subject for both of them. To Liz it was simply the way things were. To her mother it was the core betrayal that had poisoned the world. It was the fall of man.

Nothing has changed in forty years. Liz still braces herself as she enters the silent house to withstand the downward drag of her mother's unhappiness.

Today there is no voice calling from the kitchen. No doubt she is out in the garden, in the July sunshine. But there she is, sitting in her chair by the unlit fire, asleep.

Liz feels a wave of relief. Treading softly, not wanting to wake her, she crosses to the sink and fills the electric kettle. She will wake her mother with a cup of tea, as she sometimes did when still a child. Most times the tea remained undrunk, but the gesture was always appreciated. Liz has tricky matters to discuss with her mother and wishes this to be a good day.

She watches her as she sleeps, and to her surprise she feels a sudden wave of love. Beneath that thinning hair, that deeply lined face, she sees quite clearly the powerful, capricious, magnificent woman who was everything to her for so many years. Her provider, her guide, her homemaker, her comforter, her friend. Liz has never for one moment doubted that her mother loves her, and will always love her. For that alone she owes her everything. And so long as she sleeps so peacefully in her chair, the debt does not feel so burdensome.

Mrs Dickinson wakes as Liz makes the tea.

'Is that you, darling?' she says.

'Yes, it's me, Mum.'

The same old exchange rings down the years. Always her mother asks, as if there might be someone else in possession of a key, letting themselves unannounced into the house. Always she answers, completing the ritual of reassurance.

Only nowadays someone else has a key. Bridget makes a point of ringing the bell as she arrives, but then she lets herself in. No fond greeting for her.

Liz brings the mug of tea to the shelf beside her mother's chair. She takes her own usual place in the chair on the other

side of the fireplace. She watches as her mother raises the mug
in frail hands and tips it a little, so that the tea trickles to the
floor. Liz has taught herself not to intervene at such times. The
floor is tiled and will not suffer.

'So how are you, darling? Busy?'

'Yes. Like always.'

'Have you started on the building work?'

Mrs Dickinson knows all about the plans for the new house,
and takes a keen interest.

'No, Mum. We can't start for ages. We have to get planning
permission first.'

'Such a nuisance. I really don't see what it's got to do with
them.'

She manages to get her mug of tea to her lips, but she barely
drinks.

'How's Alice?' she says. 'How's my little grandson?'

'Alice is away. Caspar says he'd like to come and see you.'

'I'd like that.'

'We're out on Saturday evening. Maybe he could come then.
I thought I could ask Bridget to help out.'

'I don't need Bridget's help to see my own grandson.'

'No, Mum. But someone has to get Caspar back.'

'I can't imagine why you called him by that silly name. You
know I was hoping you'd call him John, after my father. I think
John Dickinson is a fine name.'

'He's Strachan, Mum. Alan's name.'

'Oh, yes. I keep forgetting.'

Mrs Dickinson has never believed in Alan. His continuing
existence always comes as a surprise to her.

'Are you all right after your fall?'

'What fall?'

'On Sunday night.'

'Oh, yes.' She remembers, with a gust of indignation. 'She walked out. She did, you know, Elizabeth. I know you think she can do no wrong, but she left me in the garden, in the dark.'

'You wouldn't go to bed, Mum. You refused.'

'Of course I didn't refuse. Is that what she told you? And did you believe her? Really, Elizabeth, you do let that woman take you in. She changes my pills round, you know? I watch her whenever I can, but I can't see everything. She's very sly. She gives me the wrong pills so I get confused. They do things to my brain. You're not to let her have the house, Elizabeth. Promise me.'

'Don't be ridiculous, Mum.'

'Why is that ridiculous? She's a scheming woman. She's after something. Why else does she keep coming back?'

'She's your carer. It's her job.'

'You always were too trusting, Elizabeth. You never could see through people.'

Liz draws a long breath, tells herself not to take the bait.

'Bridget is doing her best, Mum. She's the best we've had so far. She always shows up on time. She never lets us down.'

'Oh, she's keen enough. I wonder why.'

'And you know you do need someone to help you.' Liz knows she must say more. She's promised Bridget. 'I do wish you'd make more effort to get on with her.'

'Me make the effort? What about her?'

'You know you can be very short sometimes.'

'Short? What does that mean? Is that what she tells you? That I'm short with her?'

'Sometimes, Mum.'

'And you believe her rather than me?'

'It's not about believing, Mum. I've seen you with her. I don't think you mean to be, but your manner really can be quite rude.'

Mrs Dickinson's hand trembles, holding the mug of tea.

'Rude? I am not rude. I am never rude.'

'It's all a matter of how you say things. You have to consider other people's feelings.'

'Really, Elizabeth, I have no notion at all what you're talking about. What other people? What feelings?'

'I'm talking about Bridget, Mum.'

The old lady closes her eyes, the mug of tea still in her hand.

'I don't want that woman coming any more.'

'Please, Mum—'

'Running to you with her lies, telling you I'm rude. She can go away. I don't want her coming here any more.'

Liz struggles to hold down the anger that pushes up from within. No use turning this into a row. Long experience has taught her that her mother only becomes more intransigent under pressure.

'It's nothing important, Mum. It's just a matter of tone of voice, that's all. Bridget knows you don't mean it.'

'I don't care what Bridget knows. She is a scheming, interfering woman and she can think what she likes of me.'

'No, you're wrong—'

'And she tells tales about me to you, saying I'm rude, when the last thing I ever am to anybody is rude.'

'That's not true, Mum.' Liz can't help herself. The wilful lack of self-knowledge angers her, and the anger has to come out. All she can do is force her voice to sound calm. 'You can be rude. I've heard you.'

'When? To who?'

'To Bridget. To me.'

Mrs Dickinson's eyes pop open, staring, defiant.

'When have I been rude to you?'

'You've told me to go away.'

'That's not rude.'

'Actually it is, Mum. People don't usually talk to each other like that. If you go on being rude to Bridget she'll leave.'

'Let her leave!' Her voice becomes shrill. 'I want her to leave!'

'Then who'll look after you?'

'No one. I'm not a baby. I'll look after myself.'

'If Bridget leaves I'll have to find someone else, and then you'll be rude to them and they'll leave—'

'I am not rude!'

She's shouting now, as much as she can. Shouting and trembling in her chair, spilling her tea.

'You are rude, Mum.' Liz, by contrast, fiercely soft-voiced. 'You have to see it the way other people see it. You have to wake up to what you're doing.'

'You wake up. Wake up yourself.'

'You need a carer, Mum—'

'Who are you to preach at me? Are you so perfect?'

'I'm just trying to get you to see what you're doing, for your own sake. If you go on being impossible you'll have no one.'

'I don't want anyone.'

'Listen to me, Mum. This is infantile. You have to take this in. We can't go on otherwise.'

'I don't want to listen to you when you get like this.'

'You have to listen.'

'I'm not listening. Leave me alone. I don't want Bridget. I don't want you. You'd better go.'

'And how are you supposed to cope then?'

'You think you're helping me, coming here and lecturing me? Crushing me, destroying me? No, thank you, Elizabeth. You can go now.'

Liz jumps up, on the point of running from the room. She's in a turmoil of rage, she wants to hit her mother, she wants to shock her into listening. At the same time she knows the whole encounter has gone horribly wrong and must somehow be rescued.

'All right,' she says. 'All right!' Almost shouting. 'I'm sorry. Okay? I'm sorry! This is me saying I'm sorry!' Shouting she's sorry. 'I'm apologising. I'm saying sorry.'

Mrs Dickinson does not answer and does not look up. She has her jaw set in a tight expression Liz knows all too well.

'You can't go on like this, Mum. You just can't.'

Now her mother is pulling herself forward, her prelude to getting up out of her chair.

'You need Bridget. You just do.'

Now she's up on her feet. Not looking at Liz. Setting off across the kitchen to the back door.

'Where are you going?'

'You won't go when I ask you. So I'll go.'

'*Where are you going?*'

Liz is shrieking now, out of control. Her question is needless, the old lady is all too clearly going out into the garden.

She wants to scream but she traps the screams in her mouth. Forces them back down her throat, but not out of her head. Why can't you see you need help? When will you stop fighting me? How can you be so stubborn and self-destructive? Why do you drag me down with all your problems? When do I get free of you? When do you die?

Shocked by her own rage, she follows her mother's slow progress to the back door. In the doorway, holding the doorframe for support, Mrs Dickinson speaks without turning round. She speaks in a slow faraway voice, as if to indicate that all is now over between them.

'I don't want Bridget to come any more. I don't want you to come any more. I want you all to leave me alone. I'm going out now to talk to the guinea pigs.'

And out she goes.

Liz remains for a few moments in the kitchen, pondering her options. But the truth is she's too angry to produce any rational response. Her mother's blank refusal to listen, the defensive wall she erects in the face of any criticism, enrages Liz far more than her occasional rudeness. It makes her want to punish her mother in exactly the way she's asking to be punished.

You want to be left alone, I'll leave you alone. I have a life. I don't need this.

'I'll go, then,' she says, projecting the words at her mother's stooping back. And receiving no response, she goes.

20

Coming south out of Alfriston the road descends into a tree-lined hollow and then begins to climb.

'Is it almost time?' says Caspar.

'Almost,' says Alan.

He's pleased that his son remembers the road and its special cry. It must be over a year since they last drove this way.

Then with a swoop they're rising again beyond the high hedges to the summit of the hill. There, thrillingly, is the end of the world: a wide view of rolling sheep-dotted grassland, and beyond it the great glittering sea.

'Woo-oo!' cries Cas.

'Woo-oo!' cries Alan.

This is High-and-Over, the humpbacked hill that makes you shout as if you're on a rollercoaster. Coming back the other way is even better because as you go over the hump there before you – Woo-oo! – the road drops so steeply it's like you're in a plane coming down to land, and your landing strip is all England.

They head on round the fringes of Seaford and onto the Eastbourne Road.

'Will we see Rocky actually talking?' says Cas.

'No,' says Alan. 'They add all that later.'

'So how will they know what to do?' says Cas. 'I don't understand.'

'I don't really understand myself,' says Alan. 'Maybe there'll be someone there who can tell us.'

Alan has met the director, Ray Stirling, only once, and is shy of interrupting him during filming. He remembers a guarded young man with attentive eyes, who nodded a lot and asked very little. But there'll be other lesser members of the unit who'll be ready to answer Cas's questions.

Alan has his own solution to the puzzle of how Rocky talks. He doesn't talk, he thinks. His dialogue is addressed to an imaginary listener, just as Alan's own thoughts are.

'Please don't ask me to run,' Rocky says. 'Running is exhausting and undignified, and the destination is rarely worth reaching. Good things are as likely to come if you lie down and wait for them, and if they don't come, well, at least you're comfortable.'

As they cross the narrow bridge over the river by the Golden Galleon he looks out for signs of the film unit. He hasn't told Cas, but this is the first time for him too, the first time he's ever visited a location film shoot. The thought that such a mighty machine has come into being to bring to life *his story* makes him feel a little dizzy, except that it's hardly his story any more. There was no single point in the last eighteen months when he was able to say: this is a change too far, this is no longer what I intended. But little by little, draft by draft, the project crept away from him.

Through it all, only Rocky remains: sharp-tongued, world-weary, cynical, but fundamentally loyal. Rocky alone holds Alan's place on the movie, and represents his creative mind. If all goes according to the schedule, this afternoon they are to film the scene that introduces the sheepdog at the start of the film.

EXT. THE DOWNS — DAY

Sheep graze in late afternoon sunlight. Beyond, the curve of the river, the rolling green hillside, the blue sea. A MAN lies in the grass, a handkerchief over his face, an empty bottle by his side. The handkerchief rises and falls with the even breathing of sleep. A grey-and-white BEARDED COLLIE lies beside him, a second handkerchief over his face. It too rises and falls as he sleeps. A bee buzzes by lazily. The sheep drift over the hillside. Two hikers go through a gate. They fail to close it properly. The man and the dog sleep on.

The sheep find the open gate. One pushes through. Others follow. Beyond the gate is the road. Cars passing. A sheep goes on to the road. A car sounds a sharp horn and swerves to avoid it. The car horn wakes the man. He sits up abruptly, the handkerchief falling from his face. He is HECTOR, late thirties, dishevelled, friendly-looking.

HECTOR: Bloody hell!

He jumps up, sees that the sheep are through the gate. Panicking, he turns to the dog.

HECTOR: Rocky! The sheep are on the road!

The handkerchief is puffed from the dog's

face. The dog opens one eye, not raising
his head.
  ROCKY: So?
  HECTOR: They'll be killed!
  ROCKY: So what's new? Every sheep is
    born to die.

Alan sees the film unit now, filling the car park opposite the
Visitors Centre like a travelling circus: a cluster of long trucks
and smaller vans, round which men and women are coming and
going in a purposeful way.

On the facing hillside a white Landrover is crawling slowly
up the track towards a cluster of crew members. The sky overhead
remains dull and grey.

He pulls up by the entrance to the car park, where a
young man with a yellow armband stands guard, holding
a clipboard.

'I'm really sorry,' he says politely. 'Would you mind parking
just over the road there? This is closed for filming.'

'I've come for the filming,' says Alan. 'Alan Strachan. I'm the
writer.'

'Oh, sorry.'

The young man studies a list on his clipboard.

'What was the last name again?'

'Strachan.'

In front of them three men are unloading sheep from a farm
truck. Cas watches with interest. Two small black-and-white
collies run back and forth yapping at the sheep, keeping them
in a tight huddle.

'Dad,' says Cas, 'which one's Rocky?'

'I'm sorry,' says the young man. 'I don't seem to have the name.'

Alan sees Flora pass by, carrying two mugs of coffee.

'Hey, Flora!'

She turns and gives Alan a lovely smile.

'Alan! Great you could come!'

The young man lowers his clipboard.

'Should be a space the far side of the catering truck,' he says.

Flora walks beside the car as Alan drives in.

'Not a lot happening,' she tells Alan. 'We're waiting for the sun to come out. Three weeks of gorgeous sunshine and now this.'

'Can't they use lights?'

'Apparently not.' Flora gives a light laugh. 'Don't ask me why. All I know is the schedule says golden hour and for golden hour you need sunlight.'

She stops by a trailer. Unable to wave goodbye, due to the full coffee mugs in her hands, she wags her pretty head. Then she taps on the trailer door with one foot. A sign on the trailer door says Colin Firth.

Alan parks where he's been told and he and Cas walk back past the catering truck. A short line of crew members waits to climb the steps to the food counter. A strong smell of melted cheese fills the air. Ahead, the sheep are being driven round the end of a cattle grid and onto Exceat Hill. Cas wants to run after them to find out which dog is Rocky.

'I don't think either of them is Rocky,' says Alan. 'Rocky's the star. He's probably got his own trailer somewhere.'

He looks round for someone to ask, but everyone seems to be busily going about their own concerns. Alan is all too aware that he has no function here. It's an odd and not very pleasant sensation, being an outsider at your own creation. He feels an urge to get back in the car and drive away. If it wasn't for Cas, he would.

For want of any better plan they follow the sheep. Cas is watching the sheepdogs.

'How do they know what to do, Dad?'

'The shepherd gives them commands.'

'But dogs can't understand English. I mean, not really.'

'It's not exactly English.'

Alan makes one of the shepherd calls he learned while working on the screenplay, a little yipping sound. The dogs hear and look back, puzzled. Cas is impressed.

'They heard you!'

They pass a member of the crew, lumbering along with a lens case.

'Christ!' he exclaims good-naturedly. 'You don't want to do this more than you have to.'

'Are they filming up there?' says Alan, indicating the huddle of figures on the hillside.

'If we get the fucking light,' says the crew man. Then seeing Cas, 'Sorry about that.'

The track up the hillside is steeper than it looks, and is carpeted with sheep droppings. Alan and Cas keep their eyes on the ground as they climb, to avoid treading in the mounds of dark close-clustered pellets. When they pause to catch their breath and look up, they find the valley laid out in beauty below them. The wide meanders of the Cuckmere River curl down the valley floor to the shingled cove where the river meets the sea. The western flank of the Downs rises up to its graceful curving summit, and there beyond is the sea again, a line of silver against the grey sky.

'What's golden hour, Dad?' says Cas.

'It's when the sun's low in the sky and it makes long shadows on the hills, and a warm light on the actors' faces. Everyone likes filming in the golden hour. It makes everything look much more beautiful than it really is.'

'So when does it happen?'

Cas looks round as if expecting the sun to show itself from

some hiding place in the sky and oblige the waiting film crew.

'Should be pretty much now. But only if the cloud lifts.'

'What if it doesn't?'

'I don't know. We'll see.'

They walk on up the track. The huddle of figures round the camera is identifiable now. Alan makes out Ray Stirling, hunkered down on his haunches, talking to a youngish man with tight curly black hair. The camera crew are standing together, laughing at some joke. Make-up and costume have put up a wind-break, behind which stand two folding tables. Over to one side, apart from the rest, there's a stocky woman sitting on the grass with a dog.

'I think that'll be Rocky,' Alan says to Cas.

Then he sees Jane Langridge, halfway down the slope, talking into her mobile phone. She sees him and gives him a wave. She ends her call, but instead of coming up to say hello she makes another call.

Cas pulls at his hand. He wants to go and see Rocky. So does Alan. Now that the moment is approaching he feels almost nervous. What if Rocky is in some unknown way *wrong*?

The stocky woman looks up as they approach, mistaking Alan for someone in authority.

'Do you want him now?'

'No, no,' says Alan. 'Just come to say hello.'

'Say hello, Billy.'

The dog looks up and meets Alan's eyes. He's a proper bearded collie, and he's the right colouring, and he has just the right look of tolerant contempt in his gaze. Alan doesn't demean him by petting him.

'Good to meet you, Billy,' he says gravely.

The dog is all right. The dog is good. This is more of a relief than Alan has been expecting. Apparently he really cares.

'I thought he was called Rocky,' says Cas. 'Why do you call him Billy?'

'Rocky's who he's acting,' says his trainer.

'How will he talk?' says Cas.

'He won't talk,' says his trainer. 'They'll make it seem like he's talking. But he can move his mouth.'

She makes a little clicking sound with her tongue. Billy looks at her and silently opens and closes his mouth. Cas is delighted, but the little demonstration makes Alan feel sad. Billy is a mature, serious dog. He shouldn't be made to perform in this way.

Billy lowers his head once more and rests it on the ground. Alan, watching his every move, feels that he understands him. If this is what it takes to make a living for me and my trainer, the dog is thinking, then I'll do it and I'll do it well. Just don't ask me to take any of it seriously.

'What does he have to say for the film?' says Cas.

'Oh, he has pages and pages,' says the trainer with a laugh. 'Some of it's quite rude. And he has to say that line Michael Douglas said. "Greed is good." That'll be an odd one.'

'He says "Greed is good"?' says Alan.

Flora now joins them, panting and pink in the face.

'Hey, Alan,' she says. 'I see you've met Rockefeller.'

'He's called Billy really,' says Cas. 'Rocky's who he's acting.'

'My son Caspar,' says Alan.

Flora shakes Cas's hand.

'Pleased to meet you, Caspar.' Then to Alan, 'Jane asked me to see if there's any way I can help you. You should have called ahead to see what was happening. We're not having much luck with the light, so I'm afraid it could be very boring for you.'

'Oh, we don't mind, do we, Cas? I might just say hi to Ray before we wander off.'

He looks across towards the director, who is now studying a script alongside the curly-headed young man.

'I'll tell him you're here. He'll come over when he can.'

Flora goes to the group round the camera. Cas wants to see Billy do more tricks. The trainer obligingly makes the dog shake a paw. Alan moves away, not wanting to watch. There are two crew men standing smoking, watching the movements of the flock of sheep. The sheep have spread out over the flank of the hill and are grazing.

'If you was a sheep,' says one crew man to the other, 'all you'd be doing all day is eating.'

'Eating and shitting,' says the other crew man.

'Not a bad life.'

Alan joins them, nodding over towards the group by the camera.

'Not a lot happening,' he says.

'No light,' says one of the crew men.

'Not going to be any light neither,' says the other, looking at the sky in an expert sort of way.

Alan sees Flora talking now to Ray Stirling and the curly-headed young man.

'You see Flora over there?' he says.

'Yes,' says the crew man with a grin. 'I see Flora. I see Flora any time I get the chance. Don't you, Mal?'

'I do,' says Mal.

'You see she's talking to Ray? Who's the other guy with them?'

'The other guy? The little American guy?'

'I don't know if he's American,' says Alan.

'I know who he is,' says Mal.

He fumbles in his satchel and pulls out a copy of the script.

'There it is.' On the cover page it says: Screenplay by Harlan Rosen. 'He's the writer.'

Alan feels the blood drain from his head, leaving him dizzy and his vision blurred. Here on the top of the hill, with the grassy slopes rolling down to the sea, he has become untethered, no longer part of the familiar world. He thinks perhaps he'll float away, up through the layer of cloud that hinders the filming, out into the cool clear sunlight above. But of course he can't. He must stay here on earth, with his son.

He makes his way back to Cas and the dog.

'Billy's amazing, Dad,' says Cas. 'Listen to this. I hold up my fingers.' Cas holds up two fingers. 'How many fingers, Billy?'

Billy gives two short soft barks. The barks are muffled by his beard, as if he's a little ashamed of them.

'There's not going to be any filming,' says Alan. 'We might as well go.'

'No filming?' says the trainer. 'Are you sure?'

'No light,' says Alan.

'Can we come back when they're filming, Dad?' says Cas.

'Maybe,' says Alan. 'Bye, Billy.' A nod for the trainer.

They head back down the turd-ridden track, moving faster than when they came.

'Can we have a dog, Dad?'

'Maybe.'

'I could train him, like Billy. That would be so cool.'

Flora catches up with them, panting and pink-faced as ever.

'Are you going?' she says. 'I'm really sorry if you've had a wasted journey. Call me next time and I'll make sure there's something happening.'

Alan says nothing.

'So did you like Rockefeller, Caspar?' says Flora.

'He's so cool,' says Cas. 'He can actually count.'

'You wait till you see what he can do in the film.'

'Is he rude?'

'Yes, he is sometimes.' She looks towards Alan, who says nothing. 'I don't think he knows what the rude words mean, though.'

'What rude words does he say?'

'Oh, you know. The usual ones.'

'Does he say shit?'

'I think he probably does.'

'I keep treading in it,' says Cas. 'It's impossible not to. Why do the sheep only do it on the path?'

'I don't know,' says Flora, looking again towards Alan.

When they reach the concrete road at the bottom Alan says to Flora, 'So who's Harlan Rosen?'

Flora has the decency to blush, which makes her look even prettier.

'The studio insisted,' she says. 'Just a final punch-up.'

'A what?'

'You know. A quick pass for the director.'

'Ray agreed to this?'

'It was more Nancy in LA. It was a condition of the green light.'

Alan is heading for his car, wanting to be gone. There's a big crowd round the catering van now.

'Am I allowed to see the changes?'

'Yes, of course.'

'Okay, I'd like that. Email me the latest draft.' He unlocks his car. 'Hop in, Cas.'

Cas can tell from his tone that something has gone wrong, so he does as he's told without a murmur. Alan gets in, starts the engine.

'It's nothing, Alan,' Flora is saying. 'Superficial stuff.'

They drive out of the car park and onto the road back towards Seaford.

'What happened, Dad?' says Cas.

'They've got another writer in to change my script,' says Alan.

'But it's yours, Dad. They can't do that.'

'Well, you know, Cas,' says Alan, trying to sound wryly amused by the ways of the film world, 'it's not, and they can.'

'But you wrote it.'

'I wrote it. They paid me. They own it.'

When they get to High-and-Over on the way back Cas doesn't go Woo-oo! As they crest the hill and see laid out before them the great green land, a land carved and formed by people, its every smallest track tramped by people, its every house sheltering people, Alan can see only the disappointment that follows all human endeavour repeated in every home, in every car, multiplied into the far distance. The vista laid out before him is a whole world of hurt, if only we could tune our senses to the wavelength of pain.

Down into the valley. Down into the trees. Down into the shadows where real life is lived in all its grubby littleness.

I could walk away from it all. I should walk away from it all. But then what? Back to teaching? That'll never pay the mortgage on the new house.

How did this happen? How did I end up leading a life that makes me hate myself?

One of the lines he wrote for Rocky passes through his mind, making him smile even as he wants to cry.

'Life's a bitch, but you know what? Bitches have their uses.'

21

Through the kitchen window, Laura can see Carrie sitting on the low wall of the terrace, talking with Toby Clore. Toby is lying on his back on the teak outdoor table, his hands behind his head. Carrie looks animated and laughs and moves her hands about in the air. Toby's arrival has transformed her. This should make Laura happy. She and Henry have been worried recently by Carrie. She's been so withdrawn and silent. Is she depressed? And if so, why? Is it their fault? It has to be, but Laura doesn't know what she's done wrong, and why it's become so hard, so impossible, to have a conversation with Carrie. People say, Oh, she's a teenager, they go through these moody phases. But why?

Was I like that when I was her age?

With a shock Laura realises she was more or less exactly Carrie's age when she fell in love. Her boyfriend back then had been all in all to her, she has no memory of her own family at the time, only of Nick. The time she spent with him was filled by her love for him, and the rest of the time was spent waiting for him.

Is Carrie in love with Toby?

It looks very like it. Silently Laura pleads with Carrie to be careful. He'll walk away from you. He'll break your heart. But how can she say this to Carrie? And why should she say it? Loving and losing is all part of growing up.

I loved and I lost and I was wounded for years and years. Was that part of growing up? How much pain is valuable? When does it turn to plain old damage?

Laura doesn't trust Toby and she doesn't like him. Just as her own mother, she recalls suddenly, didn't like Nick. But that was different. Nick was an intellectual snob, he made Mummy feel stupid. And maybe there was something else too. Mummy could see how he treated me, how he resented my need of him, and she concluded he didn't really love me. Which you could say turned out to be both true and not true.

Did I laugh with Nick the way Carrie's laughing now? Most likely I did. Forever looking towards him to test his response to me, then looking away to conceal, or fail to conceal, my helpless obsession.

She can't see Toby's face or hear what he says, or if indeed he speaks at all. He just lies there and accepts Carrie's devotion as his right. Oh yes, he's attractive, there's no denying that. Not so much his appearance, which is too skinny and too hairy for her taste, but his eyes, which look at you with a scary intensity, and the things he says. There's no predicting which way he'll go on anything. If you disagree with him he simply changes his mind. He seems not to care about presenting a formed self to the world. This has the odd effect of making everyone else want to gain his approval. Because he doesn't seem to care how he's judged, we all submit ourselves to his judgement.

Such a boy as this will let Carrie adore him and then vanish, without trace and without guilt. Already Laura hates him for it.

She has another reason for hating Toby Clore. He mocked her for planning her dinner party. He proposed that she do nothing at all. *The guests come, you all sit down at the table, there's nothing to eat.* This image has haunted Laura ever since. Of course it's absurd, just his jokey manner, but behind it lies a criticism of her entire way of being that is a little too close to a secret fear of her own: that she leads an unworthy life. That the concerns that fill her day are not of any lasting value.

Fuck him. He's nothing but a spoilt kid from a screwed-up family. What's he ever done that makes him so great? He's living the life of a parasite, easy for him to lie about grinning at everyone, acting as if other people's efforts to make their lives work are some kind of joke.

A sudden thought enters Laura's head. Toby thinks he's Jesus. He's got the long hair and the beard and the radical philosophy. Consider the lilies of the field, they toil not, neither do they spin, yet Solomon in all his glory and so forth. There always was something flaky about all that take-no-thought-for-the-morrow stuff. Who wants to be a lily in a field? Equating Toby with Jesus does not have the effect of elevating Toby in her eyes. It reminds her of a long-held secret, that she has always found the teachings of Jesus annoying. They sound so right, but you just can't live them in your actual life. They don't fit. So you go round feeling permanently inadequate, and of course, guilty. Give all you have to the poor. Well, no. Love your enemy. Then he's not my enemy, is he? Blessed are the meek. No, the meek are a drag and a pain. The whole thing only works if you believe this world is some sort of short-lived test chamber for the real thing that's coming after death. Sure, if we're all about to die and wake up in eternity, I'll take no thought for the morrow. But if I don't die and I wake up tomorrow right here and I've made no plans, then what do we eat?

And what do I do about a hat?

This hat business is of course comical and she's ready to laugh about it, but when she's done laughing the problem remains.

She must wear something on her head at the royal garden party. Why this should be so she has no idea. That's the sort of question that interests Henry, the curious conjunction of historical hangover, social etiquette, and marking of status boundaries that is called tradition. For Laura the matter is entirely practical. A solution must be found.

She ponders the option of going shopping for a hat and rejects it. She resents the time and the cost. This is not a gathering of people she knows. The Queen won't be singling her out to compare outfits. Strictly speaking, what she will wear on Thursday has no importance at all. But not to wear a hat will be to make a statement that she is not willing to make, that she is openly rejecting the reigning convention. This mild form of rebellion would be charming if she were Carrie's age. At her age it strikes her as graceless. If she really doesn't want to be part of the circus why join the parade?

There's always the option of the 'fascinator'. The name alone is enough to make Laura wince, implying as it does a simpering and desperate attempt to attract attention. But there are perhaps ways of carrying it off. After all it's no more than a modern variant of the flower in the hair.

The words of an old song drift through her mind. 'If you're going to San Francisco . . .' Old even when she was young, from the forgotten age of the hippies, though as a teenager she was just in time to wear the long floaty dresses bequeathed by the flower children of the Sixties. She remembers with a shock her first visit to Biba, which by then was in decline, but to her was a revelation of purple and emerald, of shadowy glamour, a promise of sensuality to come. Jewel-red ostrich feathers and jade-green tights, plum-coloured eye-shadow in black pots. She wore her hair long and straight then, and floated about the store attracting glances, fully aware that her particular kind of prettiness, her Pre-Raphaelite pallor, was perfectly suited to the Biba look.

How old was I then? Fourteen, almost fifteen. My skin was so perfect in those days, why on earth did I use make-up at all? Cosmetics are no more than a doomed attempt to recreate the sole ingredient of beauty, which is youth.

But don't ask me to be young again. I've not forgotten.

Laura shivers at this brush with a long-ago past, a time of almost unbearable anguish, though over what she can no longer recall. Simply being alive brought with it such exposure, as if she was forever being stripped, forever humiliated.

Not feathers. The standard fascinator is made of three or four brightly dyed feathers, and worn on one side of the head, making the wearer look like a tipsy cockatoo. But maybe a clip-on flower, a silk flower, not too big. She has one that's pale blue and very pretty, which would go with the dress she plans to wear, but she's not sure the spring is strong enough to keep it in place for several hours.

A glance at the clock tells her it's almost seven. Henry should be home in forty minutes or so. There are tomatoes and lettuce in the garden. What else? Hard-boil a few eggs, slice them up. Some tinned artichoke hearts. Some tinned tuna. Will that be enough?

Why can't I remember where I put Henry's proposal?

She touches her engagement ring, pressing the smooth hard ruby with one finger, as she often does. She's worn the ring so long it's become part of her. But that funny little pub napkin with its question and its answers and its ticked box she seems to have hidden away beyond memory, as if the very sight of it is an embarrassment.

So I had planned my answer before the question was asked.

What's so wrong with that? It was the right answer. Twenty-seven years, for Christ's sake.

She goes about preparing supper.

The right answer but, let's face it, the wrong process. Nowadays children are taught in school not just to give the solution to the problem but to show their workings. Laura remembers all too clearly the long secret conversations with herself in which she juggled and re-juggled the pros and cons of marrying Henry. Sometimes the balance tipped one way, sometimes the other. Charles Darwin did the same thing, unwisely committing his thoughts to paper.

Constant companion and friend in old age – object to be beloved and played with – better than a dog anyhow – but terrible loss of time – an infinity of trouble and expense in getting and furnishing a house – poor slave, you will be worse than a negro – Cheer up – One cannot live this solitary life, with groggy old age, friendless and cold and childless staring one in the face – Never mind, trust to chance – There is many a happy slave.

There was a time when she knew it by heart, and used to recite it as a party trick. It always generated knowing looks among the laughter, but the assumption was that this was a male view of marriage. The woman was supposed to be sufficiently rewarded by the status granted by the man in marrying her. Or was supposed to be so in love that such calculations were beside the point.

A burst of laughter from Carrie on the terrace.

Why can't I talk to Carrie? Why don't we sit together in a dark bedroom and share secrets like other mothers and daughters? Carrie has always been self-contained, almost remote, even as a little child.

I still love you so much, darling. Maybe I don't understand you but it doesn't stop me loving you so much it hurts. I want you to be so happy. I want you to have the life you long for, whatever that is. I want you to be loved the way I love you, for ever and ever. I don't mind that you're not like me. I don't mind that we don't talk. Well, I do, but it's okay. All I want is for you to know how much I love you.

She feels tears pricking at her eyes. Jesus, I am getting soft in my old age. Where did all that come from?

She pours herself a glass of wine and stands still for the first swallow so she can feel it going all the way down. Out on the terrace Toby has now got up off the teak table and is walking up and down, smoking, gesticulating with his arms. Carrie follows him with adoring eyes. The sun is behind cloud. Dull light over the Ouse valley.

Laura boils eggs, chops tomatoes, opens tins, mixes vinaigrette in a jam-jar. Then when as much is done as can be done she opens her lined pad and reviews the menu for Saturday evening. Such thinking can only be done before a meal, when hunger brightens the prospect of food.

She called on Richards the butcher earlier, and after some discussion accepted his professional advice that a leg of lamb would not feed eight, not in July. She has ordered a saddle of lamb, which Richards will bone and roll. A saddle is expensive but not ostentatious, in a way that a fillet of beef, say, is ostentatious. This is to be classic English cuisine: new potatoes, carrots, mint sauce, baby courgettes from the garden. Everything on the plate will be familiar to her guests, but the lamb will be pink and tender, the potatoes crisp, the carrots sweet. She will make the ordinary extraordinary.

She sees then that the sardine paté is not right. Better to make a taramasalata. Smoked cod roe, olive oil, garlic, lemon juice, white bread soaked in milk. She can make it on Friday, serve it on slices of baguette oiled and crisped under the grill. Is a summer pudding too much after all this? There's always the anxiety of turning it out of the basin, you don't want it to disintegrate. The look is almost as important as the taste. But she's already bought the sliced white bread so it can be nicely stale by Friday.

Really a dinner party is like a military campaign. All the crucial decisions are taken in advance. When the signal is given to attack, all you can do is watch the battle unfold and pray you got it right.

No, battle is too aggressive. A drama, perhaps. The creation of a work of art.

She pulls a face as she frames this thought. And yet why not? All the attributes of the artist are on call here. She is making a tableau, a visual set piece, that is also a feast of the senses, and is also a play, complete with characters and plot. She will be aware throughout the evening of the tone of each player, and like a conductor of an orchestra she will exert herself to create harmony. If she's successful, by the end her guests will only be conscious that they've had a fine evening, not that they have performed in her work of art. Henry will say, 'That was quite fun, really.' One or two of the guests will drop her a line of thanks. And the evening will fade into memory.

So you could say, why bother? Other people's works of art are displayed in galleries, or performed before audiences, or at the very least survive in print form, bound into volumes that stand on library shelves, waiting to be rediscovered. Her art leaves no trace behind. And yet this is the best of her, the art which calls upon all her skills. This is herself as she wishes to be known.

She glances again at the clock. Henry will be home any minute. Laura drinks her wine and lets her over-stimulated mind run on. Behind all this, behind her irritation with Toby and her glorification of dinner parties, there lurks something that is deeper and darker. Jack is rarely home these days. Carrie will be gone soon. Her work, sporadic at the best of times, is unlikely to expand in this recessionary age. She's fifty-two years old and can reasonably expect another thirty years of active life. Thirty years! That's longer than her marriage, longer than her life as a mother. Thirty years doing what? Thirty years for what?

She thinks of her own parents. What do they do? They travel. They go to theatre and opera. They see their friends. They read books. Their lives are not empty. But you'd be hard pressed to say their lives have a purpose.

Maybe that doesn't matter. Maybe lives don't have purposes, they just happen, day by day. The trouble is, having children is so packed with purpose. Feeding them, clothing them, taking them to school, worrying about them when they get ill, rejoicing at their little triumphs, it's all so intense. You, their mother, are so necessary to every moment of their existence that you never have time to stop and ask yourself what your life is for. It's like a drug, being needed so much. You get addicted. And then it stops.

Carrie's still at home, of course, but she might as well not be. Her mind is somewhere else.

Darling, I know you're unhappy. I wish you'd talk to me. Don't let Toby hurt you. Don't smile so much for him. It'll make him think you want him too much and he'll run away.

She hears Henry's car pull up onto the gravel outside. She jumps up, going to the front door to meet him. Not something she usually does, but today's meeting was important.

He's frowning as he comes in. When she kisses him he hardly kisses her back. So it's not gone well.

'How was it?' she says.

'Oh, you know.' He drops his leather bag on the floor and kicks off his street shoes. 'Pretty bloody.'

'Oh, darling. I'm sorry.'

'Likes the idea. Wants a hip young presenter to put it across.'

'But it's your idea!'

'Yes. Funny, that. I need a drink.'

She pours a glass of wine. He sees Carrie and Toby out on the terrace.

'Carrie seems to have perked up.'

Laura lowers her voice. 'I just know Toby is going to mess her around. I can see it coming.'

'Nothing we can do.'

'No. I know. She wouldn't listen to me even if I told her.'

Henry drinks his wine quickly, in silence.

'So how did you leave it?' says Laura.

'I'm supposed to put together some kind of package. Get back to him. But that's just window dressing.' He looks up from his empty glass and meets Laura's gaze with his sad and weary eyes. 'It's not going to happen.'

She doesn't tell him it will happen. This is no time for a call to arms. That can come later. Right now, as she knows all too well, what he needs is to have his hurt acknowledged.

'After all your work.'

'All pissed away in half an hour. I know I'm onto something with this, and Justin knows it too, in some corner of his dim little brain. But it's no good. I'm just too old.'

She takes his free hand in hers and strokes it. She doesn't say no, you're not old, your best work is still to come, even though she does believe that. He is the hurt child right now. This isn't a problem looking for a solution. This is a frightened creature crying out for kindness.

'I do love you so much, Henry.'

As she says it she feels it with a force that surprises even her. She knows him so well, she admires him, she believes in him. But more than all of this, she is bound to him. Whatever is his fate will be hers too.

For now what he needs is distraction, and food, and the passing of time.

'Supper's ready,' she says.

She opens the back door to the terrace and catches a peal of Carrie's nervous laughter.

'Supper!'

Toby claps his hands, applauding her.

'There's your answer,' Toby says to Carrie. 'The solution to all the problems of life. Supper!'

Henry looks through the open door at them.

'God help me,' he says. 'I never thought I'd want to be young again.'

WEDNESDAY

22

'This is priceless, Roddy. Listen to this.' Diana has the morning copy of *The Times*, as is her way. She likes to share whatever catches her attention, unaware that other people might have other concerns. 'This man actually murdered his wife over a game of bridge. He called her the C-word and said he'd throw her off the balcony, then he stabbed her a hundred times with an eight-inch knife.'

Diana is enchanted by the story. Roddy listens, drinking his morning coffee in silence. He wonders exactly what aspect of the story it is that so delights his wife.

She relishes every detail.

'He's fifty-two. She was fifty-seven. He drank heavily, then criticised the way she played bridge. This is heaven.'

Roddy no longer makes any effort to control her. But he can't resist a low bleat of protest.

'Bit of a sad story, I'd say.'

'Sad? Roddy, these people played bridge in *Lytham St Annes*! Have you ever been there? It's even worse than Hove. Nothing but retired Tories bitching about benefits scroungers.'

She reads on.

'She didn't want a divorce. She wanted her old Stephen back, the Stephen that was not violent or drunk. She loved him even after what had happened.'

'What, after he stabbed her to death?'

'I imagine not, Roddy. Unless they've had a message from the afterlife.'

Roddy finishes his coffee and stands up.

'About this weekend,' he says.

'They printed out the hands of bridge they'd played and discussed them in the pub afterwards. These people are so *competitive*.'

'I thought I might go down on Friday evening.'

She looks up from her paper at last.

'Go down where?'

'I've been meaning to visit Worth Abbey,' Roddy says, not meeting Diana's eyes.

'What on earth for?'

'I suppose you could say, for the purpose of contemplation.'

'What do you want to contemplate?'

'Nothing, really. The idea is you go into the silence.'

'Don't be so silly, Roddy. You can go into the silence in your shed.'

'Even so.' Roddy is prepared for Diana's resistance, and has determined to press on regardless. As the great day approaches he feels increasingly reckless. To Diana's self-absorbed incomprehension he opposes a stubborn will. 'I could go on to the Broads for Friday night, and meet up with you for Saturday lunch.'

'Laura won't want you on Friday night. You'll just be in the way.'

'All I need is a bed.'

Max appears, silent and bleary-eyed. Not usually up so early.

'If you become a Catholic I'll divorce you,' says Diana.

'Why?' says Roddy.

'Why?' The question surprises Diana. 'Because converts are

sad needy people whose lives aren't working out. How would I explain it to my friends?'

Roddy stares at her without answering. Right now she seems to him to be a thousand miles away.

'So I'll get a train down to Sussex after work on Friday,' he says.

'Well, if that's what you really want. There's coffee left in the pot, Max, but it won't pour itself. I'd better get myself ready, I have a meeting at nine.'

So it's agreed: Roddy will spend Friday night with the Broads. He knows that Diana has given in because it's a matter of no importance to her. She is quite unable to imagine what Roddy has in mind for the weekend, which makes things easier for him, but is also hurtful to his pride. If he were to take up an eight-inch knife and stab her a hundred times, she would look on him in a different way. He has no desire to stab his wife, but he can't deny to himself that he looks forward to the expression on her face when he tells her just how radically things are going to change. She won't believe him at first. Then she'll ask Laura, and Laura will nod and say yes, it really is happening. Then Diana will believe him. He imagines her in shock. How will she explain it to her friends?

Diana leaves the house in a hurry, on her way to her first meeting of the day. She works as a fund-raiser, one of many, for the Royal Opera House, a function she describes at dinner parties as 'chiselling'. Roddy decides to wait a little, so that he can have his walk to the underground station to himself. He needs to call Laura, to ask about Friday night.

Max has started to read the paper in an inattentive sort of way.

'You know we're away this weekend,' Roddy says.

'Cool,' says Max, not looking up.

'Are you likely to be around?'

'No idea.'

'All I ask is that you don't drink the Barolo. That's expensive wine.'

Max says nothing to this.

'I wonder what you'd say, Max,' says Roddy, 'if I disappeared?'

Max looks up, blinking.

'I sometimes think you wouldn't notice if I was here or not.'

Max looks even more baffled.

'But you are here.'

'Yes, okay. Don't worry about it. I'll head off.'

He's actually in the hall, looking round for his phone, when Max appears, a frown wrinkling his brow.

'Dad?'

'Yes, Max?'

'You know your shed?'

'Yes, Max.'

'Some time, when you've got the time, I'd like to know what it is you read.'

Roddy is caught off-guard. This is the first time that Max has shown any curiosity about him of any kind. What's more, for all his early-morning blinking and shuffling, he says it in a way that suggests he means it.

'What I read,' says Roddy, playing for time, unsure how to respond. 'I don't think it's your kind of thing.'

'I know Mum laughs about it,' says Max. 'But I'm not Mum.'

'Diana is very tolerant,' says Roddy. 'I appreciate very much that she gives me my own space.'

Max looks at his father with his head a little to one side, as if asking himself whether or not to believe what he's just heard.

'Apparently you're looking for God,' he says.

'Am I? Yes, I suppose I am.' Roddy feels compelled by his

son's unexpectedly direct gaze to speak the simple truth. 'I'm looking for the right way to live.'

Max nods a couple of times, then smiles. He is a very good-looking young man, and when he smiles Roddy feels honoured. He gets his good looks from Diana, of course.

'Okay,' says Max. 'Cool. Let's talk sometime.'

Roddy leaves the house a little dazed. All his plans are based on the assumption that he is of no significance in his own home. This late flush of interest in him by his son presents a complication. But there's no turning back now. He's been preparing for this for too long.

Out on the street he stands by the canal and calls the Broads on his mobile phone. He prays that Laura will pick up, not Henry or Carrie. His prayer is answered.

'Laura, it's Roddy. I wonder if you could do me a favour? I have to come down to Sussex on Friday evening. I'm going to Worth Abbey. Would it be possible for me to have a bed for Friday night?'

'Yes, of course, Roddy. Just you?'

Her voice so warm and welcoming.

'Just me.'

'What time will you show up? Will you need feeding?'

'No, I'll be late. No later than ten.'

'What are you up to at Worth Abbey, Roddy?'

When Laura asks, it's not at all like Diana. You can tell from her voice that she's curious in a good way.

'It's all about silence, really.'

'Silence? God, that would be wonderful. And scary.'

'And both at once, maybe.'

'You're really going on adventures, aren't you, Roddy? I almost envy you.'

'You can have adventures too, Laura.'

'You think so? First I have a Buckingham Palace garden party, then I have a dinner party. Adventure has to wait its turn.'

'It's there whenever you want it. All you have to be is a leaf on the wind.'

'A leaf on the wind?'

'Go where life takes you.'

'Well, you can tell me all about it over the weekend.'

'I will,' says Roddy. 'I'd love to have a quiet moment to talk, just you and me.'

'Me too. See you Friday night.'

This short conversation exhilarates Roddy. He walks briskly up the canal, across Colebrook Row, and up Duncan Street, his mind filled with Laura. She has never made it so plain before that she too wants her life to change. She too is a stranger and a pilgrim on the earth.

Descending the escalator at the Angel, reputed to be the longest escalator in London, Roddy feels as if he has already gone into the silence. For all the hustling streams of people heading to work on every side, he is magnificently alone. The escalator is the stream of life, carrying him to his destiny. All he has to do is not resist.

23

It's a relief to Maggie to be out of the office and on the road. Sam's jokey insistence that she can solve all her problems by marrying him has stopped being funny, but she can't say so without revealing that she's more disturbed than she wants to admit. Also she's putting off the moment when she writes her formal letter of apology to Murray. In fact she's putting off her entire life, keeping all her thoughts of the future in a state of suspension, until she can make the decision about Andrew.

Memories of Andrew haunt her. She recalls the first time they spent the whole night together, waking to find her wrist lightly covered by his sleeping hand, and how happy this made her. Her previous boyfriend, known to her friends as 'nasty Nigel', always rolled away from her in the bed, actively repelling her affectionate touch, saying it stopped him from sleeping. He chose whenever possible to have sex somewhere other than a bedroom, on the couch while watching television was a favourite, which was exciting; but later he would announce he needed to go back to his place to sleep, and she was left feeling lonely in the night. With Andrew everything was the other way round. There were times when she wished he would go back to his place.

She remembers then – she's turned off the main road now, she's driving down one of the lanes where if you meet another car one of you has to back to a passing place – she remembers that she made him go home on Sunday evening, instead of taking the early train on Monday morning, as is his usual pattern. She tries to regain the feeling she had then, of being crowded by him, of wanting her own space, but it won't come. It seems to her that having Andrew around all the time is comforting, supportive, the way things should be.

I'm a hopeless case. I want him to stay when he's not there, and want to go when he is.

An Audi TT convertible comes fast towards her and brakes hard. Both of them check the hedges to see if there's room to creep past each other. The TT driver, a middle-aged man wearing a baseball cap, has an impatient look on his face, but when they make eye contact this vanishes. He smiles, gives her a wave, and reverses with speed and skill. He pulls into a driveway, and Maggie goes by, with a smile and wave of her own in acknowledgement. His eyes on her all the way. Not her type at all, but nice to see that he finds her worth looking at.

As she has done again and again over the last three days, she finds herself asking: is there anyone better out there? Jo had it exactly. Is Andrew the last in line? Of course there'll be men like the TT driver who are willing to give her a good long stare, but she's talking about reliable, kind men, who are at the same time a little exciting, even a little dangerous.

I'd know him if I met him. But how long will that take?

She bumps her little Nissan Micra over the level crossing and turns down the lane to Hamsey. The sign by the side of the road says Ivors Lane. There was some kind of fuss about that, years before she took on her present job, some objections to the choice of name. Ivor was a local who had died in an accident, or perhaps a suicide?

Ahead at the far end of the lane rises the knoll on which

Hamsey Church stands, its stubby square tower watching over the river valley as it has done for almost a thousand years.

Would I know him if I saw him? *Him*, the one who is not too nasty, not too nice, in whose presence all my doubts will vanish. But what if it doesn't work that way? What if the key to contentment with a partner lies not in the character of the partner at all, but in the making of an act of will? Maybe anyone would do. Maybe I'm the problem, expecting the decision to be made for me by some outside force. By love.

Is it so wrong to want to fall in love?

She sees her destination before her, just as predicted by the site plan attached to the planning application. Wayland Farm is a collection of three buildings set round a yard screened by poplars. The main house retains its original sixteenth-century hall-house layout, with an extension at the back added in the early nineteenth century. Before it, enclosing a yard that would once have been hammered chalk and is now pea shingle, a timber barn faces a brick cart lodge. The ensemble of buildings is modest, vernacular, in its way perfect.

She pulls up in the yard and takes out her file, to refresh her memory of the application. Wayland Farm is Grade II listed. The application is for a conversion, the cart lodge is to have its open bays walled in, and to have windows cut in its existing rear and side elevations, to create a workroom.

Even before she's got out of the car Maggie knows this is out of the question. The cart lodge is an oak-framed building that has retained the beam-and-brace structure, with its front posts raised on brick bases. The three open bays beneath the tiled roof have sunk and twisted over the years, but they retain a simple harmony, a delight in right proportion, that in its own domestic fashion honours the landscape as faithfully as the nearby Norman church. The cart lodge is a jewel.

She sighs to herself as she gets out of the car. This will not
be easy.

Her knock at the door produces no response. She checks her
watch: she's on time, even a little late. She knocks again. Then
she peers through the windows. There seems to be no one in.
She takes out her phone and rings the owner's number. No
answer.

She turns away, frowning. Having come this far, she might
as well make her inspection. So she unfolds the plans for the
proposed conversion and goes over to the cart lodge. She's still
standing in the yard when a voice speaks from behind her.

'Can I help?'

She swings round, and sees a tall man of forty or so, wearing
jeans and a light cotton jacket, with shaggy blondish hair and
boyish features. But the way he's looking at her is not boyish
at all. There's a sweet sadness in his face, and though his eyes
are on her, he's not taking her in. His concerns are elsewhere.

'I'm Maggie Dutton,' she says, putting out a hand.
'Conservation Officer with the Planning Department. We had
an appointment for ten this morning?'

'Did we? I had no idea.'

He looks round, clearly not sure what he's supposed to do.

'Are you Mr Strachan?'

'Yes, I suppose I am. I wish I'd known you were coming.'

'It's not a problem. All I have to do is make a site visit, so I
can write up my report. I'm almost done, actually.'

'Right. Is there anything I can do for you? I don't really know
how this sort of thing goes.'

Maggie watches him in his confusion, and she experiences a
matching confusion of her own. To her dismay, the moment
she saw him she felt a click of recognition, despite the fact that
he is a total stranger to her.

This is the kind of man I could love.

Of course it's utterly ridiculous. How can you know such a thing at a glance? And yet people do, or they say they do. Some sort of instinctual knowledge that operates at a level far deeper than the rational. And though she struggles against it, or tells herself she must struggle against it, she's doing everything in her power to attract him. She's doing that tipping-her-head-down thing, where you look up at him. She's stroking her arm with her free hand. She's making her voice soft. All this without a single conscious decision on her part.

'I just have to take some photographs,' she says. 'Then I'll be done.'

'Right,' he says.

He watches her as she moves about with her camera. She's acutely sensitive to his gaze, and takes care to stand in a becoming way; which means with the weight on one leg, so that her generally admired bum appears to advantage.

'So will it all be okay?' he says.

Maggie hesitates. Usually she takes care to give no opinion on a first site visit, but she feels a strong desire to get into a longer conversation.

'I think there may be some problems,' she says, still taking pictures. 'This is a fine example of an early nineteenth-century oak-frame lodge.'

'Yes, I suppose it is.'

'Don't you think it would be a shame to brick it up?'

He stands gazing at the cart lodge, frowning.

'It would in a way,' he says. 'But then where would I do my work?'

'What work do you do, Mr Strachan? If you don't mind me asking.'

'I'm a writer.'

Maggie's heart gives a jump. A writer! No wonder he looks so interesting.

'Isn't there somewhere in the house where you can do your writing?'

'Oh, yes. I can write pretty much anywhere, really.'

She puts away her camera and turns to him, fixing him with the full force of her charming eyes.

'The truth is I'm really not sure I can recommend approval of these proposals. I hate to be the bearer of bad news. But this is a listed building. I'm not saying there might not be some other, more sensitive way of doing it.'

So much for the words she speaks. Her eyes, her face, her body, are all saying something else. They're saying, I find you very attractive. Why don't you ask me in to your house?

'Why don't you come in?' he says. 'I'll make you a cup of tea or something.'

'Thank you. I'd like that.'

She follows him into the house. Inside, various random efforts have been made to disfigure the rooms: curtains with pelmets, an over-painted fireplace, off-the-peg panelled doors in place of the original ledge-and-brace. But the dignity of the house still shows.

'This is how it was when we bought it,' he says as he takes her through to the kitchen. 'The previous owners didn't really have a clue. There's a nice house underneath all this.'

'I can see.'

He shambles round the kitchen, makes them both a mug of instant coffee, glancing back at her from time to time. She's happy to see that he's very aware of her gaze. Also that he seems unbothered by her negative response to his planning proposal.

'We're bound by quite strict guidelines,' she says. 'English Heritage will have to give their opinion too. To be honest with you, I don't think there's much chance they'll go for it.'

'Oh, well,' says Alan Strachan. 'I suppose at least that saves us some money.'

He gives her a steaming mug.

'So what do you write?' she says.

'Plays. Films. Or I try to.'

'Would I have heard of anything?'

'I had a play on a few years ago, called *Sweetheart*. It was about an underage prostitute and her client. God, that sounds so sleazy.'

'No,' says Maggie, amazed. 'I saw it. I remember it. It was really good. You wrote that? Wow!'

'Not much wow since, I'm afraid.'

'You can't be doing too badly.'

She means the house they're sitting in, which must have cost close to a million.

'Oh, that's film money. That's not real writing.'

He's sitting down facing her now, his chin in his hands, smiling at her. His face turns out to be quite lined. This is a real grown-up.

'How old are you?'

Oh God, did I say that out loud? That's so embarrassing.

'About to be forty,' he says, not seeming to mind. 'Coming into my prime. If only.'

'That's nothing,' says Maggie. 'I'm thirty, and I feel as if my life's practically over.'

She can't believe the way she's talking. Here she is, a professional, on a visit to a married man, and she's giving him teaser lines as if this is a chat-up in a club.

'Actually,' he says, 'there's a film of mine being shot not far from here, over by the Seven Sisters. Only it turns out that without telling me they've brought in a new writer to change everything I've written.'

Maggie opens her eyes very wide.

'Are they allowed to do that?'

'They can do what the hell they want.'

He's hurt, and he's letting her see it. She wants to put her arms round him and make the hurt go away.

A car pulls up outside. He goes on looking at her, feeling her sympathy. Then the door opens and someone comes in.

'Jesus Christ! I have had it with my bloody mother!'

A woman with a hard, handsome face and unkempt hair throws her bag down on the kitchen table. Maggie stands up, puts out her hand.

'Maggie Dutton. Conservation Officer.'

'Oh, shit! Is it today? Hell and damnation.'

She looks almost frantic, moving about, eyes jumping. She goes to a calendar pinned above the fridge.

'Yes, you're right. Ten a.m. How did I miss that?'

But her mind is elsewhere.

'I stopped off to see Mum after I dropped Cas off. She won't have Bridget back. It's driving me insane.' To Maggie, 'Sorry. Batty old mother problems.'

'That's okay,' says Maggie. 'I've got all I need now. I should be getting on.'

The sight of Alan's wife has shocked her back into reality. This man is *married*. He is *not available*. What have I been thinking of?

'She'll come round,' he's saying, his voice soothing his wife. 'Give it time.'

'Alan, she can't look after herself.'

Then seeing Maggie is on the way out, she turns her attention on her, as if taking her in properly for the first time.

'So what happens next? How long will it take?'

'I'm afraid you may have to reconsider,' says Maggie. 'I don't think I'm going to be able to recommend the plans as they stand.'

This is met by a shocked silence.

'It would alter the character of the building.'

'Of course it would alter the character of the building. We're not putting hay wagons in it any more. We're turning it into a work space.'

'I do understand.' Maggie is on familiar ground here, though it's never comfortable. 'But in the case of listed buildings we try our best to preserve the original character and appearance.'

'So what are we supposed to do with it?'

The wife is getting angry now; or finding an outlet for anger that was already there.

'I don't see that it's such a big deal,' says Alan.

She rounds on him in fury.

'Not such a big deal? It's taken us four months to get this far! How much longer do we have to wait?' Then to Maggie, 'This is our property. Don't we have a right to live in it as we please?'

'Within the regulations governing listed buildings,' says Maggie, falling back on her stock of official answers.

'So what are we supposed to do? Milk cows there? This is all nonsense! This isn't a farm any more. We're not farmers. Why do we have to pretend nothing's changed? Who are these rules for? Is it so the walkers can come down the lane and say, Oh look, isn't that pretty? This isn't a museum, for God's sake!'

'I'm sorry,' says Maggie. 'You always have the right to appeal. Now I really must go.'

She beats a hasty retreat, as she has done so often before. Back in her car, heading up the narrow lane, she forgets the anger of the wife and remembers the wry smile on the face of the husband. She caught his eye a couple of times, and she's sure she saw complicity there. And what if she did? What happens next? Nothing. He's not about to leave his wife.

Not as far as I know.

The encounter leaves her in total disarray. She's ashamed of herself, conscious of having behaved badly, but no real harm has been done. No words were spoken that make her blush in retrospect. It was all a matter of looks. And yet she's quite certain that he understood her and she understood him. How extraordinary it is, this discovery of mutual attraction. Two total strangers know within seconds that they have recognised something in each other; like travellers in faraway lands who can tell a fellow countryman by the way he turns his head, by the shape of his smile.

I could be wrong, of course. The less you know about someone, the more they fill up the waiting space in your dreams. Maybe this flash of excitement is just the effect of novelty, and what's new becomes old quite quickly. Maybe that's how other people do it. They make their commitments fast, before the novelty wears off.

It was all so different with Andrew. We were friends before we were lovers. Hard to pinpoint, looking back, the exact moment at which we became a couple. People think the first time you sleep together is the watershed moment, but you can have sex and not become a couple, we've all done it. Some other process is at work that pulls you together, some recognition that you fill the gaps in each other's lives. You start seeing more of each other, you come to depend on the other person being there, and little by little your lives become intertwined. No moment of decision, and yet a decision of sorts is reached. From that point on your route is set, and it takes an act of will to diverge from it. Or an outside force.

24

Liz has just driven ten miles to take Cas to a friend's house in Folkington, which turned out to have electric gates and servants' quarters, for God's sake, and handed Cas over to a nanny who clearly thought she too was a nanny, and then all the way back to her mother's house, who she hoped had got some sense into her overnight but instead turned out to be expecting an apology from her, which not being forthcoming led to another nasty row, and she comes home to find this! Some dolly from the council simpering at Alan and telling him he can't have his office and Alan lies there like a dog with his paws in the air having his tummy tickled.

'Why didn't you tell her to piss off? Who does she think she is? I should bloody well think we will appeal! What is this British obsession with the past? No wonder we're no good at making things any more. We're so busy pretending it's still Rule, Britannia! and the empire on which the sun never sets.'

'I suppose there has to be some kind of limit,' says Alan, attempting to be reasonable at a time when reason is not called for.

'You were a big lot of use,' says Liz. 'You let her walk all over you.'

'What was I supposed to do?'

'Stand up for yourself. Argue back. Who the hell is she anyway? Why is her opinion more important than ours?'

'Well, that's her job. To protect old buildings.'

'Whose side are you on here, Alan?'

'It's not about sides. There are regulations, that's all.'

'You know she was flirting with you?'

'Oh, come on.'

'You really don't know? Jesus, Alan! Wake up!'

'Why on earth would she flirt with me?'

'I don't know. People do. She was quite pretty. Or didn't you notice?'

'To be honest I've got other things on my mind.'

'Well, you can kiss goodbye to your office. Little Miss Flirty's going to put a stop to that.'

'I can live with that.'

'Oh, sure. But what about me? I have to go on working in a cupboard.'

'Then you take the parlour. I'll have the cupboard.'

'Jesus!'

It comes out as a shout of frustration. At Alan. At life.

'I honestly don't know what else to say, Liz.'

'Anything! Say anything! Why do you have to accept everything? Why don't you ever fight for what you want? Why does it always have to be me? I'm tired of fighting.'

'Then maybe you should stop.'

'And join you in the victims' club?'

'I'm not a victim,' he says. 'Don't say that.'

She's beginning to get him angry too, and realises this is what she wants.

'Have you called your producer?'

'No. Not yet.'

'Why not? You're just going to take it, aren't you? They fuck you around, they bring in another writer without even telling you, and you just sit there and take it.'

'I have no choice!' Now he's shouting. 'Life isn't a newspaper column, Liz. You can't make all the bad stuff go away by complaining to the *Daily Telegraph*. Get some dignity, for Christ's sake!'

'Dignity? What's that? Letting everyone roll over you?'

'It's not having tantrums when you don't get your own way, like a spoilt four-year-old.'

'You think this is a tantrum? This is not a fucking tantrum! This is fury! This is the real thing, believe me. I am sick and tired of all this self-destructive misery. I'm drowning in it. There's my bloody mother poisoning herself with hatred for anyone who tries to help her. There's you letting yourself get shat on because you're so bloody sodden with self-pity. There's this house which we bought to be a place where we could both work and neither of us can do a fucking thing. Jesus, why do I bother?'

She goes out of the room and stamps upstairs. Alan stays in the kitchen, looking out of the window at the sunshine on the yard wall. Then he follows her.

She's lying on their bed, crying. Just low snuffly crying, nothing too violent. He sits on the edge of the bed beside her and speaks in a steady reasonable voice.

'I spoke to Robert at the agency about this new writer. He says there's nothing I can do. I've asked Jane to send me the new draft. If I really hate what they've done I can take my name off it. That's as far as I can go.'

Liz snuffles a bit more and dabs at her eyes but says nothing.

'You're right about the self-pity. I do feel sorry for myself right now. But it'll pass.'

So everything's all right, his voice says. No need to cry about it.

'About your mother. She won't have a carer because she can't bear to think she's old. So leave her alone. Let her get there in her own time. That's not a cruel or neglectful thing to do. It's respecting her. Let her be the one to say to you, I need help. Then she'll accept it.'

'She'll fall over. She'll break something.'

'Yes, she may. But let it happen. You can't save her from the consequences of being old.'

'I could if I had her to live with us.'

'It wouldn't work.'

'It might.'

She wants him to tell her no, he'll leave her if she brings her mother to live with them. She wants him to say it would make their life a nightmare. Anything to take away some of the responsibility that's squeezing the life out of her.

'It would drive you insane, Liz. You know it would.'

'I can't just leave her to rot.'

'It's her life.'

There's a simple brutality to his view which shocks Liz. He sees the issue as practical, almost mechanical, leaving out the surrounding swamp of duty, love, guilt, anger, memory.

She dries her eyes and sits up. He stands.

She says, not looking at him, 'What are we going to do about this planning permission?'

'Wait and see. We don't know anything official yet.'

'Do nothing, you mean.'

He doesn't respond to that. Following her up here to their bedroom, finding her crying on the bed, that was meant to be the prelude to a reconciliation. Only it isn't happening.

'Had she been here long?'

'No. Not long at all.'

'She looked very cosy in the kitchen, with her mug of coffee.'

'It seemed the polite thing to do.'

'Polite.' Liz gets up, straightens the bedcover. 'Yes. You did look polite.'

'This is stupid, Liz.'

'What's stupid?' Then, changing tack, 'Yes, I am stupid.'

'There's no need to make problems where none exist.'

'No. It's stupid.'

She walks past him and down the stairs.

What else can she do? If he doesn't understand what it is that upsets her she can't make him understand. Not without humiliating herself. And anyway, he's right. This is all stupid. All he needs to say to her is, What do I want with some other woman when I've got you? He doesn't say it because he thinks it doesn't need saying, but it does, it does.

She's younger than me, and prettier, and she was coming on to you, Alan, really she was, I'm not making it up. Why wouldn't I be just a little bit threatened? People are stupid sometimes. And they hurt each other, and are too proud to say sorry, and then everything goes silent and unhappy.

Jesus, I'm so tired of people being unhappy.

25

After lunch the sun comes out once more and floods the garden with its brittle light. Carrie has never been a sun-baby. She feels more at home in autumn, in the long shadows of evening. Now she sits on the terrace watching Toby, who stands on the lawn by her father's side, in their turn watching Terry run his dog through the orchard.

Terry himself is mostly invisible. They hear his sharp cries to his dog. 'Yip, yip! Over here, Nipper! Back up! Back up!' The small dog bursts out from between trees, racing up and down the orchard, nose eagerly to the ground, and vanishes again into the long grass.

Carrie can hear her father talking to Toby about rabbits.

'It's the weed syndrome,' he says. 'Call a plant a weed and you give yourself permission to uproot it and burn it. Do that to a rose bush and you're a murderer. Same with rabbits. Over the hedge there, in the meadow, it's all Flopsy and Mopsy and we love them. But that same rabbit, as soon as he enters my garden, he becomes my enemy and I will destroy him.'

'Have you ever actually killed one?' says Toby.

'Just the once. Shot it with an air rifle.'

'Did that give you a good feeling?'

'Fantastic!'

Carrie expects Toby to challenge this grotesque response, but

The Golden Hour

he just nods and smiles. Clearly her father was expecting a bit more kickback too. Maybe he wants it.

'I'd have thought you'd be rather against killing things,' he says.

'Why's that?'

'Well, you don't strike me as the aggressive type.'

'I don't know if I'm aggressive or not. But if you kill other creatures, it's like you're saying what you want is more important than what they want. And I do think that. I think what I want is more important than anything else in the world.'

'I suspect everyone secretly thinks that,' says her father. 'And I sure as hell think that what I want is more important than what some rabbit wants.'

'The rabbit thinks the same way,' says Toby. 'Only the other way round.'

'You think there's no difference between the rabbit and me?'

'Oh, yes, there's a difference,' says Toby. 'You're the one with the gun.'

Her father laughs at that. Terry's dog reappears, moving more slowly now, no longer nosing the grass.

Carrie resents her father for standing on the lawn talking and laughing with Toby. She resents Toby for paying her no attention. This stupid talk of killing rabbits embarrasses her. Who do they think they are? Big game hunters? It's beginning to look as if Toby's avoiding being alone with her, and this makes her feel entirely crazy inside. She asked him to go with her for driving practice and he said he would but now he won't say when. Maybe she's imagining it but it's like he doesn't look her in the eyes properly any more.

Terry now appears from the trees and his dog runs to his side.

'All clear,' he says. 'I'll lay my life there's no rabbits in the garden right now.'

'And they can't climb the fence any more?'

'No way. Squirrels, yes. Your squirrel can hang upside down. But not your rabbit.'

Carrie expects Toby to join her now the rabbit hunt is over, but he stays with the two men, discussing the habits of rodents as if he's been an estate owner all his life. When he starts asking about the dog, and if it can outrun a rabbit, she can stand it no more. She gets up from her chair, pushes it back over the brick paving so that it makes a scraping sound. Toby does not look round. She goes into the kitchen. Her mother is making a loud noise mixing ingredients in the Magimix. When the noise stops she says to Carrie, 'You haven't told me if you're in or not on Saturday evening, so I'm assuming you're not.'

'Okay,' says Carrie.

'That means you'll have to go out to a pub or something. I can't have you cluttering up the kitchen making yourself a private meal.'

'We may go out. We may not.'

'No, Carrie. I'm sorry. You're going out. You won't decide, so I've decided for you.'

'For Christ's sake, Mum. Stop trying to freeze the future.'

This is one of Toby's lines, as they both know. Carrie's frustration is with Toby, not her mother. She has no idea whether he'll still be staying with them by Saturday. If he is, she thinks it very unlikely he'll want to join the planned dinner party.

'I'm just telling you now,' says her mother.

'Fine. Whatever.'

It's all gone wrong. The sparky exciting unpredictable tone that Toby brought to the house has soured. Carrie knows she spends all her time watching him, her eyes reproaching him for his lack of attention to her. She knows this is exactly the wrong strategy. But she can't help herself.

Now she's made her mother angry. She doesn't look over towards her, but she can hear the cross clattery sounds as she gets on with her tasks. Carrie stays hovering in the kitchen, her eyes on the terrace, because she wants to be there when Toby finally tears himself away from countryside pursuits and comes in.

She hears the background hum of the dishwasher cut out, and the clunk as her mother pulls open the dishwasher door. A small cloud of steam rises into the kitchen air.

'I don't suppose you want to unload the dishwasher, Carrie.'

'Not right now,' says Carrie. 'I'll do it later.'

'Now's when I need it done.'

'I can't do it now,' says Carrie, separating the words as if her mother is being stupid.

Then comes the clinking of plates as her mother starts emptying the dishwasher herself.

What am I supposed to do? thinks Carrie. He could come in at any moment. I have to have driving practice. He may be in a good mood. This could be the time with him that changes everything.

She hears the rattle of cutlery. Then she hears her mother give a sharp cry of pain.

'Damn!' she says. 'Damn! I knew I'd do that one day!'

'What?'

Carrie turns to her in alarm. Her mother goes to the sink and runs the cold tap.

'Get me an Elastoplast, darling.'

Blood is running down the plughole.

'Christ, Mum! What happened?'

'It's okay. I just stabbed a finger, that's all.'

Carrie hurries to the medicine cupboard and gets out the box of Elastoplasts. Her mother is holding her hand under the tap, running cold water over the cut. Blood mingles with the water.

'Unpeel the tabs,' she says, tearing off a sheet of kitchen paper.

'How did you do it?'

'Reaching down to empty the cutlery. I didn't see the blade of the kitchen knife sticking up.'

The cut is on one of her finger tips. It's deep and clean. She takes the finger from the stream of cold water and squeezes it tight with kitchen paper to dry it.

'Okay, Carrie. Get the plaster on.'

The wound starts to bleed again even as Carrie pulls the Elastoplast tight round the finger.

'Don't worry about the blood,' her mother says. 'It'll stop now.'

'Poor Mum. Are you okay?'

'It doesn't hurt. I'm just cross with myself. Such a stupid thing to do.' She indicates her ring, hanging on the hook where she puts it whenever her cooking involves getting her hands messy. 'Now I won't be able to get my ring back on until it heals.'

Carrie sees what she had not noticed before, that the cut is to her mum's ring finger. She feels a pang of guilt.

'I should have helped you.'

Her father comes in from the garden, followed by Terry and Toby.

'The global economy may be on the brink of disaster,' he announces. 'My productive life may be over. But the garden is rabbit-free! They shall not pass!'

He reaches for his work bag, which is lying in the window seat where he dropped it yesterday evening, and hunts out his chequebook.

'Mum's cut herself,' says Carrie.

'Oh dear,' he says, not at all concerned. 'So what's the damage, Terry?'

'Call it a round £250,' says Terry. 'That'll cover materials as well.'

Henry writes the cheque. Carrie glances towards Toby, who seems to be interested in the contents of the Magimix.

'It's for Saturday dinner,' says Laura.

'What will I be missing?' says Toby.

'Taramasalata,' says Laura. 'It's the starter.'

'You make it yourself?'

Toby shakes his head, awed by this fact. All Carrie takes in is that he will be gone by Saturday evening.

'There.' Henry tears out the cheque and gives it to Terry.

'Cheers,' says Terry. 'And if the little buggers start climbing the gate, you know where I am.'

'Climbing the gate? Might they do that? Can't we stop them?'

'We could nail a couple of batons, raise the wire another couple of foot. If you think it's worth it.'

'Listen, Terry. This is serious. I don't want to leave one single crack in the defences.'

'It's your money.'

'When can you do it?'

'I'm on a job at Blackboys all tomorrow. I could come over Friday.'

Terry goes at last. Carrie watches Toby to see if he'll turn towards her now, give her some attention.

'I told Terry about the garden party tomorrow,' says her father, 'and guess what? He wants us to tell the Queen she's doing a great job. It's people like Terry who keep the monarchy in business.'

'Bread and circuses,' says Toby.

Carrie feels a mounting irritation, which comes out against her father.

'Why did you tell Terry about the garden party?' she says.

'I just knew he'd be thrilled.'

'You're not thrilled. I don't even know why you're going.'

'Curiosity. And after all, why not?'

He throws Toby a smile, and Carrie gets what it is that's annoying her. Her father is showing off to Toby. That is so depressing.

'Mum cut her finger quite deeply,' she says.

'Bad luck, Laura. Are you okay?'

'Yes,' says Laura. 'Nothing serious.'

'Nothing serious,' says Carrie. Suddenly she can't stand it all any more. 'Nothing serious. Nothing's ever serious.'

She goes quickly out of the kitchen and up the stairs to her room. She feels the impulse to cry and doesn't want anyone to see, least of all Toby.

In her room, the door closed, she sits cross-legged on her bed and takes up her guitar. She plucks at the strings, forming little chains of sound, not listening, going nowhere. Her thoughts are all churned up, she feels angry with everyone, most of all herself.

Dad going on about *people like Terry* because he's such a snob but can't bear to admit it. Mum wounding herself just to make Carrie feel useless and guilty for not helping. Toby acting like he cares about rabbits when all he's doing is holding up a great big sign saying: I DON'T CARE ABOUT YOU.

So what did I do wrong?

He held my hand like he wanted more. Then it was like he moved away again. Back into that private space he carries round with him, that keeps him apart from everyone else. I suppose I got a bit too close. Now I'm being trained, like he's training his mum. I have to be shown my life doesn't revolve round him.

So is that it? Do people who are different from other people and find each other and feel good together have to be different to each other too? Is everyone always alone in the end?

I don't want to be one of anything. That's what he says. That's why he likes tools. A hammer does a hammer's job and that's it. A hammer doesn't follow you round the room with wounded eyes. You can put a hammer away in the shed and forget about it until you need it again. Toby likes forgetting about things.

So fuck him.

The brief explosion of energy takes her by surprise. It's accompanied by a bristling chord on the guitar. Through the vibrating air she hears footsteps on the landing. She sees her door handle turn. No knock, no request.

He comes in.

She looks at him in silent amazement. He gives her a smile, shuts the door behind him.

'Okay if I come in?'

'Looks like you just did.'

He sits beside her on the bed, uninvited.

'So here's where I am,' he says. 'I'm not really a good person. If I've hurt you or made you angry, you just say so.'

'I don't see why I should bother.'

'Yes, you do.'

Now that he's here and he's giving her his full attention everything that has been distressing her fades away.

'People don't have to say everything,' she says.

'Okay.' He taps her guitar with one forefinger. 'You could always sing me one of your songs.'

'No way!'

'Why not?'

'Because you won't like it.'

'Why wouldn't I like your songs? Are they all posing and lies?'

'No, not at all.'

'Then I'll like them.'

It seems so simple when he puts it like that. When he looks at her so directly. More than that: it comes over like a command she can't refuse. Does not choose to refuse. So she arranges her fingers on the strings and starts to strum her very limited sequence of chords. She sings him 'It's Over Now'. She sings with a soft voice, and keeps her eyes down on the guitar, never once looking up to see how he's taking it.

> 'I know it hurts
> But it's over now
> I know you lost
> But it's over now . . .'

She's amazed at herself. She has never sung her songs to anyone, let alone someone she wants so much to approve of her. She does it because he asks her. His is by far the stronger will.

So no longer shy, no longer attempting to protect herself from whatever criticism will come, she sings her song to the end. When it's finished she lets her hand rest on the strings, deadening the last reverberations. She does not look up.

For a long moment he says nothing. Then he reaches out and puts his hand on the guitar.

'That was beautiful,' he says.

She can tell it from his voice, he means what he says. She has pleased him. A sweet blush of relief steals over her.

'It's a great song, Carrie,' he says. 'And you sing it wonderfully.'

'Thank you,' she says.

She looks up now and finds his eyes on her. She wants him to say more, to tell her more about her song, because this is the first time her song has ever existed outside herself. Any of her songs. This is the very beginning. But it must come from him, unasked, or it will be tainted by her need. Enough to see his smile of surprise, and the look in his eyes that searches her face as if to say, Where did that come from?

His hand on her hand.

'You're the first,' she says.

'Then I'm proud,' he says. 'I'm honoured.'

'Wouldn't you rather be out chasing rabbits?'

'The rabbits have all gone away,' he says. 'I have to find something else to play with.'

'And I'll do for now.'

She seems to have fallen into some deep still place where all she can say is what she really feels.

'I told you I'm not a good person,' he says.

'I heard.'

'You don't mind?'

'I'll mind later.'

'That's all right, then,' he says, 'because there isn't any later.'

He lifts his hand from her hand, and takes the guitar from her lap and puts it down on the floor. She doesn't move. She wonders if he's going to kiss her now, waiting to see what will happen. He's the one with the will.

He lies down beside her on the bed.

'Lie down,' he says.

She lies down. He takes her in his arms.

'That was a great song,' he says.

'Was it?' she says.

'But you're wrong. It's not over. It's never over.'

'Isn't it?'

'Now,' he says. 'Now. Now. Now. Now. Now.'

'Okay,' she says.

'Put that in a song. How now never ends.'

'Maybe I will.'

Now she's lying on her bed with Toby in her arms and it's never going to end.

26

Andrew is on his own in the flat and outside the long day is ending at last. So long as he's focused on the screen before him there are problems to be solved and he knows what it is he's supposed to be doing. But by the end of the day he's had enough, he's restless, his mouse-hand aches and his arms feel empty. He wants to be swimming in the ocean, beating through great strong waves. He wants to be high up on a mountainside, feeling the blast of wind on his cheeks, stopping for breath and turning to look back and seeing for miles. He wants to strive and to overcome.

Jesus, I need a break. When did I last take a holiday?

He remembers it then, with perfect clarity, the trip he made with Maggie to Bruges. Only two nights away, in March, but they were lucky with the weather. Maggie was so happy walking the streets of the old city. 'Look!' she would say, pointing out a gabled roofline or a mullioned window. 'Isn't that glorious?' They found their way into a curious tree-lined square called the Beguinage, lined with terraces of white-fronted steep-roofed houses and occupied by an order of nuns. The nuns were emerging from the church as they arrived, filing down the path between the trees. Andrew read the descriptive panel about the Beguinage aloud. It was founded in the thirteenth century as somewhere for women to live together after they'd lost their men, to war or disease. Maggie was fascinated by this notion. 'Somewhere to live, your own space, friends when you want them.'

Also in Bruges they met the ideal waffle. It became one of those little shared references that are so precious in the life of a couple, that can be named without being explained. The ideal waffle was crisp on the outside, soft within, and light as air in the mouth.

Thinking about Bruges makes Andrew want to cry. He's in a bad way, though he's fighting it. Once he starts crying he'll just fall apart, so he's pushing the temptation away. Also the unanswered question that wraps round him like a cloud, that he doesn't want to see but can't escape, which is: why hasn't she called?

Nothing has happened. They've not had a row. And yet some vital thread has snapped. It must be so, or why doesn't he call her? This is what he longs to do and will not let himself do. To call her would be to exacerbate the very fault in him that causes the problem. If Maggie has stopped wanting him in her life it can only be because he's too easily pleased, too concerned to please her. It seems unfair, being punished for selflessness, but truth to tell Andrew knows it's not selflessness but weakness. He wishes he could behave differently. He longs to be the kind of man who takes command of each social situation with confident ease, knowing always what he wants, allowing the woman in his life to accompany him or not as she chooses. But this is not who he is.

I'm one of life's pleasers. And that's just not sexy.

This is why Andrew, half crying in his unhappiness, forces himself not to phone Maggie. He adores Maggie and would do anything in the world to make her happy. So right now, because he is not a fool, because he does have some self-knowledge, because he adores her, he does not call her.

But all through the long evening spent not calling Maggie life must somehow go on. He tries watching TV, punching channels at random. *Dragons' Den* depresses him with its pathos and its nastiness. A documentary about two gay millionaires longing for babies proves a little too close to home. Though neither gay nor a millionaire, Andrew would love to be a father. He has never dared say this to Maggie, but he does so much want to have babies with her. He'd like a little girl who looks just like Maggie, who he could love without any fear that his love was too much. You're allowed to love your children totally and for ever. It's only with grown-ups that it all gets so complicated.

His phone rings. For one heart-stopping moment he thinks it's Maggie, but it turns out to be her friend Jo. Andrew likes Jo, but better still, she's a channel to Maggie.

'Jo!' he says, determined to sound strong and upbeat. 'What's doing?'

Jo is in some church hall in Fulham where she's been rehearsing all day.

'So guess who I had lunch with yesterday?' says Jo. 'I hear you're going to be a neighbour.'

'That's the plan,' says Andrew. At once he starts saying too much, to hide his fragile condition. 'Feels like a good moment to make the break from the city. The lease on this place coming up for renewal, that sort of stuff. A little inheritance coming through. Opens up the odd door.'

He realises as he's speaking that any moment now he's going to start crying and there's nothing he can do to stop it. He has no idea why this is, maybe it's the sympathetic tone in Jo's voice, or maybe it's hearing his own voice list the reasons that make this the perfect time to take the next step with Maggie. The step on which both of them have come to a standstill.

'So anyway,' he hastens on, trying to outrun himself, 'tell me the news in Jo-land.'

Then out of nowhere he starts to sob. He pushes the phone away, he tries to muffle the sounds, but it's no good. He feels the tears streaming down his cheeks. He dabs at his face with his sleeve. He hears tiny squeaks from his phone. He takes deep breaths to regain control. And so, slowly, the wrenching motion passes.

'Sorry about that,' he says.

'Andrew, Andrew, Andrew.' Jo's voice is so kind it's almost more than he can bear. 'You in your flat right now?'

'Yes,' he says.

'You got anything to eat?'

'I don't know,' he says. 'I haven't thought much about eating.'

'You stay right there,' she says. 'I'm coming round. Give me half an hour.'

After that Andrew starts to feel much better. The crying has released something that needed to be released, and knowing Jo is coming round gives the evening a new shape and colour. Shameful to admit, but he's not so good on his own. And with Jo he'll be able to talk about Maggie.

Better still, when the doorbell rings barely twenty minutes later, she's carrying two immense slices of pizza and a bottle of red wine.

'I decided to grab a cab,' she says. 'This is a mercy dash.'

'Oh, Jo. You're my guardian angel.'

She's so bright and cheerful, she fills the flat with warmth and activity, finding plates and knives and forks and glasses, laying out the pizza and pouring the wine.

'This is not good, Andrew,' she tells him, pressing a full glass into his hand. 'You've been neglecting yourself.'

'Oh, Jo. I'm so confused over Maggie. Everything just seems

to have fallen down a hole and I don't know what to do.'

'Drink wine. Eat pizza. Aunty Jo's remedy for confused lovers.'

He eats and he drinks and she's right. He starts to feel much better.

'Tell me what she said to you, Jo. She must have talked about me.'

'Yes, of course,' says Jo. 'We had a good long chat. It's all about this moving down to Lewes business. It's come a bit too quickly for her, I think.'

'Oh, God. I should never have done it.'

'It's not that she doesn't want it. But it's like the future is rushing at her too fast, and it gets her a bit panicky. Does that make sense?'

'Yes, of course it does,' says Andrew. 'I'm such a fool. It just seemed to be a great idea when the chance came up. I never stopped to think it might be too much for her.'

'Why would you?' says Jo. 'You love her.'

'I do, Jo. I want to be nearer to her. I want to be with her all the time. But if that's not what she wants . . .'

He can't say it. That way ends up in the unthinkable.

'She's not sure what she wants,' says Jo. 'She needs time.'

'Yes, I see that,' says Andrew. Then he looks up at Jo with such sad eyes. 'But I do so wish she was sure.'

'Oh, Andrew!' says Jo. 'You're so *nice!*'

'I'm too nice, aren't I? That's what's wrong with me.'

'No one can be too nice. You're lovely.'

'I'm too nice for Maggie. That's why she's not sure.'

'Then she's a stupid little fool,' says Jo.

Andrew looks at Jo across the kitchen table and he feels a surge of gratitude towards her. Her kind face is smiling at him and her full attention is on him in a way that is more than friendly. He can feel a gentle wistful longing in her, and understands that this longing is for him. This simple awareness does even more than the pizza and the wine to restore his fragile sense of self-worth.

'What do you advise me to do, Jo?'

'Well,' says Jo, 'that all depends on what you want.'

'And what Maggie wants.'

'Maggie doesn't know what she wants. She's not sure she's ready for any big moves. She needs time.'

'But what I don't understand is, what's going to change? She can take time, but how's it going to be any different when the time's up? I'll still be me, she'll still be her.'

'Ah, Andrew. You're treading on thin ice.'

'Am I?'

'I'm not here to push you into any tough decisions. I'm here to make you feel better.'

'You've done that. You're great.'

They refill their glasses with wine and move onto the only couch to get more comfortable. Andrew feels all loosened up inside. There are things he wants to hear himself say, so he can find out what he feels about them.

'Do you think maybe I'm just the wrong guy for Maggie?' he says.

'I don't see why,' says Jo. But not with much conviction.

'Remember Nigel. He wasn't at all like me.'

'No. He was a total prick.'

'But she was with him quite a long time.'

'Too long.'

'So maybe she likes pricks.'

Jo looks at him with her head on one side, like she's trying to make him out.

'But you love her.'

'Yes, I do. But it takes two. No good me loving her if she doesn't love me.'

'Jesus, Andrew. I don't know what to say.'

'Well, I suppose what I'm asking you is, what do you think?' He's discovering what it is he wants to say only as he says it. 'You know Maggie well. What I'm asking you is, do you think she'll get over this panicky feeling?'

Jo nods. Not an unexpected question, it seems. Their glasses seem to be empty again already. Andrew gets the wine and refills them.

'Do I think she'll ever love you the way you love her?'

Andrew takes a big gulp of his wine. The bluntness of her words comes as a shock. But yes, of course, this is exactly what he's asking.

'I don't know how to answer that,' she says. 'I wish I did.'

'Does that mean the answer's no, but you don't want to hurt me?'

'No,' says Jo, wrinkling her brows, trying to understand what it is she does think. 'It means I really don't know. I can't really understand Maggie's problem. I mean, if it was me I'd just open my arms and say, Come on in.'

'Oh, Jo. You're doing me the world of good.'

They clink glasses and drink some more. The alcohol is doing him the world of good too.

'To be honest with you,' says Jo, 'I can't help thinking she doesn't deserve you. I mean, where does she get off with her I-don't-know-if-he's-the-one stuff? Let's get real here. She's over thirty and you're gorgeous and solvent and actually not a prick. What's not to want?'

Andrew has taken in only part of this.

'Is that what she said? She doesn't know if I'm the one?'

'Oh, we all say that. It doesn't mean anything. I don't mean

to slag Maggie off. She's lovely, but honestly there are times
when I want to slap her.'

'She's the one for me,' says Andrew quietly.

'Oh, stop it, Andrew. I can't bear it.'

'If I'm not the one for her . . .'

He feels the tears returning. He shrugs and shakes his head,
to drive the self-pity into his body. He doesn't want to cry again.

'It takes time,' says Jo.

'How long? We've known each other for four years. We've
been going out for over a year. How much longer does it take?'

'You're asking the wrong girl, honey.'

'If she's not sure now – if she's not sure I'm the one – if she's
not sure—'

He can't hold back any more. He feels a heaving in his chest,
and the sob breaks in his throat. He leans back against the couch
and lets the tears flow.

Jo is overcome with wine and sympathy.

'Oh, sweetheart! Don't cry! No, don't cry!'

She puts her arms round him and he lets himself sink into
her soft warm embrace. She rocks him in her arms and whispers
to him like a mother comforting her child.

'You're a lovely, lovely man. Any woman would be proud to
have you. If she doesn't see it, then she's just a silly little fool.
Don't cry over her, sweetheart. If she doesn't want you, then
to hell with her. There's others that will. Any girl would want
you. You're one in a million. Let her go back to the nasty pricks
who make her miserable if that's what she wants. Why should
you let her make you miserable? Life's too bloody short and
there's enough misery to go round as it is. People should love
each other. People should want to make each other happy. There,
that's better. No more crying. There, you feel better now, don't
you?'

'Yes, Jo,' he says, holding her close. 'You're wonderful, Jo.'

'Well, I'm the same as you, aren't I?' she says. 'We all want to be loved.'

She gives him a little loving kiss on the cheek and he gives her a little kiss. Then suddenly they're kissing for real, mouth to mouth, with great intensity. He feels her body press into his, and knows that she wants him, she's hungry for him, and being wanted awakens the desire in him. They slide down on the couch until they're lying body to body, holding each other tight.

Then she's pushing herself away from him.

'This is not a good idea,' she says. 'This isn't what's meant to happen.'

But Andrew is feeling the exact opposite, he's feeling the resurgence of the simplest desire of all. This is sexual power in action, making whole what has been broken. Jo is in his arms and she wants him. People should want to make each other happy. He takes off his glasses.

'Don't think about it,' he says. 'We're drunk.'

'Drunk and incapable,' says Jo, sinking back into his arms.

THURSDAY

27

Thursday turns out to be overcast, with the threat of rain.

'Wouldn't you know it?' says Henry, dressing for the garden party in a light summer suit. He's also wearing a tie, which he very rarely does. 'My neck's got fatter.' He tries irritably to button the top button of his shirt. 'When did that happen?'

Laura tests her flower hair-clip in front of the mirror, both for position and for security. She gives her head a vigorous shake. The flower stays on. Then she smoothes the skirt of her dress, which is navy blue with white polka dots, tight-waisted, long-sleeved.

'Do you think the Queen will mind me wearing a vintage dress?' she says.

'Why would she? And anyway, who cares what she thinks?'

'That was supposed to be your cue to say how lovely I look.'

'Well, you do.'

Most of the women at the garden party will be wearing high heels. Laura can't face three or four hours standing in high heels.

'I'm going to wear flatties. After all, it is on grass.'

'We owe them nothing,' says Henry. 'A dysfunctional family from Germany with the style and culture of footballers' wives.'

Henry has been in a contrary mood for days now, ever since coming home from his meeting on Tuesday. Laura feels sorry for him and irritated by him at the same time. She ponders which earrings to wear, then remembers her ring, which is waiting for her finger to heal.

'I hate not wearing my ring,' she says.

For now the ring rests in the pretty Moroccan box on her dressing table where she keeps redundant items of jewellery, broken necklaces, single earrings. She remembers buying the ring so well, in a little shop in the Lanes in Brighton. She remembers sending it away to have it engraved with their initials.

Henry finishes tying his tie. He looks at himself in the long mirror, frowning with dissatisfaction, then looks away.

'At least Nick Griffin should stir things up a bit.'

'You're suspiciously excited by the prospect of Nick Griffin, Henry.'

'Anything for some action. We're going to be so bored.' He looks out of the bedroom window at the clouds. 'And so wet.'

'Take an umbrella.'

'Damn right I will.'

'Oh, God!' says Laura, looking in the mirror. 'This flower just looks ridiculous.'

'Then take it off.'

'I have to wear something on my head.'

Of course it's all ridiculous, but the fact is they've decided to go, and once there she does not want to feel out of place. What she wants is to be, in her own quiet way, more stylish than the rest, while remaining respectful of the conventions of the occasion. This isn't for Henry. It isn't even for the Queen. It's for their fellow guests – their fellow female guests – who she knows will be judging her appearance as critically as she will be judging theirs. There's a fine line between distinctive style and posturing for attention.

She repositions the flower hair-clip and decides it'll do. Then she gives a last touch to her make-up and goes downstairs. Carrie is in the kitchen having a late breakfast with Toby.

'We're off, darling. Should be back by seven or so.'

'You look sensational,' says Toby. 'Is that a real Jacques Fath from the real fifties?'

'Yes, it is, actually,' says Laura, surprised. 'How on earth do you know?'

'The Queen will envy you.'

'Oh, shut up, Toby,' says Carrie.

They seem to be getting on better.

'Okay if I borrow the Smart?' Carrie says.

'Who's going to go with you, darling?'

'Toby.'

'Well, yes, I suppose so.' Laura doesn't really believe Carrie can drive yet, given she hasn't passed her test. 'You will take care.'

'No, Mum. I'll drive straight into a tree.'

Henry appears clutching a fold-up umbrella.

'Come on if you're coming.'

The rain holds off until they're on the train. By the time they reach Gatwick there are puddles on the platforms, and a thin rain is streaking the windows. By Clapham Junction the sky is blue again.

They walk from Victoria Station to the Palace, having decided to enter by the front. The map they've been sent offers a choice between the Grand Entrance and the Grosvenor Place gate into the back of the palace gardens. The garden entrance is nearer but humbler.

'Might as well experience the full horror,' says Henry.

A crowd of guests has already formed outside the railings. The guests are not hard to distinguish from the tourists. The female guests wear feathered fascinators in colours that match their dresses. The male guests wear suits, with a smattering of men in morning dress. The long tail coats give the gathering a comical air, as if a wedding has been recently cancelled and the guests left with time on their hands.

Beyond the ornate black-and-gold railings the wide palace forecourt is almost empty. Red-coated guards stand by their sentry boxes wearing their enormous bearskins even on this warm July day. The palace itself presents its familiar foursquare façade with stoic dignity, resigned to acting as backdrop to a million photographs. To Henry, who looks with the historian's eye, it speaks of the nation's past: Armistice Day 1918, and the crowds in the Mall; the King appearing on the balcony on VE Day, while the teenage princesses slipped incognito into the cheering throng; Charles and Diana on the same balcony, in colour now; the Jubilee concert, when the palace became the screen for laser-beamed brightly coloured images. Our national canvas, onto which we daub our fantasies.

And we'll be entering the palace. Going through those doors to be swallowed by our own myth. And there will be the little old lady known as the Queen. How old is she now? Eighty-something? Not a real person, of course. An outline, to be filled in as each of us desires; a cartoon, two-dimensional, absurd, but in no way threatening.

Without quite meaning to, Laura and Henry find themselves taking their place in a vaguely defined queue of other garden party guests. The couple immediately behind them are both in late middle age: she large and dressed all in red, he small, in a grey suit too big for his spare frame. The woman in red is too excited to be shy, and anyway, simply by being dressed up when all the other tourists are in shorts forms the basis for companionship.

'I wish my mum was alive to see me now,' she says. 'Did you hear? Michael Winner is coming, with his girlfriend.'

'And Nick Griffin,' says Laura.

'He's had his invitation withdrawn. Didn't you hear?'

'That's a shame,' says Henry. 'I was hoping for some good old-style British aggro.'

Joan and her husband Peter are from Bangor. Joan is the one who has been invited to the garden party, in recognition of her forty years working for Bangor's Library Service. She has researched the garden party on the Internet.

'They say the drink is terrible but the food is wonderful. You're allowed to go to the tea tent twice.'

'Have you just come down for the day?' says Laura.

'For the day! If only!' Joan laughs merrily. 'You know what this trip has cost us, all in? Seven hundred pounds! Train fares, two nights in the Travelodge at Waterloo, all you can eat at breakfast, mind! He's small and don't eat much, but I'm not and I do! Then tickets for the show, and a taxi here as a treat, he didn't cheat us, it was ten pounds. Seven hundred, it's cost us, hasn't it, Peter? All in.'

Peter is gazing at the sentries in red jackets and bearskins.

'Welsh Guards,' he says. 'My dad was one of them.'

The couple behind Joan and Peter have heard the mention of Nick Griffin being disinvited. They're from Leicester. Jaspal introduces himself. He's the President of the Leicester Association of Asian Businessmen. His wife is very beautiful, and wears a white and silver sari. Jaspal introduces her, spelling out her name, Sukhjit, which sounds like Suki. She alone has no hat or decoration in her dark hair. Instead she has a vertical line of tiny jewels on her brow.

'He used his invitation for personal political purposes,' says

Sukhjit, meaning Nick Griffin. 'That's why he's been told he can't come.'

'Quite right too!' says Joan indignantly.

'When I was a girl,' says Sukhjit, 'my dad used often to come home with cuts and bruises. My mum said, what happened? Oh, I got caught in the car door. I slipped on the pavement. But really he'd been getting into arguments with the National Front. He was a real old-time socialist.'

The gate opens and the queue starts to move.

'Here we go!' cries Joan.

Henry meets Laura's eyes and sees there the same puzzlement that he's feeling. Somehow none of this is what he expected.

There are two lines of guests, crossing the red tarmac of the palace forecourt to its entrance. Everything is very well ordered. The guests proceed at a patient shuffle.

Inside the palace a glimpse of grand rooms all in red and gold with portraits on the walls, then a room with a semicircular far wall, then through glazed doors out onto a semicircular terrace.

Beneath the dull skies stretches an immense lawn, on which many brightly coloured people are strolling. At the far end, the gleam of a lake fringed by trees. All down the left-hand side of the lawn runs a long open-fronted tea tent, before which are arranged hundreds of tables, each with four chairs. On the far right-hand side of the lawn stand two smaller tents, one of which is topped with a crown. There are two bandstands, a near one on the right of the terrace and a far one by the lake. Guardsmen in red jackets are playing the theme from *Gladiator*.

The guests flow in a steady stream through the palace and onto the lawn, past smiling young women in bubblegum-pink polo shirts with labels that say: Can I be of assistance? Laura and Henry reach the lawn, walking in a little cluster with their friends from the queue outside, and all six of them gaze at the scene with curiosity and delight.

'Oh, isn't he just something!' exclaims Joan, pointing at a tall elderly clergyman in a long frock coat and a high top hat.

There seem to be large numbers of soldiers in dress uniform, and bishops in scarlet soutanes. An African dignitary passes by, in full dress uniform complete with baldric and medals, followed by four wives wearing brightly patterned African robes. The material clings tight round their bottoms and their hems trail on the grass.

Laura notes to Henry that every woman in sight wears either a hat or a fascinator.

'See? You didn't believe me.'

She says to Sukhjit, who is wearing neither, 'You're the only one with any courage.'

'Oh, I go my own way,' says Sukhjit. 'No one tells me how to dress.'

'Guess how much my outfit cost?' says Joan. 'One hundred pounds! Cheap as chips! Hat thrown in for nothing!'

They stand looking back towards the palace. The stream of guests has never ceased. Everyone carries an umbrella, but the afternoon is warm and there are patches of blue in the sky. The palace from this side is pretty, more varied than the severe face it presents to the front. Scaffolding covers up the South Wing.

'You must bag a table, Jaspal,' Sukhjit tells her husband. 'We'll get tea.'

Though the number of guests is growing larger all the time, the great lawn doesn't feel crowded. The sound of the Guards band mingles with the buzz of voices and the far-off hum of London's traffic. The guests are mostly middle-aged or elderly, but beyond that there seems to be no common denominator. Different accents, different skin colours, different styles of dress,

but all with the same look on their faces, which is a kind of shy
excitement.

They stand in line for tea. Henry, looking around at his
fellow guests, tries to identify what it is that makes this immense
gathering so unexpectedly pleasing. Then it strikes him that this
is a party without cliques. The guests are forming small clusters,
as they themselves have done, but the single factor that unites
everyone here is that they are all in an unknown place among
unknown people. Most assemblies are dominated by an elite
core of insiders. Here all are outsiders. The soldiers flaunt their
rank, the bishops their grandeur, but it's all to no avail. Lacking
the usual retinues, every guest is reduced or elevated to the same
level. This party hosted by a queen, staged in a palace, is an
exercise in egalitarianism.

Suddenly the tea is before them. The queues are shorter than
expected, because there are so many of them: perhaps as many
as fifty tea stations, stretching away on either side. Henry is
handed a rectangular dish that serves as both plate and saucer,
and asked to choose tea or lemonade. He selects his own cakes.

'You can have as much as you want,' says Joan, who sent for
the DVD on the palace garden parties and so knows the form.
'So long as you can keep it on the plate.'

Henry chooses a raspberry tartlet, a coffee eclair, an egg
finger sandwich, a salmon-and-cream-cheese roll, a slice of
fruitcake, and a square of chocolate mousse that has the royal
crest on top. He feels like a child again.

'Oh, Henry,' says Laura. 'Honestly!'

As they eat their tea a column of Yeomen of the Guard
appear, marching with an odd lurching gait between the guests
like extras in a comic operetta. Henry is on the point of making
a joke about them when Joan says, 'They're holding ground.
That's what it's called.'

'It's all a sort of a show, isn't it?' says Henry. 'We're the audience.'

He doesn't say it with a sneer. On the contrary, he feels a kind of gratitude.

'Joan and Peter saw a show,' says Laura. 'What did you see?'

'*Jersey Boys*,' says Joan. 'We left at the interval.'

'That was sixty quid down the plughole,' says Peter.

Now men in top hats and morning suits are passing among the guests, issuing polite instructions.

'The Gentlemen at Arms,' says Joan.

They wear ties in dark blue and maroon stripes, with red carnations in their buttonholes, and they carry long rolled umbrellas.

'Wonderful!' It's all beyond parody. 'Why isn't this ridiculous?' Henry whispers to Laura.

'Of course it's ridiculous,' says Laura. 'But it's wonderful too.'

The Gentlemen at Arms are nudging the crowds to form two broad lanes across the lawns. Henry and Laura find themselves in the left-hand lane until Joan rescues them.

'That's the Duke of Edinburgh's lane. Come over here. You want to be in the Queen's lane.'

The Gentlemen at Arms loiter up and down the open lanes, chatting to the guests, twirling their rolled umbrellas, smiling. Watching them, Henry is charmed. They don't take themselves seriously at all. One of them catches his eye and winks.

The guest beside him points to the Gentlemen at Arms and says, 'See the ones in the big shoes? They're policemen.' On the facing side of the lane two lads in RAF uniform are being quizzed by one of the Gentlemen. The national anthem starts to play. The soldiers in the crowd stand to the salute. Far away, on the curving terrace, there appears a tiny figure in blue.

'That's her,' says Joan.

28

The trick to a job like this is you don't hang around. No lurking in lay-bys for dog walkers to find. There's no hiding places any more, everywhere is somebody's drive or parking place. So you act like you've got nothing to hide and no one asks any questions and you get in and get out fast.

Dean drives his old van out of Lewes down the A27 and off at the roundabout into Edenfield. Then it's first right at the shop and right again down the lane and there it is, just like Terry said, with a short gravel drive and a big chimney stack on one side.

Your heart rate's up, that's natural. Got to stay sharp. You're allowed to drive up to someone's front door, no law against that. Everything you're doing this afternoon is legal except for maybe five fast minutes, but those five minutes are where you show what you've got. Mad Mac, the joker of Camp Hill Borstal, said we should get a medal every time. All Mac ever did was sheds but he was a laugh. It takes a hero, Mac said.

Dean pulls the van up by the front door like he owns the place. According to Terry the owners are out for the day but you never know till you check. Gloves on, a giveaway on a summer's day, but who's looking? From now on no mistakes, touch nothing you're not taking with you, leave nothing behind.

Mission on.

Dean jumps briskly out of the van, strides to the front door, rings the bell. Cover story ready, on the tip of his tongue, 'Delivery for Manor House', which is not the name of the property, so if someone answers the door they give you directions, you thank them and you get the hell out. But no one answers. You ring again. Don't rush it. Big house, maybe someone in the garden at the back, shuffling towards the summons of the bell.

He rings a third time, hopping from foot to foot. Like a fucking footballer waiting for the whistle.

Okay. Let's go. Do this right, Deanie. You're doing this for Sheena. Don't fuck it up, kid. Get the motor out of sight in case the owners come back while you're inside.

He reverses the van out of the drive, down the lane, pulls up by a farm gate. Grabs his tool bag, jumps out of the van, jogs back to the house. No pissing about, straight round the side through a gate into the garden behind. Senses super alert, eyes wide, ears pricked, round onto a broad brick terrace with garden table and chairs, gas barbecue, giant furled umbrella. Nice place, big garden, worth a million and counting, people like this can afford to share a little of what they've got. We're all human beings, all got just the one mouth for eating. What makes them deserve so much when you've got so little? Just luck is all. Some get lucky, others get fucked. So what you going to do about it, Deanie boy? Nobody going to stand up for you if you don't stand up for yourself.

I'm doing this for you, Sheena.

French windows at the back like Terry said. Could be bolts top and bottom as well as the door latch. He puts down his bag. He's got a heavy chisel, a felt-wrapped mallet, a can of spray foam to mute the alarm bell, a can of spray smoke to check for infra-red beams. He's ready for the alarm to go off, but a place like this no one comes running, takes the police half an hour to show up, assuming they even bother. So you let the alarm ring, you get on with the job, and that takes a fucking freezer-load of cool, pal. Easy money this is not.

He tries the French windows and what do you know? Unlocked. Come on in, Dean. Make yourself at home. So what does that tell you? Someone's in. But no one answered the doorbell. So someone just popped out for five minutes, didn't bother to lock up and set the alarm. Someone will be back soon.

Dean feels his first real tremor of fear. Getting caught is not an option. If they put me back inside I'll top myself, I swear to God. Don't give up on me, Sheena. Just this one job and I'll buy you a ring you'll be proud to wear.

For Sheena. For our future together. To show I'm not a loser all the way. It takes a fucking hero, and the rest. Ask Brad. He's been there.

Dean enters the house. From this moment on he is without doubt breaking the law. But what is this law? It's the iron rule that says the unlucky go on losing and the winners take it all. How are you supposed to fight against that? How about some law that says it's the losers who need a hand? The guy who owns this place doesn't need a hand. He's got no worries. He's the big man, the police don't stop and search his car every time he drives by just in case he's not insured. He's so fucking insured you could burn his house down and he'd get it all back.

What you do now is float like a butterfly. That's Mad Mac again. When you go in you touch nothing, your feet don't touch the ground, you're a fairy, you're Tinkerbell. Move fast, touch nothing, make no mess.

Dean heads for the hall, listening for any sounds, hearing only the pad of his own trainers on the carpet. Up the stairs to the first-floor landing, bag unopened in his hand.

Booma-booma-booma. Just his own heart beating time. Nothing else stirring. So many doors! How many bedrooms does this house have?

Dean is looking for the master bedroom. No messing about with TVs and music systems, you can't unload that crap any more, not even in a car-boot sale. People only want new stuff these days. What you want is the easy-to-carry high-value goods, which means jewellery, which means the dressing table in the master bedroom.

Two doors later and he's in. There's a big bed and wide window looking over the garden and the river valley. A wall of wardrobes, a door to a bathroom, a dressing table.

He puts down his bag, draws a slow breath to steady himself. This is where you have to be cool. No frantic rummaging. Take your time, which is all of thirty seconds. Use your brain.

So I can't read and I'm thick as fuck but hey Brad, watch this. I guarantee you I'll go straight to the jackpot.

He stands gazing at the dressing table. A line of bottles and little pots, a box of tissues, a magnifying mirror on a stand, hairbrushes, hairdryer, a stone saucer full of random items, nail scissors, buttons, hairpins. And a pretty octagonal wooden box inlaid with mother-of-pearl.

Hello Dean, says the pretty box. Open me.

He lifts the lid. Inside it's lined with pale blue silk and divided into little compartments, and in most of the compartments there are earrings. But in one compartment there's something else. Something that says to Dean that his luck is turning.

He picks it up to look at it more closely. It's a gold ring with a ruby. The ruby is smooth, a little dull on the surface, but there's a deep light beneath. The gold setting is a nest of little leaves. It's old, anyone can see that, and it's beautiful. Not flashy, just quietly confidently classy. Dean knows as soon he sees it that this is a ring Sheena will love.

The crunch on gravel of a car pulling up outside. Fuck. He puts the ring in one pocket, closes the inlaid box, picks up his bag.

The front door opens. Footsteps, voices. His mouth goes dry. He hears a pounding in his head.

Don't move. Just don't move.

They're coming up the stairs, two of them. Oh fuck oh fuck oh fuck. The bedroom door opens and closes. He can hear the sound of their voices, the words muffled by the closed door. His face is cold as ice but he's sweating, the sweat trickling over his lips.

Music starts playing.

You can do this, brother, and you know why? Because it's a job. That's all it is. So there's a hundred guns and they're all pointing your way, the worst that can happen is you die. Live or die, it's all one. You do what you do.

What do you say, Brad? We get this show on the road.

Dean stays motionless as the music plays. The volume rises, bass and drums join the intro guitar. He starts to move. Every step brings him closer to danger, but he has no choice. At the open door of the master bedroom he can now identify the room the music's coming from, and assure himself that its door is closed. He wants to run, but forces himself to move slowly, softly. Across the landing. Down the stairs. The music still playing as he enters the living room.

The French windows open with a rattle. Now he's outside, drawing the door closed behind him.

Don't look back. They may be at the window, watching him. Nothing to be done about that. Fast over the terrace, round the house, then slow over the gravel. Running footsteps always a giveaway.

Stroll, stroll, Deanie boy, stroll. Don't look like a fucking thief now. Only a hundred yards or so to the van. No one shouting after you. No one following.

He swings his bag onto the passenger seat, climbs into the driving seat, starts up the van. His hands are shaking as he makes a three-point turn, grinds back down the lane past the house, and there's still no sign anyone's noticed anything.

The shaking goes on all the way to the main road. Only when he's in the tunnel does he start to feel safe. Then all the way through town to home the sensation builds.

I did it. For once I got lucky.

On Stansfield Road there's even a space to park right outside the house. He checks the time. Almost four o'clock. He picks up his tools and takes them with him into the house. There in the bright conservatory he throws himself down on the couch and feels the blood still pounding through him. A wave of exhaustion leaves him too weak even to get himself a drink. Now that he's safe his body admits how frightened he was.

So fucking what? I did it. I nearly pissed myself, but I did it.

The original plan has not come off. He had expected by now to be on his way to Brighton, to offload a pocketful of jewels for cash. Instead, he's got the one and only thing he wanted, the perfect ring for Sheena. It has to be meant. It's like he's kept his promise to Sheena after all. Thieving is when you take stuff and sell it for money. This is more like a passing on. The ring's old, someone had it before, now it passes on to Sheena. The owner in Edenfield makes an insurance claim, she gets her money back. No one loses.

He takes the ring out of his pocket and gazes at it for a long time. It's a beauty. Sheena will adore it. He'll tell her he's been saving up, that he bought it with money from the odd jobs he's been getting, and that's not a total lie. He's worked for it. He took big risks, he stayed steady when he could have panicked, he made all the right moves. You deserve a reward after all that.

I didn't do it for me, Sheena. I did it for you. I told you I'd come good one day.

He jumps up, suddenly re-energised, and finds Brad with the rest of the squad, back in the fort. He takes Brad out and shows him the ruby ring.

Brad doesn't care shit about rubies, but he knows a good job when he sees it. You've either got it or you haven't. No need to tell the world. All you need is one good mate who knows what it takes to do what you do. Then you get back from the mission and you look him in the eye and he gives you a nod and that's it.

'Who dares wins, right, Brad?'

29

The Queen's progress down the lane walled by guests is slow and hushed. As she goes, little groups of guests are drawn out at random to stand in the open and receive her royal attention. The two RAF lads and their partners are among the chosen ones.

The royal party is preceded by security men in morning suits, their function made clear by the way they look everywhere except backwards towards the Queen. Then the Queen herself comes into view, accompanied by a tall man with crinkly brown hair, who stoops beside her, briefing her in a low voice. The Queen wears a peacock-blue crepe coat and a white high-brimmed straw hat. She has a triple string of pearls round her neck and a spray of pearls on her lapel. She wears white gloves and black patent-leather shoes. In one hand she clasps a clear plastic umbrella. She's a little stooped, her legs a little bent. She is after all a very old lady.

Laura and Henry watch as the Queen talks to the RAF lads. They hear nothing of the exchange. Henry is experiencing ever greater levels of confusion. He had expected to feel what he has always professed, a genial sense of the absurd at the pantomime of monarchy. Instead he finds himself touched. This dutiful old lady is playing this dull and repetitive part with grace and professionalism. She allows us, who know nothing of her, to

cast her in our dreams and to fulfil whatever needs we have of
her, without the interference of any clearly defined self on her
part. What discipline must it have taken, for so many years, to
retain this formlessness?

After the royal party has passed, Joan hurries over to the RAF
lads to find out what the Queen said to them.

'She said her grandson's at Valley,' they say. They are based
at Valley. 'Never tells her what he's up to, she said.'

They marvel that the Queen should be just like any other
granny. The lads' partners give a detailed account of the Queen's
make-up. Lots of foundation, blusher, mascara.

Henry asks the young men if they've done a tour of duty in
Afghanistan.

'Coming up soon,' they say. 'There's a right mess. None of
us know what's the point of the war. Don't even know who
you're fighting.'

'Oh, I do envy you,' says Joan, meaning the Queen.

'Yeah. It were brilliant.'

Waiters bring round Loseley lemon ice-cream tubs on trays.

'Now this is an initiative test,' says Jaspal. 'See if you can find
the spatula.'

Laura needs the loo. She and Henry head down the lawn
towards the lake, where the toilet block stands.

'Well?' she says.

'I don't know what to think,' he says.

'You don't have to think. It's just a tea party.'

'No, it isn't. It's something else.'

'So you're not sorry you came?'

'No. Not at all.'

While he waits for Laura to get to the front of the loo queue,
Henry walks round the lake, and stands gazing back across the
water at the great mass of guests on the lawn, and the palace

beyond. He finds himself feeling uncharacteristically warmly towards these overdressed strangers. He tries to analyse the source of this feeling. Partly it's the friendliness of the crowd, and the curious sense he's noted already that each one feels excited and special. Simply by receiving this invitation, eight thousand people across a wide social range have been made to feel equal. Then there's that social range itself. The multiracial crowd, drawn from all regions, actually does give the appearance of being a microcosm of the nation. Here in the gardens of Buckingham Palace Henry is a citizen of modern Britain in a way he can never be at home in Sussex. Even the pantomime pageantry plays its part. The well-oiled machinery of what is, after all, a very minor royal occasion has succeeded in making him proud of being British.

But why should I feel moved?

It's more than nostalgia for a lost patriotism. It's something to do with the honour accorded to people who are in the normal course of public life invisible. Joan, who plans to frame her invitation and hang it on the wall, an enthusiast whose unalloyed delight in the day has given Henry too the gift of delight. Peter, whose father was in the Welsh Guards, and arriving today finds the regiment standing to attention in his honour. Sukhjit, who refuses to wear a hat, who looks more beautiful than every woman there, whose socialist father stood up to racist thugs. The boys from the RAF, who will go to war laughing that they've no idea who or what they're fighting, even as they risk their lives.

How magnificent people are. How resilient, and generous, and unexpected.

Henry has been struggling with dark thoughts ever since his meeting at Channel 4. His shame over his lie about Alain de Botton, his fear of being found out, has come to represent for him the moment at which his career ended. And when you're judged too old to go on doing the thing you've learned to do, what happens to the rest of your life?

Now in a sudden clear light he sees the question quite differently. The regret that torments him, the failure he dreads, is not the loss of function or purpose, but the loss of status. His pitch to Justin is only half the story. Yes, we manufacture our declared tastes in order to gain status. But that's hardly important. That's just a frill, an accessory. There's something here, something that's been revealed to him this afternoon, that's infinitely more significant.

In our insecurity, we seek ways to make others feel insecure. We're like shipwrecked sailors all struggling to climb onto a life raft. We believe that each person who gets onto the raft lessens our own chances of survival, so even as we fight for a handhold, we push our companions back into the water. And then, safe on the raft, we survivors eye each other warily, knowing that supplies are limited, and each sip of fresh water drunk by another is a mouthful less for ourselves. A cruel existence, a reality-TV-show world, where each week one of the group must lose and be sent away into obscurity. There's no friendship possible in such a world, only alliances of mutual convenience. Kindness is replaced by charm, and all we understand of love is the manipulative power of seduction. This, we tell ourselves, is the harsh reality. If you want to succeed in life you have to look out for yourself.

And it's all nonsense.

This is what presents itself to Henry this afternoon with the force of revelation. This nightmare existence is self-created and self-perpetuated, an intellectually lazy borrowing from a misunderstanding of Darwin. The fittest survive, yes: but why should the fittest be the most selfish? Pursue your own goals at the expense of others and you survive, but you survive alone. There is another world, where people form and nurture bonds with each other; where the success of one is the success of all. The revelation is that so many people actively want those round them to be happy.

Why should this be revealed to him here, in the palace gardens? Why is it not evident in his own life? Because the people he mixes with are high achievers, greedy for attention, vain of their image in the eyes of others. People who see humility as a weakness.

I have been one of them. I've had my day in the sun. I've taken my bow, I've heard the applause. And ever since, the silence that follows has been working its slow poison. Once a star, for ever a has-been.

But what if that spotlit stage is not the pinnacle of dreams, but a windowless dungeon where the single light burns day and night? And what if the door to the dungeon is locked, but only on the inside? We're free to open the door and walk out into a different world. All it takes is a little humility.

Laura returns.

'We should go soon,' she says. 'You know there's that black hole after six when there are no trains for an hour.'

'Yes, sure.'

They cross the lawn to say goodbye to their new friends.

'See how the rain held off!' says Joan, as if even the weather is in awe of their special day.

'Actually, it's Jaspal's birthday,' says Sukhjit.

They all offer their congratulations. They joke that the garden party has been Jaspal's birthday party all along. Then Laura and Henry make their farewells.

As they leave by the Grosvenor Gate exit the first spots of rain begin to fall.

30

Mrs Dickinson is not quite clear how long she's been alone. There has certainly been one whole night, and quite possibly two. Because she no longer has what might be called meals, the passage of time is hard to gauge. Of course she does eat from time to time, when she realises she's hungry, but just a little muesli with milk, or some soup heated up on the stove. No, not soup. That's run out. She last had soup when Bridget was here. But none of that matters. Meals are a lot of unnecessary fuss. She can cope.

The real difficulty turns out to be the dressing and undressing. Buttons are a challenge. With her arthritic fingers, and thumbs that have lost their power to press, the undoing of buttons is a matter of long fumbling, and the doing up of buttons is an impossibility. The fingers must locate and position the button and the buttonhole at the same time, and hold both accurately in place while forcing through the button. This requires a control she no longer commands.

Why do people make clothes that are so hard to do up and undo?

Then there's sleeves. One arm can be got into a sleeve with little trouble, but getting the second arm in – well, arms just don't bend that far back and up. How do other people manage it?

On her first night on her own Mrs Dickinson succeeded in undressing herself and in getting into her nightdress. Since then she has not changed her clothes. She wears a bathrobe over her nightdress and slippers on her feet, as if she's living on a hospital ward. In itself, this doesn't trouble her, because there's no one to see. But there are a few things she needs, and it's quite out of the question to go to the village shop in a bathrobe.

A solution will present itself. For now, the important point is that she's coping on her own. She does not need a carer. Her daughter walked out on her in a rage. Very well, let her go. She doesn't need a daughter either. How does Elizabeth imagine she coped all these years without a husband? You learn to look after yourself.

She sits in the small armchair by the open window, looking out at her garden. Elizabeth spent so much time in the garden when she was a little girl, especially in summer. She had a game called Visiting. She would go visiting imaginary families in make-believe houses under the magnolia, in the big box bush, behind the crab apple tree. As she remembers, the old lady falls into a confusion and supposes that her daughter is out there now.

'Teatime, Elizabeth,' she calls. 'Your tea's on the table.'

Except of course it isn't. There's no tea on the table because she's not been to the shop. Will the shop be open? She looks at the clock, and remembers with a start that she agreed to pick Alice up from school. She must be terribly late. She becomes flustered. My goodness! She'd better ring the school and tell them she's on her way. She reaches for the phone, only to realise she can no longer remember the school's number, even though she must have rung it countless times. She turns to the telephone book to look the number up, then lets her hand fall again. She's forgotten the name of the school.

Oh, I am hopeless, she sighs. I'll have to ring Elizabeth and tell her I've forgotten to collect Alice. So she picks up the phone and dials Elizabeth's number. That at least she knows by heart. But she gets a strange high-pitched tone.

Of course, how silly of me. That's not where Elizabeth is. She's in the garden, playing at Visiting.

She wants to see her. All of a sudden she wants to see Elizabeth very much indeed. She wants to call her in from the garden and see her come running to her. She wants to hold her in her arms and make her promise never to leave her.

She shuffles her bottom to the edge of the chair and pulls herself up, holding on to the side of the dresser. She reaches for her walking stick. Slowly, carefully, she crosses the kitchen to the back door. As she emerges into the warm overcast afternoon she remembers that her daughter is grown up now, and married, with children of her own.

She stands in the back doorway looking out at the weed-clogged garden, overwhelmed by desolation.

Why has this been done to me? Why is it so hard to walk? Why don't my fingers do what I tell them? Why am I all alone? It must be my own fault, but truly I do not know what I did wrong.

She turns back to the kitchen, meaning to call Elizabeth again, but then she thinks of the guinea pigs. Has Bridget fed them properly? Bridget will just give them their dry food, when what they really like is salad. Lettuce, carrot, cucumber, tomatoes. But Bridget never listens, she goes her own way. How can you call someone like that a carer? She's a don't-carer. But try telling Elizabeth. She won't hear a word against the woman. And you know why? Because so long as she can tell herself Bridget's looking after me she can forget all about me. How often does she come to visit me? Once a fortnight if I'm lucky. My own daughter. My only child.

She stands staring into the kitchen. It strikes her that it's in a terrible mess. That's Bridget's job, clearing up. I can't do it. If I bend down to pick something up I fall over, and then I can't get up again. So it's your wonderful Bridget you've got to blame if there's unopened letters on the floor, and unwashed dishes in the sink.

But Bridget didn't come today. Did she come yesterday? Did she make sure the guinea pigs were safely tucked up in their hutch for the night?

Then she remembers. There was a disagreement. A row. She told Bridget to go and never come back.

Bridget is gone! There's a victory. If she'd stayed much longer she'd have seen me off into a home and got the house for herself. That was always her plan. But she wasn't reckoning on me. I've looked after myself all my life. I'm no pushover.

She feels an ominous stirring in her bowels. Hurriedly, almost recklessly, she makes for the downstairs lavatory. She has just managed to hitch up her nightdress and lower herself towards the toilet seat when a great eruption takes place. Most of it, but not all, goes into the toilet. The eruption ends as suddenly as it began, leaving her weak and dizzy. She remains sitting there, drained of all energy. Her phone starts to ring. She knows she has no chance of getting to the phone in time, so she lets it ring until it falls silent.

Then slowly, wearily, she cleans herself up as best as she can; also the sides of the toilet. She dare not stoop or kneel to clean the floor for fear she'll never be able to get up. The smell remains after she's flushed, but there's nothing to be done.

She hobbles to the phone. The caller must have been Elizabeth. She dials Elizabeth's number, and once again gets the high-pitched tone. She puts the phone down with an exclamation of anger. Elizabeth should answer. It's very wrong of her to place herself out of reach in this way. Just because she employs Bridget as a so-called carer she thinks she can carry on as if I don't exist.

Is that what you want, Elizabeth? Do you want me to die?

It comes to her then that this matter must be sorted out once and for all. It's been allowed to go on for too long. If Elizabeth has walked out on me the way Rex did, then let her say so. Let her say it to my face.

In the garage outside there is an electric buggy that she uses for short trips, to church, to the shop. It doesn't go very fast, but so long as it's fully charged it can go for up to twenty miles. Elizabeth's house is just the other side of town.

The old lady sets off at once for the front door. Now that she has made this decision she feels a little less desolate. Of course she must see Elizabeth. Not because she can't cope on her own. Not because she needs a carer. But because there are issues between them that can only be resolved face to face.

The garage doors are open, as they always are these days. Elizabeth says, 'That's an invitation to thieves', but what can you do? There's no way she can open the garage doors by herself. 'Bridget can help you,' Elizabeth says. Of course! Bridget can do everything! Bridget is wonderful! But now the wonderful Bridget is gone.

The old lady unplugs the buggy from the charger and lowers herself into its seat. She sets its speed to the slowest setting, and inches backwards out of the garage. Now that she's underway she feels so much more positive. She pictures her daughter's face when she opens her front door and sees her there. So I need a carer, do I?

She reverses in a semi-circle, switches to forward drive, and trundles out onto the street. After a few yards she sees ahead of her a mother with a small boy approaching on the pavement. The small boy stares at her and points. 'Mum! Mum! Look!' Only then does the old lady realise that she's wearing nothing but a nightdress, and that one side of its skirt is stained ginger-brown.

Mortified, aghast, she makes a full turn in the street, causing the car coming up behind her to brake hard and honk loudly. Her eyes resolutely cast down, she trundles back to her entrance, and returns the buggy to its place in the garage. She hobbles with her stick from the garage to the front door, and finds she has failed to bring the front door key with her.

Shivering now, not with cold but with shame and helplessness, she hobbles round the house to the back. Her strength is failing her fast. Seeing the bench outside the back door, she lowers herself down to sit on it. Broken, frightened, bewildered, she closes her eyes and slips into a shallow sleep.

When she wakes she doesn't know at first where she is or why. Before her is the guinea pigs' run, with the hutch in which they sleep at the far side. The hutch door is open, as it should be by day. There are two guinea pigs. One is running up and down as if looking for a way out of the fenced enclosure. The other is lying by the hutch door.

Have the guinea pigs been given their salad? Bridget never gives them their salad. Even Elizabeth doesn't understand. 'You spoil those guinea pigs,' she says. 'Do you think they eat chopped salad in the Andes?' But they're not in the Andes now, are they? They're here with me. As a matter of fact, Elizabeth, the guinea pigs are the only living creatures that are here with me. They're my company. When I go Visiting, they're the friends I visit. I expect that appears quite funny to you. Well, go ahead, laugh if you like. But they don't criticise me, or tell me what to do and when I'm to do it, and they're always glad to see me. They lead quite a busy little life, you know, always scampering about, always looking for something to eat or somewhere to snuggle up. Sometimes I just sit and watch them for hours.

She's sitting and watching them now. The one lying by the hutch is very still. Almost too still. She gets up from the bench, staggering a little, and goes closer. She reaches out her walking stick and gives the guinea pig a little nudge. No response. Worried now, she shuffles right up to the low fence that encloses the guinea pigs' run.

'Guinea guinea!' she calls, in the special high voice she uses to call them when she's feeding them. 'Guinea guinea!'

The other guinea pig runs towards her.

'What's the matter with your sister?' she says. 'She must wake up.'

But the motionless guinea pig does not wake up.

Mrs Dickinson executes a controlled fall to her knees. Once on the ground, she reaches her walking stick into the run, handle first, and pulls the guinea pig towards her. She knows then from the way the soft body offers no resistance that the guinea pig is dead.

She picks up the little furry creature and holds it in her arms. Its brown button eyes are open but unmoving. Its nose, always the busiest part, is still. In every other way the animal is perfect: there are no signs of a wound.

'Oh, guinea,' she says sorrowfully. 'What happened?'

But she knows what has happened. The guinea pigs were not put to bed last night. They were left with the hutch open, exposed to predators, vulnerable to night chills. Bridget should have shut them up, but Bridget is gone.

Still holding the dead guinea pig in the crook of one arm, she levers herself upright again by pulling on the hutch. She makes her way, step by trembling step, into the kitchen. Here she sinks down into her chair by the window. She arranges the dead guinea pig in her lap, and strokes the unresisting fur.

Is it my fault you died? Did I kill you? You asked for so little, only shelter, safety, a little food. Not so hard to give. And did I fail you even in this?

The little animal's needs, which have not been met, become confused in her exhausted mind with her own needs. The guinea pig is innocent as she is innocent. Both of them have suffered neglect. Both have died.

So am I dead now? If so, in whose lap am I resting? And whose hand is it that strokes me?

31

It's been a long day for Maggie, and not a good day. She's finally written a humiliating letter to Murray to get him to drop his legal action. She's been abused by two home-owners and a developer. The deadline for the Conservation Area appraisal is coming up and she's had to bundle up a mass of papers to take home. And neither Andrew nor Jo has called her. Now on her way home at last, walking down through Grange Gardens to the car park in Cockshut Road, she calls Jo and gets an answer.

'Jo! Where have you been? I've been waiting for you to call.'

Jo is in London. She's been rehearsing an oratorio, she has talked to Andrew, and he's fine.

'But the thing is, Mags, he doesn't really know what's going on.'

'Join the club,' says Maggie.

'I think he's hurt that you seem still not sure what you want?' Jo's voice rises at the end even though it's not really a question, as if to say, Don't rely on me, maybe I'm wrong here. 'I think the way he sees it, you've both had enough time to know what you feel about each other?'

'I know, I know,' groans Maggie. 'That's what's so awful about all this. It should be obvious by now, and it just isn't.'

'Maybe that's like a warning bell?'

'Maybe it is. I'm so confused. Did you tell him I just need some time?'

'Yes,' says Jo. 'The thing is, Mags, he started crying.'

'Crying! Oh, God!'

'I did a mercy dash. I went round to his place.'

'Oh, poor Andrew. This is terrible.'

'I probably shouldn't have told you. He thinks his problem is he's too nice. He asked me if I thought you'd ever get to love him properly?'

'What did you say?'

'What could I say? I said I didn't know.'

'No, Jo! That'll make him give up.'

'For fuck's sake, Maggie!' Suddenly there's a critical edge to Jo's voice. 'What's going on here? You want to keep the poor sod on a string while you decide if you want him or not?'

'Well, yes,' says Maggie, abashed. 'I know that sounds terrible. But what else can I do?'

'Let him go,' says Jo. 'Set him free.'

'Set him free? He's not locked up. He can go any time he wants.' Now she in turn feels annoyed. 'What do you mean, set him free?'

'He's a great guy,' says Jo, 'and a lot of other women would be only too pleased to have him, and if you really want to know what I think, I think you should either piss or get off the pot.'

'What!'

'Sorry, but someone has to say it.'

'He really got to you, didn't he? That nice-Andrew-crying-in-your-arms act really did it.'

Maggie is hurt that Jo has changed sides. She needs her friend. It makes her angry that Andrew has played the pity card to win Jo over.

'Actually he did cry in my arms,' says Jo.

'And you comforted him, I'll bet.'

'I did what I could. There's enough lonely people in the world already. All he wants is to be loved.'

It's the way Jo says it, more than the words she uses.

'What did you do, Jo?'

'What do you mean?'

She's playing for time. Maggie's suspicions grow.

'Tell me what you did. Tell me how you comforted him.'

Silence on the line.

'I don't believe this,' says Maggie. 'I can't believe you did this.' So now she's telling Jo she exactly believes she's done this. 'How can you have done that, Jo?'

Jo's voice reappears, now small and faraway.

'We didn't mean it to happen,' she says. 'We got a bit pissed.'

'Oh, great. You were pissed. Just great.'

Maggie is in shock. She has no idea how to react.

'Listen, Maggie,' says Jo, pleading. 'You said it yourself, to me. You said you wanted to find someone else. Someone you could really love.'

'No, I didn't. I said someone I could love more.'

'Same difference.'

'No, it's not, Jo. The difference is, I already love Andrew.'

'So why was he crying?'

Suddenly Maggie wants to end this. Whatever Jo says from now on is only going to make her feel a whole lot worse. Which she's going to feel anyway.

'Let's just leave it for now, okay? I'm a bit gob-smacked, if you want to know. Anyway, I've got to the car.'

'Please, Mags. You've got to believe me. It was nothing.'

'Right. It was nothing. I'll call you.'

She ends the call and gets into her car.

The traffic moves slowly up Station Street, and at the right turn onto West Street there's a long hold up, which means cars are backed up all the way from the roundabout on the bypass. She turns on the radio and listens to the six o'clock news. Nick Griffin has been banned from a palace garden party. His deputy Andrew Bron attended, but spoke to no one except his daughter Emma. Maggie listens as she idles in traffic but hears nothing. For the moment she has stopped thinking. Jo's revelation has paralysed her.

It turns out there's been an accident on the A27 and the road is down to one lane. Maggie switches to Classic FM and gets most of the slow movement of Bruch's Violin Concerto. The plaintive strains of the violin make her feel that everything's slipping away from her, far away, into a past that contains all happiness, and is now out of reach.

The crawl of traffic releases her at last onto the Edenfield turning, and down the narrow lane to her rented refuge. All is as she left it, the familiar little rooms welcoming her back. The message light is flashing on the phone. For a moment she thinks it must be Andrew, but he never calls her on her land line. She plays the message. It's Laura Broad, reminding her about dinner on Saturday night.

'Just checking that you've remembered, and that there's nothing you and Andrew don't eat.'

Is that a good enough pretext to call Andrew? Hi, Andrew, it's Maggie. Laura Broad wants to know if there's anything you don't eat. I want to know if there's anyone you don't fuck.

That's when she discovers how angry she feels. But she's not even sure she's allowed to be angry. That's what's so shit about all this. It's her own fault.

Piss or get off the pot.

How could Jo do this? She's supposed to be my friend, for God's sake. You just don't do it. Even if me and Andrew had decided to break up, you don't do it. You wait till everyone's moved on, and that takes months. There should be an official mourning period for relationships, like the Victorians had for bereavements. A year wearing only black and not going out to parties and quite definitely not fucking other people, most of all your friends. Then it's over and you can start again.

How long has Jo had her sticky little paws out for Andrew? Didn't take her long to make her move. Like all of twenty-four hours. So she's lonely and desperate but she's *supposed to be my friend* and you don't do that. It's wrong. End of story.

And just what did Andrew think he was doing? No wonder he hasn't called. One minute he's going to live with me, the next minute he's going to bed with Jo.

There's no way she can go through the Conservation Area appraisal material. She dumps the papers on her work table, turns on the television to make a noise, and gets herself a vodka and orange. Long on the vodka. They got pissed, now it's my turn. The TV is tuned to More 4 because the last time she watched it was to catch a repeat of *Grand Designs*. Now it's *Deal or No Deal*, which is perfect for her current mood because it's so completely lacking in anything that requires her attention.

She drifts about the kitchen drinking her vodka and orange, wondering what to make herself for supper, not thinking about Andrew. She goes into the bathroom to have a pee and there's Andrew's wash things on the shelf by the basin, and it's like a smack in the face.

Don't leave me.

This is ridiculous. He wants to move in and I'm all give-me-space. He has a fling with Jo and I'm never-leave-me. It's worse than ridiculous, it's shameful.

She makes herself remember how much he irritated her at the fête. How relieved she was when she waved him off on the train back to London. But while she remembers each moment perfectly, the feelings seem to have changed. It's as if someone has sneaked into her memories and repainted all the colours. She can see him by her side at the fête, laying his bet on one of the runners in the sheep race, and all she can think is how sweet it was of him to play along with the nonsensical pretence of competition. Then there's the way he told her about his unexpected inheritance, saying it was to be 'a nice surprise'. It strikes her now how loving and generous that was. And when she said she wanted to be on her own, he didn't sulk or make her feel guilty. He just went.

Nice Andrew, Jo calls him. Nice to Jo too, it turns out. Maggie is bewildered by the power of this one item of information to alter all her perceptions. It turns out that Andrew is not nice after all. Nice men do not fuck their girlfriend's best friend.

So why do I feel betrayed by Jo, but not by Andrew?

Because I've been treating him badly. Because I've been keeping him on a string while I decide if I want him or not. But I never said I didn't want him. I just wanted to be sure.

Deal or No Deal gives way to yet another repeat of *Grand Designs*. She watches the entire programme, drinking more vodka and orange. She still hasn't decided what she wants to eat. The truth is she's not hungry. The house in the programme is in Devon and is being built with a traditional oak frame. As always, Maggie is gripped by the drama of creating a home, even though every beat of the story has been laid down in advance. It begins with the bright-eyed dream, which is presented to the viewers in the form of an animated diagram. Then come problems with materials and weather. Then the money runs out. Then at last the happy ending, when Kevin McCloud visits the completed home, and there are flowers on the tables. The property equivalent of the romantic love story.

Maggie rises from the sofa at last, thinking she might make herself a little scrambled egg, and finds that the vodka has affected her balance. She sits down again. She picks up the remote, switches off the television, puts the remote down on the shelf by the phone. This dislodges a memory. Someone rang. Who was that?

She plays the phone message again. Laura Broad thinks she and Andrew are still a couple, and still coming to dinner on Saturday. She must be put in the picture.

Maggie dials slowly, working out what to say. Laura answers the phone herself.

'Laura, I just got your message. About Saturday. I'm really sorry, but it looks like we won't be able to make it.'

To her surprise, Laura puts up some resistance.

'Are you sure? I was so looking forward to talking to Andrew about his first editions. Could you maybe come for just a drink?'

'No, well, it's not so simple.' Maggie can feel the vodka eroding her social inhibitions. 'The fact is, Andrew and I are going through a bit of a crisis just now.'

Why am I saying this? Laura Broad doesn't need to know.

'Oh, that's different,' says Laura. 'You're let off. There's nothing worse than having to put on a happy face in public.'

She says this in such a friendly sympathetic voice that Maggie is caught unawares. She realises all at once how desperate she is for someone to talk to.

'It's not so easy even in private,' she says.

Then to her horror she bursts into tears.

'Sorry,' she says, snuffling down the phone. 'I'm fine, really. Sorry.'

She hangs up quickly, before she makes an even bigger fool of herself. What on earth will Laura think?

That I'm unhappy. And it's true.

Dazed with vodka and emotion, Maggie sets about making herself scrambled eggs on toast, even though she doesn't want it. It's a matter of self-respect. She's appalled at her collapse. She refuses to sit on the sofa and cry. Life must go on.

The doorbell rings. At half-past eight in the evening?

'Who is it?' she calls through the door.

'Laura.'

And there she is, in the last light of the day, looking so warm and lovely that Maggie wants to hug her.

'Solidarity,' says Laura. 'You sounded like you needed company.'

'Oh, Laura. I'm so embarrassed. I'm fine, really.'

'You don't have to be embarrassed, I'm probably old enough to be your mother. God, that is depressing.'

Maggie laughs. 'You'd better come in,' she says.

The truth is she does want company. She does want to talk to somebody. And Laura Broad, who she talked to for a whole train journey, who's old enough to be her mother, is the somebody on offer.

'Can I get you something? Tea? Vodka?'

'No,' says Laura. 'Nothing at all. I never want to eat or drink again. We've been in London and had a huge tea, then Henry insisted he had to have supper. I've left him clearing up. He doesn't even know I've gone. He'll ring in ten minutes, you'll see, all grumpy, demanding to know where I am.'

'So we've got ten minutes.'

'We've got as long as we want.'

Somehow Laura makes it easy for Maggie to talk. Maybe not knowing her helps. Like talking in the dark.

'It's all my own fault,' she says. 'You won't be at all sympathetic when you hear.'

So she tells Laura about how nice Andrew is, and how they

planned for him to move in with her, and how she panicked. She tells about the betrayal by her best friend. She tells how she's been crying without really knowing why, or what it is she wants.

'So when this happened with the best friend,' says Laura, 'did that make you want Andrew more?'

'Yes,' says Maggie. 'Isn't that pathetic? Like a child who doesn't want a toy until another child starts playing with it.'

'It's exactly like that,' says Laura, 'but that doesn't make it wrong. Children aren't stupid.'

'But that's not love! You can't have a love affair that only works if the other person's always off cheating on you.'

'No, you can't.'

'You have to love someone for who they are. In themselves. And you have to love them enough.'

'How much is enough?' says Laura.

'That's what I don't know.' Maggie gazes at her in comic dismay. 'That's what I can't work out. When do you say, This is it? And when do you say, No, not yet. I'm holding out for more?'

'You know what this is?' says Laura. 'This is *Deal or No Deal*.'

Maggie bursts into laughter.

'Well, it is, isn't it?' says Laura. 'Either you take the deal on offer, or you hold out for something better. Which may turn out to be something worse.'

'That is so it,' says Maggie. 'Oh my God! I'm getting my love life from Noel Edmonds!'

'We all do it,' says Laura. 'You're not alone.'

'Yes, I am,' says Maggie. 'Other people fall in love. They're crazy about the guy. They know this is the one.'

'How do you think they know that?'

'I don't know. They get lucky. They meet the right man.'

'Do you buy that?' says Laura. 'Do you really?'

'You met the right man.'

'Maybe I did. But I didn't know it at the time. I wasn't at all sure I was going to marry him. I thought about it a lot. In the end I said yes because I'd got to a point when I wanted to be married, and he wanted to marry me.'

'You weren't in love?'

'I'd been in love, years before. I had a boyfriend I was crazy about. I would have done anything for him. But he wasn't right for me at all. He was rubbish. I was plain wrong about him. I know that now. And actually Henry, who was never that special, turns out to be the person I love most in all the world.'

'Oh, boy,' says Maggie. 'Now I'm all confused.'

'You know what I think's bothering you,' says Laura. 'You think there's this huge decision in front of you, and it's all down to you. You think whatever you do there's a fifty per cent chance you'll screw up the rest of your life.'

'Yes, that's just what I think.'

'Well, maybe it's not true. Maybe your life doesn't go the way it goes because of all the decisions you make. There's a whole world all round you that's doing its own thing, and we're all being shoved and pushed about whether we like it or not. Maybe we're leaves blown in the wind. We go where we're sent.'

'Leaves blown in the wind?'

'You can fight it or you can go with it.'

Maggie thinks about being a leaf blown in the wind.

'I don't think I can be that fatalistic,' she says. 'I'm not saying I wouldn't like to be a leaf blown in the wind. But it's going to have to be one hell of a wind.'

Laura's phone rings.

'Yes, Henry,' she says. 'No, Henry. I've run away with a sailor.'

'We're done,' says Maggie, whispering. 'I'm okay now.'

'Okay,' says Laura to the phone. 'Give me five minutes.'

She gets up out of the sofa with a sigh.

'He didn't believe me about the sailor.'

'Thanks so much for coming round.'

'I've been no use at all.'

'Actually, you've been wonderful.'

And she has. It's not the advice, it's just hearing her own anxieties put into words that someone else hears too. Somehow it makes them seem more bearable.

'Do what you like about Saturday,' says Laura on the doorstep. 'I'm doing a saddle of lamb. There's enough for one of you, or both of you, if you want it.'

After she's gone, Maggie returns to the kitchen. Her unmade scrambled eggs are still in the pan. She lights the gas and puts a slice of bread in the toaster. As she stirs the eggs she thinks, I'd better ring Andrew. It doesn't seem like such a terrifying prospect any more. They need to talk.

She eats the scrambled eggs on toast first, because it turns out she's extremely hungry. Then she calls him.

'Hi there,' she says. 'It's me.'

'Hi,' he says. He sounds subdued.

'We have to talk, don't we?'

'I guess so.'

'Come down tomorrow evening?'

Tomorrow is Friday, his usual time for getting out of London.

'I can't,' he says. 'The guys are giving me a goodbye party.'

'Okay. Saturday morning?'

'Sure. I can do that.'

'Call me when you're on the train and I'll meet you.'

Now that this has been decided Maggie feels a wave of relief and exhaustion wash over her. Whatever happens will happen. They'll talk on Saturday.

Maybe I'm a leaf in the wind after all.

32

Dean knows how much Sheena loves *Coronation Street* so he waits patiently until the mournful end music plays. He has one hand in his pocket, feeling the ring. He's been silent with excitement ever since Sheena came home.

Sheena half-watches the ads as she shifts her body to a more comfortable position on the sofa.

'You okay, babe?' she says.

'How about we go out?' says Dean.

'Out? It's nine o'clock at night.'

'It's sunset. There's a sunset sky out there.'

'You want to look at the sunset?'

'Yes,' says Dean. 'With you.'

She stares at him and realises he's up to something. He never was any good as a liar. Then she looks back at the TV. Coming up next is *Homes from Hell*. Houses built too close to the sea that fall off cliffs.

'So why build there in the first place, you muppets?' says Sheena to the television. 'All right,' she says to Dean. 'I'll get my coat.'

'It's not cold out.'

'I'm not taking any chances.'

They go out together, into the dusk of the estate. The shop

is closed, but it's still brightly lit inside. They cross Eridge Green.

'So where are we going on this walk?' says Sheena.

'You'll see,' says Dean.

He's right about the sky. It rises up over the water meadows, over the railway line, over the river, a soft smudge of reds and golds. The sun itself is long sunk behind the hills of the town, but its light still colours the sky, rimming the few island clouds.

'You're a mystery man, you are,' says Sheena.

He can tell she likes it. This is Dean in charge.

They pass the playground and the allotments and head up the track. The neatly tended hedge bounding Landport Road turns to bramble and thorn. Here between the fence and the fields the track is narrow, rutted. Two boys race by on bikes, heading home.

'You like it here, don't you?' says Dean, meaning the estate, the countryside, all of it.

'I do like it,' says Sheena.

'It's brilliant, your house,' says Dean.

'Your house too, babe.'

'My house too.' He's lived there three years now. Three magic years. 'Means a lot to me, that does.'

'Course it does.'

But he wants her to know how much it means to him. Hard to find the words for this sort of thing. You don't want to sound soft.

'Couldn't do it without you, Sheen. It's like, you saved me.'

Yes, that's how it is. Sheena, my saviour.

'Oh, darling.' She squeezes his hand. 'We save each other, right?'

The track rises into the darkness of trees.

'I can hardly see where I'm going,' Sheena says.

'You keep hold of me, sweetheart. I'll look after you.'

At the farmhouse they fork right and the track descends again. Ahead they see the shine of water that's the Cut. Between the tall trees the colours of the sky are deepening. On the left of the track the hillside rises steeply, thickly wooded, its ramps of dark earth carved between the trees where generations of kids on bikes have scrambled.

Where the track reaches the meadows, right by the bright water of the Cut, there's a five-barred gate for tractors and a small kissing gate for people on foot. This is Dean's chosen destination. He leads Sheena to the gate.

'This is it,' he says.

He leans on the five-barred gate and looks at the darkening roll of meadowland, broken by lines of trees. The high railway line. The distant tower of Hamsey Church on its river knoll. The sunset sky.

'Should be more red in the sky,' he says. 'But nothing's perfect.'

'I think it's perfect,' says Sheena.

'And looky what we have here.'

He goes to the kissing gate.

'This is a kissing gate. That means you have to kiss me.'

Sheena laughs at him for that. 'You don't have to bring me all this way to kiss you,' she says.

'But I want a special kiss,' says Dean.

He goes through the kissing gate to the far side. Sheena, smiling, comes up to the gate on her side. Dean feels in his pocket and takes out the ring.

'This is for you, Sheena,' he says. And he goes down on one knee. Right there by the kissing gate, on his knee, on the dry grass. 'If you'll have me.'

'Oh, babe!'

Sheena takes the ring. She can't speak. She's silent with surprise.

'I know I'm nothing much,' says Dean, 'but I love you and I want to marry you.'

Sheena gazes at the ring in the fading light.

'Deanie,' she says. 'This is so beautiful.'

'I'm on my fucking knees, Sheena.'

She looks up from the ring with a smile.

'Then get up and give me a kiss.'

He rises, and they kiss over the gate.

'Course I'll marry you, babe.'

'You will?'

He sounds amazed. Relieved.

'Don't mean much to me either way, but if that's what you want, that's what we'll do.'

He comes back round the gate and takes her in his arms.

'So you'll never leave me ever?'

'Never ever.'

'And you like the ring?'

'It's perfect. I've never seen anything so beautiful. Where'd you get it?'

'Brighton. I've been saving and saving. Mind you, Sheena, it's not new. It's second-hand.'

'It's antique, is what it is. That's why it's so beautiful.'

'If it doesn't fit we'll have it altered.'

Sheena tries the ring on the fourth finger of her left hand. It's tight, but it goes on. She holds her hand up to see it there, shaking her head in wonder.

'It's so beautiful, Deanie. It's like it was made for me.'

Dean is happier than he ever thought he could be in all his life. Because he's done something good. Because his girl's going to marry him.

'So what was all that about the sunset?' she says.

'I wanted to propose somewhere you'd remember. I wanted you to say for all the rest of your life, There was a sunset sky.'

'Oh, babe.'

They walk back slowly, hand in hand.

'You really don't mind the ring not being new?' he says.

'Course not,' she says. 'It's got all that love in it. All the women who've worn it before me. They were loved too.'

'Not as much as I love you,' says Dean.

And they stop in the dark tunnel of trees and kiss again.

FRIDAY

33

Laura leaves home just after eight in the morning, to do her supermarket shopping. You have to get there early these days to be sure of a parking space. Her dinner party is up in the air, she has no idea any more how many she's cooking for, it could be six, it could be ten, but what can you do? She can't ask Maggie to make up her mind when she's in mid-crisis. Carrie won't answer her questions. She'd call the whole thing off except Roddy and Diana are coming anyway, and what reason could she give Liz and Alan? You can't say you need to know exact numbers to proceed. That would be ridiculous. What sort of person can't cope with a few last-minute adjustments to her plans?

A person like me. So much for being a leaf in the wind.

Waitrose is oddly comforting. She glides with her smoothly rolling trolley down the bright aisles and thinks, 'This is grace abounding.' The words come into her mind unbidden. From where? Some hymn? Searching the shelves for Maldon salt and redcurrant jelly, she remembers that John Bunyan's spiritual autobiography is called *Grace Abounding to the Chief of Sinners*. First printed in 1668, twelve years before *Pilgrim's Progress*, she handled the sale of a fine 1672 edition to Wheaton College, Illinois, for just over $50,000. Bunyan's self-confessed sins were *profanity*, *dancing* and *bell-ringing*. It was one of her jokes at the time. What would Bunyan make of Waitrose? The grace of God transmuted into the promise of everlasting plenty on ever-refilled shelves.

It's all very well letting yourself be blown like a leaf in the wind, but what if the wind's blowing you nowhere? We're all put on earth for a purpose. Who said that? Some long-ago Sunday-school teacher. Funny how you go on believing something like that long after you stop believing in God. There's no reason why it should be true. It's much more likely we all show up by accident, and lead random lives. But you go on believing, there has to be a purpose.

She finds the redcurrant jelly. There's a purpose, of a very small kind. You seek for a jar of redcurrant jelly, and you find it. Maybe it's just vanity that drives us to look for something grander.

Then there's the children. You make them your purpose for so many years, then you have to stand by and do nothing when their lives are going wrong. If Carrie's not happy, that has to be my fault, doesn't it? It means I've made too many demands on her, or too few. She doesn't have a high enough opinion of herself, which is why Toby can walk all over her. He's like a cat, that boy, you can stroke him but he'll never love you.

All the time operating with half her attention on her shopping list, Laura is filling her trolley. At the deli counter she meets Belinda Redknapp. She's deeply tanned, and wearing skinny jeans.

'Belinda, you've got even slimmer! How do you do it?'

'We've been in Syria,' says Belinda. 'Everyone who goes to Syria gets the runs. Diarrhoea, the diet. And we've been in Jordan, so Tom could see Petra. I said anywhere so long as it's hot. How about you? Have you been away?'

'We're going in September. Steering clear of the school holidays, after all these years.'

'Just the two of you?'

'Yes, I think so. Carrie may come, but I doubt it.'

'Everyone keeps telling me they can't get rid of their kids, there aren't any jobs, just wait till they graduate and they'll be home again. But we don't see Alex for months on end. And Chloe's actually got a job! Can you believe it? She claims she's told me what it is but I've still got no idea, so I expect she's a lap-dancer or something. They say there's good money to be made in lap-dancing, but I can't think why. They're not allowed to touch, you know? I really don't understand men.'

All this in her usual ringing tones. Belinda doesn't do embarrassment.

'Let's have lunch one day soon,' she says. 'I want to tell you about my new discovery. It's the answer to everything.' She lowers her voice to whisper in Laura's ear. 'Lubrication.'

They go their separate ways down the shining aisles. Laura marvels at the life force that is Belinda. Trust her to find a way to be young again where it counts.

She moves on to the dairy shelves and picks up two tubs of double cream. Roddy is coming this evening, he doesn't want feeding, but it would be friendly to offer him something. She remembers that he likes Florentines, and heads up the biscuit aisle. Funny old Roddy, going in search of silence. He must drive Diana up the wall. 'I'm a stranger and a pilgrim on the earth,' he says, just like Bunyan. Perhaps he's a chief of sinners, drawn to profanity and dancing and bell-ringing. And yet even as she smiles at Roddy she admires him. He's setting out on his own adventure.

Maybe that's what happens after the children leave home and the long empty years loom before you. You stop servicing other people and begin your own adventure. But where do you go?

She wheels her trolley along the checkout counters, looking

for the one with the shortest queue. She sees one with only two trolleys in it and is about to join it when she gets a clear view of the waiting trolley. It's the big kind, and it's full to the top. Better to join a longer line of less full trolleys.

Hell. I've forgotten my Bag for Life again.

She's always doing this, rushing out of the house in too much of a spin and leaving behind her now extensive collection of Bags for Life. She refuses to buy yet more. I'll just have to have carrier bags and be a polluter of the environment. And it is useful to have a stash of old plastic bags to wrap up the remains of meat or fish left uneaten after a meal. They can't go on the compost, and if you don't wrap them in plastic they stink. But the plastic bags end up somewhere in the Atlantic, choking marine creatures to death. Every little thing you do causes some damage further down the line.

The shopper in front of her transfers her purchases from trolley to belt. Laura waits for her to reach for one of the little plastic barriers that separates one shopper's goods from another, but she neglects to do this. Laura has to do it for herself. Surely this is wrong? She wants to tell her she's forgotten to put down the —, but she doesn't know what it's called. It'll have some specialist name that only experts use, like *cam* or *berm*.

'Hello, Laura. Out early.' It's Joan Huxtable, a stalwart of the village, in her mid-seventies now but as well groomed and upright as ever. 'Aren't we having a glorious summer! But they do say it's about to break.'

Laura is loading her shopping onto the moving belt. She takes one of the plastic barriers and says to Mrs Huxtable, 'What would you call that?'

'I've no idea. I wouldn't call it anything.'

Laura asks the checkout girl for plastic bags, avoiding her

eyes. As she pays for her shopping, pressing the numbers on the credit-card keypad, she points to one of the plastic barriers.

'What do you call those things?'

'Those?' says the checkout girl. 'I call them thingies.'

At home, putting away the shopping, Laura finds that the bandage has fallen off her finger. She examines the cut. It's far from healed, but it looks clean and healthy. She hates not wearing her ring, it's become so much part of her. She decides not to put a new bandage on, which means she can wear her ring again.

She runs up to her bedroom and opens the Moroccan box.

The ring isn't there.

She takes everything out of the box, lays all the beads and earrings out on her dressing table: but her engagement ring is not among them. Baffled, she looks round the carpet at her feet, and under the dressing table. No sign of the ring.

She goes downstairs to Henry's study. He's on the phone, but he pauses his conversation, seeing her anxious face.

'Have you seen my engagement ring anywhere? I took it off when I cut my finger the other day. I thought I'd put it on my dressing table, but it's not there.'

'No, I've not seen it,' says Henry.

He goes back to his conversation.

'I could come up today, I suppose,' he says.

Laura returns to the kitchen, thinking maybe she's misremembered and left the ring on a cup hook. She looks in all the possible places where she might have put it, but finds nothing. Can it have fallen down the sink plughole?

She revisits her memory. It's perfectly clear. She took the ring upstairs and put it in the Moroccan box. And now it's gone.

She feels a sense of panic. She loves that ring. It's not just that it's beautiful and irreplaceable. It represents her marriage. If the ring is lost, her marriage will fall apart.

This is nonsense, of course. She knows it's nonsense. She tells herself not to be so silly. But she wants with a dreadful fearful longing to find her ring again.

Carrie comes into the kitchen, followed by Toby.

'We're going out driving,' says Carrie.

'Have you seen my ruby ring?' says Laura. 'I've lost it.'

'No,' says Carrie. 'Okay to use the car? My test's next week.'

'What does the ring look like?' says Toby.

'It's antique gold, with a single uncut ruby set in gold leaves. On the inside, on the back of the setting, it's engraved with our initials, L and H. It's my engagement ring.'

'Pretty special,' says Toby.

'Yes. It is.'

'Come on, Toby,' says Carrie, taking the car keys from Laura's handbag.

'I'm good at finding things,' says Toby. 'I'll take a look when we get back.'

They go out.

Laura feels sick. She tells herself it's not an omen of disaster, but it feels as if it is. Henry's going through a difficult time. Carrie's about to have her heart broken. The hot summer's about to end. Her dinner party's in chaos. On Saturday it's the anniversary of her engagement to Henry, and she's lost her ring.

Henry himself appears, his phone call over.

'That was Aidan Massey,' he says. 'He's doing a new series, the history of India. I thought there might be something for me there.'

All Laura can think about is her lost ring. But she can feel the tension in Henry. He won't have enjoyed making that call.

'You said you never wanted to work with Aidan Massey again in all the rest of your life.'

'Oh, he's not so bad. He says he'd like to have me on the team, but it's not up to him. Anyway, he's going to fix for me to meet the series producer.'

'You hate working for other people.'

'I can cope with it, if I'm left alone.' He looks round for his leather satchel. 'I'd better buck up. I told Aidan I'd be there by eleven. Then if all goes well, I'll spend the rest of the day in the production office getting myself briefed.'

'You're going to London now?'

'Yes. Now.'

He finds his bag, his phone, his car keys. And he's gone.

Laura doesn't understand why he isn't more disturbed by the loss of her ring. But maybe he's right and it'll just turn up.

A tap on the back door. It's Terry Sutton.

'Just come to fix that orchard gate,' he says.

'Oh, right,' says Laura. She has no idea what he's talking about.

I put the ring in my Moroccan box. I know I did.

She returns to the bedroom. There lies the contents of the box, spread out on her dressing table; but no ring. She takes the box itself and shakes it. She tugs out its blue silk lining. There beneath the lining is a folded paper napkin. She opens it out, and sees on it writing from long ago.

Will you marry me?

She gazes at it. Then she starts to cry. She sits in front of her dressing-table mirror, weeping silently, because seeing the writing on the paper napkin pierces her heart. She never cried back then. But somehow the years in between have granted the moment retrospective weight, as if her future with Henry is laid out in a few faded ink strokes on that soft white paper. And that blue biro tick by the box labelled *Yes*, made by her more as an act of faith than love, was the first real step in the creation of what is now her entire life.

34

Alan comes to the end of the script emailed him by Jane Langridge. He's only skimmed through it, not wanting to torment himself with too close a knowledge of what has been changed. Most of all he has avoided the speeches of the dog. All the time that he was working on the screenplay, mocking himself for colluding in its absurd premises, he was finding ways to channel his true self.

So deep down I'm a sheepdog with a talent for financial trading. Who knew?

But of course it's not the financial skills or the dog-ness, it's the view of the world. 'The trouble with people is they're always on heat. They need a good long rest from thinking about sex.'

Jane has sent the new script with a disingenuous cover note implying it's still a rough draft, despite the fact that it says on the title page: SHOOTING SCRIPT. And as it happens they're out there right now, shooting it.

Liz looks in at the door.

'I have to go out.'

Alan knows Liz is still cross with him, but the need to vent his feelings is too strong.

'This is it,' he says, holding up the new draft. 'A quirky

character comedy now stripped of quirkiness, character and comedy.'

'I have to go,' says Liz.

'Where are you going?'

'To a donkey sanctuary the other side of Hailsham.'

'Why?'

'You know the Russians who made a donkey parasail over a beach? The *Sun* has rescued the donkey. So now Mark wants a piece on rescued donkeys.'

Henry finds this hard to take in.

'Does anyone care?'

'Mark does.'

Alan wants to talk to her about his screenplay.

'They've made the dog American,' he says. 'The only thing that was ever funny about the dog swearing was that he was English.'

'Don't tell me. Tell them. Go and tell them.'

She's heading for the front door, bag swinging. He follows her into the hall. Caspar is there, gazing at him.

'I'll tell them, Dad.'

'What?'

'I'll tell them Rocky has to be English.'

The front door closes. Liz has gone. The phone rings. It's Bridget, worrying about Liz's mother.

'She hasn't phoned,' says Alan, speaking more sharply than he needs. 'The whole point is to get her to realise for herself that she needs help. She's got her emergency-call button if she gets into trouble.'

He puts down the phone.

'If you're going to the filming,' Cas says, 'please take me with you.'

Alan draws a long breath to calm himself. He doesn't like it when there's unresolved business between him and Liz.

'I'm not going,' he says. 'It'll only make me angry. There's no point.'

'Yes, there is. You have to tell them.'

Alan looks down at his son. No self-doubt there, no self-punishment.

Maybe I should go back. Something has to give.

The mix of rage and powerlessness is making him ill. And he doesn't want to sit around the house feeling sorry for himself, waiting for Liz to come home.

Maybe I should have a private word with Jane. Ask her why they did it behind my back, as if I don't exist. No, not that. Express concern. My fear that the story might have lost some originality. Might have turned into a crock of shit.

Cas is still staring expectantly up at him.

'If I let you come, you're to buzz off when I tell you, okay?'

'Okay.'

So Alan sets out like a soldier going to the wars, and Cas runs along after him like a soldier's son who wants to go to the wars too.

The sun is bright, high in the sky. The morning golden hour is long over, the evening golden hour is yet to come. Today is scheduled to be the last filming day on the Downs. Alan wonders if they got the light they wanted on Wednesday, or yesterday. It hurts him so much, not being a member of the unit, sharing their daily triumphs and disasters, on this story that has been a part of his life for over two years.

'Dad,' says Cas as they drive. 'You made Rocky up, didn't you?'

'Yes, I did.'

'So you're the most important person of them all.'

'I don't think they think so.'

'But you are. If it wasn't for you, none of them would be there, doing the filming.'

'They'd be doing some other film. There are so many films.'

'But not *this* film,' says Cas firmly. '*This* film is only being done because of *you*.'

'That is perfectly true,' says Alan.

When they get to Cuckmere Haven they find no one controlling the entrance to the film-unit car park, and they drive in unhindered. There's a crowd of crew round the catering van.

'Mid-morning break,' says Alan.

He sees no one he knows. They park at the far end to be out of everyone's way, and walk back to the cluster of production trailers. Alan's plan is to locate Jane Langridge and speak to her in private. He doesn't want to see either the director or the new writer.

Caspar is looking round for Billy. He can't see him anywhere.

'Can you ask, Dad?'

Alan asks a member of the crew who is standing in line for coffee, but the crew man doesn't know. Then Alan sees a trailer just ahead that says on its door: PRODUCER – Jane Langridge. He crosses, and is about to tap on the door when it opens. Out steps the young man with the dark curly hair. The new writer.

He gives Alan a questioning look, tipping his head on one side.

'I'm guessing you're Alan Strachan.'

'Yes,' says Alan.

The young man shoots out his hand.

'Harlan,' he says. He gives Alan a crinkly smile. 'I'm the jerk who's fucking up your story.' He sees Caspar behind Alan. 'Hey, sorry about my language.'

'Caspar,' says Alan. 'My son.'

'Your dad did a great job,' says Harlan.

'If it wasn't for him,' says Cas, 'none of you would be here.'

'Hundred per cent true,' says Harlan. 'He's the giant. We're the pygmies, standing on his shoulders.'

None of this is what Alan has expected. He doesn't know how to respond.

'Hey,' says Harlan, 'come on in. Have a coffee.'

'Do you know where Billy is?' says Cas.

'Billy?'

'The dog actor who acts Rocky.'

'Oh, sure.' He calls out to a young woman in the line for the catering truck. 'Greta. Show this young man where the dog handlers are pitched. He's a VIP visitor, so make nice.'

Caspar runs off with Greta. Alan follows Harlan into the production trailer. They have it to themselves. There's a table with a laptop open on it where Harlan has evidently been working. A coffee machine in the galley kitchen.

'Your first screenplay, right?' says Harlan.

'Yes,' says Alan.

'You did a great job.' He pours strong black coffee. 'The morons have no idea. They fly me over to give it what they call *topical edge* –' he makes the phrase sound like a fashion accessory – 'which turns out to mean referencing a movie made all of sixteen years ago. The dog has to say, "Greed is good".'

'I saw,' says Alan.

'This dog,' says Harlan, 'is so fucking self-aware that if he were ever to say "Greed is good" he'd say it like with an up-tick, you know? Greed is good? Like he's amused by the old-time religion of it all. But try explaining that to Nancy Kravitz. You've met Nancy?'

'Only on the phone.'

'Nancy has all the thrust of the first stage of a Saturn rocket. Her job is to blast off and then fall away. She has no idea what's up there in the nose cone.'

He gives Alan a polystyrene cup of coffee and throws himself across the couch at one end of the trailer.

'Stretch out. Put your shoes up on the soft furnishings. We're just here for the ride.'

Alan sits down, sips at his coffee. He pulls a face at the bitter taste.

'Yeah, even the coffee's shit,' says Harlan.

'So,' says Alan. 'How long ago did they bring you on to this?'

'I guess it must be three months now. No one told you, of course.'

'No.'

'Welcome to the movie business, where every call is a good-news call. We don't do criticism. We do praise, and we do silence.'

'Have they done it to you?'

'Fuck, yes. I've had one screenplay made, which tanked, by the way, and no surprise to me because the director rewrote all the key scenes with his own unique brand of corpse-speak. And I've had, Jesus, I don't know how many not made. You could line the walls of a crematorium with the pages of my unmade scripts.'

'But they still hired you for this.'

'Yeah, I know. It's loony tunes. But that's how they think. It's almost touching, really, the way hope springs eternal in the studio breast. This writer hasn't quite got us there, but *the next writer'll crack it*. Or the next. No amount of evidence to the contrary can convince them otherwise. It's *new*, see? What's new is *better*. That's America. I told them when I read your drafts, I said, Stay with this guy. He's got the voice you need. Just get him to goose it up a little.'

Alan doesn't believe this, but he appreciates the courtesy.

'I don't know that I'm up to goosing,' he says. 'I expect they're better off with you. This isn't really my scene.'

'But you still show up for the races.'

'For the money.'

'Precisamento. It's just a job. Never forget that, my friend. It's like going down a mine. You do your day's work and you take your day's pay and you go home and take a shower and pour yourself a drink and you let it all float away. It's just a fucking job.'

'I guess it is,' says Alan.

'I've done what I can to keep your best stuff in there. Not that they'll ever know. Me and Colin work it together. I slip him some of the original pages and he asks for this speech or that speech to go back in. Colin is extremely smart.'

Somehow including the star actor makes it all believable. He wouldn't make that up, would he?

'I suppose I should thank you,' says Alan. 'You'll just have to give me a moment to swallow a few preconceptions.'

'What did you think? That I was part of the demolition crew? I'm a *writer*, Alan. I'm on your side. All writers get fucked over. But we know good stuff when we see it.'

'I suppose I assumed you'd want to take over. Make it your own.'

'When the project's rolling? No way. All I can do is stop them screwing it up. Then maybe the movie comes out halfway decent and does some business. Which is good for me and good for you.'

'Yes. I suppose it would be.'

Harlan leans forward and taps Alan on the knee, smiling.

'You look like you just walked in on your parents having sex.'

'I am having to make some adjustments.'

'I think this movie could make it through. Did you hear, Bobby de Niro's agreed to voice the dog?'

'No.'

'Okay, so the dog should be a Brit. But we lost that one. So if you have to have American, Bobby's as good as it gets. He's got that world-weary schtick down. I can just hear him drawling, "Every sheep is born to die." '

'Is that back in?'

'You bet your sweet tootsie it's back in.'

'Will you get a credit?'

'See, that should have been your first question. Now you're talking like a pro. Do I get a credit? The answer is no. By the rules I have to contribute fifty per cent or more, not just to the dialogue, but to the plot structure and character creation. And that I have not done. So guess what, Shakespeare? You get sole credit. Meaning for all my work, as well as yours. So who's the fucker here, and who's tied to the bed taking it up the ass for nothing?'

'Except money.'

'You're learning. I'll probably make more than you on this gig. But with sole credit on a hit movie, your quote goes way up. Next time you cash in.'

'And the movie never gets made.'

'You're there. Apprenticeship over.'

Alan shakes his head, marvelling at it all.

'How long have you been doing this, Harlan?'

'Almost twenty years now.'

He sees the surprise on Alan's face.

'Yeah, I look like I'm fresh out of school. I'm thirty-eight. I have this pact with the Devil. I never age, and he gets all the on-screen credits.'

'I'm thirty-nine,' says Alan.

'You've written a couple of good plays. One seriously good play.'

'Now I feel ashamed.'

'For wanting to make money?'

'For not taking the trouble to find out more about you.'

'Not much to know. Here's something you won't get from Google. When I was sixteen I wrote a story, it was a school assignment. My teacher said to me, Harlan, I'm not even grading this. This is the real thing. You're that rare creature, Harlan. You're a writer.'

The brittle tone falls away from his voice as he tells this story. His gaze holds Alan's eyes.

'It was like he was saying to me, You're an angel.'

'So maybe you are.'

'Yeah, sure. Maybe. You make your choices, you live with them. And we have some fun along the way, right?'

Tap-tap on the trailer door.

'That'll be Cas,' says Alan.

He opens the door and there's Cas all charged up with excuses.

'Billy had to go and I was thinking—'

'It's okay, Cas. Come on in.'

Cas comes in, looking round at the interior of the trailer.

'Wow! It's like a house!'

'How was Billy?' says Harlan.

'He was resting,' says Cas. 'Actors have to have downtime.' He finds an iPad on the table. 'Is this an iPad?'

'It is,' says Harlan. 'Have a go with it.'

Cas sets to work at once, seeming to know by instinct how to operate it. Harlan watches him wistfully.

'You have children?' says Alan.

'One boy. He lives with his mother.'

'That's hard.'

'Yes, it's hard.'

His phone rings.

'Yeah,' he says. 'Yeah. I'll be right over.'

He gives Alan an apologetic shrug.

'Duty calls.'

'Okay. We'll get back. Cas!'

Cas jumps up, his fingers still on the iPad.

'It's been a privilege, Alan.' Harlan offers his hand as he hooks up a bag full of scripts.

They go out into the now deserted space between the trailers. Harlan waves and sets off at a lope towards the film unit on the hillside. Alan and Cas walk back to the car.

'Did you tell him he'd messed up your script?' says Cas.

'No,' says Alan.

'Thought not.'

They're both silent as they drive home, each deep in thought. Then Cas breaks the silence.

'I'd do anything in the world to have an iPad,' he says. 'But there just isn't anything, is there?'

'No,' says Alan.

'Thought not.'

35

Toby feels like all he's done for days is sit on the floor in Carrie's room and watch her cry. Time to move on, my friend. Always the same story.

Everything would be so easy if people would only let go. It's the clinging on to things that makes all the misery in the world. You can't hold living things, they're in motion, if you want them to stay you have to kill them. But say this to someone and they hear something different, they hear, I want to leave you, and they start to cry.

So Carrie cries. I try to tell her, but all she hears is this won't be for ever, and if it's not for ever it's going to end, and if it's going to end it's already dying. But hey, we're all dying. Every day a step nearer the end. What's new? But Carrie cries.

'You say I should live now,' she tells me, 'now, you say, now. But you don't live now. If you did, how would you know you're going to leave? You wouldn't know it until you were doing it. So why do you have to say you'll leave?'

All of which is fair comment, but since when did I claim to practise what I preach? Since when did I preach? Say the first thing that comes into your head. Act without forethought.

Look, all I'm trying to do here is step lightly on the earth. Leave no trace. If I could shed my self I would.

'Don't sit so close,' I tell her. 'I need space.'

She moves away.

'Come closer. Lie down beside me.'

She lies down beside me. What does she want from me?

Her manner with him though not her words says, Do with me what you will. She plays at disagreement, but she has submitted. The pleasure this gives him dwindles day by day. She senses this and fears she'll lose him. In her fear she seeks to please him more, and so he becomes cruel.

'You watch me too much. Close your eyes when you look at me.'

She closes her eyes.

'Don't do what I tell you to do.'

She doesn't and so she does. Trapped in the mesh of his will. And as for Toby, caught in another repeating pattern, he grows bored.

I'm so fucking bored of being bored. Let's play a game.

'Pretend you hate me,' he says. 'Pretend you despise me. Tell me stuff to hurt me.'

'You're a cunt,' she says.

That makes him laugh. She says it so carefully, like it's a technical term. Then she's happy she's made him laugh, which isn't the idea of the game at all.

'Try harder,' he says.

'You have no emotions. You love only yourself.'

'If only that were so,' he says.

'You're a narcissist. All you see in other people are mirrors of yourself.'

'Closer,' he says.

'I don't hate you,' she says. 'You hate yourself.'

'Closer,' he says.

But still it doesn't hurt.

I am invulnerable. This is my deformity.

These are dangerous thoughts, these glimpses of the demon. He rations them, because always they come with an intoxication of the blood, a beautiful poisoning, that makes him thirsty for pain. His own pain, the pain of others. The demon feeds on shock and dismay.

I am one sick fuck.

All you can do is move on. You don't ask people to love you. You don't make promises. You don't offer gifts. You don't deceive. But they want the demon, that's the truth. They long for the demon's hurting kiss. So we're all sick together.

She says, 'Come out in the car with me.'

They go out driving.

Every time they come out in the car Toby is possessed by an urge to take the wheel and drive them into the oncoming traffic. So it's good that it's Carrie who's driving.

'Imagine driving on the wrong side of the road,' he says. 'All those cars coming straight at you. All those moments you could die.'

'You want to die?'

'No. I want to be inside those moments when I could die.'

'What happened to you, Toby? Why are you such a freak?'

'Usual story,' says Toby. 'Too much of this. Too little of that.'

Over the Phoenix Causeway, the river running low.

'I've stayed long enough,' he says. 'Time to be on the road again.'

'What road?'

'The road away.'

She drives in silence, past the old bus station to the traffic lights at the bottom of the High Street. Her body has gone stiff. She grinds the gears into neutral, brakes at the red light.

'So that's what you do,' she says. 'You start things you don't finish. You hit and run.'

'What were you expecting? Eternal sunshine of the spotless mind?'

'Oh, fuck off, Toby.'

So of course he finds her pain exciting. It's not wanting to hurt, it's wanting to be in the place where pain happens.

'You know self-harming?' he says.

'Yeah,' she says. 'I know self-harming. That your next cool idea?'

'People can do it without razors.'

'You don't say.'

The lights change, the traffic rolls on up Friars Walk. Ahead is the tricky intersection where Station Road crosses and cars come from all directions.

'So just tell me, Toby. Where do I come in? I mean, like, what is this? What are we doing here? I'd just like to know.'

'Me too,' he says.

'Not good enough. Try harder.'

Now she's negotiating the intersection, heading across into Southover Road. There are cars parked all down one side, which makes it a tight squeeze for two-way traffic. She has tears waiting in her eyes.

Bad situation. Trapped in a moving car, under pressure from demands you can't meet. The urge to break out can make you crazy. Time to kick doors, break windows.

'Don't push me,' he says.

'No, you owe me. You don't just walk away. Jesus, did I ever ask you for a fucking thing? All I want to know is, do I exist for you? Do you have any feelings for me of any kind whatsoever? On the road again. Jesus!'

'What do you want, Carrie? I stay in Jack's room for the rest of my life?'

'No! Of course you'll go! I know that! I'm not a child!'

'So I'll go.'

'Do you love anyone, Toby? Have you ever loved anyone?'

Why don't you love me? Make me suffer more. Cut my arms with your blades.

'You tell me what that means,' he says, 'I'll tell you if I've got it.'

'It means it hurts to leave,' she says fiercely.

'You could put that in a song. Loving means it hurts to leave.'

She gasps at that, as if he's hit her. The demon did that to her. Now she's driving too fast.

'Leaving means it hurts to love,' he says. 'Hurting means it loves to leave.'

He can't help himself. The demon is running free and he must follow.

'On the road again,' she says, staring ahead as she drives. 'On the road again. On the road again.'

Her mantra against pain. But she's the one who summoned the demon. You get what you ask for in this world.

'You know what, Toby.' Talking fast now, driving fast. 'This is all a joke, because I don't do the girly thing, I don't do flirting, I'm just fine being who I am. I'm not saying I'm any better than anyone else, I'm just saying I'm *me* and I'm good with that and I don't dress up as *not-me* for anyone. And you show up and I'm, how about this? Here's someone I can be *me* around, here's someone who does a really good imitation of connecting with actual *me*. So I let myself think maybe connections do happen, maybe we're not all *me*, maybe sometimes we can be *us*, and you give me this shit about being on the road again. And that's quite a joke, isn't it? That really is a good one. Because you're going nowhere. So why do I care? I'm such a fucking mess-up, look at me, Jesus! Why don't we just all roll over and die? I mean, what is there out there worth sticking round for? There's no party, right? So why am I crying? Why am I humiliating myself when you don't give a shit about anyone but yourself? Oh sure, I'll put it in a song, I'll put it all in a song. Only when I sing it you won't be there to hear, you'll be on the fucking road again—'

Rattle of noise, blur of motion, a boy on a bike *smack* across the front of the car, *crump* on the bonnet and punch through the air, bike spinning away, boy vaulting skyward, lands on a parked car, bounces, hits the tarmac, doesn't move.

Carrie jams on the brakes, she's uttering these small panic cries, 'Oh God! Oh God! Oh God!' People appear out of nowhere, mobile phones out, calling for help, taking pictures. Toby's out of the car, going to the boy.

'Don't move him!' A passer-by, an instant expert. 'Could've broken his back.'

'Crazy kid,' says another. 'Accident waiting to happen.'

'Nothing you could do,' they say. 'Came down Keere Street like a runaway train.'

Carrie out of the car now, shaking violently.

'Is he – is he . . .?'

The man who has taken charge says, 'He's breathing. He's concussed.'

'Have they – has the—'

'Ambulance on its way.'

Toby says to Carrie, 'Give me your phone.'

He calls Carrie's mum, tells her briefly and clearly what's happened.

'She's coming right over,' he says to Carrie.

Carrie nods, white-faced, shivering. The sun shines out of a clear sky, glinting on the spokes of the buckled bike as it lies on its side in the road. From far away they hear the siren of an ambulance, faint at first, but growing louder. The boy's body doesn't move.

36

Laura is trying to control her panic but the problem is she has no car. Carrie took hers for driving practice and Henry has taken his to Haywards Heath for the meeting in London. She calls Alison Critchell, gets her answer machine. Can she call Martin Linton? She stands in the kitchen looking out into the garden struggling not to picture the car crashed and what might have happened and Carrie frightened, needing her, when she sees Terry Sutton go by, carrying a roll of wire netting.

'Terry!' she calls from the back door. 'Terry!'

He comes over, and as she tells him Carrie's been in an accident she finds she's crying.

Terry turns out to be a wonder. He drops everything, offers to take her in his car, and within minutes they're on their way.

'I don't think it was Carrie's fault,' Laura says, needing to talk. 'This boy on his bike came out of nowhere. But what must Carrie be feeling? What if the boy dies?'

'These biker boys don't die,' says Terry. 'They bounce.'

He drives fast and skilfully, almost to the scene of the accident. A small crowd has formed where the police have closed the road. People are holding their phones above their heads taking photographs.

Terry acts as Laura's minder, pushing a way through for her. 'Sorry, mate. Family here. Family.'

To the policeman barring their way he says, 'Hello, Ron. This is Mrs Broad. It's her daughter over there.'

Carrie and Toby are standing just beyond Laura's car, talking to a policewoman. The boy's bike still lies where it fell on the road. Laura is let through and runs to Carrie, takes her in her arms.

'Darling, darling, sweetheart.'

Carrie cries a little. Toby speaks quietly, with reassuring steadiness.

'It wasn't Carrie's fault. The boy came out of nowhere.'

'How is he?'

'They've taken him in an ambulance.'

Laura turns to the policewoman.

'Can I take her home?'

'Your daughter can go. We'll be in touch tomorrow. But I'm afraid the car has to stay. There's an FCI unit on the way.'

'I don't care about the car.' She holds Carrie close. 'Will someone let us know about – about everything?'

'Yes, ma'am. You'll be kept informed.'

Laura keeps her arm round Carrie all the way back to Terry's car, as if she's cold. They get into the back. Toby sits in the front, beside Terry.

'I've not got a car at home,' says Laura. 'Terry's been an angel.'

'Mum,' says Carrie. 'I want to go to the hospital.'

'There's nothing we can do, darling.'

'I want to go to the hospital.'

'Sweetheart, we can't ask Terry to take us all the way to Brighton.'

'No problem,' says Terry.

So they head out onto the A27 west. Carrie starts to talk about the accident.

'I was on the right side of the road,' she says. 'I was watching where I was going. I never saw him.'

'There was nothing you could have done,' says Toby.

'They breathalysed me,' says Carrie. 'But they were nice.'

'Why didn't he use his brakes?' says Laura.

'Don't have brakes,' Terry interjects. 'That was a BMX bike. They don't have brakes.'

'Don't have brakes!'

'I felt it when he hit the car,' says Carrie. 'The car kind of rocked. Mum –' she starts to cry again – 'what if he dies?'

'It's not your fault, darling. It just isn't.'

They drive over the Downs, past the building site for the new stadium, to the Woodingdean crossroads. Here the traffic tails back, waiting for the lights to change. Laura keeps Carrie's hand in hers. Ahead the land swoops down in curving folds to the straight line of the sea, and Carrie's hand shivers in hers. Then they're moving again, past the dummy fisherman in his yellow trawler coat on the roof of the Woodingdean Fish Shop, and Carrie's holding her breath, thinking the boy's going to die.

Into Brighton over the racecourse.

'Parking at the hospital's a joke,' says Terry. 'Both our kiddies were born here. Julie can push 'em out faster than I can find a parking space.'

'Carrie was born here too,' says Laura. 'Weren't you, darling?'

Terry drives right up to A&E like he's an ambulance.

'You go in,' he says. 'I'll park and come and find you.'

'No, go home now, Terry,' says Laura. 'We can get a taxi back.'

'Have to go back the same way as you,' says Terry. 'Might as well wait.'

'You're being amazing,' says Laura.

'Got to look out for each other, haven't we?' says Terry.

Laura and Carrie and Toby go through the automatic sliding glass doors into A&E. There's a reception window with a receptionist talking on the phone. She comes off the phone and Laura tells her about the accident.

'Are you next of kin?' she says.

'My daughter was in the accident. She was driving the car the boy hit.'

'So she's not next of kin?'

'No, but she's terribly worried. She just wants to know how the boy is.'

'Do you know the name of the boy?'

'No.'

The receptionist looks at them blankly.

'Can't help, can I?' she says.

'All we want to know is that he's – well, all right. He must have only just been brought in. Maybe half an hour ago at the most. From Lewes, a boy of eleven or twelve. Couldn't you ask someone?'

'Can't do that,' says the receptionist. 'It's patient confidentiality, see?'

She looks past them to the people waiting behind.

Carrie goes to the window, speaks in a whisper.

'I just want to know I've not killed him,' she says.

'Sorry,' says the receptionist.

The people behind cough and murmur. They move away from the window.

'There's a waiting room through there,' Toby says. 'Sit down and I'll get us all a cup of coffee.'

The waiting room has lavender walls and mauve chairs and a big mural on one wall, of dolphins. There's a hot-drinks machine and a sign pointing to the WRVS Coffee Shop.

'I'll go to the coffee shop,' says Toby. 'It'll be better coffee.'

A middle-aged woman is waiting with her husband. She has a heavily bandaged hand held up above her head, as if she's hailing a taxi. She sighs and groans and says to her husband, 'Tell the nurse it's still coming through.' Catching Laura's eye she says, 'Won't stop bleeding.'

Terry now rejoins them.

'It's a joke, that car park,' he says.

'They won't tell us anything,' says Laura. 'We're having a hot drink. Then we might as well get home.'

'He'll be through there,' says Terry, pointing down the corridor. 'You could walk in. No one's going to stop you.'

As he speaks a large woman with a shock of black hair appears from the wards and heads across the reception area to the exit. Terry sees her.

'Hey, Sheena!'

'Terry?' she says. 'Oh, Terry! My Chipper's hurt so bad.'

'Chipper!'

'Only nearly killed himself on his bike, hasn't he?' Her face contorts with pain. 'Christ knows, I told him often enough.'

Terry points to Carrie.

'She was driving the car,' he says. 'She's come because she was so worried about him.'

The woman stares at Carrie in confusion. 'You was in the car?'

'How is he?' says Carrie. 'Is he going to be all right?'

'Only broken three ribs and fractured his pelvis, hasn't he? If he had any brains he might have knocked them out too.'

'So he's not – I mean, he's not . . .'

The boy's mother sees the anguish in Carrie's eyes and she's moved. She goes to Carrie and takes her hand.

'He's not going to die, love. You mustn't blame yourself. The police told me, he was way out of control.' Carrie starts to cry.

'Oh, aren't you a love! But he's my boy, see. He's a bloody idiot, but he's my baby boy. And he's a good kid, too, in his way.'

'I thought I'd killed him.'

'No, no. You never. He's going to be in hospital a few weeks. Six months he'll be as good as new. That's what they're telling me. Good as new. And maybe better. Maybe not such a fool any more. That's what I'm hoping.'

Laura is staring at the boy's mother's hand. She wears a ruby ring on the fourth finger of her left hand.

'Listen, I'm dying for a smoke,' she says. 'That's why I come out.'

She looks at Laura, sensing her close attention.

'Gave up years ago, didn't I? But a shock like this and it's back on the old fags.'

'So he's going to be all right?' says Laura.

'That's what they're telling me. They got him all pumped up with morphine for now.'

'We're so, so sorry,' says Laura.

She's thinking how she'd feel if it was Jack. Or Carrie.

'Good of you to come,' says the boy's mother. 'Decent of you. Shows there are still good people in the world. Though God knows what you're doing with this tosser.'

She gives a tired grin at Terry.

'Terry brought us over in his car,' says Laura. 'He's one of the good people.'

'He's all right, is Tel. Gotta get my nicotine now.'

She goes out through the double set of doors to the open air.

Toby reappears with a cardboard tray on which he carries four cardboard cups of coffee. He hands out the coffees.

'Sugar, Terry? I thought you'd be one for sugar.'

'We met the boy's mum,' Carrie tells him. 'The boy on the bike. He's going to be all right.'

'That's great.'

'He's broken his ribs and his pelvis. But he's going to be all right.'

'And you were so sure you'd killed him.'

'It was the way he just lay there, not moving.' She shivers. 'It was so horrible.'

They all drink their coffee.

'She's a friend of Terry's,' says Laura.

'Sheena,' says Terry. 'Friend of my Julie's.'

'She's got my ring,' says Laura.

They don't understand.

'What do you mean, Mum?' says Carrie.

'I'd know it anywhere. She's wearing my ring.'

'But that's impossible.'

'I know.'

'She can't have your ring. It must be one that looks like it. She just can't.'

'It's my ring. It'll have our initials inside. You look.'

'How can I look? Mum, I nearly killed her son. I can't go up to her and say, Where did you get that ring?'

'I know,' says Laura.

She feels a little sick, the kind of sick you feel when you lose a clear sense of up and down. Nothing makes any sense. But she knows her own ring. That's for sure.

Terry gets up and starts pacing the bleak reception area, swinging his muscular arms. He goes over to stare at the dolphins.

Toby puts down his cup of coffee, half drunk.

'Where is she now?' he says.

'Outside,' says Laura. 'Having a cigarette.'

Toby gets up.

'I'll have a word with her.'

'Toby,' says Carrie. 'Her boy's all smashed up.'

'I know how to do this,' says Toby. 'You wait here.'

And they do. He speaks with such quiet confidence that they almost believe he has some magic power. And no one else has a better idea.

He goes out through the glass doors and there's a line of ambulances, a police car. And over to the right there's a low wall topped by a green metal-mesh fence. Here's Sheena, in the afternoon sunshine, standing by a 'No Smoking Anywhere On The Premises' sign, smoking.

Toby goes over to her side and looks through the mesh at the view. Sunlit rooftops, a school playground, the top of a thin church spire. The great sea beyond.

'Spare a ciggie?' says Toby.

'Sure,' she says.

She gives him her little book of matches so he can light up.

'Not allowed,' he says, pointing at the sign.

'It's outside,' she says. 'It's fresh air.'

'Hey, if we're going to get lung cancer we're in the right place.'

'I ain't getting no cancer,' says Sheena. 'Two fags don't give you cancer.'

'You know what cancer is?' says Toby. 'It's your body turning on itself.'

'Is that right?'

'Like one part of your body wants to destroy the other part.'

'Why'd it want to do that?'

'I'll tell you why,' says Toby. 'You know how we've all got a survival instinct? How we fight to stay alive?'

'Most of us,' says Sheena.

'Well, we've got a self-destruction instinct too. We want to stay alive and we want to die.'

'I got a boy with a self-destruction instinct. He's in there now with a broken pelvis.'

'We all do crazy things,' says Toby. 'Depending on which instinct's doing the driving.'

'You're right there. Sometimes you look at what someone does and you say, What's that about? That's going to do him in. But he still goes on and does it.'

'Simple rule in life,' Toby says. 'People do what they want to do. If they want to destroy themselves, they'll find a way.'

'They do that,' says Sheena.

Gulls wheel overhead, shrilling their sad cry.

'Can I tell you a story?' says Toby.

'It's a free country,' she says.

'It's a love story,' he says. 'It's about this woman who met this guy, and they fell in love and they decided to get married. He bought her a ring, a gold ring with a ruby on it. He gave it to her, and he told her, Every time you look at this ring you're to remember I love you for ever. On the inside of the ring they had their initials engraved. Hers was L. His was H. She wore that ring every day for twenty-seven years. Then one day she lost it, and it was like she'd lost her love. That was yesterday. She looked everywhere for it, but she couldn't find it. So I said to her — you see, I'm in this story too — I said to her, Don't worry, you've dropped it by mistake. Someone will find it. They might even give it to someone else. But as soon as they know who it belongs to, they'll give it back. They're keeping it safe for you, until they find the owner. They know how a ring can mean so much. They know it means love for ever.'

Sheena stands motionless, silent. Then, slowly, she slides the ring off her finger. She turns it over and looks inside and sees the letters engraved there.

'It's a beautiful ring,' she says.

'Lucky someone found it,' Toby says.

She hands the ring to him.

'Just a mistake,' she says.

'Anyone can make a mistake,' says Toby.

Sheena takes out another cigarette and she's about to light up when abruptly she puts it away.

'Self-destruction instinct, right?'

'We've all got it.'

'Better go and see to my boy.'

She goes back into the hospital. She passes through the reception area without a word, eyes down. Toby follows.

He gives Laura the ring.

'Oh, Toby!'

Laura is astonished, blinking back tears. She puts the ring onto her finger. Carrie stares at Toby.

'What did you do to her?'

'Nothing. Just told her a story.'

Laura bows her head. She's filled with an emotion she doesn't know how to share.

'Did you make her feel bad?' says Carrie.

'No. It was just a mistake.'

Laura draws a deep breath.

'I'll never understand,' she says.

She too gets up.

'Come on, darling. Let's go home. We've kept Terry long enough.'

Terry nods at the mural of dolphins.

'I saw a programme about dolphins,' he says. 'If they see a shark attacking a swimmer, they make a ring round him to protect him.'

They make their way back through the hospital, up the long sloping lavender passages, to the multi-storey car park. Terry leads, with Laura. Carrie and Toby follow behind.

'So what was this story?' asks Carrie.

'It was a love story,' says Toby.

'Oh, right. You being the expert on love.'

37

What is it about donkeys? You don't hear of tortoise sanctuaries, or budgie sanctuaries. Go easy on the cynicism, says Mark. Don't get too clever with it. Donkeys are lovable. Five hundred words that tell us something we don't know, and leave a good feeling behind.

Pulling the car back into the yard, parking by the cart lodge that was supposed to be converted into Alan's study, Liz feels a further wave of irritation, this time at the council pixie who came and made eyes at Alan and told them their plans would *alter the character of the building*. Then she feels angry at Alan, for giving up on things at the first sign of opposition. Then she feels angry at her mother for everything. And finally she feels angry at herself for being angry all the time.

She finds Alan and Cas in the living room with the curtains drawn, watching a DVD.

'For God's sake,' she says. 'It's summer, the sun is shining. What are you doing in the dark?'

Alan comes out to join her in the kitchen, where she's getting herself an angry drink.

'It's *Babe*,' he says. 'The talking-pig film. I'm watching it for work.'

'Fine. It's work. Whatever you say. Did my mother call?'

'No. No one called.'

People don't call these days. It's all emails. She drinks wine, avoiding meeting Alan's eyes.

'We went over to the shoot,' he says. 'I met the new writer. His first words to me were, I'm the jerk who's fucking up your story.'

Liz doesn't want to hear any more about Alan's problems. She wants to unload her own frustrations.

'Good for you.'

She sees him blink as if she's smacked him. She takes a long breath. Lighten up, for Christ's sake.

'No, I mean it. It's good that you went.'

He sees she's trying, so he tries too.

'How were the donkeys?'

'What is the point of a donkey? Can someone tell me that? Why does everyone love donkeys? Is it because of Winnie the Pooh?'

Let the donkeys take the heat.

'Or Jesus,' says Alan.

'Jesus? What's Jesus got to do with it?'

'He rode into Jerusalem on a donkey. That's supposed to be why they have a cross on their backs.'

'So is that it? It's a Christian thing?'

Now Alan is helping himself to some wine too. Liz fishes in her bag for her MP3 sound recorder, which holds her talk with the owners of the donkey sanctuary.

'If you ask me,' says Alan, 'I think it's something to do with the way they look. You look at a donkey and you think, that donkey is unhappy. I can help that donkey. Actually the donkey may be fine, but that's the way you react to it. And that makes you feel good. It's that Marilyn Monroe look. The Princess Di look. I'm so fragile and only you can understand me. That's what donkeys do. Only without the sexiness.'

Liz gazes at Alan as he stands leaning against the sink, glass in hand. She's starting to feel better. She likes it when Alan says strange things with a straight face. She likes it that he's got a funny-peculiar mind.

'You're cheering up,' she says. Meaning that she's cheering up.

'Is any of that any use to you?'

'Donkeys look like Princess Di? Why not?'

She can hear the sounds of the television coming down the passage. Pulls the kitchen door closed, just in case.

'Come and give me a kiss. I'm so wound up.'

He takes her in his arms. They kiss.

'I'm turning into a bitchy wife, aren't I?'

'Yes,' he says, kissing her.

'You'd rather have that snitty little planning officer any day.'

'Any night,' he says.

His hands on her bum, pulling her closer.

'What would you do with her?'

This is a game they like to play, but not usually in the kitchen. Liz realises to her surprise that she's aroused.

'I'd put my hand up her skirt,' says Alan, putting his hand up her skirt.

'Why would you want to do that?'

'So I could feel her knickers. Get my fingers into her knickers.'

His cock hardening in his jeans as he presses against her. His fingers feeling between her parted thighs.

'Doesn't she mind you doing that?'

'She loves it. She wants me to fuck her.'

'She wants you to fuck her?'

Such a simple foolish game, playing that his desire is for another woman, even as his hand is between her legs. Why does it excite me so much? If he really was doing it with another woman I'd want to die.

'She wants to unzip my jeans and take out my hard cock.'

'And you want her to.'

'I want to fuck her.'

She has her hands on his crotch, feeling the hard ridge. The phone rings.

'Let it ring,' says Alan. 'You're not to move.'

So she stays there, pressing against him, warm with wine and melted anger and desire. Bridget's voice comes through on the answerphone.

'I'm with Mrs D now,' she says. 'Everything's fine. We've had a few little problems, but everything's fine now. That's right, isn't it, Mrs D? Just telling your daughter that everything's fine.'

The phone voice falls silent.

'See?' says Alan, kissing her neck. 'Everything's fine.'

'No, it isn't,' says Liz.

'You heard her. She said it three times.'

'Two times too many. And anyway, we can't. Cas could walk in any minute.'

Alan sighs and lets her go.

'You're right,' he says.

'I'll have to go over there.'

'Oh, Liz. That's the last thing you need.'

In a way it's a relief. The thought of her mother has been hanging over her since she walked out on Tuesday. Now, suddenly, she's impatient to be with her again. It's too wearing, the low level of anxiety and guilt. She can work on the donkey piece later.

'I shouldn't be long. Thank God for Bridget.'

'So I go back to watching my movie.'

'Which is work.'

'Actually it's a really good film.'

'Lucky you.'

She gives him a long kiss.

'We fuck later, right?' he says.

'It's a date.'

Back outside to reverse the car in the yard. She thinks of the way the snitty little planning officer stood there parroting her *regulations* and her *original footprints*. Then she thinks of Alan's hand between her thighs, and how it's her body and not the pixie body of the snitty little planning officer, and that makes everything much better.

Turning off the Brighton Road into Houndean Rise gives her the old shaky feeling. This is yet another of her many charges against her mother, that she has gone on living in the family house, and so as her own once-blazing light has faded, the shadows have reached out and darkened the memories of the past. Not that the past was all that great, but childhood is childhood, you make your zone of safety where you find it, and here is the kitchen that fed her, the garden that changed with the seasons, the bedroom that lulled her to sleep. All now overlaid by the spectre of an unhappy old woman who wants more from her than she is able to give.

How do you know what's right? How much do I owe my own mother? Where does the guilt end?

The porch has never changed. The oak door which she now knows is twenties repro, but which always seemed to her to have existed forever. The black iron ring gripped by an iron fist that was the knocker. Not fair to steal my childhood and substitute for it the miserable indignity of old age. Because face it, this is what's coming my way too. My body will decay, my friends will die, and I'll be on the phone to Alice, to Cas, and they'll groan and put off other things they'd rather be doing and climb into a car to do their duty.

Her mother is sitting in her usual chair by the window in the kitchen. Bridget is on her knees with a brush, brushing under the table. Her mother looks up and meets Liz's enquiring gaze with a look that is uncharacteristically dulled. Something has changed.

'How are you, Mum?'

Her mother shakes her head and points to the table. Bridget crawls out from under the table, dustpan clinking.

'Had a few little accidents,' she says, 'but we're all fine now.'

Mrs Dickinson continues to point to the table. There stands a tray covered by a tea towel. There's something underneath.

'She wouldn't let me deal with it,' says Bridget. 'Wanted you to see. What's the use? I said, but that's what she wants.' She raises her voice. 'You want her to see, don't you, Mrs D?'

Mrs Dickinson nods her head.

Liz lifts the tea towel. A guinea pig lies on the tray, unblemished, dead.

'How did that happen?'

'I killed her,' says her mother.

'No, you didn't, Mrs D,' says Bridget. 'We've been over all that. Guinea pigs grow old and die like all the rest of us.'

'I am sorry, Mum,' says Liz. 'I think we should bury her now, don't you?'

Her mother nods, but she doesn't seem much interested. Liz picks up the tray.

'Bridget can help me.'

She wants the chance to talk to Bridget alone. Outside in the garden she takes a trowel and digs a hole in the rose border, where Perry was buried.

'I came in this morning,' Bridget says. 'I was that worried. You wouldn't believe the state she got herself into. The mess in the bathroom! I don't think she's eaten for days. She was in this filthy nightdress, her hair I don't know how. Oh, Bridget, she says when I come in, Don't ever leave me again.'

'Oh, Lord,' exclaims Liz as she digs.

'You'd never believe the state of the place! I've been here ever since, cleaning up, putting things right. I gave her a wash and got her dressed, and she's had some lunch, I did her a shepherd's pie. Then I changed her bed and I've put in a clothes wash. But she wouldn't let me touch the guinea pig.'

'You are wonderful, Bridget.'

'Well, I couldn't leave her, could I? Whatever she says she wants. But I come in through the door and she says, Oh Bridget, don't ever leave me again.'

Liz can feel it, the enormous, almost gluttonous satisfaction this gives Bridget. She has proved her worth. She's needed after all.

'You'll have to tell me how many extra hours you've put in.'

'Oh, don't mind about that. I had two days off, remember? But I'm back on the job now. I never let anything beat me. That's not my way.'

The hole in the earth is ready. Liz lowers the guinea pig gently into the shallow grave, just as she did as a child when they found a dead bird or a mouse. You can't put animals in the dustbin. She and her friend Marianne once arranged a complete funeral service, with candles and made-up prayers. That would've been here, in this same garden, while her mother was in the kitchen preparing their supper.

She trowels the earth back over the guinea pig's body, and pats the mound down to settle it.

'Rest in peace,' she says. 'Off you go to guinea-pig heaven.' Then, to Bridget, 'Did she tell you how the guinea pig died?'

'She's in one of her muddles, your mum is. Doesn't know

what she's saying. But our Kylie had guinea pigs and they was forever showing up dead. Great ones for dying, are guinea pigs.'

Liz stands up a little too quickly, and for a moment the garden round her turns into a blur. In that moment she is pierced by a memory of shocking clarity. She's in her bedroom, standing looking out over the garden, this garden, and she's saying to herself, *I will get away from here*. Like a prisoner serving a life sentence. It's a promise to herself, an order. *I will get away from here*.

How old was I then? Fourteen? I couldn't bear it even then. I've been fleeing my mother's unhappiness all my life.

Different images collide, one triggering the next. Guy's face when she told him she was pregnant, the way he said, 'What are you going to do?' Not *we*, just *you*. Not a muscle in his face moved, but he was smiling beneath the skin, unable to conceal how well this suited him, because now he could make the break he had been too idle to achieve before. Then there came the memory of her mother's face when she told her she was having a baby, but she and Guy wouldn't be together any more. There was the same buried smile, masked by various layers of conventional shock and conventional concern, her mother comforted to know that Liz would now lead the life she had led, of loneliness and struggle. And here's Bridget, putting on the double face, finding validation for her own place in the world as she discovers Mrs Dickinson in a filthy nightdress and her hair in disarray. So we feed on each other's unhappiness, our faces assuming the same expression, a compound of pity, relief, and triumph.

Liz returns to the house to sit with her mother. She needs to confirm that some version of normality has been re-established, that Bridget will be allowed to go on doing her job.

'I hear you've had some problems, Mum.'

Mrs Dickinson gazes at her as if she doesn't hear her.

'Never mind. Bridget's got everything cleaned up now.'

Still no response. This is not like her mother. But perhaps the two days she spent coping on her own have exhausted her.

'I buried the guinea pig,' Liz says. 'I said a little prayer.'

'I killed her,' says Mrs Dickinson. She says it as a statement of fact, unburdened by any emotion.

'I'm sure you didn't, Mum,' says Liz. 'Why would you do that?'

'Because I kill everything.'

'Oh, honestly. Don't be so silly.'

She understands her mother's crushed manner now. This is self-punishment. Liz feels the anger rise within her. Why must her mother turn everything into a tragedy? There's as much egotism in casting herself as the murderer as there is in playing her more usual role, the victim.

'I do,' says Mrs Dickinson. 'I kill everything that comes near me. So you'd better not come near me.'

'That's just nonsense, Mum, and you know it.'

Her mother gently raises her shoulders and let them fall. Her head droops.

'I'm sure you know best, Elizabeth.'

Liz is overwhelmed by the desire to be spiteful. She knows of no honourable way to escape the chill embrace of her mother's neediness. But if she speaks unkind words before she leaves she will leave a part of herself in her mother's kitchen, as a bee leaves behind its sting.

'So are things a bit easier now with Bridget, Mum? She's turned out to be quite useful, hasn't she?'

Her mother answers this, but in such a low mumble that Liz doesn't catch her words.

'So you're happy for Bridget to go on coming?'

'She's won,' says Mrs Dickinson.

'What do you mean, she's won? It's not a competition. It's not a fight. She's here to help you.'

Once again her mother lifts her shoulders and lets them fall.

'Tell me what more you want, Mum. If there's anything I can do, you just tell me.'

Her mother looks up at that, and meets Liz's eyes with a gaze of such profound and inconsolable misery that Liz flinches. For once, shorn of pride and anger, her mother allows her to see how helpless she is, how lonely, how afraid. It's more than Liz can take, far more. She looks away towards the bathroom, where Bridget can be heard washing the floor round the toilet.

'Would you rather I tried to find someone else other than Bridget?'

Mrs Dickinson does not answer.

'It's just not easy getting good carers. The thing about Bridget is she's so reliable. I mean, look how she came back, even though you'd told her to go away.'

All this without looking at her mother. But it's true: reliable carers are hard to find. Bridget is a treasure. It would be madness to replace her.

'Mum, I'm going to have to go. I have to write a piece about donkeys by eight o'clock.'

She bends down to kiss her mother's crumpled cheek.

'I called you,' says Mrs Dickinson. 'Your phone is broken.'

'No, it isn't. You know we've got a new number. I gave you the new number when we moved.'

She takes up her mother's address book and finds there the old address and the old number, unchanged. She writes in the new details.

'There. You'll find that number works. I wondered why you

hadn't called. And if we're out, just leave a message. Or you can get Bridget to give me a call. She'll be in every day.'

No response to that.

'I know it's not perfect, Mum. But it works, doesn't it?'

'If you say so, Elizabeth.'

'So let's be thankful for that.'

'Yes,' says her mother bitterly. 'Thank you. Thank you for everything. Bridget is wonderful. Everything is wonderful.'

38

Tomorrow! One more day!

Worth Abbey turns out to be undergoing a restoration. Roddy refuses to be dismayed. Is he too not about to be restored? The taxi from Balcombe station delivers him to what appears to be a building site. An immense scaffolding tower rises up from a small village of Portakabins clustering round the skirts of the abbey church. This structure, built in the seventies out of beige-coloured brick, is circular rather than the traditional cruciform, and has a roof shaped like a flattened cone. Theatre in the round, once a modern approach to drama, now itself a period piece.

He makes his way to the entrance to the church, and finds himself in a long passage-like space called the Narthex. Here for the duration of the restoration works the larger religious services are held. Roddy has come for one of the humblest services, the sung office called Compline, with which the monks' day ends.

Lord, now lettest thou thy servant depart in peace according to thy word, for mine eyes have seen thy salvation.

This, the famous 'Nunc Dimittis', the Canticle of Simeon, is the heart of Compline. As the day ends and we release ourselves into the night that is also our death, we pray to be allowed to go in peace. Roddy is not a believer, or at least not an orthodox believer, but these words cast a spell over him. Simeon speaks them as he beholds the infant Jesus, and is reconciled to death. But departure takes many forms, as does salvation. Roddy too is on the eve of a journey.

A man in a red polo shirt and faded jeans appears, and busies himself with some electrical cables that run from the altar microphone. Roddy asks him what time Compline will be sung.

'Compline?' He seems puzzled.

'The monks have a little service at the end of the day?' suggests Roddy.

'Oh,' says the man, 'you mean Night Prayer. That'll be in the Unity Room. Round on the east side.'

Roddy leaves the Narthex and walks round the church, past the builders yard, as far as a gate on which is painted: Monastery, Private. Beyond the gate lies a wide, peaceful, uninhabited valley. He can see no sign of the Unity Room. The name irritates him. Unity of who, with what? This passion for all to be one, this urge to merge, strikes him as adolescent, the rhetoric of football teams and army regiments. 'We're all in this together, lads!' We are not all in this together, he thinks fiercely to himself. I am not like you. As for Christian unity, you either have convictions or you don't. The Catholic Church he admires is the self-confident monolith that calls itself universal. This late twentieth-century nervous relativism is undignified. All faiths are not one. Religion makes demands. What you believe should change how you live. Salvation can only be reached through sacrifice.

So muses Roddy, as yet unaffiliated to any church, while nosing around the scaffolding and the stacks of cement blocks and the skips for the way to the Unity Room. He finds it at last, its glass door locked, a sign on the inside saying: Night Prayer 9 p.m. He has half an hour or so to wait.

He wanders the grounds, which seem to consist largely of car parks, and so comes upon a sign that reads: Quiet Garden.

He passes through a wooden picket gate into a long narrow strip of grass bounded by a clipped yew hedge. A gap in the hedge, over which droops a long-leafed acacia tree, leads into a series of hedge-walled lawns, each with an island tree. To the south lies the immense pastoral landscape, which because it was barred by a gate saying: Monastery, Private, he likes to imagine as the paradise of the monks.

Roddy has made this trip in part to create a pretext. His true motive is to install himself in the Broads' comfortable Sussex house the night before Diana joins him there. But now that he's here in the monastery grounds with time to meditate, he's glad of the opportunity. He strolls through the beech-walled rooms of the Quiet Garden gazing at the golden evening sky, and sees there the coming apocalypse. Because his own life journey is carrying him towards an explosive rebirth – tomorrow! One more day! – he responds to all that is revolutionary in the Christian message.

Suppose ye that I am come to give peace on earth? I tell you, nay: but rather division.

The search for God is not a nostalgic reversion to a past age. It's a shattering of the vanities. Come face to face with the blazing heart of truth and nothing can ever be the same again.

This Laura knows.

'You're really going on adventures, aren't you, Roddy?'

He heard it in her voice when she said that: she wants to share the journey. She feels it as he feels it, the tingling in the air, the shining in the sky. This is the dawn of a new age.

'Laura.'

Alone in the Quiet Garden he speaks her name out loud, wanting to make her real. He feels an overwhelming compulsion to talk about her, to tell his story to some third party; but there is no one.

Father, into thy hands I commend my spirit.

Surprising how much of his half-hearted public-school Christian education has stuck. Or perhaps it's the culture, a grab-bag of resonant phrases that float to the surface of the mind in the manner of a T.S. Eliot poem. What was Eliot's original title for 'The Waste Land'? Something jokey but not funny. 'He Do the Police in Different Voices'. Ezra Pound put a stop to that nonsense. But Eliot understood that the big moments in life require big words. Lacking grandeur in our impoverished modern age we raid prestige from the past. Doesn't have to be religious, of course. Anything planted deep enough will do.

Ah, love, let us be true
To one another!

So interweaving the love of God with the love of Laura, Roddy strolls the monastery lawns, and the summer sun descends over the woods and meadows. He will stay for Night Prayer, as they choose to call it, then phone for a taxi to carry him to Edenfield.

A distant bell rings, signalling the approach of the hour. At almost the same moment his phone buzzes. It's Henry, at Haywards Heath station, offering him a lift.

'Laura told me you're at Worth, and coming to us for the night.'

'Isn't it horribly out of your way? I was going to get a taxi.'

'No problem,' says Henry. 'I can be with you in twenty minutes.'

This is just the time it will take to attend Compline. They arrange to meet in the car park. Roddy hurries to the Unity Room. The glass door is now open and inside the monks have already gathered, a dozen or so of them, taking the chairs that line three walls of the large space. On the fourth side stand three rows of maroon upright chairs for visitors. Roddy sits quietly at the back.

The room is bleak: brown brick walls support a high tray roof of steel girders and timber cladding. Lights in the shape of flying saucers hang down. In the centre of the space a patterned carpet forms an island bearing a lectern and six immense candles. The monks sing the psalms briskly, as if this is business to be done. Roddy settles his mind for prayer, but finds instead that all he can think about is Laura.

He's decided the words he's going to say and how he's going to say them. He'll choose a moment when they're alone. He'll touch her hand — touch is important, this is the contact that once made will never be broken — and she'll look at him. The look is even more important. The look will be their mutual admission. So after the touch, after the look, the first words he speaks will not be the first communication. They will enter mid-conversation. He will say, 'What are we going to do?' This claims nothing but declares everything. Her answer is not important. She may say, 'There's nothing we can do.' He's ready for that. Tomorrow is the beginning of his new life, but for a while the new life will have to remain hidden within the shell of the old. There's no hurry.

She'll be afraid. She'll be less ready than he is to cause pain to others. There'll be long hours of talk. But in the end she'll come to see what he has seen. It's no kindness to live a lie. Our partners are trapped, as we are, in false lives. Our act of love will set them free.

He hears the scraping of chairs and realises with a start that the short service of prayer has ended and the monks are leaving. Somehow he managed to miss the 'Nunc Dimittis' entirely. Roddy follows, and finds that outside night has fallen.

He walks slowly up the slope towards the car park, wondering what it must be like to be a monk. The black robe they wear, that falls to mid-ankle, is both comical and magnificent. Such a dress must change a man. Roddy imagines putting on a monk's habit, and appearing in it before his family. They would laugh, but they would also be afraid. A man who dresses like that is beyond the reach of scorn or shame.

A dazzle of headlights approaches. Henry's voice calls out.

'Here you are! Hop in.'

The odd thing is Roddy really likes Henry. Though maybe it's not so odd, since presumably Laura likes him too. Henry is one of the few people with whom he's ever been able to have a proper conversation.

'So what's this all about?' says Henry as he swings the car round the one-way system past the school buildings. 'Laura says you've been in search of silence.'

'Yes,' says Roddy. 'Change of pace, and so forth.'

'So did you find it?'

He heads out of the grounds onto the long straight road.

'Silence turns out to be quite hard to get,' says Roddy. 'I suppose I need more practice. My brain won't shut up.'

'I go on walks,' says Henry. 'High up on the Downs. Best of all where you see the Downs with the sea beyond. I find that shuts me up.'

It strikes Roddy that this is a late hour to be returning home.

'Are you usually so late getting back?'

'I've been having meetings about a possible new job. Nothing very conclusive. I'm not even sure I want it. But something is better than nothing, I suppose.'

This is all the prompting Roddy needs.

'That's not necessarily true,' he says. 'If you're trapped in the wrong something, it may be better to go for nothing.'

'But I'm not ready to pack it in yet, any more than you are. I'm only fifty-four.'

'I'm not talking about packing it in,' says Roddy. 'I'm talking about changing your life. One life ends, another life begins.'

He's discovering as he speaks that he has a powerful compulsion to tell his brother-in-law everything. Of course he mustn't, he won't, do anything of the sort. But there's a thrilling frisson of danger as he skirts the edges of revelation.

'Oh, yes, I remember now,' Henry says. 'Apparently you're looking for God.'

'That's Diana. She only understands words of one syllable.' Henry gives a gratifying snort of laughter at that. 'I don't have a name for what I'm looking for. All I know is there's more to life than I've been getting.'

Henry says, 'There could be less, you know.'

'How do you mean?'

'I'm becoming a bit of a fan of humility. Did Diana tell you we went to a Buckingham Palace garden party yesterday?'

'No. I had no idea.'

They're driving down a tree-lined road. Henry's gaze is on the beam of his headlights, dipping and undipping as cars approach and pass.

'It was quite a revelation for me. Not so much the royal side of things, though that was actually rather impressive in its way. It was the other guests. It's a very odd experience being at a party where no one knows anyone else. You realise then that your life consists of meeting people in cliques, and that all the time you're busy calculating, Am I in this group or not? Do they respect me or despise me? What do I have to do to win their approval? When you all meet as individuals, something quite different happens. You engage with strangers on their own terms. I suppose it's a bit like being in some faraway unpopulated land. Anyone you meet is automatically your friend, because there's no one else. Plus, of course, everyone who's been invited to the garden party is tremendously proud to be there, which creates a bond. So we got talking to various people, and somehow it made me feel how much goodwill there is in the world, and how we so arrange things that most of the time we never see it. I don't suppose I'm making much sense. Actually it felt like a revelation. It was like seeing a different possible version of the world. One in which people actually want to make each other happy.'

Roddy is not interested in the dynamics of a royal garden party, but he seizes on this last suggestion.

'There is a different version of the world in which we can be happy,' he says. 'I'm sure of it. But to find it we must allow ourselves to seek happiness. Most people are too afraid to seek their own happiness.'

'Do you think so?' says Henry. 'Isn't that rather perverse? I mean, why would anyone not go for what makes them happy?'

He isn't disagreeing, Roddy can hear it in his voice. He's exploring.

'Because we're afraid of hurting others,' Roddy says.

'Maybe happiness isn't after all our primary need.' Henry pursues his own unfolding thoughts. 'Maybe our primary need is respect. The need to be validated by others. And to achieve that we'll do things that may well bring us misery and suffering, even death. Look at the martyrs. Look at the suicide bombers.'

This isn't quite where Roddy wants to go.

'But why is it,' he says, 'that so many people accept a life they know won't make them happy? Why do they endure what is really only half a life?'

'It's what you say,' says Henry. 'It's fear. Why haven't I sat down and written the book I've been wanting to write all my life? Fear. I'd rather do a good job I half-like than write a bad book. And I know what you say to that. You say, How do you know it'll be a bad book if you don't try? Of course, I don't know. But I do know I don't want to be one of those sad types who followed their dream, and the dream died on them, and now they're full of envy and self-hatred.'

On the main road south he kicks down on the accelerator.

'Won't be long now.'

'You say you'd rather do a good job you half-like,' says Roddy. 'Would you choose to live a *life* you half-like? Because I think that's the real question. I'm just a couple of years older than you, Henry, and I totally agree with you, I'm not ready to pack it in. But on the other hand, I have to face the fact that I have a limited time left. I can't put a number on it, but if you count the years I'm likely to stay physically fit, you're talking about twenty-five at the most. So the question becomes, do you live those twenty-five years fully, or do you go on half-living?'

'That's what I mean by humility,' says Henry. 'If we can only get past this bloody status competition that makes us all do everything in our power to intimidate each other, then we can start to actually enjoy each other's company.'

'I'm talking about love,' says Roddy, making a determined bid to control the conversation.

'Well, yes, I suppose I am too,' says Henry. 'You could say love is the acceptance of another person as he is, and status competition is the use of another person as an instrument to boost self-esteem.'

'No, I mean love between a man and a woman.'

'Oh,' says Henry, surprised. 'Okay.'

'The love between a man and a woman is, I believe, the core energy of the universe. It's the prime act of creation. Of course, there's sex. But I go further. I believe we are made to exist in balance with a lover of the opposite sex, and without that we live only half-lives. Tolstoy believed this. Dickens believed this.'

Roddy does not elaborate, but both Tolstoy and Dickens, trapped in loveless marriages, fell in love with their wives' sisters. It was practically the norm in Victorian times, to find you'd married the wrong sister. They even had a law forbidding subsequent marriage to the wife's sister if the wife died, they were so afraid of husbands in this predicament committing murder. Henry is a historian, he'd know all about that. However, Roddy does not think it appropriate to speak of the Deceased Wife's Sister Act this evening.

Predictably Henry finds Roddy's theories comic, because Roddy himself does not conform to the stereotype of the lover.

'I don't know what to say, Roddy. You turn out to be a closet romantic.'

'There, you see. You want to laugh at me. But I know I'm right.'

'No, no, I'm not laughing at you at all. I'm just caught off-guard. You're the last person . . . I suppose it's just not the picture I've had up to now of you and Diana.'

'Who said anything about Diana?'

Henry drives in silence for a few moments. Roddy feels his heart beating. The closer he gets to confession, the more excited he becomes.

'So what are you saying, Roddy?'

'Probably I'm jumping the gun a bit,' says Roddy. 'It doesn't do to force things. I just decided some time ago to stop struggling against life. I decided to let it carry me the way it wants to go. But I can tell you that there are big changes on the way.'

'Big changes. Right. I'm not sure I should know any more.'

But Roddy presses on, doggedly pursuing his goal.

'I've realised recently it's not about right and wrong. That's part of the ego world, in which we imagine that we're in control. But once you see how it really is, once you let the ego die, then the stream takes you where it wills. That's when you become free. And of course I need hardly add, only a free man has the capacity to love.'

'Let the ego die,' says Henry. 'I think that may be what I mean by humility. But the stream – I'm not sure what this stream is. Is it God?'

Roddy shakes his head irritably. He doesn't want to talk about God.

'God is only a name. Let's say there's a force that governs all things. You might as well call it love. Though love is also intensely personal. Love presents itself in our life in the form of individual human beings.'

'I think you're losing me again,' says Henry. 'This is all getting a little too cosmic for me.'

'But it's not cosmic at all,' says Roddy, frustrated. 'There's nothing cosmic about a man loving a woman. Well, maybe there is, but you've still got a real flesh-and-blood basis for it. This man sitting in one armchair, this woman sitting in another armchair. A fire burning in the grate. A cold winter landscape outside the window.'

'What?'

Roddy realises he's overstepped the mark.

'Just an image.'

'Where do armchairs come in?'

'Don't worry about it. All I mean is, love comes down to Person A and Person B, in a real time, in a real place. And all we can do about that is say yes or no. Maybe not even that.'

'You know what you are, Roddy? You're a fatalist.'

'Or a man in love.'

Henry hesitates. 'Better not tell me anything you don't want Laura to know. I'm not good at keeping things from her.'

'Laura'll know soon enough,' says Roddy.

He feels the most delicious shiver all down his body. Then he says her name again.

'I don't think Laura will be too surprised.'

39

Carrie can't stop apologising for the accident. The police have impounded the car and say it will be returned sometime next week.

'I'm just so sorry, Mum. Now you haven't got your car and it's all my fault.'

'It's not your fault, darling. And anyway, I've got you. Don't you think I'd rather have you than the car? And my ring. I've got my ring back.'

The reappearance of the ring is a mystery. So too is the manner in which Toby got it back. Right now Toby is out in the night garden, smoking one of his roll-ups. They can both see him through the window, as he strolls up and down the lawn.

'Do you think what I think?' says Carrie.

'About what, darling?'

'About Toby and the ring.'

'No. What's that?' Then Laura does think it. 'Oh. Do you really think so? Surely he wouldn't do that.'

'Mum, someone took your ring from your bedroom. Toby has no money at all, he's told me that. And he's got his own version of morality. He believes that what he wants is more important than anything else in the world. He told me so. And how did he get that woman to give him the ring back?'

'But surely . . .' Laura feels bewildered. What has Toby to do with the woman in the hospital? On the other hand, how else did the ring disappear and then reappear? 'You think he took it and sold it?'

'He's capable of it. He'd just shrug his shoulders and say the ring has moved on to its next life or something.'

'Have you asked him?'

'No. But I'm going to.'

She speaks with a flash of anger. Laura realises then that Carrie's intense nerviness may have a cause other than the accident with the car. She wants to ask what has happened with Toby, how serious has it got, but an instinctive discretion holds her back.

'I suppose he's not someone to rely on, really,' she says.

'You can say that again.'

'Do you want me to ask him to go?'

'No, it's okay. I think he's going anyway. You know what, I really need a drink.'

So they both have a glass of Orvieto.

'Oh my God, Mum. I'm so glad I didn't kill that boy.'

'I kept thinking, what if it had been Jack? I almost wanted her to keep the ring. Well, no, I wanted it back. But you know.'

'You have to have the ring. It's your engagement ring. I've always loved seeing that ring on your finger. It makes me feel safe, knowing Dad gave it to you, and you've worn it ever since.'

'Does it, darling?'

Laura feels so full of love for Carrie right now. My proud, hurt child. Too old now for me to kiss it better.

She puts down her glass and takes Carrie in her arms. She kisses her temples.

'You know what?' she says. 'Tomorrow it's the twenty-seventh anniversary of our engagement. That's such a long time.'

'I want that too,' says Carrie. 'I want someone to stay with me. But people don't stay any more.'

'Yes, they do, darling. Just maybe not yet. You're only nineteen. When I was nineteen I wasn't stayed with. I was walked out on.'

Carrie is familiar with the family tale of Laura and her first love, Nick. It's long been a source of wonder and reassurance.

'I know,' she says, snuggling into her mother's arms. 'I do know. Only there seem to be so few people I even want to be with for an evening, let alone twenty-seven years. Then you find one, and he turns out to be rubbish. And a thief.'

Laura looks out at Toby in the garden and sees that he's finished his cigarette.

'I think he's about to come in,' she says.

Carrie goes out onto the terrace, leaving the kitchen door open behind her. Laura can hear every word.

'Toby,' Carrie says. 'We have to talk.'

Toby comes from the dark of the lawn to the pool of light falling from the kitchen window onto the terrace.

'We don't have to,' he says. 'But we can choose to.'

'Oh, fuck off, will you?'

'Okay if I fuck off tomorrow?'

'Tomorrow is fine,' says Carrie.

He doesn't move. Both of them are frozen, waiting to be released.

'Why do you tell me you're not a good person?' says Carrie. 'Why do you tell me that?'

'So you'll know,' he says.

'You think it lets you off obeying the rules everyone else has to obey? You think you can just do as you please?'

'Maybe I do. What do you care?'

'I don't care,' says Carrie. 'I just want to know what happened with Mum's ring.'

He stares at her for a moment in silence.

'What do you think happened?'

'I think you took it.'

That shuts him up.

'Did you?'

'You think I'm the kind of person who'd accept your hospitality for five days, and then rob you.'

'You could be. Are you?'

He just goes on staring at her. She looks away, her right hand tugging at her left sleeve.

'If that's the kind of person I am,' says Toby, 'then you're better off without me in your life, aren't you?'

'Yes,' she says, still not looking at him.

She hears him walk away with rapid steps. She releases her breath, which she hadn't even realised she was holding.

In the house he picks up the kitchen cordless phone, saying to Laura, 'Okay to use the phone?'

'Of course,' says Laura.

He goes into the hall. Carrie comes into the kitchen.

'He admitted it.'

'I heard,' says Laura.

'I want him to be gone. I want everyone to be gone.'

'Would you rather we didn't have all these people round tomorrow evening?'

'No, it's okay. Just so long as I don't have to be there too.'

'Where will you go?'

'My room.'

Their eyes meet, and Carrie looks back with such open sadness that Laura is humbled. Not hiding any more. And that in its way is a sign of strength.

'What do you do in your room all day?' says Laura.

'Not much.' Then she adds, seemingly as an afterthought, 'I fool about making up songs.'

'You make up songs?'

'I played a couple to Toby. He said he liked them.'

'From what I've seen of Toby,' says Laura, 'if he says he likes them it means he likes them.'

'Yeah. Maybe.'

Toby comes back with the phone.

'I called my mum,' he says. 'She's coming over tomorrow morning to pick me up.'

'Oh, I am glad,' says Laura. 'I mean, I'm glad you called your mother. I couldn't bear to think of her not knowing what had happened to you. If you were my son I'd have been frantic with worry.'

'She's not much like you,' says Toby.

'Even so. She needs to know you're safe and well.'

'Am I safe and well?' says Toby.

He looks at Carrie. Carrie meets his gaze for a brief moment then turns away.

'I'm going upstairs.'

Laura offers Toby a glass of the Orvieto, which he accepts. Then she puts on a pan for some pasta. She finds a little to her surprise that she feels no anger towards him, perhaps because he's now going. Also there's something about Toby that seems to place him outside the rules of normal social conduct.

'Thank you for getting my ring back,' she says, choosing her words carefully. 'While it was lost, it almost felt as if I'd lost my marriage.'

'I'm sorry.'

'Why do you say that?'

'I'm sorry your marriage is so easy to lose.'

Laura is too shocked to speak.

'Carrie writes songs,' he says. 'They're good. You should get her to show them to people.'

'Right,' says Laura.

'Would you mind if I went out for a smoke?'

'Supper in half an hour.'

He goes outside. Laura sees him passing up and down the lawn, a ghost in the dark, the tip of his roll-up glowing red.

It's almost ten when Henry gets home, bringing Roddy with him. Laura is full of the dramas of the day, but doesn't want to say too much in front of Roddy. She wants time to shape their version of the story before it reaches Diana, who has her own way of dramatising other people's crises. Laura can just hear Diana saying, 'You are amazing, Laura! You let some long-haired weirdo you know nothing about into your house, he steals your jewellery, abuses your daughter, and half-kills some random child! It's so bizarre it's practically performance art!' So instead she greets Roddy with a friendly kiss and goes and gets him his Florentines.

'I remembered you like Florentines. You don't have to share them. You can take them to your room and have a midnight feast.'

She asks Henry about his meeting, but she already knows from his posture that he has nothing much to report.

'There's a possibility there,' he says. 'If I can bear it.'

'Tell me upstairs. I'm utterly wiped out.'

She starts moving about the kitchen turning out lights. To her irritation Roddy doesn't take the hint and go. He stands there clutching his unopened box of Florentines to his chest and watching her.

Henry parks his load of papers in his study.

'You're in your usual room, Roddy,' says Laura. 'What time is Diana getting here tomorrow?'

'About one, I should think,' says Roddy. 'I hope you don't

mind me invading you like this. It just makes sense, what with Worth being fairly near.'

Laura doesn't want to hear about Worth right now. She goes on turning out lights. Roddy still doesn't move. So she turns off the final kitchen light and moves on to the hall, leaving him in the kitchen in the dark.

At once she regrets this act of petty vindictiveness. As he comes shambling out to the foot of the stairs she lays one hand on his arm.

'Sorry, Roddy. I've had a bad day. We'll talk tomorrow, okay?'

'Tomorrow,' he says.

He nods twice, then slowly ascends the stairs, holding his overnight bag and his box of Florentines.

Alone in her bedroom at last with Henry, Laura tells him the dramatic events of the day. She tells it in the order it happened to her, wanting him to be frightened the way she was frightened, and then relieved the way she was relieved. Henry is dismayed for Carrie and wants to go to her.

'Go and give her a kiss. She's fine now.'

But before he goes she shows him the ring. Needless to say, he hadn't noticed it was back on her finger.

'So we're still engaged,' he says.

'Just about,' she says.

'Where did you find it?'

'Long story. Go and kiss Carrie.'

While he's out she undresses and prepares for bed. For the first time in many hours she turns her mind to tomorrow's dinner party. So much has happened that it seems absurd to be worrying herself over the roasting time for the lamb. But if guests are coming, if they're to be fed, the lamb must be cooked, and she would like it to be just right.

Is making a good dinner for friends a minor decoration in

her life, or is it the life itself? It's a question of foreground and background. Her marriage remains in the background until some small shock shifts her perspective, and suddenly it becomes all that matters.

Is my marriage so easy to lose?

It's survived this far. How do you keep it in the foreground? The perversity of nature means that we only value what we fear to lose. So is the value in all things not an absolute at all, but relative to the needs of the moment? There's something here that matters, if only she could track it down. But she's tired.

Henry returns.

'She seems pretty okay,' he says. 'Could have been a lot worse.'

'Suppose she'd been hit by a car instead of a bike.'

'I don't want to think about it.'

'Something like this happens,' says Laura, 'and suddenly you realise how vulnerable we all are. Anything could happen, any time.'

Henry's undressing slowly, familiarly.

'But you can't think like that, can you?' he says. 'You have to carry on as if nothing bad will ever happen.'

'Isn't that just sticking our heads in the sand?'

'Maybe,' he says. 'But life has to go on somehow.'

'So you think it's all right to go ahead with tomorrow evening?'

'I don't see why not.'

He sounds tired. He's had a hard day too.

'So what happened with Aidan?'

'Oh, Aidan tried to dress it up, but all they've got is a bog-standard director job. I'd be working to a series producer, an executive producer, and an editor.'

'That's ridiculous. You can't do that. You've always been the one in charge.'

'It's a job.'

'Oh, darling. Did you say you'd do it?'

'I said I'd think about it.'

They move about the bedroom, both going through their accustomed rituals, exchanging information in short form, each aware of the mass of emotion that lies beneath.

'Roddy's in an odd state,' Henry says. 'He more or less told me he has some other woman.'

'Poor old Roddy. I almost wish he had. Can you imagine Diana?' In a Diana voice, 'Don't be so silly, Roddy! Put her down!'

When they're both in bed and the lights are out, Henry says, 'I'm glad the ring came back.'

'Me too.'

'What happened there?'

'Something to do with Toby, we think. Don't worry. He's going tomorrow.'

'He's a lost soul, Toby.'

'Do you think so? I thought he was just the sort that would annoy you.'

'Maybe my standards are dropping as I get older. It seems to me that just about everyone has their own mountain to climb.'

'Even funny old Roddy.'

'Roddy most of all. He wants to let the ego die and float on the stream of life.'

They can both feel each other smiling, lying side by side in the darkness. Laura reaches out her hand and finds Henry's hand.

SATURDAY

40

Maggie sits in the car in the station car park waiting for Andrew's train. It's running late. She's much more nervous than she thought she would be, and she's confused about why. Everything would be so much simpler if she knew what she wanted, but she doesn't. She doesn't even know what she feels.

I don't want to have to choose any more. I want things to happen to me, and then to have to make the best of it.

Two of the station staff stand at the foot of the steps, heads down, shoulders hunched, snatching a cigarette. A woman is feeding coins into the parking-permit machine. Maggie has her car window open on this sunny morning, and can hear the coins dropping one by one. Then comes the sound of the approaching train. It makes gentle, squealing, rocking noises, like an enormous animal settling into its lair.

As always, she sees Andrew before he sees her. She feels a little rush of affection and relief, which catches her unawares. Did I really think he might not show up? He has a preoccupied air as he walks up the platform towards the exit. He carries a small rucksack slung over one shoulder, his usual weekend bag. He could be a husband, a father, coming home after a week away working to feed his family, anticipating the comfort and rest of a loving home. She could be a young wife with a bonny two-year-old on her lap, pointing him out as he strides towards them. 'Look, here's Daddy come home!'

Jesus, what's wrong with me?

He opens the car door and folds himself into the passenger seat with a sigh of exhaustion.

'Only just caught the train,' he says. 'Really late night.'

He doesn't lean across to give her a token kiss, the way he usually does. She remembers he had a leaving party last night.

'How was it?'

'It was great. Quite emotional, actually. I wasn't expecting it to be. But I've been there over two years. Duncan made a speech.'

'Did you make a speech?'

'I said a few words. Not my thing, really.'

She can feel his nervousness, which doesn't help her own tension. She busies herself with the car, manoeuvring it through the people crossing the car park.

'So you're all set to start the new job on Monday?'

'More or less.'

He doesn't say where he's proposing to live, and she doesn't ask, but it hangs unspoken between them. Andrew has never been one to take the lead when things need to be said. In the past this has annoyed her. Now it frightens her. His silence could mean much more than she knows. Perhaps he's already sorted out a rented flat. Perhaps he's going to live with Jo. This notion of a secret Andrew, an Andrew who could be living a life of which she knows nothing, gives her the oddest sensation. She knows this man better than any other man in the world, she can tell what he's going to say before he even opens his mouth. How can he be a stranger?

'Did you manage to get any breakfast?'

'I thought I'd grab a coffee at Victoria, but there wasn't time.'

'I've got some croissants at home.'

'Great.'

Croissants. Home. Next I'll be producing the bonny two-year-old to bounce on his knee. 'Look! Here's Daddy!' Did I know when I was buying those croissants that they were for Andrew?

At some point they'll have to stop playing this game that everything is just the same as it's always been, but for now they are both in the grip of some instinctive etiquette that ordains a period of conventional courtesies. When two people meet there seems to be a certain minimum time required to pass before any real business can be transacted, as if their mobile phones have just been switched on and must search for an adequate signal before they can make or receive calls.

He looks out of the car window. There are paragliders above Mount Caburn, bright swatches of colour against the blue sky.

'Are you up for a walk later?' she says. 'I haven't got out on the Downs all week.'

'Yes, sure,' he says. 'I'd like that.'

They both know then that they've agreed to do the real talking when they're out walking. This takes the pressure off the immediate present.

Maggie pulls the car into the little cobbled parking space in front of her cottage. She sees the way he looks round as he gets out and pushes open the iron gate into the front path. She can tell what he's thinking as clearly as if he was speaking aloud. He's thinking, Is this my last time here? Such a pretty garden, Maggie knows how to make a place welcoming, I shall miss it.

All her own imagining, of course, but the odd thing is she's as grateful to him as if he has actually said the words. It's good to have your home appreciated.

In the kitchen, she fills a kettle to make coffee in the cafetière, and puts three croissants in the oven.

'Butter?' she says. 'Marmalade?'

His usual accompaniments.

'Please.'

She sips coffee, nibbles a croissant, along with him. The late breakfast makes them both feel better. He's starting to relax. He looks at her across the kitchen table, and for the first time she meets his eyes without looking away. He gives her a little smile, a little shrug that says, So here we are.

'How's your week been?' he says.

'Busy,' she says. 'Confused.'

'Me too.'

'So I gather.'

He looks away, pouring himself more coffee.

'Have you talked to Jo?'

'Yes,' she says. 'She told me what happened.'

'That was just stupid,' he says.

'How was it stupid?'

Suddenly they're in the middle of it and she feels the tension rising in her. What's stupid about having sex with someone? You do it because you want to do it. Call it disloyal, or callous, but it's not stupid. It's not like you do it by accident.

'Okay,' he says. 'Not stupid. Just a really bad idea.'

'And you were drunk, right?'

'Not very. Jo was a lot drunker than I was.'

At least he's not hiding. Not ducking and diving.

'It's okay,' says Maggie. 'I didn't mean to start talking about that.'

She's hurt, much more hurt than she ever expected. All right, so she's not blameless, but she's not been fucking someone else.

'You want to know the truth?' says Andrew. 'When you think the person you want to want you doesn't want you, it's nice to be wanted by someone else. It's like comforting the bereaved.'

'Comforting the bereaved!'

'It's been a bad week for me.'

Maggie jumps up and starts putting the breakfast things away. She had meant to be all calm and reasonable but now she wants to cry, or maybe hit him. Then she remembers something Jo told her.

'Jo says you were crying.'

'There was a bit of that.'

She stops clearing up, presses her fists down onto the table, and gives into her distress.

'You didn't have to fuck her.'

'No.'

'Did you think of me? Even for one minute?'

'Before,' he says. 'After. Not during.'

'Jesus! Don't spare my feelings. Please.'

She moves to the sink. Clatters dishes. He says nothing. When at last she turns round, there he still is, sitting at the table, his head in his hands.

'So what are we going to do?' she says.

'You tell me.'

Maggie says nothing. Words don't come.

'If this is where you tell me it's over,' he says, 'just do it fast, and I'll go out and take a walk by myself, then I'll come back and be grown-up about it.'

'Oh, Andrew.'

Now she wants to cry because suddenly she's so touched. She hadn't realised this is what he's been bracing himself to hear. His morning journey, breakfastless from London, now appears so gallant. She wants to say, 'Of course it's not over.' But is that true?

'Do you want it to be over?' she says

'No,' he says. 'No.' Then he thinks some more and says again, 'No.'

'But it's not all simple, is it?' she says. 'I mean, it's not like there's no problem.'

'Yes. I can see there's a problem.'

'Do you know what it is?'

This is unfair. Getting him to be the prosecution as well as the defence. But it's important too. She wants to know he knows what she's feeling, as then he's facing it with her, not just being the victim. But she doesn't want to say it herself because it's so hurtful.

'I think so,' he says slowly. 'Jo said something.'

'What did Jo say?'

'She said you're not sure I'm the one for you.'

'Why wouldn't you be?'

'Because I'm too nice.'

He gets up and walks over to the window, stands there with his back to her. So he's hurt anyway.

'I'm nice Andrew. I should be more assertive. That's what women want. So, great, I can do that. I can be as selfish as you like. Treat 'em mean, keep 'em keen. Then you'll say I'm the one for you. Is that how it works?'

He's speaking quietly but he's angry.

'No,' says Maggie.

'Tell me how any of this makes sense, because I can't see it. I thought when people loved each other they wanted to make each other happy. I want to make you happy, but that's not allowed, that's being too nice. Even though it's what I want for myself. I want someone who wants to make me happy. Do you want to make me happy? Maybe you don't. Maybe you're not too nice, like me. Maybe that's why I love you. Is that how it works? People only love the ones who treat them like shit? Because if that's how it is, then it's a truly fucked-up system and I don't want to be part of it.'

He falls silent. Maggie feels mortified.

'I know,' she says. 'You'd be far better off without me.'

'Maybe I would.'

'Though I did get you croissants.'

He turns to her, and he looks so sad.

'Oh, Maggie. What are we going to do?'

'Let's go for this walk,' she says.

They've done it so many times on their weekends together, followed the track that starts at the back of Edenfield Place, climbed the chalky tractor road up to the trig point at the top. Just setting out together feels like old times, and so comforts them.

They walk for a while in silence, between the high fringes of nettles and cow parsley. The steep slope makes them pant, but they press on to the top without stopping. The sweep of the coast now spreads out before them, from Newhaven to Eastbourne, a band of green and yellow land, a band of grey and blue sea.

They head east along the ridge path, with the wind in their faces. After the confusion of emotions in the kitchen, Maggie feels her thoughts clearing. Why has she assumed that it has to be all or nothing? She shrinks from the extreme decisions in both directions. Can't they find a way to muddle along until – until what? Until the decision makes itself.

I don't want the responsibility of screwing up my entire life.

It turns out Andrew's thoughts have been clearing as well.

'You have no idea how I've been punishing myself over this,' he says. 'No one can blame me more than I blame myself. But it's not just me, is it?'

'No,' she says. 'It's not just you.'

'This too-nice thing,' he says. 'I keep thinking about it. I have these arguments with you in my head, to prove to you you're wrong. Which is so stupid. Feelings aren't right or wrong, they're just what you feel.'

But Maggie wants to hear the arguments. She wants to be told she's wrong.

'What sort of arguments?'

'It's only me trying to get off the hook.'

'By making me be the one who's in the wrong?'

'Pretty much.'

'Maybe I am.'

'Actually, it's worse than that. It's me wanting to believe you're so screwed-up you'll never be happy with anyone. That way I don't feel so bad about losing you.'

'Maybe I am that screwed-up.'

'No. It's only sour grapes.'

'I'd like to hear the argument, even so.'

What Andrew says is almost exactly what she believes: she's so screwed-up she'll never be happy with anyone. It almost excites her to hear it coming from his mouth.

They've reached the point on the ridge path where they either turn back and retrace their steps, or head down the hillside past America Cottage. Andrew, following long habit, all unaware of his surroundings, takes the descending track.

'It's a pattern-recognition thing,' he says. 'You create a pattern of responses, if A then B, if B then C. You project the pattern forward to predict outcomes. It's meant to be descriptive, not judgemental.'

'Will I understand it?' says Maggie.

'Oh, yes. It's all pretty obvious. But you'll hate it.'

They pick their way down the steep diagonal path, and Andrew picks his careful way through his non-judgemental argument.

'Suppose your pattern is that what really gives you a buzz is pulling a man. You can only get that buzz from a new man. Someone who already wants you can't deliver it. And it's the buzz you want, as much as the man. That means that after the initial phase you get a choice. Either A, you move on to another man, or B, you stick with the first. But choosing B means you run out of buzz. It means you have to switch to another kind of relationship. Oh, I should have started with that. Suppose there's two kinds of relationships. There's A, conquest, and there's B, companionship. So pattern A gets you conquest, X. But it leads on to B, which gives you companionship, Y. So you have to keep repeating A to get X. And the more you do it, the harder it gets to move on to B, sticking with one man, even though you keep telling yourself that you want Y, companionship, and that if you do enough A you'll get there. You won't. The only way to Y is through B. And the only way you can ever get going on B is by giving up on A. Which you're never going to do.'

'You have totally lost me,' says Maggie.

This is not entirely true. For all his Xs and Ys, she gets the idea, which is by no means new to her. But is it true? What if somewhere out there waits a man who is so right for her that she'll know beyond doubt that she wants to live with him forever?

'I expect it's bullshit,' says Andrew. 'Just my way of telling myself it's not all about me.'

'And making it turn out to be all about me.'

'I told you you'd hate it.'

He sounds almost philosophical. How strange to be having this conversation, which in one form or another has run in her head for years, with an actual boyfriend who is personally implicated in the outcome. Except there never is an outcome.

'It's the Mr Right question,' she says. 'Does Mr Right exist? Or does Mr Right, however right he is, turn into Mr Ordinary once you've spent enough time with him?'

'He has to, doesn't he?' says Andrew. 'You have to settle down to another way of loving.'

She thinks about that as they scramble down the last of the steep track. On one side New Forest ponies graze behind electric fences. Ahead, the low drone of the distant main road as tiny cars pass up and down.

'Here's what I don't get, Andrew. If you think I'm stuck in this stupid pattern, why on earth do you want to stick around me?'

'For the same reason,' he says. 'No one's perfect. Why should I do any better with anyone else? You're a bit screwed-up, but you're good enough for me. The problem is I'm not good enough for you.'

'No. That's not true.'

She stops, making him stop. This is important.

'It's not true you're not good enough for me. It's just . . .' She pauses, summoning her courage, looking away over all England as she speaks. 'How do I know there isn't someone out there who's even better?'

He says nothing.

'There. I've said it. That's the worst thing I could ever say to you.'

Still he says nothing.

'Did you hear what I just said?'

'I knew it already. Jo told me.'

'Don't you hate me for wanting someone better than you?'

'No. I think it's dumb. But I don't hate you.'

'You think it's dumb?'

'Sure,' he says. 'According to my theory you're going to have to wind up making the best of it with someone who's less than perfect. So why waste time? You might as well get on with it with me.'

Maggie is amazed. None of these thoughts is new to her. What's new is sharing them with Andrew. Just hearing him talk this way changes her view of him. It takes away the guilt. He becomes someone much like her, trying to make life work and finding it's full of faulty parts.

They're out of the field path now, and passing the uninhabited cottage. The weeds in the garden have grown higher than the surrounding flint wall.

'Look at that,' says Andrew. 'Someone should look after this place.'

'It's got no utilities,' says Maggie.

'All it needs is a little love and care.'

The coach road is shady after the open Downs. They walk side by side, one in each tyre track. Maggie recalls what Laura Broad said to her.

'It's like *Deal or No Deal*,' she says. 'Do we settle for what we've got, or keep on hoping something better will turn up?'

'Or take what we've got and turn it into something better.'

'You think we could do that?'

'If you're up for it.'

'You just want somewhere to live near your new job.'

'True.'

'What if it doesn't work?'

'Then I go.'

He makes it sound so simple, and it just isn't simple. But maybe it's something else. Maybe it's possible.

'Stay tonight, at least.'

'I'd like that.'

'How about going to dinner with the Broads?'

'Okay with me.'

So instead of making a big decision about their future they make this small decision. They will go to the Broads' dinner party as a couple. Maybe it's pretending. Maybe it's practising. But no one's deceiving anyone, and that makes everything possible.

41

'Where did you get it, Dean?'

'Brighton.'

'Where did you get it?'

'So someone nicked it and sold it on to the shop in Brighton. How was I to know?'

Sheena just goes on gazing at him and he feels like something's about to burst inside.

'She lost the ring on Thursday. Which is when you gave it to me. I'm not stupid. I can add up.'

'Well, fucking add up, then. What do I care?'

He looks round the room, and the thing inside is going to burst. His eyes are hot, his palms are sticky. He wants to hurt someone. His eyes fall on the toy fort.

'Fucking stupid kid's toy,' he says.

He picks it up off the table and throws it down hard on the floor. The guard tower snaps off. Plastic soldiers scatter over the carpet. He stamps on the fort, crushing it. Stamps again and again. Sheena just watches.

The fort breaks easily, it's only cheap matchboard. Soon it's nothing but a mess of fragments. He stops stamping on it, stands staring down at the wreckage, breathing hard. The thing inside still hasn't burst.

'You done?' says Sheena.

He doesn't answer.

'Now you listen to me,' says Sheena. 'My boy's in hospital because he was stupid, and he's not going to be walking for three months. That's enough stupid for me, all right? I don't need it from you. Now tell me where you got the ring.'

Dean throws himself down onto the couch, and lies there face down.

'Nicked it,' he says to the cushions.

'You nicked it.'

'Yeah.'

'You're a bloody fool, Dean Keeley. What else did you take?'

'Nothing.'

'What other jobs have you done that I don't know about?'

'Nothing.'

'Just the one house? Just the ring?'

'Yeah.'

'You're a bloody fool, Dean Keeley. You don't go nicking stuff, you hear me? And if you do, you don't give it to me so I can wear it and the woman who lost it sees it on my hand.'

Dean groans into the cushion.

'What's that?' says Sheena.

'My fucking luck,' says Dean.

'Right,' says Sheena. 'You're right about that. You got lucky, you did. Your stroke of luck was it was her daughter's car Chipper hit, so she's sorry for me. Otherwise you'd be answering questions down the station, wouldn't you? So you can thank your stars you caught a bit of luck, you can.'

Dean groans again.

'Now you clear up this mess on the floor.'

She removes herself to the kitchen.

Left alone, Dean can no longer hold down the feeling. He gives a great gulping sob and starts to cry, the tears stinging his eyes, the sobs wrenching his chest. He wants to howl, so he pushes one fist into his mouth to block the sound. Then, still sobbing, his nose now running, he gets off the couch onto his knees on the floor, and starts picking up the pieces of the smashed fort.

When his hands are full he looks round blinking for somewhere to dump the debris. There's a wastepaper basket by the TV but it's too small. So he gets up and goes out through the conservatory to the garden and makes a pile on the pavers outside. He has a notion that he'll burn it later.

Back and forth he goes, clearing every last little stick. Sheena likes a job done properly. He picks up the plastic soldiers too, throws them onto the pile. Then he finds Brad, some distance away from the others.

Brad wouldn't have broken down like this. Brad would've given a shrug and said, 'Win some, lose some.' This is what Brad does when a mission ends: he checks the damage, he cleans up any wounds, he rests. And then he moves on. He doesn't look back. Never look back.

Dean pushes the plastic soldier into his jeans pocket and goes out through the conservatory door, closing it softly behind him. He jumps the fence at the bottom of the garden and walks away fast down the road. Past the allotments, up the narrow path into the trees. Some kids on bikes messing about on the earth bank. He pays no attention, walks on. Past the gleam of low water in the ditch and out into the meadow, to the five-barred gate, to the kissing gate. Here he sinks down onto the grass and lowers his head, and sobs like a baby.

Never cried this way when Dad belted me. Never cried this way when I got sent down.

He pulls the plastic soldier out of his pocket and stands it up, facing him.

'Can't do it, mate,' he says. 'Can't do it on my own.'

Someone is coming. He looks up. It's Sheena.

'Sorry,' he mumbles.

'Me too,' says Sheena. 'I'm sorry too.'

'It's okay. I'll go.'

'Go? Where have you got to go to?'

'Don't know,' says Dean. 'Not your problem.'

His mouth feels as if it's full of glue and the words come out with difficulty.

'I don't want you to go. I want you to stop behaving like a bloody fool.'

'Did it for you,' he says, very low. But she hears him.

'You think that makes it all right?'

But he can hear it in her voice. It does make it all right. There's that old tenderness come back. A rush of sweet relief flows through him. If Sheena will stick by me, nothing else matters.

'Did it so we could be married,' he says.

'That doesn't make stealing right, babe.'

'You weren't supposed to know.'

'You know what, Deanie? I didn't mind one bit giving that ring back. It felt like that was the only reason Chipper didn't die. They told me at the hospital he was lucky to be alive. So she got her ring back, and I got my boy back.'

'Talk about luck.'

'It's not luck, babe. It's meant. These things don't go the way they do for no reason. Now come here. Give me a cuddle.'

He gets up and goes into her soft white arms and presses her close, smelling her sweet warm smell.

'Least you didn't nick the sunset,' she says.

That makes him smile.

'Now wipe your nose. We're going out.'

'Where are we going?'

'We're going to the hospital to see how Chipper's coming along. But we're stopping at the shops on the way.'

They drive out in Dean's van and park in the Priory car park. Sheena leads Dean over Cliffe Bridge past the Big Issue seller and his dog to Argos on the far side.

'What do we want in Argos?' he says.

'You know what we want,' says Sheena.

She opens the catalogue at the jewellery section and finds the pages of rings. Dean is silent, watching her as she searches the plastic-coated pages. His heart is too full for words.

Sheena pulls over an order form and picks up one of the stubby pens, made specially short so no one will want to steal them.

'This is what we need,' she says. 'This is perfect.'

It's a nine-carat-gold ruby-and-diamond heart ring. It costs £49.99. Not real ruby and diamond, of course. They call it 'created ruby and diamond'.

'Created just for us,' says Sheena.

There's a bundle of plastic rings by the counter you use for sizing your finger. Then you wait your turn in the queue to order. Then you wait for the item to be brought up from the stockroom. Throughout this process Dean says nothing. He assumed their engagement ended when the stolen ring was given back to its true owner. Now here comes another ring.

He can't believe Sheena's generosity. She hasn't said she forgives him but here she is buying another ring.

It comes in a little hinged plastic box. They take it out of the shop into the sunlight. The street is crowded with Saturday shoppers. They find a bench on the bridge by the Big Issue seller and sit down side by side. Sheena gives Dean the box, and he takes out the ring.

'You haven't changed your mind?'

'No,' she says.

'Do I go down on my knee again?'

'No. You've done that bit.'

'Here it is, then.'

'Here it is, then?' She laughs as she repeats his words back at him. 'Is that the best you can do?'

'It isn't as good as the other one,' says Dean, 'and I haven't even paid for it, but my love's the same. More, even.'

'That's better.'

She puts the ring on her ring finger. Then they kiss.

'All right for some,' says the Big Issue seller. 'All I've got is a bloody dog.'

42

Henry sits in his study, gazing out of the window at the garden. He's shut himself away here because he has a decision to make about his future, or supposes he has.

The view out of his window is deeply familiar: the garden framed by tall elms, dominated by the great heave in the land that is Mount Caburn. The ridge at the top that was once an Iron Age fort pulls him back down the centuries, places his present concerns in the majestic and merciful sweep of time. And there, in his nearer view, on the grass of the lawn, representing a beginning rather than an end, sit Carrie and Toby, cross-legged on the grass, deep in conversation.

How am I supposed to manage this business of growing older? Don't tell me the best is now past.

He remembers then how as a boy he would always pace his passing days round delights to come. He was a great one for looking forward. It could be something as small as knowing there'd be pizza for supper, or it could be one of the grand holidays, birthday, Christmas. Always the present moment was made brighter by a light shining from the near future. Such an arrangement works because we live our lives forwards. If the bright lights are in the past, their glow no longer carries the excitement of expectation. Turn that way, look back that way, and all you feel is the ache of regret.

His unseeing gaze catches a tremor of movement in the long
grass beyond the border. His attention returns with a snap. Was
that a rabbit?

He goes to the window and looks out into the orchard. Yes,
he sees it clearly for a brief moment. A rabbit making for the
fence.

He goes out onto the terrace, not hurrying, knowing he's too
late, wanting only to discover where the defensive wall has been
breached. As he crosses the lawn, Carrie and Toby don't look
up, don't even seem to notice him. He patrols the orchard fence,
looking for holes in the wire, but finds nothing. Then returning
down the close-mown strip beside the fence he spots rabbit
droppings. A little further into the orchard, by the roots of an
old apple tree, he finds a rabbit hole. They've tunnelled in.

You have to hand it to rabbits. They don't give up. Such a
deal of effort, and all to break in to a garden that when all's
said and done is much like the meadow outside. Surely it can't
be worth it? Then it strikes him that maybe his mental map
is wrong; or rather, meaningful for him, but not for the
rabbits. In his map there is a strip of land bounded by tree,
fences, walls, that belongs to him and is called his home and
garden. In the rabbits' map there is only land. The land extends
in all directions, and the rabbits' imperative is to roam ever
further in search of food. The obstacles they encounter have
no meaning. Meeting a barrier, they press onwards, going round
and over and under, seeking any passage through, in the way
that water will always find a channel. Think of the rabbits as
water, as wind, as weather, and the goal of shutting them out
of the garden becomes laughable. All you can do is stuff the
leaks with newspaper, and make repairs in the fabric after each
winter's storms.

He hunts out a medium-sized log from the woodpile and

hammers it with his heel into the rabbit hole. He knows this won't stop them. They'll dig round it. But it'll slow them down.

So have I surrendered? Have the rabbits won?

It feels like something else, something that has wider-reaching implications. It's a kind of a truce, something less than victory but more than defeat. A realisation that the conflict will never end, but that this state of affairs is in fact manageable. An acceptance of imperfection.

Humility again.

So returning slowly through the orchard, his recent thoughts combine in his mind, and together they add up to a revelation. That dark cloud of dread that rolled towards him down Artillery Row was no external reality, as he supposed, not the unbearable truth of his own meaninglessness, but a hallucination, a projection by himself of his own fears. Demand a life of ever-mounting achievement and of course disappointment lies ahead. But such a demand is self-created, unachievable, foolish. Life is not a staircase. To each age certain ways of being are appropriate. There are high points and low points, the graph tracks many lines. Income, status, health, happiness, all peak and trough at differing times. How then can you ever say the best is past?

Look on your life not as a race which must end in victory or defeat, but as an adventure into the unknown. As long as you live there's more to be discovered, more to be enjoyed. The magical virtue called humility sets you free.

Henry knows this moment too won't last. The human condition is too volatile, too fickle, too vulnerable to gusts of self-doubt and envy of others. But for now he's experiencing a kind of tranquillity, and he feels an overwhelming sensation of gratitude. He wants to say thank you for this home, for this family, for this life. For these rare few weeks of high summer. For the passing of regret. But who is he to thank?

He returns to the house. In the kitchen, Laura is chopping mint leaves with a mezzaluna and Roddy is sitting in the chair by the window, a newspaper unopened on his knees.

'Oh, Henry,' says Laura, 'thank God you've emerged. Now you can talk to Roddy.'

'I was perfectly happy talking to you,' says Roddy.

'Yes, I know, but I don't really understand a word you say. Henry loves all that kind of stuff.'

Henry understands from this that Laura has a lot to do and Roddy is getting in her way.

'Come along, Roddy,' he says. 'Laura much prefers to listen to Radio 4 when she's cooking. Come and tell me about stuff.'

Laura shoots him a grateful glance. Roddy gets up, newspaper in hand.

'Wrong moment,' he says. 'I never seem to get it right.'

Laura turns on the radio and gets the start of *Money Box*. She switches to Radio 3 and the last few minutes of *CD Review*. Roddy follows Henry into the living room.

'Hasn't it been an amazing summer?' says Henry. 'I suppose it'll all change soon, but really we should appreciate it while we've got it.'

'To be honest,' says Roddy, 'I'm entirely indifferent to the weather. I'm just as content in a blizzard, so long as I myself am warm and dry.'

'Really?' says Henry. 'That's very philosophical of you.'

Roddy settles himself down in the most comfortable chair in the room.

'Ah, well,' he says, 'there is a philosophy behind what I say. Away with arrogance. The weather won't be commanded. The wind blows where it will.'

'I think I detect the stream of life,' says Henry.

'Let yourself be carried away by the stream of life,' says Roddy. 'Let yourself be swept along, you know not whither nor why.'

There he sits in his cord trousers and brogues and his heather-green jumper, his squat and crumpled features earnestly asserting a freedom of spirit that is mocked by his mottled balding head, and Henry feels for him a grudging admiration. It can't be easy being married to Diana.

The doorbell rings. Henry is already out of his chair when Laura calls from the kitchen, 'Get that, will you, Henry?'

Henry opens the door to see a Mercedes convertible with the hood down, and a woman standing not on the doorstep but on the gravel of the drive. She has her back to the door, a light cardigan over her shoulders, and one hand on her hip. He senses at once that this is an attitude assumed on purpose. He notes a slim figure, a full head of blonde-streaked hair, tight jeans, stylish red trainers. Then she turns to greet him, and like one of those pictures of faces that changes completely when you turn it upside down, he sees an old woman.

'Hi,' she says. 'I'm Toby's mother. Sally Clore.'

Unfair to call her an old woman: she looks about fifty, almost certainly younger than Henry himself, and was clearly once good-looking. But she has aged early, and the strenuous make-up is unable to disguise the brittle skin, the puckered lines. She wears dark glasses up on her forehead, holding back the mane of tawny hair. This hair, this slender body, by raising such expectations of youth, makes a sad mockery of the ageing face.

'Henry Broad,' says Henry, holding out his hand.

'So good of you to put up with Toby. I'm sure he's made a perfect nuisance of himself.'

'No, not at all. Come on in.'

Sally Clore comes into the house, bringing with her a wave of expensive perfume. Henry calls to Laura in the kitchen.

'It's Toby's mum.'

He leads the visitor through into the living room. Roddy lumbers to his feet. Sally Clore doesn't notice him: her gaze has already discovered Toby out in the garden. As if drawn by a magnetic force, she goes out through the French windows onto the terrace.

'Toby,' she says.

Her voice is low, but it has immediate effect. Toby starts as though stung, and gets up off the grass. He turns towards Carrie, then back towards his mother.

'Hi, Mum,' he says.

She holds out her arms. He comes to her, bounding over the terrace wall, his expression suddenly that of a small boy who has stayed out playing too long.

She takes him in her arms and holds him close.

'Who's a naughty boy?' she says.

Carrie comes up onto the terrace after Toby. Henry looks on in surprise. The maternal embrace goes on. Toby, far from trying to hold back, seems content to remain like a child or a lover in his mother's arms.

Henry makes further introductions. Toby's mother doesn't even pretend to take these in. Her eyes are only for her son. She strokes his face, draws his long hair back from his cheeks, tugs at his beard.

'Still that horrible beard, darling? When are you going to get rid of it?'

Laura joins them.

'Toby's mother, Sally,' says Henry.

'Oh, I'm so glad Toby called you,' Laura says. 'I gather he's been away for ages.'

'He has!' Sally Clore smacks her son lightly on the cheek. 'He's so unkind to his poor old mama! I haven't set eyes on him for weeks and weeks!'

'Weeks?' says Carrie.

Toby turns his gaze on her and she says no more. His look is not a warning of any kind: it's the look of one who no longer knows her, and turns to hear what she has to say out of common politeness.

'I'd got the idea he'd been away much longer,' says Laura.

'It's been long enough, believe me,' says Sally Clore. 'But we have a very special relationship, my bad boy and me. We know when we've been apart for too long. As soon as I start to feel it, he feels it too. Don't you, Boby?'

'Let's go home, Mum,' Toby says.

'Your carriage awaits, Master.'

She gives a silvery laugh, and holding Toby by the hand, leads him back through the house. The three members of the Broad family are too astonished to intervene. Mother and son seem to have lost all sense of normal social behaviour. For a moment it seems as if they will go skipping out of the house together without a word of farewell.

'You're wearing Jack's clothes,' says Carrie.

'Give me a moment,' Toby says to his mother, and runs upstairs.

Sally Clore stands in the hall smiling at nobody in particular.

'Would you like a drink or something?' says Laura.

'No, thank you,' she replies. 'I drink only water, and only a very particular kind of water. It's one of my silly little fads, and causes no end of nuisance, but if you knew what they put in the water you'd think twice too. I'm not just talking about human waste. I'm talking about male sex hormones.'

'Goodness!' says Roddy.

Toby comes back downstairs in his own clothes, swinging his backpack.

'Thanks for everything,' he says.

As he gets into the convertible beside his mother, Diana's BMW pulls into the drive.

'We must absolutely run!' cries Sally Clore. 'Come along, Bobes. You've outstayed your welcome as usual.'

The Mercedes disappears in a screech of gravel as Diana gets out of her car. She stares after the convertible in awed fascination.

'Who on earth was that?' Then turning to the group on the doorstep, she issues a sharp command. 'Roddy! Bags!'

Roddy unloads the car. Diana follows Laura into the kitchen, carrying a bottle of champagne. She puts the champagne in the fridge, her inquisitive eyes scanning the bright shelves.

'Summer pudding! Ooh, yummy. Have you tried making Jane Grigson's summer pudding? You line the bowl with sponge cake and mix the fruit with whipped cream. It's sensational.'

'Diana, I've already made it.'

'Oh, so you have. So who was the kept woman?'

'I don't think she is kept. She's the mother of a friend of Jack's called Toby. Toby's been staying here for a few days.'

'Ooh!' says Diana, ogling Carrie. 'Nice for someone.'

Carrie turns and runs upstairs to her room.

'Honestly, Diana.'

'What did I do wrong?' cries Diana. 'Doesn't she want a boyfriend? She must be getting just a little desperate. When Isla was her age she'd worked her way through half her year group.'

Roddy struggles across the hall and up the stairs with a suitcase and a heavily laden basket.

'Not the basket, Roddy! That's house gifts. What do we want with a bottle of olive oil in the bedroom?' To Laura, 'Chance would be a fine thing!' Then, seeing Henry, she inclines her cheek for a kiss. 'Hello, Henry. How was the garden party? I felt for you on Thursday afternoon. Was it utterly ghastly?'

'No,' says Henry. 'I loved it, actually.'

'You loved it?' Diana stares, incredulous. 'You can't have loved it. I don't see how that's possible.'

'When did you last have an experience you loved, Diana?'

'Oh, heavens! Loads of times! I adored the Polly Morgan sculptures at the Haunch of Venison. Did you see them? Gutted animals and balloons. Incredibly powerful. And I'm wild about XX. I've been playing a download Isla got me all the way from town.' She looks at her watch. 'I have to make a business call before lunch. I have one very rich but very elusive donor.'

She takes out her BlackBerry and heads through the living room onto the terrace.

'Drink,' says Laura. 'Get me a drink.'

Henry pours them both a glass of wine.

'Should I find Roddy and offer him a glass?'

'He'll be lying down in the spare bedroom. Diana has that effect on him.'

'And Carrie.'

The phone rings. It's Maggie Dutton to say that she and Andrew will come this evening.

'That's wonderful,' says Laura. 'Don't come too late, the early evenings are so lovely. Any time after seven.'

Carrie comes creeping downstairs, looking around warily as she comes.

'Where is she?'

'On the terrace. On her phone.'

'I'm starving.'

She goes to the larder.

'Can I have what's left of the ginger cake? There's almost nothing.'

'Yes, if you must,' says Laura. 'But we'll be having lunch in an hour.'

Carrie comes out of the larder, cake in hand.

'What about Toby's mum?' Laura says to her. 'Did you hear? She called him Boby!'

'Something very odd going on there,' says Henry.

'He's very, very screwed up,' says Carrie. 'I mean, very.'

'Are you a bit relieved he's gone?' says Laura.

Carrie thinks about that, nibbling away at the cake.

'I think maybe every single thing he said was a lie,' she says. 'But I don't know. It doesn't seem to make much difference. He's not like any one else I've ever met. He told me when we were talking this morning that he thinks he has a demon inside him.'

'A demon? That's a bit worrying, isn't it?'

'It sort of made sense to me.'

Diana returns.

'Where's Roddy?' she says. 'Has he come down?'

'No,' says Henry. 'Not yet.'

'That means he's gone to sleep on the bed. Honestly! Take your eyes off him for a minute and he'll find somewhere to lie down and go to sleep.'

Roddy comes down a little later, holding a book he's found in the spare bedroom. It's Michael Cunningham's novel *The Hours*.

'I've just realised,' he says. 'The river across the fields here. That must be where Virginia Woolf drowned herself.'

'That's right,' says Henry. 'She lived in Rodmell, the other side of the river.'

'She just walked out of her house, across the fields, and into the river.'

'Yes, Roddy,' says Diana. 'We know. It's quite well known, you know. We saw the film.'

But Roddy seems powerfully struck by the discovery.

'Just out there,' he says, pointing out of the window. 'Just a short walk away. According to the novel, she didn't throw herself in, she just walked in.'

'She wasn't in her right mind,' says Laura. 'She was terrified she was going mad again.'

'Does anyone know exactly where?' says Roddy.

'Oh, for heaven's sake, Roddy!' exclaims Diana.

'Not exactly where,' says Laura. 'Her body wasn't found for three weeks.'

'She left a note for her husband saying, I can't go on spoiling your life any longer.'

'Yes,' says Laura. 'It's so sad.'

Henry hands Roddy a glass of wine.

'Here,' he says. And raising his own glass, 'Moriturus te saluto.'

43

Cas sits very still, watching the old lady. They're in the garden, on green plastic chairs, in the shade of the magnolia tree, near the straw-littered run where the guinea pig is eating his evening salad. Cas likes Granny's garden, it's got a little patch of lawn, but beyond it's mostly wild. He imagines little creatures creeping about in the thickets of overgrown shrubs, making their homes there, though he's never actually seen any. They'd be much smaller than the guinea pig, of course. Tiny voles and field mice. Also beetles and spiders and woodlice and ants. If you lie with your face to the ground after a while you start to see them. There are little things living just about everywhere, some of them so small they can't even see you, you're as enormous and invisible as the sky.

Granny sits with her shoulders slumped and her eyes closed, but she's not asleep. You can tell that because from time to time she opens and shuts her mouth and mumbles words you can't quite hear, as if she's arguing with someone in a dream. Her hands move up and down on her lap. The skin on her hands is amazingly wrinkled. Now she's making one hand stroke the other hand, it's like she wants to smooth out the wrinkled skin. Cas, watching, wants to reach out and touch her hands too. He wants to see if they feel scratchy or soft.

Mum says Granny has been unhappy all her life but surely that's impossible, you'd just die. You can't be unhappy all the time. You'd get tired of it, you'd have to have a rest. Maybe that's what Granny's doing now, having a rest from being unhappy. Bridget is in the house making supper for them both, then after supper Bridget will put Granny to bed, then after that she'll take Cas home and he'll go to bed. Cas likes it that Granny will go to bed earlier than him, it makes him feel that he's more grown-up than her.

He doesn't mind that she doesn't talk to him, sitting here in the evening garden. He just watches her, keeping very still, not frightening her, waiting for her to feel safe. And after a bit he sees her eyes open and she looks at him. He looks back at her, but she doesn't speak or smile or do anything. You have to just wait. When they feel safe they start to make little noises. Then you can make little noises back.

She's staring at him and she's frowning, trying to remember.

'Who are you?' She says.

'Caspar.'

'Caspar? What sort of name's that?' She speaks in a small cross voice. 'They should have called you John.'

'Why?' he says.

'It doesn't matter. No one listens to me.'

Cas is listening to her. He doesn't say so, he just goes on listening. She's started making her little noises now.

'What are you doing here?' she says.

'You're babysitting me, Granny.'

'Am I?'

'Mum's gone to a dinner party.'

'Has she?'

'Bridget's going to take me home after supper.'

'Bridget? Is she here?'

'Yes, Granny. She's in the kitchen, making supper.'

The old lady closes her eyes, not to sleep but to ponder this information. When her eyes are closed she has a nice face. Quite suddenly Cas sees something he's not seen before, which is that Granny looks very like Mum. If you don't look at the grey hair or the wrinkles, just at the way the nose and mouth and chin go together, it could almost be Mum. And Mum is the person he loves most in the world.

'She's won,' says Granny. Then she opens her eyes again. 'Bridget has.'

'What's she won?' says Cas.

'She does as she pleases. I can't stop her. This is her house now. I'm surprised she lets me go on living here. But I shan't live much longer. Then she can have it all.'

Mum said to Cas when she drove him over, 'You know Granny is not always quite right in the head. She gets muddled about things. But Bridget will be there, so you mustn't mind.'

Cas doesn't mind. He's interested.

'Bridget shouldn't have the house,' he says. 'It's your house.'

'That's what I say,' exclaims the old lady with sudden force. 'This is my house! What's she doing here?'

'She's making supper,' says Cas.

'What do I want supper for? I don't want to go on living.'

'I want supper,' says Cas. 'I'm hungry.'

'Oh, well then. She can make supper for you.'

This thought seems to calm her. The fit of anger passes.

'Granny,' says Cas. 'Does your guinea pig talk?'

'Oh, yes. She talks a great deal. They talk to each other all the time.'

'Are there two guinea pigs?'

Cas can only see one, still steadily working its way through the bowl of salad.

'Oh, I forgot. One of them died. That was Bridget. She killed it.'

'Then she should go to prison.'

'She should! She should go to prison!' She smiles for the first time, a cruel little smile on her wrinkly face. 'Then she'd get a taste of her own medicine.'

'I think rabbits talk to each other,' says Cas. 'But they do it without making any sounds. It's a kind of silent talking.'

'I talk to Perry,' says the old lady. 'I tell him everything that's happening to me.'

'Who's Perry?'

'Perry's my little dog. You remember Perry.'

Cas doesn't remember Perry. But there's no need to say this. She's got her wrinkly hands on her lap, moving one over the other, pushing at those fine wrinkles, making him want to touch them.

'Does Perry talk to you, Granny?'

'No, darling. Perry's gone now. But I talk to him anyway, because it makes me feel he's not gone so far.'

'Dad's got a dog in his film that talks. It doesn't really talk, it's only film tricks. But if you hold up two fingers, or three, he can count them. He does it with barking.'

He holds up two fingers to demonstrate.

'Woof! Woof!'

The old lady is delighted.

'Woof! Woof!' she repeats.

'You like animals, don't you, Granny,' he says.

'Oh, yes. I do.'

'So do I.'

'Animals are innocent, you see. They don't tell lies. They don't want to hurt you. But they have just as much love to give as people. Really they're much better to have round you than people. I wish I could have a carer who was a dog.'

'Like Nana,' says Cas.

'Who's Nana?'

'The dog in *Peter Pan*. It looks after the children.'

'Oh, yes.' But she looks confused.

'Why didn't you get another dog after Perry died, Granny?'

'I couldn't bear to go through that again,' she says. 'When Perry died, I wanted to die. I loved him so much. It was much worse than when Rex left me. No, I'd rather be alone. And I can still talk to Perry, you see. He's not so very far away.'

'And you've got Bridget.'

'I don't like Bridget. I have to do what she says. My father was a solicitor, we lived in Farnborough, we were gentry, the butcher delivered every Friday. It said it on his van, Supplier to the Gentry. Who is this Bridget to tell me what to do?' She lowers her voice to a theatrical whisper. 'The working classes have no manners, you know? Bridget has no idea how to lay a table. She calls me Mrs D!'

Cas ponders the situation.

'So what will you do, Granny?'

'There's nothing I can do. I've lost.'

'But you can't spend all day being unhappy. Not every day.' He says this earnestly, unable to believe that there aren't moments of relief from the misery. 'You're not unhappy now, are you?'

'No,' she says. 'Not so much right now.'

'So if I come and see you sometimes, you won't always be unhappy.'

'Oh, my dear.'

'And Mum can come and see you.'

'I'm such a burden to your mother. She works so hard, she doesn't have time for me.'

'Yes, that's true,' says Cas.

'She must be just waiting for me to die.'

Cas wants to be truthful. 'I don't *think* she wants you to die.'

'I'm just a nuisance,' says the old lady. 'That's all I am. A burden and a nuisance. Do they think I don't know it? Do they think I can't see it in their faces? Oh, they're thinking, what does she want now? What's she demanding now? Why can't she just go away? But you see how it is, I can't go away. I'd love to go away, but I can hardly walk any more. So of course it's them who do the going away. It's always been them who go away, and I'm the one left on my own. Why is that? I don't understand that. Can you tell me why everyone always leaves me?'

'No, Granny,' says Cas. He thinks about it for a moment. 'Maybe it's because you get so cross.'

'Cross? I don't get cross,' she says crossly. 'Who told you I get cross? Was it Bridget? I tell her when she's doing things wrong sometimes, but that's not getting cross. You have to tell servants when they do something wrong, or they get lazy and sloppy. It's just something you have to do. Not that Bridget listens to a word I say any more. No, I'm the one who has to listen to her. Come in now, she says. Go to bed now, she says. And I have to do it. She's got me where she wants me, all right. I've told Elizabeth, but she won't listen. Nobody listens. I might as well be talking to the trees.'

The guinea pig has finally had enough salad. It waddles off to its hutch.

'I listen,' says Cas.

'Well, maybe you do. But you'll go away too. In the end everyone leaves me.'

'So really,' says Cas, 'you're unhappy because you're lonely.'

'Well, yes.'

'Isn't it horrible being lonely all the time?'

'Yes,' she replies. 'It's horrible.'

Cas reaches out and strokes her hand, so he can feel the wrinkles. They're soft as soft, not dry or crackly at all. She looks at him as he strokes her hand and it's like Mum looking at him, only her little eyes have gone shiny.

'Soft,' he says.

'Old,' she says.

'When I feel lonely,' he says, 'I go and visit the rabbits.'

'What rabbits?'

'There's a warren in the field behind our new house. They don't know I'm visiting them, of course. But you don't feel at all alone watching rabbits. Mostly they just eat grass and stuff. But sometimes they play with each other. It's called binking.'

'Called what?'

'Binking. They jump about in the air just because they feel happy. They go binky.'

'Go binky?'

The word delights the old lady.

'So you could watch rabbits when you get lonely.'

'But I don't have a warren in my garden. We don't want rabbits in here.'

'So if you don't have rabbits, watch your guinea pig.'

'One guinea pig doesn't do much.' She eyes the guinea pig as it noses in the straw of its hutch. 'I don't think guinea pigs go binky.'

'Then,' says Cas, in a moment of illumination, 'watch Bridget.'

'Watch Bridget!'

'So you don't get lonely.'

'Bridget!'

'You don't have to like her. You just watch her. See all the funny little things she does.'

'I don't think Bridget will go binky.'

'You never know. She might. You just have to keep watching. It's easy to miss the best moments. You have to sit very quietly, so they forget you're there. And then, all of a sudden, they start binking. Up and down, jumping all over the place, out of just being so happy.'

'Perry used to jump like that,' says the old lady. 'Oh, Perry! I hope you're happy now, Perry.'

'Where is he?' says Cas, interested.

'He's in animal heaven. And when I die, that's where I'm going to go. I don't want to go to people heaven. I don't think I really like people very much. I shall go and live for ever with the animals.'

Bridget comes out of the house.

'Supper on the table, Mrs D. You can run on in and start, if you want, Cas. I'll help Mrs D in. We take our time, don't we, Mrs D?'

Cas jumps up eagerly.

'Do you mind, Granny?'

'Off you go, my love.'

Caspar runs into the house. Bridget comes to the old lady's side and readies her arm so she can pull herself up. Mrs Dickinson fixes her with an unblinking stare.

'I'm watching you, Bridget,' she says.

'You do that, Mrs D. Now come on. Up you get.'

44

Early evening on Saturday. Sunlight bathes the west-facing terrace, and the air is mild. Laura has made her decision. They will eat outside tonight. They will sit down to the main course at half past eight, in just over two hours time. Now begins the most complex and intense phase of the entire operation.

The rolled saddle of lamb, the expensive centrepiece of the meal, is the source of greatest anxiety. As she works away at its preparation, piercing holes, poking in sprigs of rosemary and wedges of garlic, massaging it with olive oil and salt and pepper, she reruns the sums in her head to determine the cooking times. Six pounds at sixteen minutes a pound, ninety-six minutes roasting time, twenty minutes to rest: just under two hours. So it should go into the oven in ten minutes or so. But what are the chances the guests will be in their places ready to eat at eight-thirty? Better the lamb too pink than overcooked. So put it in the oven at 6.40 p.m. and take it out at 8.15 p.m.

Time before that to top and tail the courgettes and slice and toss them in olive oil and butter. Then there's the baguettes to slice and grill for the taramasalata. And oh God, someone needs to pick some flowers.

She goes out onto the terrace, where Henry is sitting talking with Diana and Roddy.

'I think we can eat outside, don't you?' she says. 'Henry, I'm leaving you to lay the table and deal with drinks. Diana, I don't suppose you'd like to pick some flowers?'

'I've just been telling Henry about Max,' says Diana. 'That boy never ceases to amaze me. I've always known he was bright and, of course, exceptional, really, but he's becoming so *wise*. Yesterday he gave me quite a lecture about taking life more seriously. He's becoming almost *formidable*.'

'Maybe he gets that from Roddy,' says Henry.

'From Roddy?' Diana sound surprised. 'Roddy isn't formidable in the least.'

'Why don't you give everyone a drink?' says Laura to Henry. 'And bring me a glass in the kitchen.'

She returns to her vegetable preparations. In her mind she is slotting the various tasks into the time available. Clearly Diana won't be picking the flowers, so she'll have to find five minutes for that. Then at some point after the lamb's in the oven and before it's time to cook the vegetables she must steal a quarter of an hour to change and make herself presentable. And what is Carrie to eat? She may choose to lurk in her room but she still needs to be fed.

Roddy appears, bringing her a glass of wine.

'I'm an emissary from Henry.'

'Oh, thank you, Roddy. It's a bit early, I know.'

She drinks gratefully. Then she starts work cutting up the baguettes.

'So when are the other guests coming?' says Roddy.

'In half an hour or so. I asked them to come early while there's still sun on the terrace.'

'Half an hour!' Roddy sounds shocked. 'We haven't had any time to talk.'

'Yes, I know,' says Laura. 'Everything's been a bit up in the air, what with Carrie's accident and all the rest of it. And now

I'm afraid I'm going to be a bit frantic until we're all sitting down and eating.'

'Would it bother you if I hang about in the kitchen while you work? I've been so looking forward to telling you about – well, you know.'

'Your adventures.'

'Yes. My adventures.'

Roddy is visibly pleased. Laura would far rather be left alone at this point, but she hasn't got the heart to turn him away.

'I don't suppose you feel up to picking some flowers for the table, do you?'

'I don't think I'm much good with flowers,' says Roddy. 'I'd pick all the wrong ones.'

'There aren't any wrong flowers. You just pick ones you like, that you think will go together.'

'But what if you don't like what I pick? Or Diana. I'm quite sure Diana wouldn't approve of my choice.'

'Oh, Roddy.'

She meets his uncertain gaze with a smile of sympathy.

'You really are a saint with my sister.'

'Oh, well, Diana and I . . .' He looks out to the terrace where Diana and Henry are talking. 'It's been so long since we've been . . .'

His voice trails away into silence. Then before Laura can say something vague and consoling, he starts up again.

'You have to look at these things objectively, don't you? And objectively speaking, I don't see that I have all that much to offer Diana these days. I suppose that sounds hard. But you can see how we are together.'

Laura's heart sinks. It's worse than she feared. This is not what she needs right now. She reaches for a pair of scissors.

'Roddy, I'm the first to admit that my sister must be impossible to live with, and God knows how you've managed it all these years. But this is really going to have to wait for another day, I'm afraid.'

'Yes, of course,' he says. 'It just helps to know that you — that you understand.'

'I really do have to go out and pick some flowers.'

To her slight irritation he follows her to the flower borders. She cuts handfuls of alchemilla, laying it in foamy yellow-green heaps in the trug she carries on her arm. She moves briskly, aware of her deadline for the lamb. Roddy trots along behind, talking in a ceaseless semi-coherent stream.

'You get to an age,' he says by the magnolia, 'when you realise you're not living the life you were created to live. Of course I realise that's something of a presumption. That there is a creator, I mean . . .'

And following Laura to the banks of pink cosmos, 'After all, we're not either of us getting any younger, though I dare hope for at least another thirty years of vigour and good health—'

And by the fringe of the orchard, where the bright blue cornflowers grow, 'In one sense we're all borne along by the stream of life, but in another sense we must act, we must be the authors of our own destiny, when that destiny at last presents itself.'

Laura has only a general idea what Roddy is talking about, and isn't really paying close attention. He comes at last to a stop, saying, 'I think we understand each other pretty well, don't you?'

'Yes, yes, absolutely,' she replies.

It's almost time to put the saddle of lamb in the oven. She returns to the house with Roddy half a pace behind.

'Talk to Henry, Roddy,' she says as she crosses the terrace

where Henry and Diana are sitting with their drinks. 'He understands all this so much better than me.'

'All what?' says Henry.

'And don't forget you're laying the table, Henry. Roddy can help you.'

By this means she sheds Roddy. She parks the trug of flowers on the table, checks the time once more, and slides the lamb in its roasting tray onto a high rack in the top oven. She makes a mental note to baste the roast in half an hour. Within that time she must trim and arrange the flowers in two vases, tidy the mess in the kitchen and living room, sort out serving dishes – oh, and put out the redcurrant jelly, bought rather than home-made, but you can't do everything. Then there's the sliced baguettes to oil and grill for the starter. Might as well take the taramasalata out of the fridge now. Get down a long platter to lay the slices out. And some olives, they'll go well, the big sweet Spanish olives from Bill's in Lewes, everyone loves them.

More wine. Now to see to herself.

She runs upstairs and changes into a light cotton summer dress. She brushes her hair and does a little work on her make-up. A bolder red on her lips, some eye shadow, some mascara. Then she picks out a pair of shoes with heels, pretty and rather fragile. She checks her appearance in the long mirror, unconsciously assuming a pose that presents her body to advantage and slightly protruding her lips. From the terrace below comes the sound of voices and the clink of cutlery as Henry puts out knives and forks. She checks her watch. Almost seven o'clock. Still so much to do.

She looks in on Carrie before heading back downstairs. Carrie is sitting on her bed with her guitar on her lap and a pad of paper and a pen in her hands.

'You okay?'

'Yes. Fine.'

'I'm going to make a plate of food for you. You'll have to eat it in secret.'

Carrie doesn't even look up. 'Thanks, Mum.'

Maggie and Andrew walk over to the Broads from Maggie's cottage. The Broads' house looks so substantial, so rooted in the world of tradition and convention, that Maggie hesitates, assailed by doubt, on the gravel before the front door. Suddenly she's not sure she can do this. Sounds of teenage music come from an open upper window. A glimpse into an unoccupied drawing-room shows framed photographs of smiling children on a sideboard. This is family land. All the guests will be in couples.

'Maybe this is a mistake,' she says. 'I feel like I'm here under false pretences. What if they ask us about our plans for the future?'

'People don't ask people about their plans for the future.'

'They might.'

'Then we say we're thinking of setting up a commune,' says Andrew unexpectedly.

'A commune?'

'Shared property. Free love.'

Maggie grins at that.

'Seriously, Maggie,' says Andrew, 'if it all gets too much we can leave. We could have a code word, and if you say it, I'll come up with an excuse, and we'll leave.'

'What sort of code word?'

'Something you wouldn't normally say in conversation, but not so weird that everyone notices. Like Basingstoke. Or Purley. Rhymes with *early*, as in Let's leave early.'

All this is a side of Andrew that has been in hiding in recent weeks. Her confession of uncertainty seems to have liberated him.

'How do you get Purley into a conversation?' she says.

'It doesn't have to be Purley the place. It can be pearly like in a necklace.'

'Pearly necklace? That's just odd.'

'It's got to be odd, or it'll come up in ordinary conversation. The code word could be *girly*, but you might say it not as code, and I'd think you wanted to leave, and you wouldn't.'

'Girly? I never say girly. When does anyone ever say girly?'

'Girly laughter. Girly night out.'

'All right,' she says. 'Purley it is.'

Such a ridiculous conversation to be having. She takes a deep breath and rings the doorbell. Henry Broad answers the door.

'The lovely Maggie! And you must be Andrew. What terrible neighbours we are. You've not been round before, have you? Come in, come in. I blame the Internet.'

He leads them through a big, warm-toned kitchen, where Laura Broad is turning a rack of toast on the hot plate. The air is heady with the aroma of roasting meat. Laura greets Maggie with a kiss. A quick friendly glance at Andrew shows that she at least is following the plot.

'I have to find a moment to talk to you, Andrew,' she says. 'I've been learning a few things about your uncle's collection.'

Henry ushers them out onto the terrace, where a thin elegant woman stands with an ugly middle-aged man, quarrelling in undertones. As they're introduced Maggie finds herself actually blushing, not at anything anyone says, but because in the eyes of these strangers they are effectively married already. She wants to say, 'No, you don't understand, we only met on the doorstep.' Or more truthfully, 'We've come as a couple but we've had a rocky week and may be splitting up tomorrow.' Instead she dips her head and smiles and allows the illusion to remain. Everyone here is tidily paired off. Everyone has a home and a life companion. There's no call to confuse matters.

'Maggie's job is in conservation,' Henry says.

'Whenever I hear that word I think of jam-making,' says the thin, elegant woman.

Diana takes against the newcomer on sight. Maggie is exactly the kind of woman she finds most tiresome: pretty in a girly sort of way, without sophistication, the sort who grew up in pony clubs and feels at home in Wellington boots. Maggie's smiling at her in a placatory way because that's how people behave in the provinces, where they value social cohesion above intellectual stimulus. So instead of smiling back Diana looks away, not to talk to anyone else, but to indicate that she at least won't be playing the tedious game of nicey-nicey that passes for an entertaining evening out in Sussex.

'You're thinking of conserves,' says Maggie.

'So I am,' says Diana. 'But actually there is a connection. You know when you make jam there's a vital ingredient that makes the jam set? It's called pectin. There's bound to be an equivalent in the conservation of buildings, something you have to add to the process to make it really last. I wonder what it is.'

'What on earth are you talking about, Diana?' says Henry.

'I'm making small talk,' says Diana. 'I'm being sociable.'

She can feel without actually looking how the person called Maggie is entirely out of her depth, and this gratifies her. Why should people put so much effort into making each other comfortable? Life begins when you leave your comfort zone. Her talk with Max this morning, just before she left, had just this effect. She still feels a little shaken by it. But she recognises that Max had the energy and the originality to challenge his own mother's preconceptions, and Diana applauds that.

'What makes you think your views are superior to Dad's?' he said. 'Has it occurred to you that you might occupy a far smaller mental universe than he does? Has it occurred to you that he's grappling with the really important questions, and you've never asked them because your mind is clogged by triviality?'

Many mothers would have found that quite hurtful, but Diana has always prided herself on the freedom she's given her children to be themselves. She takes Max's criticism in the spirit it's given, not as an attack, but as a sharing of his own evolving outlook. She stays open to new experiences. That's the difference between the life she leads and the life Laura leads in Sussex. And if that openness exposes her to the occasional sting, then so be it. That's the price you pay for staying alive. She knows Max is still both her beloved son and her friend. This is what she's most proud of in her life. Her children are her friends.

'I'm useless at being sociable,' says Roddy. 'Diana's always telling me I have no small talk.'

'Oh, for heaven's sake, Roddy.'

It really is more than she can bear to have Roddy drooping about the place pandering to other people's insecurities. If they want to have a shy people's tea party, let them all move to Cheltenham and do it where it won't bore the rest of us to death. Then, abruptly, she remembers that Max has offered her a different perspective on Roddy.

'Tell them about your search for God,' she says. 'Max has been telling me I'm too trivial. Do you search for God?'

She addresses this to the dull-looking young man in spectacles who has come with the jam woman. She has entirely failed to retain his name.

'No,' he says, 'no, I don't. Do you think I should?'

'Absolutely. You wouldn't want to be accused of having a mind clogged by triviality, would you?'

'Shut up,' says Roddy.

Diana is startled.

'What did you say, Roddy?'

'I said shut up.'

At this point another couple joins them, and Henry makes introductions and passes round drinks. Diana is bewildered. Did Roddy just tell her to shut up in public?

'Diana. Roddy. This is Liz and Alan.'

Liz answers Henry's courteous enquiry about her mother by telling the story of her week. She tells it as if it's a comic anecdote about a maddening but lovable old eccentric.

'Every day she was telling me she didn't need her carer, she hated her carer, she wanted me to take her carer away. So I took her away. She lasted three days. Now she's saying to her carer, Never leave me.'

But as she speaks her real attention is on one of the other guests, who she recognised as soon as they came out onto the terrace. It's the council pixie who made eyes at Alan, and who is making eyes at Alan even now. Alan too has recognised her, and they have begun a conversation. Liz is thrown by this. The encounter feels embarrassing, almost indecent, like meeting your gynaecologist at a swingers' party.

Half picking up on their conversation even while conducting a conversation of her own, Liz gathers that the pixie knows about Alan's other writer. She's sympathising with him over his predicament. How does she know this? Have they had more than one meeting?

'What's your view on donkeys?' she says to Laura's brother-in-law.

'I think I can truthfully say,' he answers, 'that I have no view whatsoever on donkeys.'

Laura comes out with a plate of something or other on toast, and gives Liz the plate to hold.

'It's taramasalata,' says Laura. 'To keep you going.'

She heads back into the kitchen. Henry refills glasses. Alan remains deep in talk with the pixie. Liz feels old and ugly and incompetent. Laura is a far better cook than she is, and a far better hostess. She catches herself hoping for some social disaster to overtake the evening.

'These are *delicious*,' says Diana. 'Roddy, you've already had your share.'

'My point is this,' says Henry. 'We've all lost confidence in our ability to make artistic judgements.'

'Have you lost your confidence to make artistic judgements?' Liz says to the young man in glasses.

'No,' he says. 'I never had any confidence to lose.'

'So what is it you do?'

'I work in IT.'

Liz barely hears him. She's watching Alan, his face so animated, talking so eagerly, while the pixie smiles up at him.

'I'm so sorry,' she says to the man in spectacles, 'I didn't catch your girlfriend's name – your partner—'

'Maggie,' he says. 'Maggie Dutton.'

'I don't think she remembers, but we met just a few days ago.'

Alan finds to his surprise that he's enjoying the evening. Henry is assiduous at refilling his glass, and he's flattered that Maggie remembers not only what he does for a living, but what has been causing him grief this week. He responds to her friendly interest with a comic tour-de-force on the fate of his poor sheepdog movie, which secretly impresses even himself.

'And best of all,' he concludes, 'I get to tell total strangers at dinner parties about Colin Firth and Robert De Niro, neither of whom I have actually met, who are speaking words written by someone else, for which I will get the credit. How sublimely wonderful is that?'

Maggie laughs, visibly enchanted.

'But you do write plays as well,' she says. 'Those are your words.'

Liz joins them, carrying a plate of something or other on toast.

'Hi,' she says to Maggie. 'I'm Liz.'

'Maggie's the conservation officer,' Alan says. 'She came over the other day.'

'I remember,' says Liz.

Alan sees at once that Liz is going to give Maggie a hard time, and this irritates him. She's only doing her job. When you meet socially you put all that stuff aside.

'We're not even going to think about all that,' he says. 'This is a social event.'

'I'm sure Maggie is used to it,' says Liz. 'Like being an off-duty traffic warden. You must keep meeting people you've given parking tickets.'

'Like you keep meeting people you've misquoted in print,' says Alan.

Liz gives him a stare. Then she turns to Maggie.

'I've been talking to your husband. He tells me he's in IT.'

'We're not married,' says Maggie. 'He fixes people's computers.'

Henry comes to refill their glasses.

'Did Laura tell you we went to a Buckingham Palace garden party?' he says. 'It was rather wonderful. We came to mock and stayed to pray.'

*

In the kitchen, Laura has basted the lamb, and moved it to the bottom of the top oven. Serving dishes are in the bottom oven to warm. The carving board is out, the carving knife sharpened. Time to put the potatoes on. A glance through the open door onto the terrace shows her guests, lit by the golden light of the sinking sun, drinking their wine and talking happily.

The water is bubbling in the pan. She lowers the steamer basket over the boiling water, sprinkles salt onto the new potatoes, and covers them with a lid. As she turns round from the stove she sees Roddy standing in the doorway staring at her.

'You've changed,' he says.

Roddy is in hell. He doesn't understand how it happened, but something has come between himself and Laura. The unspoken understanding they had before has gone, to be replaced by something hard and shiny and impenetrable. He feels as if the words he says to her no longer reach her, they're blown away by some cruel wind. He watches her all the time to see if she feels it too, but she's in motion, always busy. Roddy hates the dinner party. He hates the people here, with the sole exception of Laura. What are they but noise and interference? A great change is destined for this weekend, and it's unable to come into being because of this bustle and chatter, this pointless worthless nodding and smiling that has in it no reality, no substance, no love. If he could remove Laura from the party for the shortest time, for half an hour, for ten minutes, if they could walk out across the meadow, down to the river bank, and be silent in each other's company – then the true Laura would meet his eyes, and he could speak the simple words that he has so far failed to utter.

Roddy blames himself. He knows he has a tendency to ramble. It's because he's nervous. Alone, feeling her loving gaze on him, the nervousness will fall away, and his tongue will speak the truth of his heart.

How beautiful she is. How radiant and womanly. Even as she moves out of his reach she becomes more perfect. All he wants in life is to be with her. Others talk of the search for God and have no understanding. Only those who live the true and destined life know God. With Laura I am with God. Without her I am in hell.

'Do you have a moment, Laura?'

'Look at me, Roddy. Do I look as if I have a moment?'

Henry appears by his side and speaks low in his ear.

'Roddy, do me a favour. Rescue Andrew.'

Andrew is the soft-faced young man with glasses. He's standing talking to Diana, or rather, listening to Diana. Diana is doing that thing she does, talking to someone while her eyes gaze in all other directions, transparently in search of some person or object of more compelling interest.

Bowing his head as if to his own execution, Roddy does as he's asked.

'Roddy,' says Diana. 'You're behaving very oddly this evening. Are you ill?'

'I expect so,' says Roddy.

'Well, don't be. It's such a bore. Andrew and I have been talking about computers. More your kind of thing.'

She goes into the kitchen to bother Laura. Roddy looks wildly at Andrew, overwhelmed with anger at Diana. Why now? Why this evening? Not that there's anything new. She's been behaving this way for years. But today was to have been the day of his liberation. He feels like a prisoner whose term has expired, only to find as he is led to the prison gates that a new sentence has been imposed, and he will never be free.

'We weren't exactly talking about computers,' says Andrew.

'We were talking about why some people seem to have a blind spot about computers.'

'You work with computers, do you?'

'Yes,' says Andrew. 'I fix computer problems. Though of course it's very rarely the computer that's at fault, it's the user. So you could say I fix people.'

'You fix people?'

Dimly, through the haze of pain and anger, Roddy is aware that this is interesting. At any other time he could take pleasure in pursuing the insight. But through the open kitchen door he can see Laura at work in the kitchen, and Diana leaning against the table, where he should be, saying empty nothings to her, when he could be changing lives.

'I suppose that sounds a bit pompous,' says Andrew. 'But you know what I mean.'

Maggie joins them, slipping one hand through Andrew's arm.

'Has Andrew told you?' she says. 'We're thinking of setting up a commune.'

'Really?' says Roddy.

'Shared property and free love,' says Maggie.

'She's teasing you,' says Andrew.

'Oh, right,' says Roddy. 'I never get it when people make jokes. Diana says you have to ring a bell for me.'

'I'm only partly teasing,' says Maggie. 'There isn't nearly enough love in the world. We could set it up in Basingstoke.'

'Why Basingstoke?' says Roddy.

'Because it's near Purley.'

'How near?' says Andrew.

'Quite near,' says Maggie. 'But we're not there yet.'

Maggie is already a little drunk. Henry is so good at refilling the glasses that without noticing it she must have drunk half a bottle or more already. The encounter with Alan has thrown her off-balance, but it has also sharpened her senses. Those first impressions have not deceived her. This is a powerfully attractive man. She can't keep her eyes off him. All the while they were talking she was longing to touch him. For some reason this quiet man with the lined, weary face and the mass of soft brown hair has aroused her sexual desire. It's not anything he says or does. It's just what he is. She's had to walk away from him, afraid she if she remains close for any longer she'll start undoing his trousers and saying, 'Let's fuck.'

He himself seems to be oblivious to her response, but his wife is more than aware. Maggie can't blame her, but what can you do? Her conversation has been entirely innocent, she has no designs on Alan, she's walked away from him, hasn't she? But she can feel him still, behind her, by the terrace table. Her back feels him and tingles. Her bum tingles.

She pulls a little tighter on Andrew's arm. Maybe they should leave. There's no one here she has any desire to talk to except *him*. But Laura has been so kind to her, and it would be so rude to walk out. Also if they left early, would she tell Andrew the reason? You can't say something like that, can you? You can't tell your boyfriend you're wetting your knickers for another man. So you don't tell him. You bury it, and you behave yourself. And then what?

'Free love is an interesting concept,' Roddy says. 'People think it means orgies, but you could argue it means true love. In that there's no true love without freedom.'

'What about married people?' says Maggie. 'They're not free. Does that mean you can't be married and have true love?'

'It might mean that,' says Roddy, his eyes gleaming. 'It might indeed.'

'There, you see, Andrew,' says Maggie. 'It's your A and B and X and Y.'

'It's a theory I was trying out on Maggie,' Andrew explains to Roddy. 'The intense phase of love rarely lasts.'

'But it does,' says Roddy with sudden earnestness. 'With the right person it not only lasts, it grows deeper and stronger with every year that goes by.'

'You're a lucky man,' says Maggie.

How strange people are. This ugly man and his sharp-tongued wife have clearly found a way to make marriage work. She wants to ask him their secret. It can't be sex, surely? But you never know. In the privacy of the bedroom perhaps they call each other baby names and do things to each other with their fingers that excite them both to ecstasy.

Henry stands gazing at the teak terrace table, now laid, made pretty with two vases of pink cosmos and blue cornflowers, and three red candles in glass wind-shields. He's puzzling over where to seat his guests. He'll put himself at the head, as host, and Laura on the far right corner where she likes to go, so she has easy access to the kitchen. Andrew on her left, so she can talk to him about books. That means Andrew had better have Liz on his left and Alan opposite, which puts Roddy at the other end of the table, with Maggie on his right. Henry mentally surveys the arrangement. It means he gets Diana, but he can cope with that, and at least she's as far from Roddy as it's possible to get on a table for eight.

Have I brought up enough wine? Red for the main course, eight people, four bottles should be enough, surely? The white has been disappearing faster than expected. Still light on the terrace, that sweet gentle light of summer evenings. Too soon to light the candles.

The moon is rising, almost a full moon but not quite, a squeezed disc low over the rim of the Downs. Barely a breeze. What a summer it's been so far. A summer to be grateful for. A day to be grateful for. A day that is now slowly, beautifully, ending.

He looks back at the house, its windows glowing in the twilight. He sees Laura at work in the kitchen, reaching for the oven gloves that hang over the rail of the Aga. Things have their places. Little by little, the tools you need for daily living discover and occupy their rightful niches, as if the house is a garment that is tailored to fit over time. The gap between the dishwasher and the sink becomes a slot for trays. The Deruta bowl on the dresser holds string, glue, Sellotape, drawing pins. Rarely used serving dishes and big vases are stored in the cupboard under the stairs. Laura's nightdress and his own bathrobe hang on hooks above the bedroom radiator so they're warm for wearing at night. These arrangements are all unremarkable, obvious perhaps, but each one represents a decision they have made over the years. So a house grows in familiarity and rightness, just as a person does; just as a marriage does.

Roddy enters the kitchen with a determined stride and takes Laura's wrist in his hand.

'Come with me,' he says.

Laura has the oven gloves in her hands. She's about to take the lamb out of the oven. She's so surprised by Roddy's manner that she doesn't resist.

He leads her into the hall, which is not overlooked from the terrace. Keeping tight hold of her wrist, he fixes her with his eyes, revealing there the turmoil of his spirit. Laura understands that this is all about his troubled marriage, and she wants to be sympathetic, but he has chosen the worst possible moment.

'Laura,' he says.

'Please, Roddy—'

'You know what this is about.'

'Later, Roddy.'

'I just need one word. One word, Laura.'

She pulls at her hand, but he only holds it tighter.

'Look, Roddy, I really will listen, but not now. The lamb has to come out of the oven—'

'The lamb!' His face darkens and his voice rises. 'I don't give a fuck about the lamb!'

The obscenity releases Laura's last qualms of conscience. She snaps her wrist out of his grasp.

'You're drunk, Roddy. Go and stick your head in cold water.'

His face crumples.

'I'm not drunk,' he says.

'Then go back to the others and behave yourself.'

She hurries back to the kitchen and opens the oven door. Hot air and the smells of the joint engulf her. She draws out the saddle of lamb on its roasting pan and transfers it to the bottom simmering oven, leaving it there with the oven door ajar to rest. Has she left it too long? With lamb two or three minutes can make all the difference.

What's wrong with Roddy? He's having some sort of breakdown, evidently. Laura realises she'll have to have a proper talk with him, but it can wait till tomorrow. Time now to put on the carrots and sauté the courgettes. Then there's the gravy to make, from the juices in the roasting pan. Then Henry can carve.

Andrew takes Maggie to the end of the terrace to show her the moon rising between the trees. Here he can speak to her in private.

'Look,' he says, 'if you want to go I can fake an emergency call on my phone and we can just go.'

'But I'm having a wonderful time,' says Maggie. 'Aren't you having a wonderful time?'

Her eyes dart about as she speaks and she moves her feet as if dancing to some music in her head.

'No, not really,' he says.

'Well, you should, Andrew. These are lovely people, and they're our neighbours, so you should make more effort.'

She performs a little pirouette in the twilight.

'And it's such a lovely evening.'

'You're not usually like this,' he says.

'Aren't I? Well, we can't be usual all the time.'

He can't tell if she's drunk or just playing at being drunk. All he can see is that whatever it is that's happening to her does not include him.

'Come on,' she says, drawing him back to the others. 'We mustn't be antisocial.'

They join Alan and Liz and Diana.

'Have you seen the moon?' Maggie says. 'I think it might be a full moon.'

'Couple of days to go,' says Alan.

'Are you sure? Do you know about things like that? Are you one of those people who knows things?'

'Just don't ask him what day it is,' says Liz. 'Or where he put his reading glasses.'

'Oh, I have the answer to that,' says Diana. 'You buy lots of pairs, and scatter them round the house. The average German owns six pairs.'

'Andrew never loses his,' says Maggie, 'because they're always on his face.'

Henry summons his guests to the table and assigns them their places.

'Roddy, you're at the other end. Why don't you give everyone a glass of red? It's a nice Rioja. Well, I hope it's nice. Maggie, you go there, by Roddy. Liz, you're by me.'

Laura brings out dishes of vegetables. She displays the saddle of lamb before it's carved.

'I just hope I haven't overdone it.'

Roddy fills glasses as the others take their seats. Henry takes the lamb back into the kitchen to carve. Diana, finding herself facing Liz, does her conversational duty.

'You live in the village too, do you?' she says.

'No,' says Liz. 'We're about four miles away.'

Laura says, 'Liz's daughter Alice goes out with Jack.'

'Oh, yes,' says Diana, remembering. 'You write for the *Telegraph*. Didn't I read something the other day about men and women being friends, or not being friends, or something?'

'Yes, that was me,' says Liz.

'Why can't men and women be friends?' says Maggie. 'I've got lots of men who are friends.'

'Because of sex,' says Alan.

'Friends can have sex,' says Maggie.

'Doesn't that change friendship?' says Laura. 'I thought it did.'

'Of course it does,' says Diana. 'If you're having sex, you're not friends, you're lovers.'

'But friends can have sex,' insists Maggie, 'and still just be friends. It's not as if they have to get married. I mean, they can, but that's a whole other thing. They may just want to carry on being friends.'

'Doesn't happen,' says Alan. 'Sex is rocket fuel. Once you start, you're airborne. You have to keep flying, or you fall to earth.'

'Keep flying?' says Maggie, holding out her glass, already

empty, for Roddy to refill. 'Flying where? Flying to marriage?'

'Could be,' says Alan.

'And what then? Is marriage still flying?'

The married ones all laugh at that, except for Roddy. He sits at the end of the table in silence. Henry appears with plates of lamb.

'Oh, Lord,' says Laura. 'It is a little overdone.'

'It isn't overdone at all,' says Liz. 'Mine's a perfect pink.'

'I don't know how you can say that,' says Diana. 'I can't see a thing.'

They all fall to helping themselves to the vegetables, and the gravy, and the mint sauce, and the redcurrant jelly. Henry, now at the table too, sees that everyone's glasses are topped up. Then he lifts the cylinders and lights the three red candles. The flames burn steady and strong shielded by the glass. All at once the evening changes. The sky is still light, but here round the table on the terrace the candlelight draws them together into its flattering glow.

Liz says to Maggie, 'So I take it you've not been married yet?'

'That's a strange way to put it,' says Alan. 'As if all marriages exist in the past.'

'No, not yet,' says Maggie. 'I'm up for any tips.'

'Tips about how,' says Liz, 'or tips about who?'

'Have we got any tips, Henry?' says Laura. 'We're the longest married here.'

'As it happens,' says Henry, 'today is the twenty-seventh anniversary of the day I proposed to Laura.'

'Bravo!' says Alan. 'We should drink to that.'

'We will. I mean to propose a toast, after we've eaten.'

'You're not going to make a speech, are you, Henry?'

Laura smiles at him down the table, through the blur of candlelight.

'I might,' he says.

'Well, here's what I want to know,' says Maggie. 'Does falling in love make a good marriage? Or is it nothing to do with it?'

'Nothing,' says Diana.

'Everything,' says Liz.

'Falling in love,' says Diana, speaking a little fast, blinking her eyes, 'happens over and over. If you got married every time you fell in love you'd spend your life in a wedding dress.'

'This is new, Diana,' says Henry. 'I didn't know you were such a romantic.'

'I'm helplessly romantic,' says Diana. 'I fall in love with every pretty boy who gives me a smile. Doesn't everybody? It doesn't mean anything.'

'That's not falling in love,' says Liz. 'Falling in love is something that takes you over completely.'

At the other end of the table Laura starts talking to Andrew about his inheritance.

'You know it's my field,' she says. 'If you're thinking of selling, don't just accept the first offer you get. That collection is very special. It could go for as much as a hundred thousand.'

'Good God!' exclaims Andrew.

Maggie, who sits opposite Laura, wants to be part of the conversation about love. She leans across Alan, one hand on his arm, to question Liz.

'That's what I want to know about,' she says. 'I mean, I do know about it. But I want to know if falling in love is what leads to a successful marriage.'

'Have we got a successful marriage?' Liz says to Alan.

'Ten years and counting,' says Alan. 'Not bad.'

'How long have you and Roddy been married, Diana?' says Henry.

'Twenty-four years,' says Diana. 'That's right, isn't it, Roddy?'

Roddy nods, but does not speak. He's drinking steadily, and his eyes gaze before him at nothing.

'This is terrific, Laura,' says Alan, tapping his plate with his fork. 'Best lamb I've ever had.'

'I get it from Richards,' says Laura. 'He's a proper butcher.'

'Roddy,' says Diana, 'what are you doing down there? Are you going into the silence? Because if you are, please come out again.'

'There's more lamb,' says Henry, 'if anyone wants it.'

'I can see I'll never get an answer to my question,' says Maggie. 'I expect there isn't an answer. Don't you have an answer?' She addresses this to Alan, by her side. 'You're the one who knows things.'

'I've forgotten the question,' says Alan.

'Maggie wants to know if she should follow her heart,' says Liz. 'Assuming her heart is giving her directions.'

'Of course you should follow your heart,' says Alan, looking directly at Maggie. 'Anything else is half-hearted. Who wants to go around with half a heart?'

Maggie holds his gaze for a moment, then she blushes and looks away.

So the first course passes, and the sun sets, and all are agreed that on such a beautiful evening as this, in a summer like this, England's the only place in the world to be.

Then Henry goes round with the Rioja, charging the glasses.

'This is for my toast,' he says.

He goes back to his end of the table and remains standing, glass in hand.

'Laura doesn't approve of speeches at dinner,' he says, 'so this isn't a speech. It's just me saying this and that. Actually it's really me saying thank you. Thanking has to be done in public, doesn't it? Otherwise it doesn't count. I want to say thank you for this summer. We've been stay-at-homes here in Sussex, Laura and I, and haven't we been rewarded?'

'Who are you thanking for the summer, Henry?' says Diana.

'Oh, the powers that be, I suppose. Who I must also thank for keeping Carrie safe in her car accident. And for returning Laura's lost ring.'

Laura holds up her left hand to show the ruby ring.

'There's something else, too. It so happens that this week it's been made clear to me that my professional career is effectively at an end.'

'No, Henry!' cries Laura. 'You know that's not true.'

'Of course I shall go on working,' says Henry, 'but careers are meant to career, don't you think? They have momentum. And then one day the momentum runs out, and you know that in a while you'll roll gently to a stop. When you see that time coming, you face a choice. You can fight it, or you can let it go. I know Roddy has been having similar thoughts recently.'

'Yes,' says Roddy, his voice a low groan.

'This is all getting a little funereal, Henry,' says Diana. 'Some of us aren't ready to die quite yet.'

'Nor am I, Diana. Quite the reverse. That's what I mean when I say this is me saying thank you. You see, the person I'm really thanking is Laura. Twenty-seven years ago today I wrote on a paper napkin, *Will you marry me?* And she ticked the box marked *Yes*. Out of that moment has grown – well, everything, really. This home, this family, thanks to Laura. My daily happiness, thanks to Laura. This excellent dinner, thanks to Laura. So you see, it doesn't matter about my career. I'm learning the virtue of humility. I don't want to live any more in a world where people envy and fear each other. I want to live in a world where people treat each other with kindness.'

He looks round their faces, silent in the candlelight.

'There, now. I've confused you by turning serious.'

But his eyes are on Laura, who is gazing at him with a queer smile on her face, biting her lower lip, blinking her eyes.

Henry raises his glass high and says, very quietly in the evening hush, 'This is for Laura, on our not very important anniversary. With all my love, till the day I die.'

He puts the glass to his lips. The others are not sure whether to clap or to echo the toast or just to drink, and attempt a confusion of all three. Only Roddy does not move or speak. He too has been watching Laura's face. Her skin smoothed by the soft candlelight, her eyes bright with unshed tears, she radiates beauty, but not for him.

'Thank you, Henry,' she says. 'How very unexpected.'

Afraid she's about to cry, she jumps up from her seat.

'I think I'd better get the summer pudding.'

As soon as she's left the table the others all start talking at once, as if anxious to break the spell.

Liz says, 'I wish I'd been recording you, Henry. That was so sweet.'

Alan says, 'You're right, of course. This ambition thing puts a curse on everything one does.'

Maggie says, looking at Alan, 'It's just what you said. It's following your heart.'

Henry takes up the fourth bottle of Rioja and refills glasses. Roddy stands up and mumbles that he needs to have a pee. Diana holds Henry by the arm, as if to tug him down from a too-risky flight of fancy.

'Even so, Henry, admit it,' she says. 'You and Laura bicker as much as anyone. I've heard you.'

'Actually we're on the point of splitting up,' says Henry. 'I only said all that to put you off the scent.'

'Splitting up!'

'Very sad. After twenty-seven years.'

'Oh, you're joking. That's a rotten joke, Henry. You have to be careful what you say, or it may come true.'

Laura comes out with the summer pudding on a large white dish.

'It came out of the basin perfectly,' she says. 'You can all admire it while I get the bowls and the cream.'

She sets the glistening pink and purple mound down before Henry's place. He is the one who will serve it.

'I just love summer pudding,' says Alan.

'Me too,' says Maggie.

'There's a way of making it with sponge cake and whipped cream,' says Diana, 'that's an absolute revelation. Do you remember, Roddy? I made it when we had Peter and Rebecca round.' Then, realising Roddy has not yet returned, 'Roddy is a serious pudding man.'

Laura reappears with a stack of pink-and-white bowls, a jug of cream, and a triangular-shaped slicer.

'That's for you to cut it up with, Henry.'

Her hand resting on the back of his neck, stroking the short hairs there. Henry starts to slice. He cuts into the soft crust and the dark purple juice runs out.

In his absence, and on Diana's instructions, Roddy is given a large slice of the pudding. The cream jug makes the round of the table. Alan takes so much cream the pudding in his bowl disappears.

'Oh, Alan,' says Liz. 'What a pig you are.'

Maggie too pours herself a liberal helping of cream.

Alan, noticing this, says with a smile, 'The road of excess leads to the palace of wisdom.' Then, to the rest of the company, in apology, 'Blake, not me.'

'We don't have puddings like this in Purley,' says Maggie.

'I know Purley,' says Henry. 'Purley is basically a traffic jam.'

'Don't say that, Henry,' says Laura. 'Maggie probably grew up in Purley.'

'No,' says Maggie. 'I've never been there in my life, and I don't see any reason why I ever should go there. If you go to Purley you leave too early.'

The others laugh at this without understanding it, because it has the sound of a joke.

'What's happened to Roddy?' says Laura.

'He went to the loo.'

'He's been very quiet during dinner,' says Henry. 'I hope he's all right.'

'Why don't you go and see, Henry? Tell him his pudding's waiting.'

Henry gets up and goes into the house.

'My God, this is heaven,' says Alan, meaning the pudding. 'I would get so fat if I was married to you, Laura.'

'Thanks,' says Liz.

'Oh, this is only for special occasions,' says Laura. 'Usually I can't be bothered to do puddings.'

A trill of high birdsong sounds from a nearby tree, invisible in the darkness.

'Is that a nightingale?' says Alan.

No one knows.

'Aren't we useless?' says Alan. 'We live in the countryside, but we know nothing about birdsong.'

'I don't live in the countryside,' says Diana.

Henry comes out.

'I can't find him,' he says. 'He's not in the downstairs loo.'

'Maybe he's gone to lie down.'

'No, I've looked. He's nowhere in the house.'

'Nowhere in the house?' says Diana. 'He must be.'

She goes into the house and can be heard calling him in shrill tones. 'Roddy! Roddy!' Then she returns, arms spread in bewilderment.

'Where can he be?'

'He hasn't gone off to get something in the car?' says Liz.

'No. The car's there.'

'I suppose he's taken himself off for a walk,' says Laura. 'He's been in an odd mood all evening.'

'A walk?' says Diana, her voice rising. 'At night? Where would you walk to?'

'I don't know. To the river, maybe.'

'To the river?'

A moment of silence. Diana turns to Henry. All at once her face looks pale and lined.

'He's not having some sort of breakdown, is he?'

'No,' says Henry. 'No, of course not. But I'll tell you what. I'll get a torch and go out to have a look for him.'

'I'll go with you,' says Alan.

Diana has started to tremble.

'He was drinking rather a lot,' she says. 'He has been in an odd mood all evening.'

Henry and Alan cross the dry meadows in the moonlight. There's no need for the torch. To start with Henry calls out every few minutes. 'Roddy! Roddy!' Then they make their way in silence. The lights of Lewes glow amber in the distance. A cool night wind on their faces.

'You don't think he'd do anything silly,' says Alan.

'No,' says Henry. 'But something's not right with him. He was going on earlier about how this is the river where Virginia Woolf drowned herself.'

'Bloody hell.'

Ahead a strip of water glints in the moonlight.

'Actually,' says Henry, 'it's not the same river here, it's a tributary called Glynde Reach.'

'Is it deep?'

'Deep enough.'

They tramp on over the close-grazed grass. The ground is hard beneath their feet. Too many weeks without rain.

'Roddy!' calls Henry. 'Roddy!'

No answer.

'He's probably sleeping it off under a hedge,' says Alan.

'Hell of a lot of hedges,' says Henry.

He turns on the torch and rakes the land all round them, more to feel he's doing something than in the expectation of any result.

'Your speech at dinner,' says Alan. 'It was wonderful.'

'Too much information, I expect.'

'No. These things need saying.'

Now they've reached the river. It runs bright and straight between deep banks. Henry flashes the beam of his torch over the water's surface, but there's nothing to be seen. They make their way along the river bank, following the water's flow. Ahead, the raised line of the railway embankment.

'How far do we go?' says Alan.

'This'll do,' says Henry, turning round. 'If he's thrown himself in the river he'll be halfway to Newhaven by now.'

'But he wouldn't do that,' says Alan.

'No,' says Henry. 'Of course not.'

He flashes his torch round the fields once more.

'Roddy!' he calls. 'Roddy!'

They tramp back along the way they've come, no longer expecting to find him. And then, suddenly, there he is. He's crouched by the river's side, sitting on the grass of the bank, his legs in the water up to his knees. He's hunkered down, both hands wrapped over his head, as if to protect himself from some imagined storm.

'Roddy! You bloody idiot!'

Henry's rough anger gives away his relief. Roddy looks up, his eyes confused, not recognising them.

'Get your feet out of the water, you chump!'

He does as he's told. As he straightens up they see he's clutching something that has been resting in his lap. He totters slightly as he rises to his feet, and it falls to the grass. Henry gives him his hand for support. Alan picks up the fallen object, and holds it out in the moonlight. It's a box of Fudge's Florentines.

'Come on, now. Pull on me.'

Henry gets Roddy up the bank and onto the level ground.

'Are you all right, old chap?'

Roddy nods.

'I'll tell you what. You've ruined a perfectly good pair of shoes.'

Roddy doesn't look up or speak, but he allows them to lead him back towards the village.

'So what's our story?' says Henry. 'You were pissed and decided to go for a paddle in the river?'

Roddy says something, but too low and indistinct for the others to catch.

'My fault,' says Henry. 'Sloshing out too much wine. Typical host anxiety, I'm afraid.'

'Not drunk,' says Roddy.

'Best to say you are,' says Henry. 'Better to be drunk than to be off your head.'

'Stick my head in cold water,' says Roddy.

'You do that.'

Roddy comes to a stop and looks round in panic.

'My Florentines!'

'Here they are,' says Alan, giving him the box.

Roddy takes the box and hugs it to his chest. They tramp on over the night field in silence. As they approach the lights of the village Roddy says with a tremor in his voice, 'Don't let them make a fuss, will you?'

'No fuss,' says Henry. 'We need to get you straight to bed.'

But the other members of the party are looking out for them, and seeing them approach they come to meet them. Diana has put on Wellington boots that are too big for her, but careless of her dignity she comes running, floundering.

'Roddy!' she cries. 'Roddy! Thank God!'

She wraps him in her arms and clings to him, now openly sobbing.

'Thank God! Thank God! Thank God!'

Laura and Maggie have come too.

'He's fine,' says Henry. 'Drunk too much. Needed to cool off.'

Henry and Laura move away from Roddy and Diana, not wanting to intrude on the unexpected spectacle of Diana's disintegration. Alan and Maggie move off in another direction, for the same reason.

Henry and Laura are the first to return to the house, where they're quick to reassure Liz and Andrew. Then a few moments later Diana appears, clasping Roddy tightly by one arm, and without a word to anyone leads him up the stairs to their bedroom.

Alan and Maggie, following behind, pass from the strong moonlight of the open field into the black night of the copse of trees bordering the lane. Maggie reaches out her arm and draws Alan close. She presses her body against his, feels in the blackness for his face, finds his lips with her lips. She kisses him fiercely,

straining her whole body to reach him, wanting to touch all of
him. He returns her kiss, but only for a moment. Then his hands
are gently detaching her, and he's drawing away from her.

They come out of the trees and cross the narrow lane into
the gravel drive of the Broads' house. Neither of them speaks
a word. Maggie enters the kitchen first, and there's Andrew
waiting for her. Laura is making coffee for them all.

'Roddy's gone up,' she says. 'Diana's with him.'

'We should go soon,' says Liz to Alan. 'It's not fair on Bridget
to stay out too late.'

They drink their coffee and talk in subdued voices, because
although no one has questioned the cover story, they all saw
how Roddy's legs were half-soaked.

Then Liz and Alan leave.

'So what was going on there?' says Liz as she drives out onto
the main road.

'God alone knows,' says Alan.

'She was all over you. I couldn't believe it.'

'She was drunk.'

'Were you drunk too?'

'Oh, come on, Liz. What was I supposed to do?'

'You could have stopped smirking at her, for a start.'

'Was I smirking?'

'Yes, you were smirking.'

'Oh, God. I don't know,' says Alan. 'I suppose I'm not very
used to that sort of situation. I mean, you've got to admit it
was all coming from her. Christ alone knows why.'

'She fancied you. Is that so surprising?'

They drive in silence for a few minutes.

Then Alan says, 'Maybe she'll give us our planning permission
now.'

Liz smiles at that.

'You might have to fuck her for it.'

'That's going a bit far, isn't it?'

'I'll have to think about that,' says Liz. 'It's a tough one.'

Now Alan too is smiling in the dark of the car.

'What happened with Roddy?' says Liz.

'We found him with his feet in the river. I think he had some half-arsed plan to drown himself.'

'Poor bugger. Wouldn't you, with a wife like that?'

'I don't know. People are infinitely mysterious. She was all over him when he came back.'

Turning off the Offham Road into the lanes, the river valley lies before them in the moonlight, calm and still.

'Didn't you love Henry's speech?' says Alan.

'I was jealous,' says Liz.

'I'll make you a speech like that,' says Alan. 'But it has to be in public. That's what makes it count.'

'What will you say?'

'All the things Henry said. How loving you is all I really care about. But I'll leave out the bit about humility, and put in a bit about how you're a wonderful fuck.'

'In public?'

'I may use euphemisms.'

'So you don't want to run away with the pixie?'

'No. I want to run away with you.'

'Well, you don't have to run far.'

'How about tonight?' he says. 'Are you still on for our date?'

'I may fall asleep,' she says. 'Henry never stopped filling my glass.'

'Is it okay if I fuck you while you're asleep?'

'Yes, it's okay.'

His hand strokes her thigh, feeling her bare leg under her skirt.

'I may wake up,' she says.

Walking back through the night village, Maggie expects Andrew to speak, but he says nothing. After a little while she says, 'I suppose I should say sorry.'

'Quite an evening,' he says.

'I kept on saying Purley. You were supposed to make an excuse so we could leave.'

'I didn't want to,' he says.

He doesn't sound angry, or hurt. Just far away.

'You weren't having a good time,' she says. 'I could see you weren't.'

'No. I wasn't having a good time.'

'I drank far too much.'

Then, because he doesn't say anything, she says, 'I kissed him. Out in the lane, when they came back from finding Roddy.'

He doesn't say anything to that either. If he's surprised, he's not showing it.

'Actually I don't know why I did it,' she says.

'I expect you wanted to find out,' he says.

'Find out what?'

'If there's someone out there who's better.'

How can he be so reasonable? It makes her jumpy.

'Don't you mind?'

'Yes,' he says. 'But I couldn't stop you.' Then after a pause, 'I didn't want to. I wanted you to go as far as you could.'

'Why?'

'So you'd find out.'

'I didn't find anything out,' she says. 'He acted like I hadn't done it. I expect he thought I was too pissed to know what I was doing.'

They walk on in silence. Through the half-open windows of a house they see the flicker of a television, hear the muffled excitement of a match commentator and the muffled roar of a crowd. In the lane ahead a fox lopes out into the moonlight, turns to stare at them, lopes into darkness.

All at once Maggie feels desolate. Here in the cool summer night, walking beside Andrew but not touching, she feels as if she's lost in space. She wants him to reach out and take her hand. She remembers how Henry said to Laura, 'With all my love, till the day I die.'

'So I suppose you can't wait to get away from me,' she says.

'I don't know,' he says.

'After my little exhibition this evening.'

She needs him to say more, so she keeps on raising the stakes, probing for the breaking point.

'I suppose you hate me,' she says.

'Not really.'

'What, then?'

He doesn't speak.

'Please,' she says.

'What is it you want from me, Maggie?'

Now at last she can hear the hurt in him, and something that was clutched tight inside her begins to let go.

'I don't want you to hate me,' she says.

'I don't hate you.'

'I know how badly I've behaved tonight. I don't really know why I did it. I think maybe I wanted to push things, you know, to the edge. Or over the edge. So that then there'd be no decision to make after all.'

'Because I'd walk away.'

'Yes.'

'Is that what you want?'

'Oh God, I don't know. I don't know why you don't hate me.'

'Well,' he says slowly. 'I was watching you this evening, and maybe I've got this wrong, but I thought, this is all an act. She's not having a good time. She's putting on an act. It's like you were saying to me, Look, I'm not a nice person at all. If you want to go on being with me, this is what you get. You think you love me, but can you love this?'

She can't speak. Such a strange muddle inside, of relief and fear.

'But it's not about can and can't,' he says, as if he reads her thoughts. 'I just do.'

'Love me?' she says.

'Yes.'

'Oh, sweetheart. I don't deserve it.'

'You know what, Maggie? You have to let other people make their own mistakes. I'll decide what I want and what I don't want. And you have to do the same. If you want me to go, all you have to do is tell me, and I'll go.'

'I don't want you to go,' Maggie says.

So there it is: her decision after all.

They've stopped in the lane and he's looking at her, but it's too dark to see his face.

'At dinner this evening,' he says, 'I was watching you, I felt you were just so unhappy. I wanted to put my arms round you, like you do with a child who's had a bad dream. I wanted to hug you and say, It's only a dream.'

'You should have done.'

'Should I?'

'You could do it now,' she says.

So he wraps his arms round her, as if the night is cold and he's undertaken to warm her. They stay like this for some time, silent, holding each other close.

Henry and Laura clear away the dinner party together.

'You go on up,' says Henry. 'I'll turn out the lights and lock up.'

When he comes upstairs he finds Laura sitting on the top step, near the door to Carrie's room. She motions to him to stay silent and sit down beside him.

Through the closed door he hears Carrie's sweet light voice singing to herself, to the accompaniment of occasional chords on her guitar.

> 'You told me there's no future
> Only now, now, now
> But then one day you left me
> And it's now, now, now . . .'

Laura takes Henry's hand in hers. She moves his fingers so that they feel her ring. Then she raises his hand to her lips and kisses it. Light falls from the half-open bathroom door across the worn landing carpet. They listen to Carrie's song.

> 'So now I know the future
> Is the time when you have gone
> And I'm living in the future
> And it's lonely in the future
> On my own . . .
> On my own . . .'

Author's note

My novels are of course fiction, but I care very much about the authenticity of the details and build my inventions as far as possible on a solid ground of fact. In this I have been greatly helped by the real people to whom I turn for details of their experiences.

I would like to thank Chris Morris and Katya Bowen, the Design and Conservation Officers for Lewes District Council; Terece Walters, Associate Chief Nurse, Clinical Operations at the Royal Sussex Hospital; Dave Gaylor; Brian Davis; Nigel Lee; Jaspal and Sukhjit Minhas, real people whom I met at a Buckingham Palace garden party in July 2010; and Alain de Botton, who is also real.

MSW